The Alpha King's INNOCENT Bride

(Book 1)

POOJA RAO

DEDICATION

This book is dedicated to all my readers and family that supported me in every step. Love you all.

CONTENTS

AUTHOR'S NOTES

Books have always given me space to breathe but the idea of writing my own book was always one of my dreams. The day I created my first world that would be found in my first book it became my passion. I began my journey writing a dark romance but never expected that people would love my writing. Later, I kept trying different genres with my next books, young adult, LGBT+, action, and fantasy.

My Mom's support in all things in my life everything. Taking a month's gap after the completion of each book to contemplate readers' criticism helped me to improve my upcoming works.

My editor at Dreame, Victor West, was the best thing that happened in my writing journey. He is one of the calmest and most respectful person, he always guides and encouraged me. Trying genres at Ringdom/STARY is always the most challenging for me but with my book 'Reborn In The World Of The Undead' I was honored with an award. The 'Academy star, the outstanding performance in Stray writing academy in STARY 3rd Anniversary. It was one of the most amazing moments of my life, and that was all thanks to STARY.

Thank you.

1. Personal Whore

Elaine

"STUPID BITCH!" he yelled over the sound of flesh hitting flesh as it bounced off the walls of the small room. Curled up in a ball I covered my mouth with my hand, to prevent any scream from escaping. I was terrified to the point that I had forgotten what it was like to breathe properly. I sat curled in on myself in that musty cupboard trembling uncontrollably coated in a layer of cold sweat as I looked through the crack provided by the door of my hiding place for the last hour.

"You dare ask me for money," the man emphasized every word out of his mouth with another hit to Nora. I had long ago stopped trying to keep count of the number of times he had landed blows to different parts of her body. I knew that Nora was trying her hardest to avoid letting so much as a whimper escape her lips despite suffering through a brutal attack. As I watched a small bit of blood leak from her busted lip, I could not help but think that a regular person would never be able to stand this torture never mind survive it.

"If you don't give me any money, how am I going to eat? Please sir, give me something, even just a few coins for my service," Nora pleaded. She had once again fallen victim to hunger, this had led her down the dangerous path of begging that monster for money. He seemed crazed as he continued to land blow after blow to her body until her screams of torment stopped bringing his sadistic heart any joy. It was at that point that he allowed her to slump into a semi-conscious heap on the floor that let out a steady groan of pain.

"YOU OMEGA'S WERE BORN WITH NO OTHER PURPOSE THAN TO BE FUCKED! YOU'RE A WHORE! HOW DARE YOU ASK ME FOR MONEY! I COME HERE EVERYDAY BECAUSE YOU HAVE TO FUCK ME LIKE THE HUNGRY LITTLE BITCH YOU ARE. I DON'T HAVE TO GIVE YOU A CENT! the man roared as he towered over her. My eyes grew as wide as saucers when I watched him brutally drive his foot into her stomach as if he were kicking some kind of ball. Nora screamed out in pain at his latest attack while a small dribble of blood leaked from the corner of her mouth. I was on the verge of leaving my hiding spot in the cupboard to make an attempt to save her as I knew that he would not stop tormenting her when I noticed Nora gesturing to me. She was warning me not to leave the safety of the cupboard, otherwise both of our lives would be at stake. I knew at that moment that no matter how much it pained me, I had to remain where I was. Though it didn't prevent me from recalling how all of this had begun.

Flashback...

I had come into Nora's room to check on her as she'd been feeling sick, I found her lying motionless on the bed.

"Nora, are you okay?" I asked as I helped prop her up into a

more comfortable position with a pillow behind her head. She nodded her head to assure me that she was fine, though I knew it wasn't true.

"Have you eaten?" I couldn't help but ask, taking in her weak disposition. My dear friend was paler than the white sheets that she lay on.

"My customers haven't seen fit to give me any money. So, I haven't been able to buy any food," she explained quietly. I knew then that it had been two days since she had eaten anything, the same amount of time as me. Our pack members did not see fit to provide me with food either, not so much as a drop of water.

Nora and I belong to a pack that served under the Alpha King's territory, due to this fact it was one of the largest packs in the country. Not that it mattered to us, Nora and I were little more than slaves in this pack. Our ability to eat was left to the whim of those around us, if we pleased them we might be given scraps. The problem was it was nearly impossible to please anyone in this pack. I would say that they treated us like animals but that would be a lie, they treat the livestock better. I have wondered on more than one occasion if they enjoy watching us whither slowly away from prolonged malnutrition and dehydration. Then again, what do I know? I don't even know who I am, other than an Omega.

"It's going to be alright Nora. Once I finish working tomorrow, I'll go and get you something to eat. I'll even ask for some money to get you medicine, to help you feel better," I told her as she weakly nodded. She knew that the glimmer of hope I was trying to give her was as likely as either of us being accepted by fated mates. At twenty-one Nora was already well versed in pack dynamics, the two of us had been slaves our entire lives.

However, unlike me Nora had been brought to the pack after my pack had defeated hers. Despite the fact that we were children, no one showed a drop of mercy to either of us. When Nora, three my senior, turned sixteen the Alpha made the decision to make her the whore of the pack. Now my eighteenth birthday loomed ahead tomorrow and I had no idea what fate had in store for me.

I brought a cup of water to her lips, helping her drink a few large sips. It was the only substitute we had for food to fill our bellies and it came with the added satisfaction as we hadn't had anything to drink in a while. I stared at the water longingly wanting to have a drink of my own. My mouth and throat were bone dry while my lips were a bloody cracked mess from dehydration. As much as I wanted that water, I knew that I couldn't take a single drop or the outcome could be dire.

"Have a drink, Elaine. I know that you're just as bad off as me. They aren't here right now. No one will see. Do it quick, before it's too late," Nora urged me. She knew that as similar as our situations were, I was still worse off. While she was a whore, I was a slave with no value.

"It's alright Nora. There isn't much left. You need it more than I do," I lied, placing the cup back on the little table.

"For the moment I just want you to get some rest and not worry about money. Just trust that I will do whatever is necessary to get you food in the morning," I reassured her as I helped her lay back down. Slaves of this pack like Nora and I needed to obtain our food and water from the Luna. The catch was even if she granted us food and water we still had to provide some sort of payment, whether it was on our backs or working without food, water, or sleep for two days.

This was what I was doing. For a measly amount of sustenance, I had been working myself to the bone for the pack. My brain was consumed with thoughts of how I was going to procure food for Nora when I hadn't been able to secure a single crumb of bread for myself. That was when there was a knock on the door, causing panic to raise up inside of me. Nora sat up in bed, the plain terror in her large eyes fearing the worst was about to happen.

In truth it hadn't been a knock at all but a bang, like someone wanted to slam their fist threw the sorry excuse for a door. It was the wee hours of the morning; I had thought it a safe time to check on Nora as no one in the pack was aware that I would sneak in to see her sometimes. I always came at this ungodly hour when no men would be here visiting her, tonight it seemed our luck had run out.

"OPEN THE FREAKING DOOR!" the man bellowed his frustration clearly building the longer he was made to wait. Nora was panicking while I stood there frozen in fear.

"If he finds me in this room then I'm done for," I whispered to myself. It seemed that death was eagerly waiting to greet me on the other side of Nora's bedroom door. I figured that it was most likely a pack member as that was mostly the "clientele" that Nora serviced though there were guests of the Alpha on occasion. Nora's sharp ears had heard my whisper, she tightly clasped my trembling hands, a serenity coming over her.

"You need to go hide in the cupboard, don't come out until I tell you it's safe alright?" Nora murmured. I couldn't control my eyes when they widened out of fear, that meant she fully planned to let whoever was on the other side of that door in here.

"Please Nora, don't do this. You don't need to open that door. We both know what he'll do to you if you do. You're too sick to handle it. I won't be able to bear witnessing that," I urgently whispered in an attempt to persuade her from opening the door. If she opened that door she was not only inviting my death but her own as well. I watched her eyes flicker back and forth between me and the door before settling on me.

"You know as well as I that you won't be able to get food for me, at least let me try before I'm too far gone. Without some money I will die of starvation. You don't need to worry, this happens multiple times a day. You just need to do as I've asked," she softly encouraged forcing a smile to her pale face. I could tell from the glazed look of her eyes that she was talking absolute nonsense.

"I refuse to let you do this. You're too weak! If you do this you'll die!" I whispered not realizing that she had led me over to the cupboard until she shoved me inside. She used some spray inside and outside the cupboard to cover my scent, it was what we always used to hide my visits. She hurriedly closed the cupboard doors before donning an air of normalcy and opening the door.

"WHY DID IT TAKE YOU SO LONG TO OPEN THE DOOR?!" the man barked as he barged in, almost managing to shove Nora to the floor. His head turned from side to side as if he were searching for something or someone. Observing their interaction through a small hole in this dilapidated old wooden cupboard made it impossible for me to catch a glimpse of his face, all I could tell was that the man in question was tall. I also had this strange inkling that I knew him. Who was he?

"I apologize. I was sleeping deeply and didn't hear you," Nora explained, closing the door behind her before she dared to steal a glance at him.

"Here I thought you were just fucking another man," he crudely pointed out as he yanked back on her hair. He was still turning his head this way and that suspiciously searching the near barren room for a man that didn't exist.

"Like I said, I was sleeping," she blatantly lied as her eyes went to the cupboard silently advising me not to make a sound. It was at that moment that he turned slightly, my eyes widened out of sheer terror when I saw his face. It was the Beta of our pack! He came to see Nora too? I didn't understand, he always acted like he hated her around everyone.

"That's good to hear. Now, you need to take good care of me, we'll start with..." he chuckled darkly. "You should know by now," he ordered while giving her a harsh push. Nora nodded; I knew her well enough to be able to read the awkwardness she was feeling in her body language at having to service the Beta while conscious of the fact that I was in the room. She did manage to cram what modesty remained down as she did what she was told.

That was when I noticed Nora's eyes drifting closed, she must have felt dizzy. Despite the world spinning around her she didn't stop what she was doing, it seemed to go on forever. All I wanted was for it to end probably more than Nora did. I thanked the Moon Goddess herself when he finally stopped. I thought that he would finally leave having slaked his lust, I couldn't have been more wrong. The Beta wasn't a man, he was a monster. I forced myself to close my eyes and cover my ears to block out his actions.

"You aren't satisfying me properly like you usually do. Are you sure that you weren't with another man today?" he mockingly asked. She just shook her head, reassuring him that she hadn't. When Nora glanced in my direction I could see the pain in her eyes, it was deeper than I'd ever seen before. I understood why she was doing this, for money, for food, for her own survival. She was desperately clinging to the last crumb of hope she had left that she would be able to accomplish this small feat.

An hour later once he finally felt fully sated he left her in a heap on the mattress. Nora didn't so much as twitch, her body was consumed with nothing but agony as a pain filled whimper spilled passed her lips. Even though the last hour had been hell for me, it had been hell on Nora. Nora noticed that the Beta was putting his clothes back on and used all the strength she had to get up off the bed.

"Please give me some money," Nora begged, standing up with the help of a small bedside table. He ignored her, shoving her away. Every time she asked him for money the only thing she would receive was a beating.

Flashback ends…

It didn't matter how many he kicked her in the stomach, her eyes pleaded with me to remain hidden from that monster. She was helping me keep my secret concealed from the pack. The secret that would inevitably destroy my life the same as it had hers. I was a virgin, the only Omega left in the pack that was.

They've told me that my mother was a pack whore that my father would never have married. She had been used and discarded like a dirty handkerchief. When I was small my mother was sentenced to death after committing a crime against the Luna. Having been labeled the daughter of a traitor I was forced into the shackles of slavery

As a slave to this pack, they could demand that I do whatever they wished without argument. I never did it for food or money, only so that I was allowed to continue breathing. I never dared to so much as dream of a better future for myself. I had no delusions when it came to the truth of my existence, the Alpha, his son, and the Beta used every Omega in the pack as their play things.

They felt it was their right as they owned us. I had learned that all the men in the pack were the same, they loathed us yet still had no issue using us for their own satisfaction in bed. I would turn eighteen tomorrow and still desperately clung to my virginity in secret. Over the years I had done my best to hide myself from them. I suppose it was a blessing that I was the daughter of a traitor, they didn't seem to want me like the other women.

Finally, the Beta exited the room leaving Nora cold and naked on the floor with her eyes closed. I waited a few minutes after he left before pushing the door to the cupboard open and crawling out. On weak legs I walked over to the bed to grab the torn and dirty blanket then fell to my knees beside my friend. I covered her battered body with a thin blanket then gently placed her head in my lap as Nora opened her eyes.

"We need to get up off the floor, Nora. This cold isn't going to help you," I coaxed trying to help her up. Instead her eyes fluttered closed without ellisting a single sound.

"Nora are you…" I couldn't force the rest of the sentence out of my mouth, I was petrified. Her eyes weren't open, there weren't even any tears leaking from them. Left with no other option I held my trembling hand below her nose, tears instantly blurred my vision with the realization that she wasn't breathing.

"Nora!" I loudly wailed. My only friend had died right in front of me and I could do nothing to save her.

"Nora please…please wake up. I promise I'll get you food in the morning. You won't have to go through that again, please just wake up," I bargained with her lifeless body.

"YOU BITCH!" Those two words were the only warning I had before it felt like my scalp was on fire as someone dragged me away from Nora by my hair. There was no way for me to see who it was, but I didn't need to. I knew that it was the Alpha's son, Lewis. He yanked me down the hallway and tossed me into my room. I was unable to prevent my head from bouncing off the floor nor the cry of pain it caused from escaping my lips.

"What the fuck where you doing in there?!" Lewis growled as the Beta stood guard beside him pinning me to the floor with his withering glare. This meant he had been the one to tell Lewis that I was in Nora's room, he'd known I was there the entire time and done nothing.

"That bitch should be beaten to death for disobedience!" Natasha shrieked, stepping into the room. Lewis's sister smiled at her father's Beta as if she were congratulating him for a job well done before she glared at me. That was the moment it hit me, this had all been planned. They had already known that I was in that room when the Beta had shown up, he'd done everything to Nora under Natasha's orders.

"I told you to bring me tea! How dare you ignore a direct order to go check on some whore!" Natasha squawked, slapping me hard across the face over and over again until I curled in on myself on the floor. I no longer had the energy and was in too much pain to stay up right any longer. Not that it mattered but I knew she was lying, she never asked me to fetch her tea. She was always doing things like this though, just to have an excuse to beat me.

"Are your ears failing you? Answer the question that Natasha asked you! Why were you in the whore's room?" Lewis loudly reiterated. It was clearly meant to be my final warning, if I didn't start cooperating, I would not enjoy where things went next.

"Nore, she...she's dead," I stuttered out by way of an explanation causing his eyes to burn like flames. He strode and delivered a swift kick to my stomach. I was already in pain from starvation. I couldn't even muster a gasp when he added more, I just curled further in on myself holding my stomach.

"She was an Omega whore! Born to do little more than spread her legs and die. What does it matter that she is dead?! Do you expect me to pay my respects to a whore? That I will leave all the important work I need to do behind just because a slave is mourning her?!" He snarled, and I could hear Natasha chuckling in the background.

"It's true, she must expect something along those lines. It's either that or she went to learn how to become a whore. I think now that Nora's death has left a vacancy Elaine should be made the pack whore," Natasha pointedly suggested with sharpened polished nails. My eyes widened in horror. Understanding that she had gotten the better of me, she gave me an evil smirk as she clutched my jaw in her hand.

"When the sun rises you should be ready to become the pack's new whore," she warned, revealing the hate she held for me in her eyes as her nails dug into the skin of my cheeks.

"Let's go, the stench of this bitch's room is giving me a headache," Natasha whined then delivered a kick to my midsection with her high heeled foot exiting the room, the Beta trailing after her. That left Lewis and I alone, he moved closer, holding my jaw in his hand as he gently rubbed his thumb across my cheek giving me the chills. I had to control the shiver of revulsion from moving through my body at his lust filled gaze and repulsive touch.

"There's no need for you to be scared of becoming a whore,

Elaine. In the morning, I promise that you will become a whore that exclusively serves me. Do you know why?" he sadistically questioned me as I tried to move away from him, but he held me tight while clenching his jaw.

"No matter what it's inevitable that you'll become my personal whore," he confidently promised then left the room. Once I was alone I let the tears I had been holding back spring free. I was to turn eighteen in a matter of hours, shortly after that my worst nightmare would also be realized.

I never thought that my pointless little life would turnout like this, living my life never daring to want anything. Actually, I was lying to myself, there was something that I wanted. Just like every other werewolf I wanted my mate. I wanted him and him alone.

Using one hand to brace my stomach as I sat up on the floor my hand went under my torn blanket on the floor. I pulled out my most prized possession, a picture that I had admired my entire life. All that I wanted was the chance to see him one more time before I became untouchable.

2. Saved

Elaine

ours had passed, yet I had been unable to tear my gaze for the clock in my room. It was six in the morning, by now I should have been in the kitchen making breakfast for the pack. I had been assigned that duty since I was a small child, though cooking wasn't the only chore that I was responsible for. The list was too long to name them all, though the among the worst had to be hand washing Natasha's underwear.

If I was ever late reporting to the kitchen, they kept a whip hung on the wall to discipline me. That morning the atmosphere in the kitchen was different, I realized that they had already appointed someone else to take my position. I suppose there was no time to waste in training someone else if I was to become a whore. I hadn't been able to stop thinking about it all night nor had I gotten a wink of sleep as Lewis's works kept repeating over and over in my head.

By eight o'clock the shock of Nora's death that I had cloaked myself in to make it through the night had worn off and tears steadily streamed down my face. I didn't have a clue what they were going to do with her body or if they would lay her to rest, what I did know was that I was responsible for her death. If I had just had the courage to come out of the cupboard I could have saved her, maybe then things would have been different. Just maybe she would be alive, but it was too late now.

I braced my hand on my stomach, attempting to stave off the hungry pains. The cramps had grown so intense that it felt like I would die soon, I hadn't eaten or had anything to drink in three days. I was fully aware that if I didn't have any water today that I would die of dehydration.

As I was contemplating this I heard the click of my door being unlocked from the outside. The fact that they had locked me in my room brought a weak smile to my lips. I knew they were attempting to prevent my escape, the question remained where exactly would I escape to? This pack was all that I had ever known. The door to the room was unceremoniously kicked open, causing me to flinch and let out a gasp of fear as a group of pack members stormed into my small little room. Beta Dale was the last to enter with a wave of his hand, his men moved to surround me, causing me to crawl away from them in fear.

"No, please!" I yelped, just as one of them was about to wrap a hand around my arm. I pushed that hand away from me only to be slapped hard across the face by Beta Dale as he gave me a frigid glare.

"Girl, you do not want to test my patience today. Come quietly or I'll have no issues dragging you out of here without a stitch of clothes on," the Beta warned. His threats brought a fresh wave of tears to my ears, which led to an evil smile spreading across that sadistic man's face.

"Lewis has requested that I deliver a message to you personally. If you decide to cause a scene then he will make himself available to come down here, strip you of every last piece of clothing, then drag through the pack by that long beautiful hair of yours to the Alpha," Dale passed on the message while staring into my eye. Of course, his words sent a shiver down my spine. I was well aware that if the message was indeed from Lewis that no one would step a toe out of line to stop him.

"Do you understand?" he asked pointedly with a quirked brow. I quickly nodded my head, not wanting to test his or Lewis's patience. It had been Lewis's goal for years now to have me naked before him. I had achieved this in the past by not giving him a chance to use my disobedience against me. Beta Dale gestured to his men with a flick of his wrist and disinterested look, in less than a second they pounced grabbing me by the arms as they dragged me from the room.

It was only a matter of seconds before I was tossed to the floor at the feet of the Alpha and Luna. I couldn't stop the small whimper of pain that slipped past my lips, I was in so much pain that I felt like I was dying in front of them. I tilted my head, looking up through my lashes at Alpha Fabian and Luna Wilma sitting on their throne like chairs staring down at me like I was little more than a bug they wanted to crush. In this open room there was nowhere for me to hide from Luna Wilma's hate filled eyes as they burned into my flesh. Without having to look I knew that Lewis would be to the right of his father and Natasha would be standing beside him. I had no desire to see the knowing smirks on their faces, it would be as if they were telling me without a word that now that I had turned eighteen my world would be turned upside down.

I could safely assume that Lewis had already discussed his wishes with the Alpha and Luna during the night. One thing about Luna Wilma was she would do anything to make her son happy. Unfortunately for me, the one thing that would bring Lewis pure joy would be to tie me to his bed as his permanent personal plaything. I squeezed my eyes shut out of fear, I was waiting for the Alpha to declare that I was officially becoming Lewis's whore. I knew without a doubt that once the Alpha said those words Lews would drag me to his room where I would have every one of my hopes and dreams stolen from me. I would lose any hope I had of seeing him again.

"What is she doing here? Get out!" the Alpha barked, I couldn't stop myself from giving him a wide eyed look. He was demanding that I leave the hall? What was going on? The Alpha was the one that had made me a slave as a small child, why would he spare me now? I darted a glance at Luna Wilma, the angry shock was clearly written across her face at her Alpha's words. Next my eyes went to Lewis's panicked face as he watched the bottom fall out of his glorious plan. He seemed like he was ready to erupt into a murderous rage. I didn't bother glancing in Natasha's direction, I already knew that whatever her reaction was it would be five times worse than that of her brother. After all she had made it her life's mission to torment me the last eighteen years.

"But father…" Lewis started to whine as he spoke to the Alpha. "Mother and I discussed it last night, Elaine is to be my personal whore." With every word out of Lewis's mouth it was as if he forgot that he was speaking to the Alpha, his voice rose higher and higher in frustration. In response he received a warning growl from the Alpha for his impertinence. Luna Wilma quickly intervened to calm the Alpha in order to shield her son from his wrath.

"I think that the time is long overdue that we give this daughter of a traitor to our son to serve as his personal whore. After all, I believe that Lewis would agree that this is the gift our son would like most for becoming the Alpha in a few days time. We should want to see our son happy. That piece of trash is just an Omega, she was born to serve. So let her serve him in bed as his whore," Luna Wilma persuaded while staring me down. I lowered my gaze back down to the floor as I began to tremble, I knew I was done for. The Alpha wasn't going to refuse a direct request from his Luna. A mind-link from Lewis, made my head snap up.

'Go to my room now, Elaine. Go there and strip. When I arrive I better not find a single strip of clothing on that milky white skin of yours otherwise I'll be forced to peel of some of that delicate skin with my claws before I fuck you,' Lewis cautioned with a wicked smile. The tears that came to my eyes were beyond my control, I was subconsciously aware of Natasha chackling at my misfortune situation.

"IS THERE SOMETHING WRONG WITH YOUR EARS GIRL?! I SAID GET OUT!" Alpha Fabian roared, as I scrambled away on the floor. I couldn't believe that he still wanted me to leave, that he wasn't going to make me the latest pack whore. I wasn't sure what the proper reaction to the situation should be, but bracing my aching stomach I hurriedly got up off of the floor and exited the room.

"You fucking bitch! Where do you think you're going?!" Lewis yelled as he caught a handful of my hair in his fist then used it to turn me so we were both facing the Alpha.

"Father, why are you doing this? You know that I want her. That I want her under any circumstance!" Lewis whined like a toddler having a tantrum, stomping his foot and yanking on my hair in his frustration at his father's decision. I let out a cry of pain after a particularly brutal jerk that felt like he was going to pull my hair out by its roots. A low rumbling growl emanating from the Alpha's chest was Lewis's final warming. The scent of fear permeated the room, it oozed from the pores of every pack member in the room, myself and Lewis included. It did, however, scare Lewis into letting go of my hair.

"GET THE FUCK OUT!" Alpha Fabian reiterated one last time. It was enough to prod my flight or fight response into action, holding my cramping stomach I raced out of the room like it was on fire. I could not believe that by some miracle I had been saved. I hadn't been made a whore. I was still pure and meant just for him. I was snotty nosed and tear streaked when I finally fell to my knees in as safe of a place as I was going to find. I sobbed loudly, unsure of how long I would be kept safe from their clutches.

I had know idea when I would be able to see him or if he had a mate already. What would I do if he had a mate? Bawling my eyes out I looked up at the sky letting the rain cool my heated skin. Opening my cracked lips I collected the rainwater in my mouth to drink. I knew that after I had left whatever transpired in that hall would not lead to the betterment of my well being. I would like usual be treated worse than livestock, yet I still needed to survive and endure this place. I had to, for him. It did not matter whether he was mated or not, I at the very least wanted to see him one final time before I left this world.

Lewis

I watched as Elaine sprinted out of the hall, not being able to lift a finger to prevent it due to my father's order. I was growing incensed thinking about not being able to have her, that I wouldn't be able to fuck her the way I had always wished.

"Clear the room now. I need to speak to Lewis alone!" father commanded. I could feel Natasha's rage, a burning flame to match my own, not far away from my side. Mother motioned for Natasha to join her in leaving the room, their exit would be seen as far from ladylike with stomping and setting up quite a fuss. Eventually, father and I were left alone in the hall. I knew better than to look him in the eyes, but I had to clench my fists to prevent myself from saying or doing anything that I might regret at a later date.

"Lewis," father called. I raised my gazes while sucking in an angry breath.

"Why? Why did you do this father? You know all about this, it's not like I've kept it hidden from you. I want...no, I need to have Elaine!" I demanded answers from my father as he looked down at me passively.

"There are already more than enough whore and other women in our pack. Hell, there are some in every age range, many are far more beautiful than Elaine. Choose one of them, forget Elaine," was my father's answer. I had reached my breaking point.

"WHY CAN'T ELAINE?! SHE IS THE ONLY ONE I

WANT!" I bellowed only to be slapped sharply across the face by my father, my wolf instantly submitted to his superior wolf.

"You won't enjoy the consequences of your actions if you raise your voice to me again. I am still the Alpha, seeing you act like this is making me seriously reconsider my decision to hand over my position to you," my father warned. My eyes grew round in shock, he had never threatened me before.

"It is my decision that you are not to have Elaine! Do you understand me?! You aren't to so much as lay a finger on that girl. Otherwise, you can kiss your dream of becoming the next Alpha of this pack goodbye. I hope that you've gotten that through that thick skull of yours!" my dad barked at me before leaving the room, but he hadn't used his Alpha tone on me. I screamed in frustration, wanting nothing more than to kill someone at that moment. Even bathing in someone's blood wasn't going to ease my foul mood, just like I knew my hunger for Elaine wouldn't be sated until I had her.

"Why can't I have her?!" I yelled, then felt Natasha rest her hand on my shoulder.

"You can, and I'll help you," Natasha promised with a wicked grin.

"You're right, I will have her."

3. Mating Ball?

King Emmett

The front gate of the palace opened prior to my arrival as the guards had received my mind-link while my horse barreled towards them at a full tilt. Any talk amongst them was drowned out by the pounding of horse hooves as the rest of the party that had gone hunting with me flooded through the gate.

I reined in my horse a short distance from the palace steps. Rex, my Beta, dismounted his own horse before quickly approaching me in an attempt to intercept me. All I wanted at that moment was to retreat to my quarters. We had spent the last two days without food or sleep, now my bed was calling to me. As was the usual custom everyone stood by the front door of the palace to welcome me home. When I scan their bowed heads anger reignites in my blood reminding me of why I had gone hunting in the first place.

Rex, having sensed my rising anger defused the situation before someone was brutally punished.

"Alpha, none of the wolves present are mated and marked. I assure you that these are all unmated wolves. I'll take full responsibility if a situation like that ever happens again," Rex confidently assured me as my eyes searched the crowd. Everyone in the crowd was trembling slightly and staring at the ground while they awaited my inspection. I was sure if it were physically possible they would have acted like ostriches, willingly shoving their heads in the dirt at the first sign of my displeasure.

"Alpha, I would like to formally apologize once again for the incident that occurred a few days ago and assure you that it won't happen again," Rex affirmed. Without saying a word I began walking.

It was a simple truth that any time that a wolf stood before me and I caught sight of a mating mark on their neck, my blood boiled with rage. Whenever someone that worked or lived in the palace found their mate they were swiftly transferred to another packhouse. It was well known that no marked wolf was allowed in my presence upon penalty of death.

I was born cursed. Cursed to forever feel incomplete, to remain mateless, to only ever be half of a whole. I would always be searching for her. It was the unbearably painful truth of my existence, one that no one, even those closest to me, could ever begin to imagine. Not that any of them were even aware of my curse, only my Beta and Vincent, my best friend that was the Alpha Prince of his own kingdom were the exceptions to this. While I remained the cursed Alpha King.

Upon entering the palace I found Amanda, my stepmother waiting for me with a welcoming smile. She was my father's second chance mate. A few months after my mother died when I was five, my father discovered that her younger sister was his second chance mate. From that moment on my aunt turned stepmother raised me as if I were her own. Waiting alongside

Amanda was her son Raymond, my stepbrother, and his mate April.

"Emmett, where have you been? I've been so worried about you," Amanada asked, coming forward to hug me tightly.

"Everything is fine, mother," I replied with a half smile as I deftly placed distance between us, forcing her to let me go. She didn't hide the slightly offended look on her face, yet she was well aware of the fact that I disdain being touched. Whenever someone touched my bare skin it elicited a horrible burning sensation. Since infancy it had only been my mother's touch that was able to sooth me without pain, I've always assumed that it was connected to the curse.

"Welcome home Alpha," Raymond greeted with a respectful bow of his head. My gaze skated over to April, she hurriedly lowered her own gaze as she proceeded to bow her head like her mate.

"Emmett, you must be ravenous. Let's adjourn to the dining room, we've all been awaiting your return," Amanda suggested as my eyes landed on the dining table. Amanda had a preverbal feast prepared for my return and every dish looked mouthwatering. I could smell from the hall that the kitchen had prepared all of my favorites. Despite the tantalizing display I didn't utter a single word, Amanda knew well enough to understand that meant I wanted nothing more than to sleep.

"Please Emmett, can't you do this for me?" she sadly asked.

"Please brother, we just want the chance to spend some time with you," Raymond piped in, getting me to finally concede.

Sharing a meal with them wasn't the worst idea, seeing I was hungry. I quickly sat in my chair at the head of the table and requested that Rex join me. The seating arrangements were always the same Rex sat to my left while the chair to my right was left empty. I didn't know why I continued to delude myself into thinking that someday my mate, my Queen, would take her rightful place beside me in that chair. While I was intent on the vacant chair everyone around me had begun eating. Then as if on cue everyone's attention focused on me.

"Emmett dear, don't you think the time has come for you to choose a mate of your own?" Amanda suggested, forcing me to tear my gaze away from the coveted seat to my right.

"Take a chosen mate?" I asked in shocked confusion.

"Yes," she delicately placed her fork down on her plate before continuing. "Tomorrow you will turn twenty-eight and people are beginning to gossip. Everyone in this room knows that you've been searching for your mate far and wide, but I've come to believe that she isn't part of our Kingdom. I firmly believe that the best course of action is for you to choose a mate of your own rather than continuing to wait for a woman that you might never discover," she gently advised me with a concerned smile.

Of course, Amanda had made this suggestion not knowing that I was cursed to be mateless. Everyone in the Kingdom was under the pretense that I had been searching every corner of my Kingdom to find her to only come up empty handed. Rex had also informed me of rumors that some had been circulating about me, the perpetrators had been caught and sentenced to death. However, I was beginning to see the writing on the wall and knew I should consider what Amanda had to say.

"What do you think, Emmett?" she inquired, pulling my attention back to her from my thoughts. I wasn't sure how to respond, so I elected to just nod my head. I had honestly not expected her to get so excited that she jumped out of her chair.

"Oh Moon Goddess! This means that you're going to have a chosen mate!" she squealed as she looked at Raymond beaming happiness at the news. Raymond, on the other hand, seemed to be in shock. In the past whenever the topic of my mate had come up I had always pushed it to a later date or never given a definitive answer. Today had felt different, I had come to the realization that a 'chosen mate' was really the only option left for me.

"This is good news brother. I'm happy that you're finally considering this option. Mother has been worrying about you for some time," Raymond added while sharing a smile with April.

"If you aren't opposed to it…" Amanada began to say, seeming hesitant. "We will plan to have the mating ball tomorrow on your birthday," she finished. I observed Rex to gauge his feelings on the matter.

"Tomorrow? How can a mating ball be put together that quickly?! Rex exclaimed, staring at me with wide eyes.

"I can understand your concern about this Beta Rex. I just ask that you trust that I will have everything handled. Our Kingdom wishes to celebrate their King's birthday. Every pack in our Kingdom with every member of their pack will be invited to attend," Amanda sought to convince my Beta as I thought over the situation.

Who would I choose in the end? Would she only wish to marry me for the position and power that I could provide her by becoming Queen? Just the thought of being stuck with someone that self-centered sparked the dormant coals of rage inside causing me to break my silence.

"Rex, do as my mother wishes. Assist her in organizing the mating ball, but I want it to be held in my palace," I ordered as everyone's jaws dropped to the floor.

"What? You want it in your palace?" April wondered aloud, breaking the silence.

"That's correct, you're to invite every unmated noble woman that is a member of one of our packs. If there isn't one among them that I deem good enough to choose then I'll feed them to my pets," having delivered by ultimatum I left the dining room. However, I didn't miss the shocked pale faces of those sitting at the table at my announcement. It had been for everyone's benefit, there were far too many women that had tried their hand at seducing me over the years. Greed, lies, and betrayal were among the things that I hated most in this world, I certainly didn't need them in my chosen mate.

Raymond

Once Emmett left, Beta Rex, and my mother followed in short succession. I glanced up at April, she gave me a glare that would have chilled lesser men to their bones as she left the room, her high heels angrily snapping against the floor in the wake. In short order I left the dining room to follow her to our room, softly closing the door behind me. I found April staring out the window with her arms crossed over her chest.

"April," I cooed, wrapping my arms around her waist. He gained no response from her, so he began kissing his way up her neck. That was when she abruptly turned in his arms then shoved him away.

"What in the Goddess' name do you think you're doing Raymond?!" she shrieked, her shrill voice drilling into my head.

"Why the hell are you yelling at me? Especially where someone can overhear you?" I grumbled, through gritted teeth.

"Really? You don't have the slightest inkling as to why I might be upset? Alright then, your brother is at the center of every one of my problems. Thanks to that man my life has become a living hell," she snapped, closing her eyes and pinching the bridge of her nose in frustration.

"I am fully aware of your feelings, that was why I had mother suggest to Emmett that he take a chosen mate. This is the most surefire way for us to be able to live the way we want," I cajoled as I watched her face turn as red as a tomato.

ALPHA KING'S INNOCENT BRIDE

"Trust me I see exactly what the hell you did! Look what happened after your fabulous idea was set in motion! Were you not listening to what he said? That is he doesn't find a woman that is suitable to be his chosen mate, every woman that attends the mating ball will be fed to his pets!" she exclaimed in a huff while turning away from me. Emmett's pets were a lion and a crocodile both of which he'd cared for and handled himself since they were born, making them docile with him but vicious with others. Of course, Emmett was a beast as well. Maybe that was why they had responded so well to him. The Goddess knew that I'd lived in this palace with him for years, yet I was without a doubt afraid of him.

"Okay, I see your point. Things didn't exactly go as planned, but I still don't understand why you're so worried about it? We don't know any of those women. Why are you so concerned with Emmett's affairs?" I inquired as I lazily reclined on the bed. April turned, giving me a look of utter disbelief.

"Has the existence of my sister Naomi completely slipped your mind?" she asked rhetorically, allowing all the puzzle pieces to click into place explaining her foul mood. "She will be expected to attend the mating ball. You know that she would do anything within her power to coerce Emmett into selecting her as his chosen mate. She's been infatuated with him since she was a small child. When she learns that there is to be a ball at which the Alpha King will choose his Queen, she'll refuse to listen to anything that I have to say. I'm terrified for her well being, Raymond. Emmett won't hesitate for a moment before tossing her into the cage with his lion. My life has been in shambles thanks to being paired with a useless mate. I refuse to allow her to ruin her life in the same manner," April rambled on in a fit of anger as I grabbed her arm.

"What do you mean exactly by useless, April?" I inquired, tightening my grip on her arm only to have her shove my hand away.

"Do you see this?!" she asked, motioning to her bare neck. "Since we met I've been dying inside for you to mark me! For crying out loud it's already been a year, yet you won't even contemplate it out of fear of the King. So please, tell me what you would like me to say," she snarled while I took deep breaths in an effort to control my temper. There was nothing in the world that I wanted more than to mark her, it just wasn't possible at the moment.

April, you need to listen to me. The reason that I haven't marked you yet is because I've been thinking ahead to our future. Every werewolf that marks their mate isn't allowed to live in the palace. You know that this is one of Emmett's laws. It's not a new law either, it's been in effect for years even though I don't know the reason behind its existence. I have dreams, if I ever hope to achieve them I must continue to reside in the palace which is why I'm waiting to mark you. Despite whatever you may think I've been slowly dying to lay claim to you since the day we met the same as you. You aren't suffering in this alone," I told her before exiting the room and slamming the door behind me. I could hear April sobbing through the heavy wooden door, which just caused my burning rage toward Emmett to grow.

4. My Life is Going to Change

Elaine

I was already back working in the kitchen before lunch had to be served. The other Omega that they had used to replace me in making breakfast for the pack that morning had not provided a satisfactory meal, compared to the food that I usually prepared for them. That Omega had been punished while I'd been sent to the kitchen early to prepare enough food as everyone was famished and demanding extra food. The Alpha was furious about the entire situation. Personally, I didn't understand what the big deal was seeing as I'd gone without food for three days and they'd only had a single unsatisfactory meal. I guess what I've always felt was an unspoken rule in this pack was true. Alpha cared about his pack members as long as they were ranked above an Omega.

By this I felt completely drained of energy, I was barely able to keep myself standing. Despite this fact I'd been left alone to handle everything in the kitchen for the last hour, making food for the pack as usual.

Every so often my eyes would move to the door that separated the kitchen from the dining hall, fear slowly crept in clouding my mind further as time slowly passed. Alpha had announced his decision concerning my fate early this morning, since then I've been waiting for Lewis to seek out his revenge against me for the humiliation he received by giving me a beating. The fact that he had yet to appear was only causing my anxiety to ratched higher. I felt like a mouse waiting for a cat to pounce on them at any moment. I could not help but think that the fact he was taking so long meant that he was creating a perfectly evil ploy to torment me with.

I had not seen Natasha since that morning either, it made me wonder what new forms of abuse she was secretly coming up with. Her harassment had begun two years ago after a mating ball when a Beta from another pack that she had a crush on insulted her by saying that I was far more beautiful than her. It was at that moment that she swore to make me one of the pack whores just to prove that she was and would always be better than me. Both Natasha and Lewis were twenty-two years old as they were twins, but neither of them had been fortunate enough to find their mates yet. Natasha liked to blame me for her mateless status, she had wanted to take that Beta as her chosen mate two years ago. In my opinion she was just being an impatient bitch, she didn't want to quietly wait like the rest of us for our mates. Nope she wanted to take a mate of her choosing as soon as possible.

Since the night of the mating ball she has dragged a different man from the pack up to her room to use as her own personal fuck toy. She uses them to slake her sexual frustration over not having found her mate. Of course there had been several such evenings that she demanded that I attend her in her bedroom while those men were servicing her. Witnessing that hand had made me want to vomit but I could not refuse a direct order otherwise I would be punished severely.

When lunch was prepared a different female Omega was the one that carried out the platters of food to the crowded dining hall. I stayed hidden in the kitchen, only sneaking a peek at the hall from behind the shelter of the door. There wasn't a rule stating that I wasn't allowed into the dining hall, it was just that after everything that had transpired that morning, I didn't want to chance taking any further risks.

Truthfully, I was just worried that if the Alpha caught sight of me he would change his mind just to please his Luna and son. It wasn't the Alpha that noticed me stealing looks into the dining hall, but the Luna. I instantly flinched back concealing myself completely and lowered my eyes to the floor. Just as I was about to retreat into the kitchen, my eyes fell on Lewis. I realized that he had been searching for me amongst those in the hall for a while. As I watched from my hiding spot his lips curled into an evil smile, it sent a cold shiver down my spine as my eyes grew large and my heart stopped beating for a moment. I scurried away from the door and found a quiet corner of the kitchen to sit on the floor with my knees pulled to my chest. My mind spun with questions: What had that meant? Why was he smiling? I didn't have a good feeling about the behavior he was exhibiting, it wasn't what I had been anticipating. The unexpected tended to spell my doom.

"Elaine," a woman called my name, almost eliciting a scream from me when she touched my shoulder. I slapped my hand over my mouth to stifle my scream as I watched the door with baited breath. It wouldn't be unheard of for the Luna to come and investigate what had disturbed their peaceful lunch. Minute by minute time slowly ticked by, but the Luna never appeared. Eventually, I lowered my hand from my mouth, realizing the coast was clear though not understanding the why of it.

"Elaine," the woman called again, drawing my attention back to her.

"Ye...yes?" I asked, attempting to disguise my fear behind a half smile as I peered up at her from the floor.

"We did it! We haven't had anything to eat or drink for the last two days. So, according to the pack laws we get to eat today," she was brimming with excitement.

A genuine smile grew on my lips, I quickly got up off of the floor to fetch us both plates. Once I handed the other Omega her food and she left the kitchen, I stared down into the bottom of the pot. Tears of relief swam in my eyes at the sight of the small pile of rice. It wasn't much, only enough to fill my small shriveled stomach but it was enough to help me endure another two days. It seemed that the Moon Goddess had decided to smile down upon me on my birthday.

After the tragic events of last night, things were beginning to go well for me. Or I should say as well as they ever could for an Omega in this pack. I scooped up my portion of rice into a small bowl adding a small amount of salt to make it edible. I wasn't allowed to add any egg, meat, beans, or protein. Anything that delicious was meant only for the other pack members, not for Omegas. I wasn't even sure what those foods tasted like, I've only ever eaten old bread and rice. Whenever I watch the other pack members eating all of those flavorful delicacies, my mouth waters with my desire to taste them even once. However, any time that thought crossed my mind I remembered the punishment I had suffered when I was young for having dared to eat something that was off limits.

When I was seven, I had picked up a piece of red bean that had fallen to the floor when I was clearing away people's plates. I had picked it up off of the floor, just as I was about to put it in my mouth, Natasha chucked a glass at my head. The pain caused by the impact led to me dropping the bean. Of course, the Luna had witnessed the entire event and beat me for it. From that moment on I understood that delicious food was reserved for pack members that mattered like them, not for me.

I took my small bowl of rice back to the quiet corner I had been sitting in earlier, then began to eat. From the very first bite I would

30

have sworn that I was the best tasting rice that I had ever had the pleasure of eating. I shoveled a couple of spoonfuls of rice in short succession out of sheer hunger only to have some of the rice get stuck in my throat which led to a coughing fit. I swiftly got up off the floor and rushed out to the well to collect a cup of water for myself. I was permitted water today as well, to keep from descending completely into dehydration.

Once I had dislodged the rice and eased my parched throat I returned to the kitchen to finish my meal. The moment I walked into the kitchen I discovered that my bowl of rice had been knocked over onto the floor with dirt and debris covering it. It was too much, I fell to my knees in tears. I'd only managed to eat three bites of food, but now it was ruined. Before I'd left the kitchen I had carefully placed it on the countertop so that it would be out of the way, there's no way it could have fallen on its own.

That was when I caught the scent of a familiar fragrance, Natasha had been in the kitchen. What I didn't understand was what she could possibly have been doing in the kitchen, she never came here. The only plausible explanation that I could come up with was that she had come into the kitchen when I had gone to the well and had dumped my food on the floor to get revenge on me. I could even hear her loud cackling laughter coming from the dining hall.

"Bitches don't deserve to be fed!" She yelled from the other side of the door. I bit down on my fist to keep the sounds of my sobbing from making their way back to her. I knew without having to be told that the whole pack was laughing at me as she explained to them what she'd done.

The hunger pains had grown so severe that I could no longer bear the starvation. I used my hands to scoop the dirty rice back into my upturned bowl. Logically I knew that I didn't have much of an option other than to eat the soiled food, it was either that or attempt to make it another two days before I could possibly eat again. I opened my mouth for a spoonful of the tainted rice.

"Elaine, what in the world are you doing?" someone jerked the hand holding the spoon away from my mouth. I glanced up, I had been so focused on the rice that I'd missed Marvin approaching me.

"Marvin, what are you doing back here in the kitchen?" I asked him, surprised. He had somehow made it into the kitchen without anyone in the dining room noticing. His hand still firmly grasped my wrist preventing me from eating.

"That food is inedible, you will make yourself sick if you eat it," Marvin warned as he helped me up from the floor. He led me out of the kitchen to the other side of the packhouse where no one would be spying on us. I looked back longingly at my rice that was still lying on the floor of the kitchen as we left. I was fully aware that if I left the kitchen now, that I might never have another chance to eat.

"Marvin, what are you doing?! That was the first thing that I've had to eat in two days. Today will be day three, if I don't eat soon I will die," I explained which caused him to stop, we were alone in the pack garden.

"Do you even realize what you're saying Elaine?! You're just as likely to die of food poisoning if I let you eat that!" He argued with me.

"Does it really make a difference whether I die of starvation or food poisoning? I'm going to die one way or another, I am sick of slowly crawling towards my death at the hands of famine. You have no concept of what it's like to miss a meal, nevermind starve!" I snapped. He stood there silently assessing me for a few moments.

"You're right Elaine, I've never experienced so much as missing a meal. I still hate seeing you like this," he told me while gently stroking my cheek. I lowered my gaze and moved away from his touch. His hand would get dirty from touching someone like me.

"It's my fate," I stated flatly before walking away from him. I already knew what he was trying to say, that he had feelings for me. He has claimed to have been in love with me since we were children. Similarly to the pack that I belong to his was also rich and was part of the Alpha King's territory. Both of the packs were allies since the Alpha of his pack and my Alpha were brothers. This meant that while we were growing up he was allowed to visit as often as he wished.

When we were small it used to be my responsibility to run behind, Marvin and Natasha holding their shoes in my hands, to prevent them from getting dirty. The pair would play together while I would watch from afar. Slowly over time Marvin grew closer to me, he would start sneaking me his leftover food. He's always worn his pity for me on the surface.

"I refuse to accept that it's your fate. Become mine," he suggested while reaching for my hand.

"Why in the world would you possibly want me?" I asked, looking at him like he was insane, he just smiled.

"The answer to that question is simple, I love you," he admitted.

"This isn't love Marvin, you just feel sorry about my situation. I'm just the Omega that sits obediently at your feet and give your scraps to when you see fit. Don't mistake your pity for love, you'll only be hurt in the end when I'm gone," I corrected him. He tried to turn away before I saw the look of disappointment on his face.

"You say that every time I confess my feelings for you so that you can shut me out, yet I still continue to say it to you. I love you," he earnestly claimed as I continued to stare at the ground. I wasn't allowed to leave until I was dismissed or ordered to do so.

"Here, take this," he gently offered as he handed me a small bag.

"What is it?" I asked as he forced the bag into my hands.

"It's your birthday present," he replied. When I opened the bag I saw that it was filled with grapes. Once again Marvin was taking pity on me. All I could do was stare at him, he knew that in my current state I couldn't afford to refuse the gift. My next allotment of food wouldn't be for another two days. That of course meant that I would have gone without sustenance for four days if I didn't eat the grapes. I wasn't sure that my body could survive that long, my hunger pains were growing intense.

"What do you want in exchange for this?" I asked suspiciously, he smiled.

"I just want you to keep smiling and never run away from me," he laid out his conditions, I nodded in agreement.

"ELAINE!" Natasha angrily screamed my name. "Where in fucking hell did that whore go?!" she yelled, this time it caused me to drop the bag of grapes in my hand. I glanced down to find that they were dirty, though that wasn't important as they could be washed. All of my attention was focused on why Natasha could possibly be calling me. I stared at the packhouse as fear gripped me.

"I'm sorry, but I need to go," I apologized to Marvin, he grabbed my arm as I walked passed him.

"It's alright, don't worry about the grapes. I'll have some fresh fruit put in your room," he assured me before I ran towards Natasha's bedroom.

I sprinted up the stairs to her room, knowing it was best not to keep Natasha waiting. I knocked before entering as was expected, but as I walked in I was surprised to see all of her dresses laying in disarray on the floor. She had pulled every item of clothing out of her closet. I had no idea what she was up to. I found Natasha sitting in front of her largest mirror admiring herself with the expensive bracelet Luna Wilma had given her for her last birthday.

"Why are you looking at my bracelet, bitch?" she snarled. I tore my gaze away from the glittering bangle. I had just been admiring it, it's not like I had a need for such expensive trivialities. Access to food and water were the only things that mattered to me.

"Well, are you going to stop standing there like an idiot and start handing me dresses," she snapped and I scrambled over to the piles of dresses. I carefully began to handle the dresses one by one holding them out for her, to prevent any wrinkling. I repeated this process dozens of times.

"Bring me the red dress," she demanded, extending her arm. I handed it to her and she began trying it on. Once she was clothed, she stepped in front of the mirror to assess herself. Until then she'd tried all the dresses on quickly, but with this one she was blushing and smiling like a loon. It was obvious that she was thinking about something or someone. From what I had been able to gather she was going to be attending a special event somewhere. It had turned her into a love struck puppy, she was so happy, jumpy, and not able to stand still.

"What do you think about this green one?" she asked with a raised brow. I knew that if I said something that was even construed as neutral she would bash my head into that large mirror.

"It...it's beautiful," I stammered, causing her to smirk.

"Of course it's beautiful, It was made for a beautiful woman like me. Not for an Omega like you that has grubby hair, an ugly face, is chubby, and has an awful body odor,' she laughed with a wrinkle of her nose.

The joke was on her though as none of her insults fazed me any longer. I had been insulted by her and the rest of the pack my entire life, my skin has grown thick beneath their barbed tongues. My hair wasn't grubby, I just didn't have a proper brush for it. I knew I had a distinct smell, but it wasn't body odor, it was from the water in the abandoned well that I used to bathe behind the packhouse.

"This is what I will wear for tomorrow's mating ball," she announced, then gently placed the dress on the safety of the bed. It was at that moment that I noticed the invitation for the Alpha King's birthday party, it stated that it would be a mating ball at which he would choose a mate for himself. My heart began to beat rapidly in my chest when I read the words mating ball. That meant that men from all over the Kingdom would be attending. Natasha was going to the party with the hope of finding her mate. Now that I had also turned eighteen there was a possibility that my mate could be out there waiting for me, it made me excited. I couldn't care less about who the Alpha King took as his chosen mate, I was only interested in my own mate. Of course, I was only an Omega so I wouldn't be allowed to attend.

"You'll be coming with me," Natasha informed me, my eyes almost popping out of my head.

"You're taking me with you?" I asked, surprise clearly written on my face.

"Were you daydreaming about becoming the Alpha King's chosen mate? Well you can forget about that. I am going to become the Alpha King's chosen mate. I'm bringing you with me as my personal slave. You'll do anything and everything that I ask without question," she crowed while shoving me out of her room.

Despite all the work that lay ahead of me in the coming days, there was a smile on my lips as I made my way back to my room. If I had to attend a mating ball to serve Natasha then there was a chance that, no matter how slim, that I might be able to find my mate. What if he was my mate? It seemed like my life might soon be changing.

5. I am Trapped

Alpha Fabian

W hen I arrived in the dining hall the entire pack was already seated waiting for me. I swiftly took my seat at the head table, Then Elaine along with the other Omega's entered the hall to deliver the food. I watched her small hands tremble as she placed my meal before me. I growled lowly until she flinched away, it had been meant as a warning for her to keep her wits about her and be extra careful.

"Apologies Alpha," Elaine whispered while moving away. My Luna refused to be served or have her food touched by Elaine. So, a different Omega had been designated to attend to her during meals. Once they had been served the pack began eating, I was discussing business with Beta Dale when I noticed something. Elaine was serving Lewis his meal, for whatever reason my son couldn't keep his hands to himself and was grabbing her ass. She continually attempted to escape his grasp but all he did was smile at her. Both Wilma and Natasha seemed to gain great enjoyment from watching Elaine's discomfort over the situation.

"Lewis!" I snapped, slamming my fist down hard onto the table with a snarl. Everyone in the dining room was shocked as they stared at me, in the meantime Lewis slowly moved his hand away from Elaine.

"Yes, father," he muttered as I glared at him from down the table.

"Eat quickly, then get the fuck out of my sight!" I commanded with a clenched jaw.

"As you command," I could feel the hate filled glares of both he and his mother on my person for having yelled at Lewis publicly.

"Eliane!" I bellowed, she quickly ran forward.

"I never want to see your face in the dining hall again, do you understand me? Otherwise, I'll be forced to remove both your legs," I warned and she swiftly scurried into the kitchen for cover. Soon after I rose from my chair having completely lost my appetite after what I had witnessed.

"Darling, where are you going you haven't eaten anything?" Wilma tauntingly inquired. Instead of answering I glared at her over my shoulder then continued to exit the dining hall without uttering a word. I made my way up to my office, Beta Dale followed close behind me.

"What's going on Alpha?" Dale asked while I inspected a paper that was laying on my desk.

"Elaine needs to be removed from the pack at our earliest convenience. It definitely needs to be before Lewis becomes Alpha, otherwise all that we have worked for will turn to ash. That boy's lust for Elaine is making him stupid, he won't be deterred any longer. He's letting his feelings for her affect his judgment to the point that he's not even looking for his mate," I groused.

"What are your orders, Alpha?" Dale inquired with a deep breath.

"Just figure out a way to make Elaine disappear! No one ever needs to know that there was a girl in this pack named Elaine, otherwise we're all doomed," I advised Dale. He just nodded his head until his eyes fell on the paper on my desk.

"Alpha," he shivered in fear as his eyes widened over what he saw written on the page. "Did someone... I mean, did Elaine..." he stumbled over his words unsure of what the sensible thing would be to ask, then out of fear decided it was more prudent to shut his mouth.

"Yes, they are," I answered the question he'd been trying to ask before ripping the paper into pieces and tossing it into the fire. No one needed to discover this.

"Just remember, this stays between the two of us," I swore my Beta to secrecy.

Elaine

Since the moment the sun had broken the horizon that morning the pack had been bustling with frenzied activity. None of the unmated women were able to sit still, they were all too excited about the Alpha King's birthday and the possible prospect of being selected as his chosen mate. It seemed like I was the only person in the whole pack that was working, running from place to place, delivering whatever item was needed only to be told I needed to immediately do something else.

Despite the fact that I had already finished making both breakfast and lunch then cleaned the kitchen. I had yet to have the chance to even sit for a moment to rest my feet as Natasha sent me to the market for make-up over and over again. Of course, if Natasha was dissatisfied with the quality of the item that I brought her, she would order me to return the product, and demand I return with more options. I was well aware that she was purposefully being difficult just to give me a hard time.

My legs were beginning to ache from trudging up back and forth from the market to Natasha's room at least ten times. It was just approaching five in the evening and I was absolutely exhausted, I had no idea how I was going to make it through the rest of the night. It had been a boon that Marvin had left some fruit in my room like he had promised, it was the only source of nourishment that I had available. Though I wasn't selfish enough to horde the fruit all to myself, I shared it with the other Omegas. I knew that if I was starving then it was highly likely that they were as well.

"Elaine!" Natasha screamed for me again as I was running into her room with her replenished glass of juice. I quickly placed her juice on the side table before taking in the utter disarray that Natasha's room had become since I had left. Somehow in the time it took me to refill her glass, Natasha had pulled every one of her dresses from her closet and scattered them around the room to once again assess her wardrobe options. I was beginning to question whether she had lost her sanity over this mating ball and the possibility of becoming the Alpha King's chosen mate.

I have never seen the Alpha King in person before. Though I had heard all the rumors that spoke of his handsomeness that had droves of women willing to sacrifice themselves in his bed. Of course that was the more positive gossip surrounding the King. It's said that he has a terrible temper, that he never lies, and that he brutally kills anyone that attempts to deceive him.

I didn't understand why every unmated female in the Kingdom was clamoring to become his chosen Queen when he seemed so volatile. I had always had a difficult time grasping why someone would decide to take a chosen mate when they could have their fated mate, even if their chosen mate were someone as powerful as the Alpha King.

"What the hell are you doing?! Why the hell are you staring at my dress like a blithering idiot?!" Natasha shrieked at me then shoved me out of the way as she stormed into her closet.

"You called for me?" I asked demurely, I still had heaps of work to finish in the kitchen. Natasha turned around, assessing me with her beady eyes from head to toe.

"You will be coming with me to the palace. Of course, you can't actually step into the mating ball but that's perfectly fine. You'll just wait outside the palace gates for me in case I need you to do anything. It doesn't matter how long I'm at the ball or even if I ever come out again, you are to wait. If the Moon Goddess smiles down upon me I'll be chosen by the Alpha King, which means he'll be screwing my brains out in his royal chambers," Natasha murmured while rubbing her thighs together having gotten lost in her own fantasy. On the other hand, I felt like the ground that I'd been standing on had crumbled beneath my feet. If I couldn't go into the ball, there was no possible way for me to find my mate. I didn't understand the logic behind me accompanying her.

"Seeing as you'll be waiting outside there is no need for you to wear a decent dress, no one will look at you anyways. Not when there are Princes, Princesses, and members from various noble families. Plus, you shouldn't delude yourself into thinking that your mate will be there. Someone like you would have an Omega or slave as a mate…if they're even still alive. You really shouldn't waste your time looking for him," she cackled. All of her barbed comments had hit their mark as both my wolf and I flinched.

To even think that one's mate could be dead was a curse. I couldn't help but wonder if what Natasha said was true. I had always been unlucky, why should this be any different. Perhaps it went even deeper than that. Maybe the Moon Goddess made the decision not to bless me with a mate from the very beginning. So that I would spend my entire life pining for someone to come and rescue me from my pack. The heavy weight of disappear wrapped around me like a blanket making my eyes water.

"You'll wear whatever it is you call the rags you're wearing now," she ordered with a sneer and I nodded in understanding. "I'll be heading to the palace in half an hour's time. You will be arriving on foot," she informed. I couldn't stop my jaw from dropping at her latest order, the palace was a fair distance from the pack using a vehicle nevermind walking. The distance was too great, that was not taking into consideration the other dangers that lurked in the woods on the lands between here and the palace. It wasn't just animals that I would have to contend with but rogues as well. There had been an escalation in rogue attacks in the area recently.

"How will I get there by myself? Please let me go with you, I'm worried something is going to happen," I pleaded but she just laughed at me.

"Do you think that you are special or something? If someone grabs you in the dark of the woods then its a rogue, don't fight, let him have a quick easy fuck, and you can be on your way. If I can't find you outside the palace waiting for me, I will have you killed," she warned, letting her wolf come forward in her eyes. I nodded in understanding.

"Don't just stand there! Get the fuck out, before your ugly face ruins my day," she barked, looking disgusted. Once I left Natasha's room and walked down the hall I saw the Luna. She was sitting on one of the sofas watching me. I tucked my head down as I made a beeline directly to the kitchen to hide.

"Elaine!" She yelled my name, forcing me to halt my escape. Apparently she had been waiting for me to appear.

"Yes, Luna," I answered with my head lowered while making sure not to get too close to her. When I was a child she had made it clear that I was not allowed to let my shadow fall on her person or

I would be severely punished.

"You're aware that the Alpha family is attending an event at the palace tonight," she stated plainly with a single raised brow. I nodded my head in response.

"Good, then you won't be wandering the packhouse like a lost puppy while we're gone. Instead you'll be catching up on all of the housework you've fallen behind on today, like the cooking, cleaning, and whatever else it is that you do around here. Do you understand me?" she asked while examining her long perfectly polished nails while I tried to control my panic. She wanted me to attend to all the housework when I had just been ordered to wait outside the mating ball by Natasha. I wasn't sure what to do, I couldn't disobey either of them.

"You unruly brat! Are you even paying attention to me? Or do you think you are above answering me?!" the Luna screamed, causing me to jump. Honestly, I had gotten so lost in my thoughts that I had forgotten to answer her.

"I'm sorry Luna, I understand," I apologized quickly as her eyes blazed with anger. When she got up from the sofa I made sure to keep a safe distance from her to avoid being slapped. It was a good day as she didn't beat me for insubordination.

That was the moment that I noticed Lewis coming towards me, he had just exited his room. He was dressed in an expensive personally tailored suit that showed without words that he came from wealth. It was clear that he planned to attend the mating ball as well, even though from the look on his face he had other less savory acts in mind where it concerned me. I could feel the intensity of his gaze as it roved over my body despite my head and eyes being lowered in submission. I tried to ignore him so that I could be on my way to the kitchen, but he blocked my path and refused to move.

"Please let me pass," I quietly request as he uses a finger to lift my chin to force me to look him in the eye.

"How do you expect me to let you go when I've done nothing but crave you?" he asked, his voice gravely while his lust perfumed the air. I swiftly stepped back from him out of fear, needing to place as much distance as possible between the two of us. I knew what Lewis wanted from me, it was what he always wanted from me, and it made both my wolf and I quake. Lewis chose that moment to strike, grabbing a fist full of my hair and violently yanking my head back.

"Elaine, don't forget to do exactly what Natasha said. Make sure that pretty ass of yours is waiting outside the palace tonight. Otherwise, you'll have the pleasure of being fucked by me in front of the entire pack," he whispered in my ear as I clenched my eyes tightly closed.

"Does that itty bitty brain of yours understand?" he asked, giving a sharp pull on my hair. I couldn't help the yelp of pain that escaped my lips from his actions.

"Yes," I answered and he let go of the grip he had on my hair.

"That's a good little bitch," he praised me while gently running a hand over my hair. Then he gave my ass a hard smack before sauntering out of the packhouse to the car that was taking him to the mating ball. Even from this distance I could hear his evil laughter through the door. I had to bite my lips to keep the sounds of my sobs from escaping. What in the Goddess' name was I supposed to do? If I obeyed Natasha and Lewis then the Luna would have me killed. Of course, the same was true if I followed the Luna's orders, no matter which way I turned I was trapped.

6. Trapped by Lewis

Elaine

The purr of a car engine as it left the pack drew my attention to the window, unsurprisingly the Alpha and Luna were the first to leave for the ball. Though Lewis and Natasha left in their own vehicles respectively in short succession. I quickly made my way down to the kitchen, I wanted to finish as much work there as I could as fast as possible. Of course, it wasn't until I stepped into the kitchen that I realized that it was almost seven o'clock at night, I had no idea how I was going to handle this situation.

It was going to take me until well past midnight to complete all the work that the Luna had left for me. That meant if I finished everything for Luna Wilma, I wouldn't be able to make it in time to wait for Natasha outside the palace walls as she had instructed. Really, it didn't matter whose command I followed either way I would be punished, I couldn't be in two places at once. I dropped the serving spoon that I was washing back into the soapy water in the sink and curled up on the floor as anxiety ridden panic caged me firmly in its grasp.

It was impossible for me to problem solve my way out of this situation, no matter what option I chose the night would end in my painful unjust death. For one Lewis would go stark raving mad the moment he discovered that I didn't follow Natasha's orders. His latest threat from earlier this evening was still fresh in my mind, making my skin crawl anytime I thought about it. I still struggled to grasp why any of this concerned him to begin with. Of course, if I made the decision to disobey a direct order from Luna Wilma, she would take the issue straight to the Alpha. It was a damned either way situation.

"Elaine, why are you huddled on the floor?" A fellow female Omega asked when she entered the kitchen. "I thought that you were supposed to be going to the palace, to attend to the Alpha family. So, why are you in the kitchen?" she continued, causing my anxiety to rise.

"Before she left, Luna Wilma commanded me to complete all the work that needed to be done to set the kitchen to rights for the night then move on to clean the entire packhouse. If she returns from the mating ball and discovers that I ignored her orders in order to attend the mating ball, she will have me killed without a second thought," I answered. I could read her fear for my situation in her eyes.

"But if you don't go to the palace, it will be Natasha that kills you for disobeying her," the Omega pointed out. I nodded, desperation oozing out of my pores as my fear continued to grow.

"I think I have a solution! You head to the palace to take care of Natasha while I handle all the work here in the pack for you," she suggested, shocking me.

"I don't understand, you're willing to help me?" I asked as she gently placed her hand on mine.

"Yes, now go get ready," she urged nugging me in the direction of my room. I hurriedly grabbed my tattered scarf, wrapping it around my head and neck as I slipped my feet into my shoes.

"You aren't going to change into nicer clothes?" the Omega asked when I came back through the kitchen. I couldn't contain my laughter.

"You're new here aren't you? This is the only set of clothes that I own. I wash them every night in my room before I go to bed so they will be dry in the morning. I'm prohibited from having anything nice, including clothing. I received this set when I was fifteen, I'm eighteen now. I've grown over the last three years, so they are a little bit tight. That's why there's a small hole along the seam, every time I put it back on another stitch tears making it bigger," I explained, giving her a sad smile.

"You're going to the palace though, will they let you in if you aren't wearing at the very least suitable clothes?" she inquired, I glanced back at her over my shoulder.

"It shouldn't be a problem. I just need to wait outside the palace for Natasha. Due to my status in the pack I'm not allowed inside the palace walls like the others anyway, I'm going there as Natasha's slave," I clarified further for the new girl though this time I couldn't force myself to smile about the situation. The circumstances surrounding tonight's events were far too distressing, the fact that I was going to be at the palace yet unable to go into the ball to look for my mate was torturous. What if he was there? What if his mate was with him? I reasoned that I would be able to bear that if I at least had the chance to see him one last time.

When I passed by a window I checked my reflection, taking the time to tuck any stray hairs underneath the scarf wrapped around my head and neck that way no one would recognize me as I left. All too quickly I was in the woods and on my way to the palace, despite fear of rogues gripping me I was nimble and my feet swift.

Utilizing my wolf speed I was able to cover over half the distance to the palace before I began to get lost in thoughts of him.

When I was young I would pray every night to the Moon Goddess to make him my fated mate. Even back then I knew that he came from a wealthy family while I was just a slave. I had been completely heedless about our vast differences in rank and had fallen in love with him the moment I laid my eyes on him. Every werewolf grew up knowing that they would be given a mate by the Moon Goddess, I just dared to dream that mine would be him. I did my best to keep my status as both a slave and an Omega hidden, worried that I would be on the receiving end of further humiliation and reprimand. If I were being completely honest I hid my status for my own self reasons as well. It was so that I might have another chance to catch just one more glimpse of him. I wasn't delusional though, I was fully aware that it was highly likely if he were to see me in my current condition he would kill me for deceiving him.

I slowed my pace to a walk then stopped as I stared down at the picture of him in my hand, it was the only image of him that I had. Logically I knew that he must have found his mate by now, he was considerably older than me, yet I still hadn't been able to let him go. Perhaps it was better that the Moon Goddess was preventing me from attending the mating ball. At least this way the question of whether or not he was my true fated mate would never be answered. It would also spare me the pain of having to witness another finely dressed woman on his arm as his mate. I knew that as much as I longed to see him, it was better that I continued to cling to my idyllic dream of him being my mate than have to confront the possible truth of it not being true.

I hadn't even realized that I was crying until a couple of my tears splattered on the picture in my hand, I wiped off the tears before tucking the picture back into my pocket. I needed to stop dilly dallying and get to the palace.

Before I knew it I had been running again for another half an hour when I heard a loud crash that caused me to shout out in alarm. I realized that the loud crash had been a speeding car that had collided with a stout tree on the side of the road. I sprinted toward the crash site to find out if there was someone that needed help.

"Hey, does anyone need help in there?" I yelled while banging my hand against one of the car windows. In response a woman let out a pain filled groan a second before the driver side door creaked open and a woman tumbled out landing on the torn up earth with a bleeding cut on her head. I reacted quickly, pulling her away from the car and leaning her against a nearby tree.

"Oh my Goddess. I need to stop the bleeding. Are you injured anywhere else?" I asked as I unwound my scarf to use as a bandage for her bleeding head. I was worried that she was going to slip into shock after the accident. Add the amount of blood coming from her head wound and I knew that I could quickly lose her to blood loss if I wasn't able to get her to help in time. Apparently she had other ideas in mind as she shoved my hand away from her head.

"It's already too late for you to be of any help to me," she managed to pant out between wheezed breaths while her eyes frantically searched for someone or something in every dark shadow. I couldn't help but notice the bag that she clutched to her as if it were a child.

"I…" She began to tell me something when she started to cough up blood. I was unable to contain my shock, her internal injuries were far worse than how she appeared on the surface. This woman could die any minute, but I refused to let that happen.

"Don't move, I'm going to get you some water," I told her as I got up to leave. Despite the fact that she was knocking on death's door the woman was able to pull me back down her side while shaking her head.

"No, there isn't any time. You have to listen to me," she pleaded with me between short gasping breaths and groans of pain as she clasped my arm for dear life.

"Okay, okay," I assured her while making sure that my scarf was still securely wrapped around her head but she pushed my fussing hands away.

"There are members of the Opal Moon Pack that are chasing after me so that they can kill me," she explained. My shock was clearly written on my face, why would my pack be trying to kill her? If her car and outfit were any indication she came from a wealthy family, definitely from among the nobility of the werewolf community. It didn't make sense for them to be after her. That was when I heard the howl of an approaching wolf, it also drew the attention of the injured woman in front of her.

"They're...they're already here. They've found me," the she-wolf nervously whispered while clutching her handbag and looking up at me with wide eyes.

"Why are they trying to kill you?" I inquired.

"They're almost here, there's no time to explain. I don't have much time left any ways," she wheezed and coughed up some more blood. "No matter what it's inevitable now that they'll find me, but I can't let them have this bag. You must take responsibility for it now, it's the only way that I can keep it safe. You can give it to the right person eventually," she said as she handed me the bag. My curiosity got the best of me as I took a quick glance into the bag to see for myself what was so important, there were some clothes and a mask, the perfect party attire. This hurt she-wolf must have been on her way to the Alpha King's Mating Ball. I felt more than saw the wooden box as the bag clunked against my leg, really I couldn't understand what about this woman or the bag was special enough to die for.

"No, I can't take this! Let me help you instead. We'll get you somewhere that you can be treated then you can be the one to give this to its rightful owner," I proposed in an attempt to get her to work with me to save herself but she was having none of it.

"That's not going to happen, I can't stand nevermind walk," she pointed out pulling up the hem of her dress to reveal the grizzly sight of her mangled severed leg. I couldn't believe that I hadn't noticed, the smell of blood coming from her head wound and coughing must have covered the copious amount oozing out of her mutilated leg. It must have happened before she got into the car, sorrowfully for this woman it was probably also what led to her crash. This new information shot a fresh dose of fear through my system, it was proof that everything that she had told me was true. The she-wolf seemed to sense my panic building because she reached out and grabbed my hand drawing my focus back to her.

"Good, you understand now that it's impossible for me to go anywhere. You will have to carry out this task in my stead. You must go to the palace, attend the Mating Ball, there you will be able to find Alpha Prince Vincent. He is anticipating my arrival, he'll be waiting. It's imperative that you give him that bag," she spelled out for me. My brain was attempting to process everything that she had told me while simultaneously trying to figure out how I was going to accomplish the near impossible task this she-wolf had just assigned me.

"I don't even know how I'll get through the door. I'm just an Omega slave, I'm not allowed to step one foot inside the palace without my mistress," I couldn't help the hysterical laugh that slipped past my lips. "To make matters worse, my mistress has ordered me to wait outside the palace walls for her," I laid out all my cards for her. She just clamped her mouth shut in an attempt to queal her wheezed cough and shook her head.

"Trust me you'll be allowed to enter, my dress and mask are in the bag. All you need to do is change into them before you approach the palace wall. As long as you do it like you belong there the guards won't recognize you and let you in. It's imperative that you understand that you hold eighteen years of someone's hard work combined with the sacrifices of countless individuals in your hands. The future of the kingdom and the life of an innocent princess is now your responsibility," she gestured to the wooden box. I managed to nod my head in agreement, a peaceful smile came over her face before she winced in pain.

"Blast it all, put your noses into it! That stupid bitch has to be around here somewhere!" The frustration was evident in Beta Dale's voice even from this distance. I knew that if I could hear them they weren't very far away. That also meant that everything the dying she-wolf had told me was true. My pack was hunting her, they wanted her dead for whatever reason, and they were the ones responsible for mangling her leg. I was fully aware of the dynamics within my pack, there was no way that Beta Dale was stepping one paw out of line without a direct order from Alpha Fabian. That meant that the Alpha wanted this she-wolf disposed of. I wondered what could possibly be going on in the pack. I had thought that the Alpha and Luna had left for the ball before Natasha and Lewis.

"You need to go, run away from here. Otherwise they'll kill you just due to the simple fact that they saw you with me. Those wolves are far more savage than any monster from legend," the she-wolf warned, shooing me away. If only she comprehended how much she didn't have to caution me about the sadistic cruelty of those wolves, I had lived under their oppression my entire life. Of course, she might not have felt so comfortable entrusting me with this life and death task.

"Run!" She urged. I didn't hesitate as I got up from my spot in front of her and sprinted into the woods before my pack members had a chance to see me. There was no question that I would be dead the moment they laid eyes on me since I was supposed to still be home at the packhouse.

I could tell by smell that I was getting close to the palace, so I glanced back to see if any wolves were trailing me or not. The muscles in my legs quivered in exhaustion from the overuse and lack of proper nutrition, the rest of my body was shaking out of sheer panic. In the back of my head though, I knew that I couldn't stop running. No matter how much it hurt, how nervous I got, I kept running as fast as I could because someone's life depended on me getting there. I had already steeled myself to withstand whatever horrific punishment Natasha and Lewis decided to meet out for me disobeying a direct order. At least I would be able to save a princess. Of course, to succeed I need to figure out how to remain hidden from Lewis.

By the time I focused my attention back in the direction I was running in it was already too late, Lewis was running straight at me. The second I registered the lust in those creepy eyes of his, my blood rain ice cold. Lewis came to a slow halt a small distance away from with a wicked grin splitting his face. It seemed almost as if he had been waiting for just this moment, or waiting to finally catch me, whichever came first he didn't seem to care.

"Finally! The guest of honor has arrived, the real game can begin," he cheered, stalking closer to me. Panic clamped my lunges, in response my legs began to run towards the palace as if they had a mind of their own. The only thing that I was certain of was that I did not want to find out what Lewis meant by a game. This was too much of a coincidence, Natasha and Lewis must have planned this together. For some reason those two must have set it up so that I would be outside of the palace and therefore outside of the minimal protection of the pack.

7. Drugged

Elaine

Traveling alone in the forest hadn't left me with any other option than to run especially when faced with one of my most seasoned tormentors. I could see the lights on the towers of the palace blinking over the canopy of the forest. Even though the palace was within my sights I was still too far away when Lewis stepped out from behind a tree into my path like a barricade. I must have been delusional to think that I could out run an Alpha like Lewis, that wasn't even taking into consideration my physical condition.

"You couldn't have made a bigger mistake in running away from me, Elaine. I plan on fucking you so mercilessly that you won't be able to walk for at least a week," he threatened closing the space between us as I backed away. I whimper escaped my lips when Lewis began divesting himself of a new piece of his clothes with every step he took towards me.

"Pa...pa...please, Lewis let me go," I stuttered left with little other recourse than to plead with him as tears coursed down my cheeks. I knew that there was nothing in this forest that would stop him from doing exactly what he had been dreaming of. He was going to take the only thing I had left to offer my future mate, once he was done with me I'd have nothing left to live for.

"Stop fighting it and just come here you bitch!" He yelled, wrapping my hair around his fist until my face was so close to his that I could smell his fetid breath.

"I've fantasized about this moment for years, you've purposefully fueled my lustful hunger. The entire time you were aware of the perilous situation that you were placing yourself in by stoking a man's sexual desire. You even went so far as to fuck other men in the pack but not me!" he accused, shoving me to the ground. I managed to stifle any sounds of pain from escaping my lips as I stared up at him only for my eyes to grow huge at the sight of his hands moving to undo his pants.

"Please, don't..." I pleaded as I scurried back but it was no use. He grabbed me by my ankles and yanked me towards him then ripped the bodice of my dress. It honestly took me a moment to realize that I was the one that those horrific screams were emanating from until Lewis reached down and tore the rest of my threadbare dress off. So that I was left struggling to hide my nudity with my fraile arms.

"For fuck sake! I can't believe that you've been concealing this temptress's body from me. I mean Goddess! Look at how hard you've made me just from looking at you. I can only imagine how my cock will react when he finally gets a taste of you," he rambled while stroking his engorged member and I could feel his stare focused on my most intimate of places. I tried to close my legs so that he would stop, but that just ignited his anger further as he forced my legs wider apart and slapped me across the face.

"After all of this you still have the gumption to hide my obsession from me?" He snarled, placing his full weight on my spread thighs as he settled himself between them. "You should be offering yourself up to me like the pack whore that you are. Stop pretending as if you are protecting your virginity for your mate or some other ridiculous notion," Lewis snickered, squeezing my breast painfully hard until I let out a whimper of pain. I had felt his claws begin to extend when I hadn't reacted to his torturous treatment.

"Lewis, please you're hurting me. Please let me go, I'm begging you," I tried to persuade him though he just slapped me hard across the face again.

"Just be quiet you stupid bitch! You know this will be easier on you if you stop struggling. No one is going to save you, this isn't some fairytale that's told to pups, it's real life." An evil smirk spread over his face, "Plus, this is just the start of our time together, Elaine. I fully intend to leave marks from my loving all over your perfectly smooth skin so that every one of our pack members can see exactly who you belong to. That way they'll be too scared to touch what's mine," he told me with a deranged light in his eyes as he looked pointedly at my neck.

No, no, no, no! It took every bit of my self control to keep that one word from slipping passed my lips. I had lived with heaping amounts of injustice in my life but this was even beyond what I had thought Lewis capable of. He wanted to mark me, but I wanted nothing to do with him. When he leaned in for a kiss I began frantically struggling, instead of slowing him down he slapped me again before going back in for a kiss.

I was a sobbing, snotty nosed, mess as I continued to shove at Lewis trying to fight him off. I knew from conversations with Nora that sometimes a man's wolf could take over during sex. At that moment I fully believed every word she had told me. Lewis' facial features seemed to have sharpened as he snapped and growled at me in his fervor to claim his prize while slipping in a few strategic hits to sensitive body parts to keep me subdued. I could feel myself begin to slip away from reality as a way to deal with the horrors of the situation. It wasn't until Lewis started touching me between my thighs that in an act of desperation I used the last of my strength to put some distance between our two bodies.

"You feisty little bitch!" he roared, rearing back. I seized the opening that he left me to bring my knee up and nail him hard in the groin before shoving him away from me. He fell to the ground so concerned about holding his injured junk in his hands that his head slammed into a rock eliciting a painful groan.

With all of the training that Lewis had undergone I was well aware that he wouldn't be out of commission for long. That's why I hurriedly got up from the ground holding the shreds of my dress together, located the bag, picked it up from where I had dropped it by a tree, then sprinted flat out towards the lights of the palace as if the hounds of hell were nipping at my heels. I knew that the only place that I had even a slim chance of hiding was among the crowd at the palace. Even though I had managed to put a fair bit of distance between Lewis and I, his mutterings to himself about exactly what he planned to do to me when he caught me again still reached me. I knew if that was happening he was far closer than I had originally thought, I was running short on time. She needed to seize the only opportunity that she had to escape him. In a rush she plucked the photo from the pocket of my destroyed dress, tucking it into the bag. With no other option I changed into my wolf midstep holding the bag firmly in my muzzle, at least in this form I could run twice as fast.

I knew that Lewis couldn't be far behind. Even as I thought that I spotted the palace walls in the distance, I couldn't control the hope that I might actually escape from growing in my chest. There weren't any visible guards patrolling, it allowed me to throw caution to the wind as I hastened my step and leapt over the palace wall. Never in my wildest dreams would I have thought that I would ever be able to jump that high, I suppose adrenaline could go a long way in making the impossible possible.

I landed with a splash into a body of water, the bag that I was holding in my muzzle slipped out in surprise. I let out a small groan of relief at making it inside the walls as I shifted back into my human form. Of course, the sense of relief was short lived, the second I was back to my usual self I was seized by panic over the fact that I didn't know how to swim. I did feel rather sheepish after I had already begun to panic and I tried to stand up only to realize that the water wasn't even over my head. I could easily make it out of the water safely, I had never been in any danger of drowning especially seeing I had jumped into a fountain of all things. Though I didn't see anyone in the immediate vicinity, I was sure the loud splash that my landing had made would draw a guard or two to this location. I needed to get dressed and quickly vacate this area before I was found.

"Did anyone else just hear that?" A man yelled followed by two sets of footsteps echoing off of stone stairs.

I held my breath, I knew what awaited me if they discovered me, an Omega, in the palace breaking a royal law. It equaled a death sentence. I scrambled out of the fountain after retrieving the bag that was floating nearby. The one positive thing I had going for me in all of this was that I had fallen into the fountain and the water would mask my scent. That meant that neither Lewis nor the palace guards would be able to sniff me out from the fountain anyways.

I sprinted into the lush palace garden hoping that the well tended greenery would offer me ample cover. Once I entered the palace gardens I realized that there really was nowhere for me to go, there were guards crawling all over the place like ants on a cupcake. I also needed to take care of the fact that I was walking around the palace naked, that's when I thought to look in the bag. That's right the woman had mentioned there being a set of woman's clothes in there that I could wear. I just prayed to the Moon Goddess that the contents of the bag hadn't gotten soaked when I had gone for a swim in the fountain. When I opened the satchel I was astonished by what I found.

As if by some magic the entire contents of the bag were bone dry. I found what appeared to be a gorgeous hand sewn gown fit for a princess among the items in the bag.I hated to admit even to myself how transfixed I was by the beauty of the dress, so much so that I had even forgotten that I was still naked. It felt almost as if the dress was coaxing me, with a shake of my head at my own ridiculousness I pulled the dress on then looked down at myself. Despite being intimately familiar with the many types of fabrics in Natasha's wardrobe, I had never seen anything that was even remotely similar to the material of the dress I was wearing. It felt as if I was almost still naked, the woman from early had been correct. This dress was indeed meant for a princess.

My hand nervously fidgeted with the long wet rope of hair as it trailed down my back. It was a wild mess but I did not have a comb so the best that I could do was run my fingers through it before twisting it up into a semi presentable bun. During my time at Opal Moon I had become an expert at fashioning elaborate updo's in Natasha's greasy unwashed hair. There was no way for me to check how bad I looked, I just had to hope that it was good enough to pass. I reached down to the open bag to check on the contents before going on my way only to find the bag empty. The wooden box was no longer there.

"Oh Goddess!" I whimpered in fear as I frantically checked the bag again even though there was no place for the box to be hiding in the bag. It wasn't like the bag was cavernous and the only other items in it were the mask and my photo. I was going to lose my mind trying to figure out where that box was. Could it have fallen out while I was running? Or maybe when I had landed in the fountain? I bit my knuckle to force myself to calm down enough to breathe through my nose, panicking right now wouldn't end well for anyone. The woman from the woods had entrusted me with this important task and I had carelessly lost the object I was supposed to deliver.

No! I refused to let that happen. I would find it and deliver it to its rightful owner.

"Hey, who's out there?" A palace guard yelled, nearly giving me a heart attack when I realized how close he was. I was so dead, it was imperative that no one saw my face while I was here. I hurriedly pulled the mask on, tucked the empty bag under a shrub behind me so that I looked less suspicious, then turned in the direction I could hear him approaching from. When I finished turning around the guard stopped leaving more than the appropriate distance between us.

"I apologize for my rude behavior, please continue on your way into the palace," he said with a bow of his head refusing to look me in the eye. I did my best to control the trembling that had taken over my body due to fear. Though it seemed that the dress had the desired effect as the guard believed that I was a she-wolf from a noble family pack. I was too nervous to respond, so I just nodded and started to walk away.

"Wait a second, miss," he called and waited until I turned back towards him. Had he somehow figured out the truth? Was he going to inform the Alpha King? Was I going to be given a death sentence? I had all I could do to control my breathing so that I didn't fall victim to a full fledged panic attack.

"The Mating Ball is that way," he said pointing in the opposite direction that I was walking with a smile on his face. I let out a long sigh of relief as I finally went in the right direction. Though I wasn't sure what I was going inside the Mating Ball when I was no longer in possession of the wooden box. What exactly was I going to tell the Alpha Prince seeing I didn't have the item I was meant to give him? It wasn't even possible to run away or just hide in the garden seeing as the guard was still standing there watching to make sure I made it to the ball.

As I finally approached the doorway my legs stopped on their own accord at the sheer number of people that were milling around the ballroom. Many of the people in attendance appeared to be Princes and Princesses in their own right. While others were more of what I had anticipated being in attendance, members of affluent packs and families. I did notice that everyone from those in the most lavish of outfits all the way down to those serving guests each wore a mask. That was what gave me the confidence to step into the Alpha Prince's grand ballroom, the understanding that I would be able to remain anonymous behind my mask. That did not however alleviate any of my other concerns. I was all too conscious of the fact that if I held the skirt of my gown just a little too high someone at the ball might catch a glimpse of my well-worn slippers that in no way went with the gown I had on.

The further I moved into the ballroom the harder it became to resist getting lost in the beauty of the palace. The Alpha King was unbelievably lucky that he got to live in a place brimming with such opulent refinement. Never once in my life did I think that I would have the chance to see something like this nevermind stand in the palace. I quickly lowered my gaze when I realized I was attracting the attention of not only the men but also the ladies in the room. That was the last thing I needed, someone to recognize me.

I slipped into a shadowed area to watch a couple that had just discovered they were mates. The girl had jumped into his waiting arm in her excitement before they were lost to a series of joyous kisses and hugs. The smile that curled my lips was wistful as I watched them. The newly mated couple was indescribably beautiful in their newly blossomed love that my eyes could not help but scan the room for a particular someone. Would he be here? He was quite wealthy, so there was a possibility. However, the smile slipped from my face the second that his mate popped into my mind. I had to be satisfied with being able to see him this one last time.

"A drink, miss," a waiter stopped next to me offering a tray of cold beverages.

"Thank you, but I am all set," I politely refused.

"There's actually a rule stating that you can't be in the ballroom empty handed. You have to take one of these," he explained with a smile.

I glanced around the room, everyone there had a drink in hand, so it would seem oddly suspicious if I were the only one in the room that did not. I took the offered glass, giving it a delicate sniff as the waiter walked away. From the smell of it, the contents were definitely alcoholic. Having just one small sip wouldn't hurt, I was surprised that it was nowhere near as bad as I thought it would be. I had a hard time believing that the liquid in the glass contained any alcohol at all. I had drunk half the glass before I remembered that Natasha, though in a mask just like me, was somewhere in the palace. If I was in danger of anyone recognizing me in my mask it was from her. I also knew that if Natasha was the one to find me she would not think twice about killing me on the spot.

I placed my half empty glass on a nearby table as a wove between party guests trying to make my way to the main entrance to the ballroom until I was hit by a wave of dizziness. The vertigo was so profound that I had to reach out to steady myself with the table. I had no clue what was going on. Why was I getting dizzy all of a sudden? My entire field of vision had gone from normal to blurry so fast that I knew I was going to collapse if I didn't do something. Passing out in the middle of the Alpha King's Mating Ball was the worst possible option, I needed to get out of here. The only problem was my vision had grown so blurry that I couldn't see the door any longer.

"Excuse me…can you please…tell me where…the ladies' restroom is?" I managed to ask through slurred speech of one of the waiters. I tried to focus hard enough to see exactly where in the room he had pointed but everything was a blurry spin. I began walking in that direction using the tables and chairs as supports for my wobbly legs. I did my best not to jostle anyone, the last thing I needed at the moment was an altercation. Luck was on my side as I made it quickly through the crowd then continued exiting the ballroom using the wall to support myself. Eventually my legs completely gave out and I slid down the wall to slump on the floor. What was happening to me?

I wasn't sure how long I lay on the floor before I heard someone's footsteps approaching me. I tried to get my eyes to focus but they wouldn't adjust. The only thing that I could make out about the individual coming towards me was that it was a tall shirtless man. Who was this man? Had he come to help me? Even this close to me his face was so blurry that there was no way that I could identify him. My eyelids drooped like they were suddenly made of lead when the stranger gently stroked my cheek.

When I next opened my eyes I had no idea where I was or how long I had been unconscious.

"Aaahh!" I groaned in slight discomfort that was quickly overshadowed by pleasure when I felt someone thrusting between my thighs. I opened my heavy-lidded eyes trying to figure out what was happening to me. There was a man hovering above me, he was pounding himself into me in a fast and steady rhythm. He was delivering untold pleasure that my body was willingly accepting. There was no way that I could deny I was enjoying every touch under his masterful hands. This was an entirely new experience, the pleasure unforeseen and unfathomable. All I could do was listen to the occasional sounds of pleasure that he made and accept every bit of bliss he showered on me. It was only as my eyes grew heavy and I drifted away that I came to the realization that the stranger had taken the one thing of value I had left, my virginity.

8. She Was My Mate

King Emmett

S prawled across the couch in my private suite with a glass of wine in my hand and the moonlight filtering in through the sheer curtains I had to admit that even on this of all days I was relaxed. It had alright been quite a night even though it wasn't even half way through yet but I just needed to take a break. It seemed that my solitude would short lived as the endless chatter and bustle of all the guests in the ballroom below. The Mating Ball had been meant to be a celebration not just of my birth but also of my taking a chosen mate. Though for whatever reason I couldn't seem to force myself to join them. Why wasn't I brimming with nervous enthusiasm? For Goddess's sake finally having a mate of my own was the one thing that I've always longed for, today was the day that I would choose one for myself. Of course, like any other wolf I wanted to be blessed with a mate by the Moon Goddess herself. That one person in all the world that was meant just for me, to be mine alone.

"Alpha," Rex called with a knock on the door. This was his friend's third attempt to get me to join the guest at the ball. Just seconds before he had knocked, I had come to the decision to cancel the rest of the evening and send everyone home. All so that I could simply enjoy the moonlight in solitude. Just as I was about to deliver the command to Rex, canceling the ball, Emil, my wolf, grew relentlessly distracted.

I got to my feet and made my way out to the balcony, hoping that some fresh air and the night sky would calm me. I leaned back resting my hip against the railing as I stared up at the Moon. I wasn't sure what had come over me, I had certainly never experienced anything like this before. Whatever it was had affected Emil as well. Now instead of having the relentless desire to cancel the ball, that desire had been reversed to attending the same ball. How strange.

"My King," Rex called again more tersely this time from the doorway.

"I'm coming," I told him with a slightly chagrined nod. The change in Rex's body language was visible as the tension left his body at my change of heart. Rex immediately went to my wardrobe in search of appropriate attire for me for the evening, I just narrowed my eyes at him. This wasn't the first time that I wondered if my two closest friends, Alpha Prince Vincent and Beta Rex, were somehow more enthusiastic about me taking a chosen mate than I was.

Despite the fact that I was the Alpha King with all the curses and benefits that entails, I had never spent much time around maidens. I spend very little around people and never around so many in a confined location. It was discovered when I was an infant that if anyone other than my mother so much as brushed my bare skin with theirs I experienced a horrific burning sensation all over my body. Hence the law my father passed soon after my birth essentially forbidden anyone from touching me otherwise it was a swift and immediate death sentence.

"Alpha," Rex called for my attention as he hung the tailor made absurdly expensive suit that had been made for the ball. In all honesty I hadn't looked spared the blasted thing even a cursory look since Rex set it in the wardrobe yesterday. Now that I was taking the time to inspect the suit more closely Emil was growing restless.

"My King, is everything okay?" Rex hesitantly inquired, seeming cautious of any possible fluctuation in my mood that his question my allicit.

"Why? Do I seem different to you?" I sternly countered, not sure of the response I was going to receive after he shook his head.

"It's just that you're smiling, my King." His response truly astonished me. I was smiling, of all people. "As far as my memory serves, I think the last time I saw you smile was before your sixteenth birthday. Though today is also a fighting occasion to smile, Alpha," he went on to explain.

I really wasn't sure what had prompted this change in me. What I did know was that I was not in the mood to discuss these changes with anyone. So I dismissed Rex, allowing him to go back to the ball and mingle with the other guests. Even after some soul searching for the reason behind this shift in a willingness to practice to self torture in the form of watching marked and mated couples be deliriously happy together, I still had this urge to attend. I was breaking one of my own cardinal rules. What the fucking hell was going on with me, these feelings had me at my wits end.

After hurriedly changing, I inspected my reflection in the mirror then with a satisfied shrug I left the room. Once I exited the quiet solitude of my suite the clammer of my guests' chatter as the maidens' strategize the best way to garner my attention were so overwhelming they were almost like a physical blow. I clenched my jaw in frustration when I overheard some she-wolf proclaim how she would become my Queen through the use of her body. She was lucky I didn't order a guard to have her dispensed with.

I studied them from above using the mezzanine that wrapped round the ballroom. My gaze drifted over each and every woman in attendance, everyone of them was the same. Every one of those beautiful faces concealed a black heart filled with nothing but lust and desire for power behind a thin veneer of makeup. All that I wanted was to kill every last one of them for their attempts at deceit, then feed what even parts were left to my pets.

"Rex" I mind-linked my Beta that was somewhere on the ballroom floor below with Vincent waiting for me to make my grand appearance.

"Yes, Alpha King?" he answered via mind-link.

"Remove every last one of these wolves from my home this instant! I refuse to stand the sight of all of these gold digging bitches for another second. They have exactly five minutes to vacate the palace otherwise I will see to their death sentence personally!" I roared my commands through mind-link, I could feel his panic coming back at me in waves through the open link even though he never said a word. Not wasting a second of time Rex set to work while I stepped back from the railing of the mezzanine. Neither Emil or I had any desire to join the ball now, not that there was a ball any longer. Had it really ever been a Mating Ball? Or had it always been an auction and I just happened to be the most valuable item for sale tonight?

"Hey, that she-wolf is going into heat!" I heard a male voice exclaim, making me stop. I looked in the direction the voice had come from, keeping my eyes trained on that area as I walked toward the situation.

"Ple…please le…let me go," a young woman pleaded as she was surrounded on all sides by three men. The mask clad woman was huddled in on herself on the floor, tightly securing her dress to her body out of fear. She knew that the scent of her heat had turned all the unmated men crazed with lust.

"There's no need to fret sweetheart, I'll make you feel all better," one of the men promised as he reached out to touch her cheek. Only she shoved his hand away and shook her head no, denying him. She was in a great deal of pain from her heat, but she wasn't willing to just give up and let anyone have her.

"Fuck this! I'm not waiting any longer," one of the men grumbled as he staked toward the woman. The other men seemed to take this as the signal that it was open season to begin touching her though all it did was cause her to shriek in pain and fear. Even stranger it was when the three men began to touch the woman that Emil began to lose control.

"GET THE FUCK AWAY FROM HER!" I roared, leaving all three males quaking a few steps away from her as their wolves' automatically obeyed their King's command. Once they realized I had been the one to intervene on her behalf they fell to their knees to plead for my mercy, in not taking their lives.

"Fuck off! Before I think better of it and change my mind," I barked, leveling a venomous glare to instill more fear. They tripped over themselves in a rush to escape my wrath leaving the faint scent of urine in their wake. It left me alone with the woman groaning in pain on the floor, unsure as to why I had saved her. No one would ever make the mistake of referring to me as kind. I never took much of an interest in what happened to others, she was the exception. I believe it has to do with the fact that I couldn't sense any duplicity in her. Of course, Emil began acting strangely again the moment I laid eyes on that woman.

At that moment a wave of her heat hit me square in the nose, sending me to my very knees before her. Despite the mask obscuring a majority of her face I could read the terror in those big dark brown orbs. Even knowing that I would suffer under my curse, experiencing that skin peeling burning sensation, I longed to touch her. My large hand slowly reached toward the soft skin of her cheek, I was surprised by how hot it was like fire. Just that simplest of touches from me had caused her to moan erotically as another fragrant wave of her heat hit me. In the advent of that second wave Emil lost all control while my own lust was being fueled by all those sweet little sounds she was making. Hold up, it had taken me a moment to realize something. Why wasn't I writhing in burning pain on the floor after touching her?

The only person that had ever been able to touch me without causing me horrific pain was my mother. So it made zero sense for this woman to be able to do so without inflicting pain. Heck, I couldn't even rationalize to myself why I had interceded on her behalf in the first place. Other then if I had just left her here, it wouldn't matter if it was those men or some others would have been raped. Unlike with the other males she wasn't afraid of my touch nor was she pushing me away. Somehow this woman was making me hungry for her, to the point that I refused to let any other male have her. Only I had that right.

I scooped her petite figure up into my arms then took her to the opposite wing of the palace from my suite. I knew better than to return with her to my room as Rex or Vincent could appear and interrupt us at any moment. For some unknown reason I didn't want Rex to witness this young lady in the throws of her heat. I would never be able to bear it if he lusted after her, the last thing that I wanted was to have to kill my own Beta. What the hell was I thinking? Was I really willing to kill my best friend and Beta over a woman that I had just met? I carried her into one of the many spare rooms in this wing of the palace and gently put her down on the bed. She let out a sultry groan and arched her chest into me when I began to release my grip on her. Emil was screaming at me to just get down to business, but I wouldn't. She hadn't wanted to be touched in the ballroom earlier.

She was in the full throws of her heat, no one could say she was in her right mind. I had no way of knowing if this female already had a mate out there and that was what had caused her to go into heat. I had come to the firm rational decision to lock her in this room by herself until her heat had passed, that way she would not be in danger from other males. I was backing away from the bed when she grabbed my by the lapels of my jacket, yanking me down until I was level with her departe___ eyes and parted plump lips

"Pa..Please…don't go," she begged, quickly pulling me back in undering her spell. I was so turned on that my hardened length rested against her hip as she asked me to fuck her.

"Please," she whimpered pitifully as another wave of heat hit me. The tattered threads of my resolve unraveled no match for the seductive power of this woman as if hypnotized I silenced her whimper with my lips. After I tasted her I groaned, I couldn't remember anything sweeter than her. I reached down grabbing both of her wrists and pulled them over her head, if I was going to have her I was going to feast.

The enchantress leaned forward nipping my lower lip, lighting my entire body up like a fireworks display. She didn't have a clue what she was doing to me. I, however, knew exactly what I was about as I nipped her plump lip then plunged my tongue into her waiting mouth needing a deeper taste of her. As our tongues were plunging and swirling she rubbed her feverish body against me like a cat wanting loving from its owner. All of her lust had been laid bare before me by her heat, she needed me inside her to soothe that ache. I was well aware that just continuing to feast on those plump pink lips of hers wasn't going to alleviate her pain yet I didn't want to overwhelm her either. With that in mind my hands went to the neckline of her gown, rending it clear down the middle. I leaned back so that I could fully appreciate the beauty of her body.

The sight of her flushed mouthwatering body laid out before me like a feast was enough to almost bring tears of joy to my eyes. I quickly divested myself of all my clothing, looking forward to experiencing the bliss of skin-to-skin contact. I planned to worship every bit of her body with my lips and tongue, until both of us were lost in a delirium of pleasure. As my lips cruised over her skin, dipping into bends, or nibbling and sucking on sensitive flesh I became transfixed by the bounce of her pert breasts topped by eraser hard nipples. Unable to resist the temptation any longer I latched onto one the hard pebbles giving it repeated long hard sucks. When I released it from my lips I blew cool air on the hot wet numb and watched her riggle beneath me with a moan before giving the other nipple the same attention.

I wasn't sure why I found her so addictive, after my first taste of her it was like a drug I just continuously needed the next dose. Some small subconscious part of my brain wondered if there was a strange reason behind what I was experiencing with her that was driving me crazy.

Any hot blooded male would admit that the woman laying under me undeniably has the body of a goddess, yet I still yearned to see the rest of her face that the intricate masquerade mask covered. It didn't make sense for me to be losing my senses over a woman that I wouldn't be able to pick out of a group of women. Who was she? How was she able to drive Emil crazy as well?

My hands reached up towards the ties of her mask so that I could try to remove it from her face, but I couldn't touch them. Why the hell couldn't I touch the mask? It was as if some unseen force was forcing my hands away from it, like there had been a spell placed on it to prevent anyone other than the wearer from removing it. Could this woman be a witch? That didn't seem right though, I didn't sense any magic in her blood. She was a pure-blooded werewolf.

While I sat there contemplating the situation she let out another whimper of pain pulling my attention back to her. I watched as the tears leaked from lust hazed eyes and trailed under the mask disappearing. Her long elegant fingers were white knuckling the bed sheet, she was in so much pain. The sight of her squirming in pain on the bed was more than enough to shove every bit of my remaining hesitation aside and focus on relieving the ache that was burning her from the inside out.

I didn't wait another second, I settled myself between her thighs then slid myself inside her waiting warmth. Neither of us bothered to control the breathy groans that escaped our chests, the pleasure I was experiencing bordered on pain. The tight clasp of her was unbelievably intense, I was also pretty sure that I had felt something give under the first thrust of my member. As I slowly withdrew from her, I glanced down to find my length speckled red with blood. That was when I came to the realization that she was a virgin and shit eating grin broke out on my face before I placed a sweet kiss on her forehead. My earlier assumption about her being different from other women was true, she wasn't only innocent of the mind but the body as well.

I slowly glided back inside of her, trying to be conscious of how tender she would be after losing her virginity. At least I was attempting to be gentle, it was just proving to be an exercise in futility. No one would ever accuse me of being a gentle or patient man even under the best of circumstances and the scent of heat in my nose made that impossible. Especially when she started to urge me to move faster, deeper, and more roughly as we had sex.

It wasn't that she actually said a single word other than to let out sounds of pleasure. She communicated everything to me with the movements of her body. For the most part she lay beneath me with her eyes closed, her heat combined with with my hard fucking of her petite figure seemed to be combining to bring her in and out of consciousness. It was only ever for a few seconds before she woke up again moaning and grasping at me with her arms and legs wanting more. She wanted me to stay buried deep in that tight little channel of hers and if I were being honest at that moment my cock wanted nothing then to live there.

"Show me your face," I whispered in her ear before giving the lobe a nip. I could feel her pebbled nipples rubbing against my chest, driving us both wild with my frenzied pounding. Wait a second was she kissing my throat? My eyelids closed overwhelmed by the bliss conjured from the simple action, to the point that I stopped moving inside her. That was when I felt her canines sink in the soft spot on my throat, causing my eyes to snap open in utter surprise.

Wait...she was actually marking me?! Her canines sunk deeper and deeper into my skin until our fates were sealed and I was completely hers, then licked the wound clean. I stared down at her small pale face in shock, she had fainted once she had finished marking me. My hand subconsciously went to my neck, touching the mating mark, and coming away with a very faint amount of blood and salvia. That hadn't been my imagination at all. I had truly been marked, though I had no idea how it was even possible. My wolf hadn't announced her as my mate in our mind nor could I smell her specific scent. In fact I couldn't seem to smell any scent on her at all, it was as if she was scentless. The only issue that remained was that soulmates were the only ones that had the ability to mark each other. Seeing as how I was the cursed Alpha King, this situation didn't make sense unless…she was my mate.

I finally realized why Emil had been so relentlessly possessive of her when those other males had been sniffing around her earlier. It also explained why I had smiled for the first time in years, it had been another subconscious reaction to finding the other half of my soul. On the night I had planned to give up and take a chosen mate, the Moon Goddess had sent my soulmate to me instead. Fearing that somehow this was all some sort of dream I clutched her to me as I began to move inside her desperate to complete the mating and marking. As I sped up my thrust, she moaned and writhed under me until I was on the verge of climax. My gaze was focused on her throat where I would place my own mark on her. I leaned forward with my canines out more than ready to claim her as mine. Just as I gave a final thrust and began to cum deep inside of her, I went to mark her throat. The problem was that I couldn't.

This made no sense, why could she mark me but I not mark her? I wanted to claim her as my own, she was mine! The Goddess had chosen her for ME! I tried again with no success. What the hell was going on? I had found my mate, but was unable to claim her. Could this be because of my curse? I didn't know. What I did know as I gently pulled out of her and tucked her against my chest was that I was willing to accept whatever fate handed me as long as it meant getting to keep my mate with me. Now that I had finally experienced having her in my arms, I refused to ever let her go.

9. She Died

King Emmett

With a single swing of my sword, his head was cleanly severed from his neck. The blood seeped out creating a puddle of red on the floor. Not one of the one hundred and fifty people that had been gathered in the throne room let so much as a peep escape their lips, at this point they would rather walk into the arms of the Devil himself than upset their Alpha King further. Everyone closed their eyes in an effort to conceal their dread despite the fact that their heads were bowed. None of them wanted to take the risk of accidentally making eye contact with an enraged Alpha King, which would inevitably lead to their untimely death.

I ever so slowly lifted my head as I examined my subjects that knelt before me. I then raised a single finger in the air, it served as a signal to Beta Rex that it was time to haul the monstrously large soldier out from holding that had been assigned to guard the main palace gate when the incident occurred. Rex didn't waste a second, he grabbed the man in question by his hair then tossed him at his Alpha's feet. The man in question reeked of fear and sweat, yet he never made the misguided error of pleading with his King to spare his life. He was familiar enough with me to understand that if he muttered even a word in an attempt at charity I would relieve him of his head utilizing my claws rather than a sword. Death by claw was a far more painful way to meet the Goddess when compared to a sword strike.

"Where is she?" I calmly repeated the question that I had asked all ten guards that I had previously interrogated. The little patience that I had left reached its end as I simultaneously asked my question and raised my sword, blood dripping from the handle to land in the kneeling guard's line of sight. I wanted to make it crystal clear to him exactly what happens to those that fail to provide the answers that I seek.

I noticed that the guard held his breath as I raised my sword, whether or not he was doing it because he lacked information, to cover for himself, or someone else. The distinct fetid odors of panic, anxiety, and pure primal fear that wafted up to me from the crowd behind the guard as they witnessed my interrogation and anticipated his impending death.

I was well aware of this particular soldier's accolades, for valor, honor, and his tremendous strength. He had been instrumental in my fight against numerous enemies. Every one of those deeds faded away into oblivion in the face of my desperate rage to find her. The only thing that mattered to me now was getting an answer to my fucking question. I was sure that it had never crossed this hulking brute of a soldier's mind that one day his life could possibly end in something other than either glory or old age. I watched as he unclenched his jaw, ready to please me in an endeavor to save his own neck.

"I…I'm really s…sorry my King…" his stuttering apology died on his lips when my sword separated his head from his shoulders. I wasn't satisfied with just lopping his head off, I dropped my sword, then extended my claws to eviscerate him. Once my subjects witnessed that ghastly display then went from kneeling to laying in subjugation before me. I was sure that my eyes had turned into obsidian pits, I could feel myself beginning to lose connection with humanity as I glared down at my sniveling subjects with aversion.

"Where the hell is she? Where is my mate?" I roared over the back of their heads as they kissed the stone floor of my throne room. I knew that the overbearing dominance of my wolf was forcing their wolves to submit before my supreme wrath. I allowed the tip of the sword in my hand to drop so that it dragged along the floor as I circled around my subjects creating a sound akin to claws being raked down a chalkboard.

I came to a halt beside a man laying prone before me. Without my having to move a muscle Rex reached out, snatching the man by the hair then yanking his head back so that he was looking at me, though honestly it was over my shoulder.

"Where is she?" I asked, having lost touch with all emotion except my obsession with finding her.

"We really don't know my King," a different soldier offered, he was the one responsible for overseeing the security of the palace.

"Can someone please explain to me how the fuck a five foot three inch slip of a woman managed to flee my FULLY MANNED palace?! She would have had to evade multiple guards to make it through the gate, yet not one of my guards saw a thing? How is this even possible? It's not as if she just snapped her fingers then magically teleported herself!" My frustration came to a boiling point as I reached out with a single swipe of my sword separating the head of the soldier that had just spoken from his neck.

The people on the floor laying near him whimpered in alarm, shying away from me as much as space would allow. I stared down at my quivering subjects attempting to keep my lips from curling in utter distaste while simultaneously containing the raging inferno burning within me at their failure.

When I had woken up earlier that morning the first thing that I had noticed was that I was alone in the bed, my mate was gone. I immediately sent my soldiers to search the entire palace from top to bottom, yet there was no trace of her anywhere. She had disappeared, if they hadn't mated I might have questioned whether she was a ghost. After the initial search came back fruitless, I commanded that every pack member that was part of my security team was to report or be dragged to my throne room.

Unsatisfied when the search conducted by Rex and my soldiers turned up with nothing, I carried one out myself. I personally checked every room, I didn't stop there. When every room inside the palace came up empty I searched outer buildings like the stable, gardens, even the royal crypt but no matter where I looked nothing changed. The only certainty in my world right now was that with every second that ticked by my crazed desperation to find her grew. I was down right furious that my mate had slipped through a palace full of soldiers undetected when I had never seen her face therefore had no way to actually identify her.

Once I had guaranteed with my own senses that she was nowhere on the palace grounds I ordered that the rest of my Kingdom be immediately searched for any trace of her. I sent my soldiers out to begin raiding the pack closest to the palace to look for evidence. There was to be no place overlooked no matter how large or small, I did not care if it was the Alpha's bedroom itself it was to be searched.

I had issued the command that anyone caught hiding my mate stood to be responsible for not just their own ruin or that of their family but their entire pack. I knew that it would take more than one person to successfully hide my mate from me. That meant the only way to snuff out who was responsible was to make it crystal clear to every one of my subjects that not only would the traitor be subjected to my wrath but their entire pack as well. I found it far more motivational when the lives and happiness of a whole pack hung in the balance of one individual's poor decision making skills.

I had added the order that anyone discovered to be involved with her disappearance was to be apprehended then brought to me immediately. That way I would make sure to extract every possible bit of information from him before bringing the unimaginable punishment down on their head. The news of my command had spread as if on the wings of a bird to every pack in my Kingdom, yet she was still nowhere to be found. The tense in my palace was so thick that I could cut it with my sword. Every person that I walked passed or spoke to was worried, wondering whether they might be the next to bear the brunt of my wrath.

During my interrogation of the guards assigned to manning the walls and gate that morning I had learned that my mate had escaped the palace. The problem was I had no clue how even after killing eleven of my own people. It was at that point that I had to accept that none of them knew a blessed thing and that I was wasting valuable time.

"Rex!" I barked.

"Yes, my King," my Beta bowed his head ready to receive my order.

"Those guards were on the receiving end of far too easy of a death for my tastes. Their corpses have not earned the right of a proper burial. They can serve as meals to assuage my pets' hunger," I commanded with a wave of my hand.

Everyone that was left in the throne room hurriedly scattered as the soldiers began carrying out my order. I could feel Rex's eyes on me as I tossed my sword down next to my throne then continued walking out of the room. The two of us had been friends for so long that I had no need to tell him that I was going to search for my mate myself. Of course, Rex probably thought that I would take one of my cars or maybe a motorcycle, he'd be wrong. With every step I took I shed another piece of clothing until I was naked, that was when I shifted into my wolf.

I ran out the door of the palace then through the huge iron gates that my soldiers opened for me once they saw a large white Alpha wolf sprinting towards them. Without having to look back I was certain of two things, the first was that every wolf that I passed was on their knees in submission. The second was that Rex was no more than five steps behind me, having made a solemn vow to me earlier to not leave me for a moment.

I quickly reached the forest, after crossing the main road and the ditches filled with thick brambles. I was distantly aware that my rage was blocking my brain from registering any of the pain my body was experiencing from the harsh terrain. Less than ten minutes later I was on the verge of crossing the border into the most infamous pack under my command, Opal Moon. Something inside me had suggested that Opal Moon should be the first place that I check for my mate.

It was at that exact moment that an excruciating pain seared through me causing my wolf to let out an anguished howl before I was forced to shift back into my human form. Rex found me curled up on the forest floor, what could have only been moments later but felt like hours.

"My King, what's wrong? What happened?" Rex asked in a barely controlled alarm, not knowing what to do. Having been one of my longest friends Rex understood explicitly the pain that I experienced when someone touched me, even though he had never seen me like this.

I let out a tormented howl while holding my hand over my mating mark. I could feel more than see Rex take a step back from me weary over the fact that Emil had come forward in my eyes. I yelled again, my entire body arching off the ground. I sunk my claws deep into the soil for purchase as the pain coursed through me as the burning in my mark grew in intensity. I was distantly aware at this point that my mouth was open in a perpetual scream, the all consuming annoying that had seized my being had me convinced that I was on the verge of death.

Eventually, I felt my body relaxing infinitesimally, allowing me a second to take in Rex's trembling figure standing guard close by. My body was covered in a sheen of cold sweat but my eyes were slowly returning back to their normal color. In an attempt to allow my body time to reacclimate to not being in pain, I continued to lay on the forest floor for a short time regulating my breathing. I wasn't sure exactly what had just happened but I knew that I felt off.

Rex walked up to me with eyes as wide as saucers while they focused on my neck. I recognized exactly where my Beta's gaze was drawn to and reached up a hand to brush my fingers reassuringly over my mating mark. The only problem was my fingers felt nothing but smooth taught skin, my mark had vanished.

"No, no, no, no, no! My mark it's...it's gone!" I released a grief ladened wail from deep within my chest as I fell to my knees. It wasn't the pain from the loss of the mark that was all consuming it was, the realization that I had waited my entire life for my mate only to have her stolen away by death less than twelve hours later. Everything from that moment forward had now become pointless in my life.

"No, you can't be dead!"

10. Beginning of My Revenge…

King Emmett

My agonized howl permeated the forest as Rex watched on from the side trying to be supportive and control his own emotional reaction to my suffering. I was consumed with a sense of bitterness over the fact that I hadn't even made it twenty four hours into marked and mated life before my mate ran away and died. I was downright furious over the fact that I had waited twenty seven years for the woman that the Moon Goddess had chosen just for me only to have her stolen from me before I even had the chance to see her face.

Neither my wolf nor I were in any position to be able to willingly accept the worst torment that could be dealt to a werewolf, which was why I allowed Emil to take control. Once we had completed the shift Emil tilted his large white head back releasing a long mournful howl before taking off into the woods. It was only belatedly that I even had a second's thought over the fact that I had taken off so quickly that there was no way that Rex could have possibly seen which direction I had gone in after my initial turn North. When Emil had originally started on this run he hadn't really had a particular destination in mind, we had sprinted across our territory aimlessly having just lost the last reason we had to really keep living. Both Emil and I had moved beyond the state of being broken that we had been living in before our mate had entered it last night to utter devastation.

I was subconsciously aware, as I darted between trees, that Emil and I were probably moving too quickly for Rex to be able to track us using scent when he finally shifted into his wolf. Honestly, I didn't care whether he was following me or not. Hell, I wasn't even sure where I was going at the moment. I had just completely surrendered myself to Emil and our misery, wondering if the only thing left to us was death. I had waited twenty-seven grueling years for the Moon Goddess to finally deem me worthy of granting a mate, only to have her snatched away the following day. What was the point? Why bother giving someone cursed like me the hope of a happy future like that in the first place if it was only going to be brutally torn away? Why was the Moon Goddess seeing fit to play with my heart so cruelly?

As all these thoughts spun on repeat in my brain, I grew further agitated with righteous indignation over what had happened to my mate. Before too long my righteous indignation honed itself into the sharp blade of revenge. I had decided that I would make whomever was responsible for killing my mate's life suffer in complete and utter torment. My first order of business was to discover who had murdered my little mate, so that I could begin executing my vengeance. If I had learned one thing in my time as Alpha King it was to never leave a known enemy alive and waiting on the field. Now on the off chance you did decide to keep them alive, make sure that they wished for death with every breath they took before you so generously take their life. That was exactly what he had planned for whomever was responsible for taking his happy future away.

Admittedly, I was occupied with rather macabre thoughts giving Emil heed to go wherever he wished. Long before we saw the river the rapid currant echoed off the trees alerting me to its presence. Once Emil broke through the tree line on the crest of the hill overlooking the river I took in the beautiful scene. Between the rumble of the water and the sparkle of the sun off the water I was quickly entranced by watching the water flowing downstream.

When I was young I used to come here regularly, it had been my secret place where others weren't allowed to follow. I had squirreled it away refusing to tarnish the place where I could revisit my most cherished memories. Though if my memory was correct it had been twelve years since I had last come to this spot to experience the natural wonder of the river and recall happier times.

I gave my head a shake having decided to leave, I gave the water one last look making a mental note at just how quickly the current was flowing. That was when something in the water caught my attention, there was a body floating in the water. As I looked closer at the person in the water I realized that they weren't moving other than along with the water. Both Emil and my thoughts of grief filled revenge vanished when the critical situation presented itself. I didn't even give it a second thought before I skidded down the hill on all four paws then plunged into the river while shifting back into my human form to make it easier to swim.

Just as my legs were being swallowed by the freezing water Rex must have caught up to me because I heard him yell "Alpha!" then I'm not sure with the rushing water if what I heard him mutter next to himself was "Is he committing suicide?" I honestly didn't much care, I was just relieved that there was someone else here to assist me with saving whomever was in the river.

He asked himself, pulling his hair. He wanted to strangle himself for even having such thoughts. The man whose very name scares his enemies to the point that they would choose to take their own life instead of confronting him, the cruel Alpha King Emmett can't commit suicide, Rex thought and peered over the edge, changing into his human form.

Rex's breath stopped when he didn't see Emmett in the water. The flow of the river was so strong that if someone drowned, only their corpse would get out. Rex decided that he himself would jump into the river after Emmett. When was readying himself to jump, he saw Emmett's head pop out of the water. It was so deep!

Once my head broke the surface of the bracingly cold water I immediately swam toward the body. While I fought to make progress against the flow of the river, I realized the body was heading rapidly toward a huge sharp boulder that jutted out of the river. The problem was that I wasn't sure if I would be able to reach the person in time to prevent them from slamming into it and no doubt sealing their fate.

I had to close my mouth to prevent water from choking me as I laughed at the errant thought of what my Beta must look like at this moment on the riverbank. Rex was probably questioning the rightness of the world as there was no way that I the merciless Alpha King would ever lower myself by saving someone else. It would have been sheer lunacy to even suggest such a thing. The absurdity of the situation gave me the burst of energy that I needed to reach the middle of the river. There the current was impossibly strong, unless you were some that had trained regularly, like I was expected to, there was no way that you would be able to escape this river with your life. Even with all my additional strength and prowess from being Alpha King I struggled keeping myself afloat while reaching the body in time.

The moment I was able to snag my hand into the persons' clothing to drag them closer, I wrapped an arm around their chest before turning back to the riverbank. In the swiftly moving current the limp body in my arms was nothing more than deadweight making getting the both of us to shore seem like an insurmountable task.

The reasonable thing to do would be to let go of the person I rescued, lucky for them today I was far from reasonable.

The moment that Rex saw me emerging from the river with my charge I almost laughed at the utter relief that caused his entire body to sag. He quickly recovered then ran over to join me.

"My King, have you been hurt? Are you alright?" Rex asked, his anxious eyes searching me from head to toe for so much as a scratch. He was so frantic in his examination that he almost reached out to touch me, he quickly regained his bearings and snatched his hand back as if shocked by his own lack of thought. I was pretty sure it was at that same moment that Rex noticed the beautiful unconscious woman sagging in my arms. I could tell that was when the reason behind my suicidal swim registered.

Even though I was peripherally aware of what Rex was doing, my gaze never left the slight figure cradled in my arms. I had always found those banal expressions that people always say like I knew it from the moment I saw her or when our eyes met it was like I was struck by lightning overly cliche. I never would have believed for a second that when I first laid eyes on the woman in my arms it would feel as if the world itself stopped spinning. It wasn't that she was beautiful, trust me I had seen far more than my fair share of gorgeous women be they Queens, Princesses, or noble ladies. It was everything from the dark mass of long wet tresses that clung to a body that would tempt even the most devote of holy men, yet this young woman seemed to radiate an innocent beauty from within.

"My King, I'm sorry to say this but the girl is dead," Rex gently pointed out. I was well aware that the young woman that I pulled out of the river wasn't breathing. The thing that I found strangely absurd about the entire situation was that the thought of leaving her here made my heartbeat quicken. Rex's gaze bored into the wide swath of shoulders as I bent forward to do what to him would be considered the unthinkable. I tilted her chin up to begin giving her mouth-to-mouth resuscitation, hoping to force the water out of her lunges and maybe just maybe save her life. I had no thoughts for decorum or whether it was appropriate for the Alpha King to touch a dead body, my sole focus was on reviving the young woman I'd fished out of the river consequences be damned.

"My Ka...Ka...King, there isn't any use. Please..." the anxiety was coming off of Rex in waves, not that he bothered to continue with his pointlessly idiot comment once I leveled a venomous glare at him. No one, not even my oldest friend was going to stand in the way of me saving this woman. I continued performing mouth to mouth on her, adding in chest compressions now that I was certain that she didn't have a heartbeat.

I couldn't be sure if it had been seconds or minutes into my cycle of mouth to mouth and chest compressions, when her body jolted. I quickly turned her to her side as she coughed up all the water that was in her lungs. I looked at Rex out of the corner of my eye as he stood there shocked over the fact that I had just managed to bring the girl back from the dead. Despite the fact that the woman I had rescued was violently retching to remove the water from her system she had yet to open her eyes. Even now that she had returned to resting on her back having expended all of her energy, the only perceivable movement of her body was the slightest rise and fall of her chest denoting her breathing.

To reassure myself that the woman had not been reclaimed by death, the hand that had just a second ago gently caressed her cheek hovered inches above her nose and mouth to ensure she was still with us. As luck would have it, it seemed that she had just passed out from sheer exhaustion and the trauma of whatever had befallen her. Discovering that the worst was behind us I allowed some of the tension to ease from my body, Rex quickly followed suit all fear of me losing the tenuous grip on my sanity gone.

Less than half a second later both of our heads snapped in the direction of the forest on high alert, where we could hear a wolf sprinting towards them. Once the wolf became visible, I recognized him immediately, it was Zach, my personal bodyguard.

Zach used all four paws to skid to a halt on the gravelly soil of the riverbank a respectable distance away from me, before shifting back into his human form in a kneeling position before me.

"My King," he bowed his head, staring down at the ground as a sign of respect. Not that I was paying attention to Zach when there was a beautiful mysterious unconscious woman laying on the ground in front of me.

"What do you have to report?" Rex asked as Zach glanced up at him before quickly looking back down.

"It grieves me to inform you my King, but the remains of our Luna were found in the Opal Moon Pack," the news that Zach carried came as no surprise to me, I had already experienced my mate's death earlier that day.

"What was her business with that pack?" Rex inquired attempting to piece the puzzle together.

"I was told that our Luna was Alpha Fabian's youngest daughter, Emily. They are uncertain as to how this tragedy unfolded, they can only assume that she ran home in a panic after waking up in a strange place. Every member of the pack was standing in mourning at the grave side when I arrived having just finished burying her," Zach relayed every minute detail of what he had witnessed to me. Of course, with every word out of Zach's mouth the joy that I had felt at bringing the woman from the river back to life eked away until there was nothing left but endless pain.

"Who killed her?" I asked in a voice so dangerously calm that Zach was shivering from the chill.

"It was explained to me that our Luna was murdered by one of the pack's Omega slaves, a young woman by the name of Elaine. When the she was confronted with her crimes, rather than face the consequences of her actions Elaine jumped into the river committing suicide," Zach revealed to me.

"Elaine!" A man broke through the treeline near the riverbank at a run while screaming the name of the Omega slave that I had just learned murdered my mate. I watched as Zach instantly rose from his kneeling position on the ground to intersect the man before he could get any closer to Rex or myself.

"Stop, right there! Who are you, that you have the balls to approach the Alpha King himself?" Zach questioned the man in out right challenge at his blatant audacity.

"Please, I'm Alpha Marvin the nephew of Alpha Fabian of the Opal Moon Pack, can you just tell me if she is alright?" Marvin pleaded, proper etiquette apparently being the furthest thing from his mind as he had forgotten to at least bow his head in acknowledgement of my position as his King. He was far too focused on the young woman I had fished out of the river than lay on the ground before me.

"Elaine, I need you to open your eyes!" Marvin yelled from the same spot yards away from us where Zach had stopped him. Though when it finally dawned on me that he was referring to the woman laying on the ground before me by that murderous Omega's name, it felt as if someone had thrown me back into the icy river.

I stared down at the beautiful that had enchanted me mere minutes ago, I never would have guessed that fate would have been quite so cruel. To have me the cursed Alpha King rescue the woman that murdered my mate less than twelve hours after I had found her. Others would have thought it a story or a badly written joke but no it was my reality. My fists clenched at my sides, my vision going red around the edges due to my need for vengeance as I glared at my enemy. Crouching down low near the woman I now understood would be the focus of my retribution.

"My vengeance begins now," I whispered in her ear a wicked gleam in my eye.

11. Meeting The Alpha King

Elaine

Before I had even opened my eyes the first thing that I noticed was that I was freezing. As an Omega slave I was intimately familiar with being persevering through cold. Despite all of that experience, it felt like someone had dunked me in a frozen lake then stuck me in a refrigerating unit to turn me into a she-wolf icicle.

The acrid scent of cigarette smoke wrinkled my nose. I had never really liked the smell of cigarette smoke, but this one in particular had a spiced note to the smoke making it district. That was odd, the only reason that I was aware of that brand was due to Alpha Fabian's penchant for handing them out to any wealthy or royal guest that visited the pack. Alpha Fabian always loved to exhibit his magnanimousness to pack guests by showering them with expensive gifts, like cigarettes and alcohol to make them happy. The one thing that I couldn't understand was why the smell of the smoke was so potent. It was so thick with smoke that it almost seemed like I had been placed in a sealed room with someone that was chain smoking, but that couldn't be right. Where was I? Was I in the palace? Oh my Goddess, the palace!

The more that I thought about the palace the more anxiety built in my chest yet I couldn't manage to open my eyes. That was when my memories began flooding back, if I hadn't experienced it all myself first hand I would have thought it a wildly concocted tale. The night had started out like any other, I'd been given more work then I could possibly handle but the Moon Goddess had smiled down on me and I had been able to leave for the palace racing into the foreboding forest. While traveling to the palace I had come across the woman that had been in a car accident that was trying to escape from the Beta of my own pack. After helping her from the car she had given me a bag and charged me with another task, seeing she was dyeing. Once I had continued on with my journey towards the palace there was when Lewis had caught up to me in the forest then tried to rape me but I was able to escape but sneaking into the palace. Of course, that was when I realized that I had somehow lost the very box I had been tasked to bring to Alpha Prince Vincent by the woman earlier that night. Admittedly, I hadn't had much of a chance to look for the box as I'd been forced to join the party, then unknowingly consumed a spiked drink. My emotions surged when I remembered what had transpired next, that stranger taking my virginity.

My virginity had been the only thing that was truly my to give, which was why I had been saving it for my mate. I suppose that I shouldn't have been surprised that the one thing that I had to offer was taken from me without consent. Then again after what happened when I returned to Opal Moon that somehow seemed far worse. I no longer had any desire to continue living, I just wanted to curl up into a ball and die. Why hadn't I died in that river?

The smoke had so permeated the area that my irritated lunges began to protest with loud hacking coughs that wracked my petite frame until I placed a hand on my chest to steady myself. Even as my lungs burned from the hacking cough the rest of my being was still enveloped in that severe cold. I concentrated on opening my eyes, understanding that if I was going to survive this that was the first step. Slowly as if they had been coated in glue my eyes pried themselves open, I found myself staring up at what I believed to be the thatched roof of a hut. It was hard for me to be certain given the haziness that hung in the air from the cigarette smoke. It wasn't helping that I could also sense another presence in the room, an incredibly high ranked wolf if the aura coming off of them was any indication. It just added another layer to the puzzle I was trying to solve as I reached my hand up to my forehead exploiting every bit of energy, I had to keep my eyes open.

The only other thing that I could discern about this other wolf was that they were a rolling storm of emotions, informing me what a dangerous situation I had found myself in. Who could possibly have sat in this hut with me? I forced my head to turn left then right but still wasn't able to make anyone out through the thick smoke. I gingerly attempted to prop myself up into a seated position, discovering that the dirt floor of the hut might as well have been mud. That could have been caused by the rain that I heard coming from outside, all I knew for certain was that it was not helping me with the chill. The only information that I had was that I was in a hut and I could sense someone close by. I had no recollection how I got here or why. I was also relatively certain that I wasn't still on Opal Moon territory.

In the next moment I felt someone crouching down across from me, they were studying me like one does a particularly interesting bug while the smoke obscured their face. To be perfectly honest the mere presence of this individual in the hut with me sent a chill down to the marrow of my bones. Who was it? Another round of rasping coughs escaped from my chest as the smoke ever so slowly filtered out of the hut. Once the air cleared I began to be able to make out the figure of a man, broad shoulders, and long muscular legs. He was the one that was smoking.

A second later the was flung open as a beam of light shone directly into my eyes forcing them closed. After giving my eyes a few moments to adjust to the light I was vaguely able to make out the man holding the flashlight beam that was burning my eyes through the smoke and shadow.

"How dare you sit there when you are in the presence of your Alpha King! Show some respect! Bow your head before I remove it from your neck," the man barked at me.

Without a moment's hesitation I tucked my chin to my chest bowing my head in alarm. I had no clue how I had come to be in a hut with his majesty the Alpha King but this could not be good. I could already feel the sickening cold sweat collecting on previously chilled skin just at being in the same one room hut as the cursed Alpha King. I didn't understand why things like this kept happening to me. There was no way that I could have possibly known the man crouched down in front of me was the Alpha King. There was no need for me to know what he looked like, he was a tiger while I was an ant easily crushed beneath his mighty paw. What worried me was that I had no clue how I had gotten to this hut nor did I have an inkling as to what the Alpha King's presence here meant for me.

Seeing as neither of the men in the hut with me seemed inclined to fill me in on exactly what was going on, I deduced that the man that was not the Alpha King must be his Beta. What I could not wrap my head around was what the Alpha King was doing here. Even better, why was he lowering himself by being in the same room as an Omega slave. I was still trying to piece together exactly what was going on in this situation. Erroring on the side of caution I kept my head lowered waiting for their next command. I continued kneeling in the cold mud that served as the floor even though my legs were growing numb and neither of the men had spoken a word for some time. I was quite positive that if the situation went on like this that the terror collecting in my system would overload my heart stopping it mid-beat.

I could see movement in the periphery of my vision, the Alpha King had moved from a crouch to a chair across from me. He had even begun to impatiently tap his foot while he waited for me to do the unthinkable and meet his gaze. Slowly I peered through my lashes first getting snagged on his shiny expensive shoe then moving on to a fleck of dirt that marred his damp pant leg below one knee where a hand rested. My eyes hesitantly continued the journey up his intimidating figure, whether it was my nerves or something else I wasn't sure but I realized that I was noticing small details about the Alpha King. Like for example he had paints that were zipped but they had been left unbuttoned, did that mean he had donned them in a rush?

My eyes snapped shut out of pure panic. Why in the world would the Alpha King wish for me to take in the ominousness of his being when his pants were undone? He persisted in waiting for me to look at him. The only positive thing that I could find was that at least there was only one button that had been left undone, so there was not much that I could accidentally see.

Once again, the restless tap, tap, tap of his foot against the floor as his annoyance grew. I attempted to center myself before garnering the courage to resume their tour, he wore an unbuttoned jacket that molded to his broad shoulders and revealed all the muscles of his chest. At Opal Moon I'd always been running around doing whatever the Alpha family had commanded of me, that had meant that by this point in my life I had seen far more than my fair share of shirtless warriors. I would swear to the Moon Goddess herself that I had never seen a man whose muscles were even half as pronounced. There was not a single doubt in my mind that if the Alpha King were to step onto a battlefield every one of the Kingdom's enemies would wet themselves in pure terror before tucking their tails between their legs and running.

My eyes quickly glanced over his strong unmarked neck to his lips, they were in a stern line at the moment but still full red and mesmerizing. I couldn't remember ever thinking that a man's lips were mesmerizing, I was almost consumed with the desire to kiss them. I ripped my gaze away from that temptation, finally meeting his chocolate brown eyes. I had never seen so many different shades of brown and gold, I couldn't recall ever seeing anything more beautiful even as they peered into the depths of my soul.

The moment that his face registered in my brain, I forgot how to breathe. If I were anyone else I might have laughed at how fickle fate was, placing me in front of this man out of all others. Nevermind the fact that he was the Alpha King. I wasn't sure how I had managed to miss that fact but I had to collect myself and get some of my fear under control. Two facts were warring with each other in my mind, the first was that somehow the Alpha King was the man that I had obsessed over for the last ten years. The other was that I couldn't seem to force my eyes to blink as if my subconscious was worried that he was a figment of my imagination rather than physical reality. It was hard for me to accept that he was here, I had only ever seen him that once but it had been enough. He was my first love, that was why I had kept that photo of him.

Not once over the many years that I had spent years yearning for him with an unending devotion had I even dared to imagine that he was the Alpha King nor that we would be reunited under such odd circumstances. I remember lamenting that I would never get to see him again after everything that I had gone through the night of the Mating Ball, yet here he sat across from me in all his lethal beauty. Was it possible that I was still asleep?

As my surprise began to wear off I realized that it wasn't just that his pants were damp, water dripped from his hair and along his skin unnoticed. With his gaze never wavering from me he brought the hand hold his cigarette to his mouth for a long draw. Despite how gorgeous I found his eyes, the way that he was staring at me unwaveringly was beyond unnerving. It was the unadulterated loathing that brewed like a storm in his eyes that was focused solely on me. My chin sunk to my chest and my eyes to the floor in utter dejection.

Out of the billions of scenarios I had concocted in my head over the years, him despising me from the moment I knelt before him had never been one of them. Could that mean he was aware that I had lied to him when I was younger? I had just wanted to keep my identity as a slave hidden, but if he had caught wind of this information there was no way that he would have possibly let me live. Getting caught red handed in a lie to a member of the royal family never mind the Alpha King himself was one of the worst crimes you could commit, it was considered an act against the Kingdom. Just on the basis that he wasn't demanding my head on a spike that meant that he didn't recognize me. Honestly, I wasn't surprised in the least. After all, what need did the Alpha King have to remember an Omega slave at a pack that he once visited? The thing that I couldn't understand was why I was upset over him not recognizing me or this unwavering desire that had to touch him regardless of the contempt he was exhibiting towards me.

"Elaine!" A voice that I recognized as Marvin's called from somewhere I could not see outside the hut.

"Are you alright? They haven't hurt you in any way?" Marvin yelled from wherever they were holding him. When I finally caught a glimpse of Marvin through the hut's open door, he was down on his knees in the rain. Another man stood behind him with one hand on his shoulder holding him in place, the other had its claws extended as they dimpled the fragile skin of Marvin's throat. For the moment I could only assume that the man was the Alpha King's bodyguard and was more than willing to rip out Marvin's throat at the slightest provocation.

"Marvin, what's going on? What are you even doing here?" I asked worried for his life. My panic had overroad my common sense when the questions just spewed out of my mouth undeterred by the fact that I wasn't allowed to speak without permission while in the presence of the Alpha King. I was forced to watch as the bodyguard sunk his claws deeper into the skin of Marvin's throat until blood began to flow and whimpered in pain. No, no, no, no, no! It didn't matter what the Alpha King did to me but I couldn't let him kill Marvin. Marvin was the next in line for the Alpha position in his pack, he was supposed to be nearly untouchable. Well, he was untouchable to any one other than the Alpha King. Obviously, the Alpha Kings' bodyguard was just following the commands that he was receiving from his King via mind-link, therefore nothing could be held against him.

"Please don't kill him," I pleaded, lowering my entire upper body to the dirt floor in a bow up subjugation. I had no idea what unforgivable transgression I had committed, nor did I understand how we had gotten to the point where Marvin's life was being threatened. The one thing that I had resolute clarity on was that I needed to save Marvin's life no matter the personal cost. He was the only person left that had treated me with anything resembling common decency. It was after I had made that decision that I felt the insistent pressure of a single finger under my chin compelling me to meet the Alpha King's shrewd gaze. He had silently shifted closer at some point, I realized that I was now caged between his long bent legs in an almost intimate position.

"Allow him to live?" He asked rhetorically. That was the first time I had heard him speak in ten years, well knowing that it was him anyway. I had achieved my ultimate goal in life, I had gotten to experience being in his presence again. I would not have thought it possible but he had become even more handsome than the last time I had seen him. Admittedly just being this close to him was giving me heart palpitations.

"That's rich, a cold-blooded murderer begging for someone else's life," the venom laced comment that slipped off his barbed tongue was finally enough to knock me out of my thoughts and back to the grim reality of the situation.

"Murderer?" I inquired in utter astonishment. I couldn't comprehend why the Alpha King was referring to me as a murderer, it didn't make any sense.

"Of course you're a murderer! You slaughtered the youngest daughter of the Opal Moon Pack's Alpha in cold blood, she was the Alpha King's mate. When you were about to be caught so that you could be brought to justice for your crime, you attempt to commit suicide by jumping off the castle wall into the swollen and freezing river. You stole the life of our future Luna Queen and you will be punished in a manner deemed by your King!" The Beta snapped, laying out each of my supposed crimes as my head spun.

How could I have killed the future Luna Queen? Especially when Alpha Fabian only had one daughter not two. Therefore, there was no youngest daughter, there was only Natasha. I glanced up at the Alpha King whose anger was palpable in the hut after listening to his Beta recount the events of the day.

"You MURDERED my mate!" he roared mere inches from my face, so that I could feel the heat of his breath as my wolf coward in my mind.

"No, pa...pa...please there's been a horrible mistake. I've never hurt anyone, never mind murder, I..."Just as I was going to begin my version of what had happened the Alpha King wrapped a single large hand around my throat then lengthened his claws until they devoted my skin. He pulled me towards him by the throat until I was on my knees at the juncture of his legs, face to face with him once more.

"A horrible mistake?! Do you think that I'm a fool?" he growled, the only defense I had against the terror briming inside me was to close my eyes. There was nothing I could do, my wolf had submitted to her Alpha King. Even if I had wanted to I wouldn't have been able to tell him what had truly transpired over the last twenty four hours. Like what had happened when I woke up not in the palace but back in the packhouse, in my own bed this morning.

12. ALPHA KING'S
INNOCENT BRIDE

Elaine

Flashback...

*A*fter *the series of tragic events that had culminated in having my virginity stolen by a stranger I had welcomed the peaceful oblivion of sleep, only to open my eyes in the morning in my own bed back at the pack. I didn't have the slightest idea how I could have gotten back here, had it all been some sort of weird dream? The gorgeous gown that I had worn the previous night was nowhere to be found. Instead I was back in the same outfit that Lewis had shredded the previous night when he had* *tried to rape me but they were magically back to state they had been before I left the pack.*

I was having a hard time accepting the fact that not only had I miraculously been transported back to the packhouse but my clothes had been mended as well. Again I found myself questioning my own mind, until the dull ache coming from between my thighs registered. No, that alone proved everything that I remembered from the previous night had occurred. That comfort was short lived with the revelation that I was now ruined with nothing to offer my mate. I didn't bother stemming the flow of tears that streamed down my cheeks unchecked at that realization.

I swear that it wasn't even three heartbeats later there was a loud crack as the wood of my door splintered then flew across the room due to someone kicking it open. The commotion from the incursion into my room had startled me so terribly that I had fallen out of my bed in the chaos. When my head popped up over the bed I learned that it had been Beta Dale that broke my door down as he still stood in the doorway with Luna Wilma standing further back in the hallway behind him. With the barrier of the door now disposed of, Luna Wilma sauntered into my room, her temper already a physical entity in the room ready to explode like a bomb on its next unexpecting victim. Just like with everything else that morning I was at a loss, I had no clue why they were here or why Luna Wilma was seething in rage.

Her claw-like fingers struck out snatching a fistful of my hair that she then used to drag me out of my room without warning as my feet tried to gain purchase on the bare wood floors. I tried to muffle my whimpers of pain knowing how much they annoyed her while simultaneously pleading with her to let me go for whatever crime it was I had committed against her this time. Unsurprisingly, she continued trudging through the packhouse using my hair as little more than a leash as she led me up the security wall around the pack that sat next to the river. Once we had come to a stop I realized that the Luna and Beta were not the only ones that would witness whatever punishment I received, every Omega that was part of the pack also stood on the battlements. I wasn't sure what to do about the slight itching sensation that occurred in the recesses of my brain when I spotted the Omega that had offered to assist me the previous night. I couldn't be certain if the sensation was over due to her not making eye contact with me or had to do with something else entirely.

"Where the hell were you last night?" The Luna spat out a millisecond before slapping sharply across both sides of my face a few times. This made me incredibly nervous, it meant that she was aware that I had left the packhouse last night. I just couldn't connect the dots as to how she could have known? Was it Lewis? No, that wasn't it. If Lewis had been the one to turn me in he would be standing here gloating, waiting to steal whatever pound of my flesh that was left when his mother was done with me. That only left the Omega...

"I...I.. was just following Natasha's order..." I tried in vain to explain the situation only to have the Luna cut me off mid-sentence when she sliced her nails down one side of my face until I felt warm rivulets of blood dripped from my chin.

"Don't you dare even think about lying to me, that Omega bitch that you pawned all your work onto told me every detail already! What the hell did you think you were doing? Did you really think that there would be no consequences when you didn't follow a direct order from me? Instead, you pass your work off onto another Omega so your skanky ass could go for a walk around the pack. Did you think in that pea sized brain of yours that I wouldn't find out what you'd done? Who exactly do you think you are that you believe you can disobey a direct order from your Luna, hmm?" Luna Wilma shrieked while pinching my jaw with her hand. I had the fleeting thought over all the pain she was causing me that the Luna wanted to ruin my face. I did try to catch the eye of the

Omega that had lied to me the previous night but she wouldn't look up from staring at her feet.

The Omega must have been one of Luna Wilma's spies that had been commanded to observe my every move just in case one toe went out of line. If that had been the case I couldn't help but wonder why she would have even bothered to put on the show of promising to help me to begin with. Especially, seeing as the Omega hadn't even told the Luna the scarce information that I had given her, which was that I was leaving under the orders of Lewis and Natasha.

"Mother, don't believe their lies. She wasn't out on a walk last night!" Natasha's shrill voice broke through the chill morning air as she dramatically burst through the door.

"What do you mean? If this bitch wasn't out on a walk last night what was she doing?" The Luna demanded, unwilling to relinquish the vice grip she had on my hair.

"She secretly ran off to the palace, I saw her there with my own eyes. She thought that she was being clever by dressing up like a proper lady, the problem is that I would recognize her no matter what mask or clothing she wore," Natasha scoffed. Of course she had failed to mention anything to her mother about the small fact that she had ordered me to meet her outside the palace wall, nor would I be given a chance to defend myself against these accusations. I had known in the moment that if she spotted me amongst the crowd that it would spell my doom. That's why I had tried my best to stick to the shadows, not that my plan had been successful. I had known last night that this was a lose-lose situation, yet I had still accepted the other Omega's assistance. All my efforts from last night to escape a bad situation just landed me in a far worse one less than twelve hours later.

"Why in the Goddess's name did you ignore all of your work in the packhouse to galivant at the palace last night? Did you get it in that pea sized brain of yours that you were going to find your mate?

Haven't you realized yet that the only thing that a little whore like you is good for is spreading her thighs for whichever man has taken an interest in you? Just like your skank of a mother did! The Moon Goddess isn't going to deem you fit enough to deserve a mate! I've been trying to beat that fact into your thick skull since you became our responsibility, not that you've managed to learn that lesson!" Luna Wilma screamed at me like a raving lunatic as she snatched a nearby flashlight from the belt of one of the guards then began raining blows down on me.

The first strike to my head caused my knees to collapse beneath me, depending on how I wanted to look at it I was lucky enough not to pass out from the pain and location of the hit. The beating came to an abrupt halt as I watched Natasha saunter closer then used my hair to drag me back up to drag me up until I knelt before her. Once I was arranged to her liking she commenced beating me with the flashlight much to the delight of her mother, when that was no longer sufficient to satiate her I felt myself being dragged. It was only when we came to a stop that I cracked my swollen eyes open to discover that I had been let to the break in the top of the battlement. Looking down on the other side of the wall the treacherously swollen river with a current that would carry a full grown man away in a matter of seconds. I was positive that no one could escape that river with their life.

"Natasha, please reconsider! There has to be some other option," I pleaded in a hushed whisper clearly reading her intention to toss me head long into the raging river. I began to struggle in her grasp giving no thought or care to the hair that I lost in my fight to get away.

"Do you recall the moment that I warned you to never get in my way?" she said quietly enough so that only I would be able to hear it over the rushing of the river.

"What are you talking about? Please this doesn't need to go any farther," I attempted to convince her while unsuccessfully trying to extract myself from her clutches. The problem was that after

102

receiving so many blows to the head and torso, I was left in a weak and vulnerable state that a toddler would be able to overpower. It was at this point that she yanked my hair all the way back so that my face was fully exposed for her to deliver a vicious backhand to stop my jerking about. Bit by bit she eased me up to the edge of the wall until my toes hung over, the slight breeze ruffled through a few loose strands of hair. I knew without having to be told that at any moment I was going to be pushed into a watery grave.

"You've spent years drooling over the man that I've been in love with my entire life, then last night you slept with him. Did you think that I didn't know the lengths you went to poach what was mine last night? You stole the one thing that has meant anything to me," Natasha revealed but only loud enough for me to be able to catch. I was left in a state of shock, the man that had taken my virginity was the man Natasha had been infatuated with all of her life...that was quite the unhappy coincidence. I just wished that I could actually recall what he looked like. There were only a few things that would come to mind when I thought of last night, one was that he hadn't been wearing a shirt. Other than that, I vaguely remember that he brushed his fingers over my cheek before positioning himself between my thighs.

"Natasha please, you must have misinterpreted something that you saw. I...I don't even know who that stranger was. I haven't stolen anyone from you," I pleaded in an attempt to convince her but she was beyond all rational thought. Angered beyond words Natasha delivered a series of harsh kicks to my exposed stomach as a way to vent her frustration.

"He belongs to me! You wait, within the next few months I'll be his wife and Luna! It won't matter then whatever sick or twisted reason that he loved you, his future will be with me. I'm just truly sorry that you won't be able to witness all of this yourself first hand," Natasha spat venomously at me a split second before shoving me off the battlement into the raging river.

I knew that I had nowhere near the strength necessary that it would take to escape the river. Of course, that would mean someone would have had to care enough to teach me at some point. No one had, leaving my only recourse as my threadbare dress was weighed down with river water to allow my body to drift along with the current. I had been aware from the millisecond that Natasha began to shove me over the edge that these were likely the last moments of my life. Before long, my lungs were burning as they strained under the lack of oxygen, it became so unbearable that I instinctively inhaled sucking in a lungful of water. My body reflectively tried to rid itself of the water I just inhaled, only to replace it with more water. It wasn't long before my vision dimmed to black.

Flashback Ends...

Considering the litany of injuries that I had sustained to different parts of my body, I was still questioning how I had made it out of the river with my life. Though if I was being perfectly honest with myself the situation, I found myself in now was worse than death. Being accused of murdering the cursed Alpha King's mate in cold blood was tantamount to killing the Moon Goddess herself.

"I've never hurt anyone, never mind killed someone, please believe me," I had tried to explain but he just grew more enraged.

"I find it frustratingly interesting how everything out of your mouth is a falsehood in some manner. I wonder if you're aware that lies or even half-truths are among the things that I hate above all others in this world?" He informed me as I quivered in terror. I had no evidence to substantiate any of my claims, not that he was inclined to believe me at the moment anyway. Not when I had fed him a huge lie the only other time we had ever met, when I had purposefully hidden my identity as a slave from him.

"My King, I swear to you that I'm not lying. Please believe me when I say that Alpha Fabian only has one daughter," I attempted to explain one final time only to notice a hint of surprise in the Alpha King's expression.

"What did you just say?" He snarled with bared teeth.

"I'm sorry my King but it's true. I have spent every day of my life in the Opal Moon Pack territory, Alpha Fabian only has one daughter. As a slave to their family wouldn't I know about this supposed second daughter of the Alpha?" I attempted to spell it out for him as logically as I could, what I had said was beginning to register through the rage infused haze that was clouding his brain. Evidently what I had said had clicked as his grip on my throat loosened.

"If anything, you've just said even the minutest of detail turns out to be false, not even your imagination will be able to come up with the things that I'll do to you," he ominously warned as he took a step away from me. I was thrilled that there was even this small amount of distance between myself and the bloodthirsty Alpha King. After pinning me to the ground with nothing more than a glance he turned to his Beta.

"Confirm whether what this girl said is true or not. If what she says is even remotely true, that my mate wasn't the daughter of Alpha Fabian, then head will roll over this grievous mistake!" He barked as I trembled at his feet. I was just hoping that the Alpha King's Beta wasn't miraculously able to provide evidence that I was lying, what lay at the end of that road was my certain death. From all of the rumors I had heard about the cursed Alpha King I could only begin to imagine the warped tortures that he had in his arsenal.

"Of course, my King. I'll see to it immediately," the Beta replied as he quickly stepped out of the room to gather the information. I knew that he was just stepping away so that he could mind-link the warrior they had left at Opal Moon in the inevitability that this situation arose.

The one room hut was small to begin with but when the massive frame of the Alpha King jammed into the already matchbook sized space made it claustrophobic. I tucked my back into the farthest corner of the room, huddling there in an attempt to make myself completely invisible. Not that it worked for a millisecond, his furious gaze was burning a hole into my skin. This wasn't the first time that I had been glared at with unwavering intensity. I wondered if the ruler werewolves were taught this skill at an early age. Every second that passed felt like an eternity, though I knew with a certainty that the King would have to correct information soon. It would be at that point that I could save myself, but in the meantime I would remain a bundle of nerves tucked into the corner.

"My King," the Beta called as he stepped back inside the hut, squeezing into the last bit of space. My eyes snapped open as I waited for my exoneration.

"Well, what did they have to say? Repeat everything they had to tell you word for word," King Emmett commanded. I wasn't sure why the confidence that I had been filled with just moments earlier had elected to vanish, replaced with a chilling sense of foreboding. I wasn't able to shake the idea that whatever the royal Beta was about to say wouldn't work out well for me.

"I sent your bodyguard back to Opal Moon earlier after you fished her out of the river, that way he could conduct a thorough investigation into anything and everything that had taken place in that pack if you so desired. He found blood spatter all over our future Luna's room. From what he could surmise it appeared that our Luna had been stabbed repeatedly in the chest with a silver knife. The knife had even been used to disfigure our Luna's face. This wretch's claim that Alpha Fabian only having one daughter is complete fabrication on her part. There have always been two Natasha, the older of the two, then Emily your mate. From what he could gather this girl," he gestured at me, "was the one to murder our future Luna in a jealous rage. Apparently she wanted nothing more in this world than to replace our Luna," the Beta reported out. All I could do was sit there in the corner in stunned disbelief as my teeth sank into my lower lip and I shook my head.

Panic seeped into every cell of my being as I watched the massive bulk of the Alpha King rise from his chair, somehow, I had been proven a liar when I had told them nothing but the truth.

"No, that's all a lie. I've never raised a finger to anyone," I broke down into full body wrenching sobs, petrified of what the Alpha King planned to do once he finally reached me. I was babbling as tears streamed down my cheeks in an attempt to convince him this last time of my innocence.

"Please...please...please," was the only word that I could manage to utter as the Alpha King yanked me towards him, throwing me off balance both physically and emotionally. Our faces were so close that I watched as his eyes flickered between black to a lighter that couldn't make out in the dim light of the hut, I knew it was a sign that he was seconds away from slicing my throat open with his claws.

"I warned you not to lie to me," he closed the small distance between us until our faces were a hair's breadth apart, it wasn't until that moment that I noticed his Beta had already left the hut. I'd been left alone in the hut with the cursed Alpha King known for his cruelty, that didn't exactly elicit warm fuzzy feelings.

"No, I swear I didn't," I promised again.

"You really have to gall to lie to my face! He roared then there was a flash of movement and I was partly naked. Instead of using his claws on my throat he'd elected to slice off some of my dress. Of course it all happened so quickly that I could do nothing about it, not that I could have either way.

"No! I screamed, not that it had any effect on him whatsoever.

"Pa…pa…please don't ra…rape me," I begged taking hold of his hand with both of mine. His entire body stiffened as he stopped what he was in the middle of to stare down at my hands clutching his. I immediately dropped his hand as if it were made out of burning hot coals. I had realized the horrible mistake I had just made, I had touched the Alpha King. The punishment for that particular transgression was death.

"I apologize, my King. I never meant to touch you," I offered as he stared down at me blankly. It was at that moment that I noticed the slightest of changes come over him before he reached out and roughly clutched my cheek.

"It may not have been your intention but you did it all the same. Though I'm beginning to sense a pattern, every time you feed me a lie you attempt to cover it up with a thin veil of tears and innocence," he accused, using every inch of his towering build to crowd me into the wall. "You used that pure facade, that seems to ooze from you, to get me to buy into the idea that in essence all the evidence my bodyguard and warriors have collected was a lie. It is evident that you are the individual solely responsible for the murder of my mate, you then attempted to lie directly to your King's face to cover it up," he growled in my face as I frantically shook my head.

"Bu…but, I didn't, I swear," I stammered as he swiped at my tears with his fingers.

"Let me guess, you killed my mate out of jealousy for her place beside me, am I correct?" He inquired with a dark chuckle while staring down at my lips. "So I'm going to grant your deepest desire, the two of us will be wed," the ground crumbled beneath my feet at his announcement. "The only way for you to properly pay for your heinous crimes is to chain you to me through marriage. Within a month's time you'll be on your knees begging for the mercy that only death could provide you, but all you'll receive is endless torment and humiliation at my hands. You'll come to lament the day you were even born. I may be becoming my wife, but it is in name only you'll have no power instead you'll be my slave," he declared. I couldn't keep my eyes from widening the size of saucers at his statement, I was to marry the man I had dreamed about all my life only to be his slave.

"No, please I don't want to marry. Please, just let me go," I pleaded with him in between sobs as he stared down at me with a maniacal smile and gleam in his eye.

"Hmm, I wonder why you've suddenly had a change of heart? Could it be that it's finally sinking in the full magnitude of what you've done? Or even better, all the things that I'll get to do to you?" He asked while his gazed skated over the curves of my body. His hand reached out towards me, I tried to prevent it but he tore the front of my bodice even further. In a moment of pure instinct I made yet another terrible mistake when faced with the imposing force of the Alpha King, I ran.

With a hand clutching the ends of my tattered dress together over my chest, I ducked under his arm, and sprinted out of the cramped hut. I slipped and slid in the mud with my bare feet, unable to find any traction during my unplanned escape. My mind was searching for a place that would be safe for me to hide. That was an issue, I had spent my entire life in Opal Moon then to make matters worse the Alpha family had rarely allowed me to leave unless it was on an errand for them. Okay, I would just have eventually come up with somewhere to hide eventually. That left me with the conundrum of how to protect myself from the Alpha King? I had barely made it through the last fifteen odd years of my life as a slave, it had only been my firm grasp on the dream of finding my mate and him taking me away that had helped me endure. My mind refused to accept the pure injustice of weathering further torment at the hands of my King, master, and would-be husband until the day I left this world.

I was still having trouble wrapping my mind around the idea that he wanted me to become his slave wife, a man I'd always secretly longed for.

I had only run for about ten seconds when suddenly my foot landed on a sharp, pointed stone and I fell to the ground in pain. The rainwater was falling on my body. When I looked back, I saw that he was getting closer to me. I closed my eyes crying and still tried to drag myself away. I continued to crawl on the ground in hopes that I could somehow get away. This wasn't possible, however, because I felt my clothes slowly sliding away from my body as I crawled forward. I paused at noticing this and saw that someone had put their foot on my clothes.

"Please, I don't want to marry you. Can't you just let me go?" I pleaded while using one hand to hold up what remained of my dress after the tatters had been caught under on something. When I glanced back, I found that I had been stopped by the Alpha King's foot on my dress. Tears rolled down my cheeks unchecked at the knowledge that I had been well and thoroughly caught by the man that not only wanted to keep me bound in servitude but as his wife.

"I'm sure that others would agree that I should be compensated for the murder of my mate," he pointed out while giving a sharp tug to what remained of my dress. The seams rent further apart, holding together in some places by a single thread and the Goddess' will that all of my flesh wouldn't be revealed to is lusty gaze.

"Pa...pa...please don't do this. I've never hurt a soul, nevermind killed someone," I attempted to reason with him, but that didn't stop him from ripping what remained of my dress from my body. Listening to me deny any part in his mate's murder must have provoked him, I watched as his eyes became the color of pure obsidian. My rags forgotten in a pile on the ground he yanked my head back using my hair forcing me to look him in the eyes.

"Do you really have the balls to continue lying to my face?! He roared while towering menacingly over me until I was bending backwards in an attempt to escape. I let out a whimper of pain, I watched his expression change as his eyes went blank. The last time he had looked at me that way he had said something about me having innocent eyes, I thought. Not that it mattered, the soft look was quickly overtaken by a sadistic smile that would make Natasha giggle with glee.

"Mmhm, still playing the innocent are we?" He asked in a sinfully deep voice while gentling his touch and pulling me into his body.

I shivered with his sudden change in attitude. It was like he was a devil wearing an angel's mask. He looked deep into my eyes.

"Please no…" I begged, having no idea what was coming next.

"It's been decided, you'll be the Alpha King's innocent bride," Alpha King vowed.

13. Brothel

Elaine

"It's been decided, you'll be the Alpha King's innocent bride."

I had always found it immensely interesting how there were always those among any group that fervently believed that any pain or slight they experienced was the epitome of torment, therefore everyone else should bow down in subjection of their fortitude. Of course, I had also come to the conclusion that most of these individuals haven't experienced anything more inconvenient than having a favorite toy no longer being available for entertainment. Unlike individuals such as myself that seemed to face a different abuse at every turn. Though I honestly couldn't blame the Alpha King for his reaction to the murder of his mate. I definitely hadn't been the person to kill her whomever she had been, but the loss of a fated mate was the worst possible thing that could happen to a werewolf eliciting empathy for his situation.

However, my empathy as it was paled in the light of the realization that my life, meaning everything I had suffered at the hands of the Opal Moon Pack, would seem like child's play in comparison to what the Alpha King had in store. As if the Moon Goddess had a twisted sense of irony, she had indeed paired me with the man I had always loved and desired from afar only not to be his cherished mate. No, instead of vows of undying love I received pledges of unending torment at their hands.

With my latest revelation the dark clouds hanging low in the sky decided that moment was the perfect time to unleash the new torrent of rain as if they too understood my sorrow. The pure loathing emanating from him as he glared down at me succeeded where all others had failed until that point, a deep fissure opened up in the recesses of my soul. The only outward display of my inner turmoil and acceptance of defeat were the tears slipping silently from my lashes to mix unnoticed with the rain. Every ounce of fight that I'd once had left my body, there was no point in struggling or raging at his unjust and brutal treatment of me. He had already come to his own desired conclusion, refusing to change course as he tightened his grip bursing grip on my arm to drag my back to the hut.

"Please believe me. Please let me go..." I pleaded, saying the same thing over and over again while trying to hold onto some semblance of hope that he would let me go, but he didn't. He was taking me back to the hut. I hadn't no idea what he planned on doing to me, but I knew enough to understand that he wasn't going to kill me. Whatever, I was about to face would make me wish for death.

"PLEASE...WHAT ARE YOU DOING?!!" I screamed at him, hugging the ends of my torn clothes to me. He dragged me so mercilessly that the foot I had injured while trying to run away was beginning to feel an intolerable amount of pain.

"AAAAHHHHH..." I yelled out in pain. I couldn't walk anymore. My foot was causing me too much pain, so I just fell to the ground and he looked back at me. He looked very serious, maybe he thought that I was acting. If I continued walking in my current state then I feared that I would lose the ability to walk at all. It felt like there was a piece of that stone still lodged in my foot.

"Get up!" he barked as I peered up at him from the ground.

"You either get up right now or I have no problem fucking you right here in the mud. That way everyone will be able to witness the beginning of your punishment," he threatened, slipping in a trace of his Alpha tone to ensure my compliance. I had to summon every crumb of strength left inside of me in order to stagger to my feet, even knowing that I would inevitably collapse under the strain in a matter of minutes anyway. I should have guessed that before I had the chance to fall that he would prevent it by grabbing my elbow.

"Please, don't take me back to that hut. Please, I have no desire to marry or do anything with you," I pleaded only to have him pinch my chin painfully tight between his thumb and index finger.

"If you continue to persist with this drivel, you will leave me no other choice. I won't just fuck you, I'll force you to watch while I kill Alpha Marvin then feed what remains of him to my pets," at his mention of Marvin alarm rose like a wave inside me. As the Alpha King continued to haul me back to the hut I frantically searched the woods for the barest of clues pertaining to Marvin. The problem was that I couldn't find a sign of Marvin anywhere, to make matters worse I hadn't seen him since he was with the

Alpha King's bodyguard. What could the Alpha King have done with him? Had his bodyguard killed Marvin?

"What crime have you charged him with and where have you taken him? It doesn't really matter to me just please don't kill him," I asked, causing him to halt.

"His most egregious crime is the love that he bears for you. When you combine that with the blatant concern in your eyes for his well being, it's more than enough reason for me to call for his death," he explained nonchalantly, eliciting a shiver from me.

"Please, Alpha Marvin is only in danger because of me. There could never be anything between us, he is to be the Alpha of his pack while I'm a lowly Omega slave. Surely, he would never love someone as inferior as me. I'm only concerned for his well being for the sake of his pack. I harbor no romantic feelings for him, just please don't cause him any harm," I attempted to clarify without arguing but he still squeezed the delicate bones of my wrists painfully hard.

"Just stop! You are in no position to beg for his life, especially when you can't do anything for your own! The concern that is plainly written on your face for him that anyone could read like an open book is just going to led to the rest of your existence being truly fucked up!" He snapped, shoving me away. For a startling moment I was sure that I was going to fall back into the muddy ground, instead I hit something hard. I glanced over my shoulder finding the Alpha King's bodyguard standing directly behind me.

"Zach!" Alpha King called to the bodyguard.

"My King," he answered with a bow of his head. I watched as the King's Beta joined us as well, stopping to stand behind the King.

"Take this woman to the brothel near the palace immediately!" The Alpha King commanded. His use of the word brothel struck fear to the core of my being. I couldn't go to a brothel, I would never survive that. I knelt on the muddy ground with rain pouring down on our heads in subjugation before the Alpha King while clutching at his feet.

"No, please don't...I don't want to go to a brothel...please. You can kill me or torture me in other ways just please don't send me there," I begged of him as he roughly pulled me up from the ground by my arms.

"Do you think I am sending you there for your own enjoyment? Don't be so misled..." He said as my throat went bone dry.

"What do you mean? Why are you sending me there then?" I asked, I could just make out the evil expression on his face.

"You are a worthless murderer and a good-for-nothing whore that doesn't deserve to be anywhere other than a brothel! Don't worry though, you'll still become my bride. You'll still get what you coveted most in the world, just not in the way you had hoped," he sneered as my face turned white. He hasn't given up on the idea of marriage then.

It was at that point that Zach took over responsibility for dragging me. Though I continued begging for mercy from the Alpha King, he never bothered to look towards me or did he listen. Just watching his back turned towards me as I was being dragged away to a brothel took the last bit of hope I had in my heart. He never looked at me once.

Marvin

As soon as the car stopped in front of the Opal Moon Pack, I immediately jumped out of the car and strode into the packhouse.

"MARVIN!!!" Father got out of the car with Alpha Fabian and called after me, but I didn't turn around.

"Stop right there!!!" Father barked using his Alpha tone. I stopped and looked back as he stood in front of me boiling in anger.

"DO YOU HAVE ANY IDEA HOW DIFFICULT IT WAS FOR ME TO GET YOU OUT OF THERE ALIVE? HOW HARD IT WAS TO GET YOU AWAY FROM THE CLUTCHES OF THE ALPHA KING?" Father yelled at me. Alpha Fabian was also giving me an angry glare.

"But who told you to get involved in my affairs, father?" I said, earning a hard slap across the face.

"I HAD TO GET INVOLVED BECAUSE YOU ARE THE FUTURE ALPHA OF MY PACK!! I HAD TO GET INVOLVED BECAUSE YOU ARE MY SON, I WAS NOT GOING TO STANDBY AND WATCH YOU DIE BECAUSE OF SOME MURDEROUS SLUT OMEGA SLAVE!!" He roared in my face and I clenched my fists in anger.

"Why did you need to get involved with the woman who murdered the Alpha King's mate?!!" Alpha Fabian asked.

"That's a lie. It's all a lie and you know it. You have no daughter other than Natasha. So how could Elaine have killed the mate of the Alpha King who's apparently your non-existent second daughter? You have accused an innocent woman who's now going to be a prisoner of the Alpha King then tortured out of revenge for the death of someone who doesn't exist!" I pointed out to both of them, trying to kee[control of my anger. However, I didn't mention that the Alpha King was going to force her to marry him, actually no one knows that fact. I hated it. It had been unbearable to listen to the Alpha King's pack members talking about it. I was blindfolded, but I could still hear everything going on around me. I still could not believe that I had lost Elaine. I lost her to the Alpha King. I lost her to the point that there was no way that I could ever bring her back. Father refused to let me tell the Alpha King the truth.

"I won't let you destroy my pack over some Omega slave! You will keep the fact that your uncle has no second daughter to yourself. Do you understand?" Father ordered me using his Alpha tone, I looked at Alpha Fabian and my father in a silent plea. The two brothers were only thinking about their packs. They weren't thinking of the innocent life that was being ruined by their lies. Their greed for power has ruined my life and led to the loss of my love.

I didn't respond before I walked away, as I was walking I noticed Lewis getting into his car. My eyes turned red at the sight of him. I charged towards him, grabbing him roughly by the collar as I punched him in the face.

"WHAT THE FUCK ARE YOU DOING!!!" Lewis shouted at me as I landed another blow. I didn't bother to give him a chance to try and fight back. Natasha came running out of the packhouse closely followed by Luna Wilma. Everyone watched the scene in shock.

"MARVIN!!! STOP THIS INSTANT!!!" Alpha Fabian and father yelled at me, but I wasn't going to stop.

"LET GO MARVIN!!!" Lewis screamed while trying to get out of my grasp.

"DON'T YOU DARE THINK THAT I DON'T KNOW WHAT YOU DID TO ELAINE!!" I roared in his face.

"What do you mean? I didn't do anything!" He blatantly lied even as his face turned white. He shoved me away as hard as he could, but he couldn't seem to look me in the eyes.

"YOU CAN TRY TO PRETEND TO BE INNOCENT FOR AS LONG AS YOU"D LIKE, JUST REMEMBER THAT KARMA

IS A BITCH!! WHATEVER YOU HAVE DONE TO THAT INNOCENT SOUL YOU'LL COME BACK TO YOU DOUBLED!! I'LL MAKE SURE OF IT!! I'LL GET MY FAIR SHARE, BUT NOT BEFORE DESTROYING YOU!!!" I snapped at him then stared down my father and Alpha Fabian who were glaring at me. Everyone knew what I was alluding to.

Emmett

The sun had set, but the twin flames of hatred and anger still burned inside my heart. Whenever she would plead with me, my anger just kept increasing. As soon as the sound of her screaming could no longer be heard, my hand went up to my neck to the place where my mark had now completely disappeared.

Rex was watching me, I could feel the sorrow in his heart. It made me wonder if anyone could feel the sorrow in mine? The only one that was capable of feeling my anguish was dead. She left me alone again, just after finding her. I clenched my fists and swore an oath that I would have my revenge. I would make that Omega's life a living hell.

"Rex, prepare everything," I ordered him, he bowed his head. I started to walk away, Rex followed right behind me.

"Alpha Marvin was taken captive by us, but when this was discovered by Alpha Fabian and Alpha Marvin's father, Alpha Alfred, the two brothers came to plead the boy's case to us. They confirmed that Marvin was not involved with the Omega slave Elaine. According to them, she was a prostitute in their pack who trapped Alpha Marvin in the web of her beauty for her own selfish desires," Rex quickly filled me in. Alpha Alfred had begged for his son's life to be spared.

"As per your order, his life has been spared and his father has taken him back to their pack," Rex continued to inform me when I didn't reply. I hated how he had been screaming for her. I wanted to break his jaw when he had been acting like he would die if something happened to her.

"Alpha, might I be permitted to ask you something?" Rex quietly requested, I just nodded my head.

"Why did your body not burn from her touch?" Rex asked and his words made me stop in my tracks. I looked down at my hands. I had realized this earlier when I saved her from the river, but hadn't really processed it or tried to figure out what it might have meant. My body had not burned from her touch.

"Perhaps it's due to the loathing and fury I hold in my heart towards that woman, perhaps it is overpowering the curse that affects my body. So much so that I can't even feel the burning sensation from her touch," I replied, clenching my fists as I began to walk again.

14. Marked

Elaine

The King's bodyguard, Zach, roughly dragged me away from the hut. He was like a machine, never stopping to take a break. I couldn't tell where he was taking me because I had never been allowed to leave the pack. I was only allowed to go fetch different items from the market from within the pack when Natasha needed something. This area was completely unknown to me. When I had woken up after being thrown in the river I had already been placed in the hut which appeared to be surrounded by dense forest, I could still hear the sound of the river nearby.

I had finally stopped trying to get out of his grasp, coming to the understanding that he was too strong for me to get away from and that he wasn't going to listen to my pleas. He wasn't paying attention to me at all actually. It was as if I was just a bag of flour that he needed to deliver. That being said, the more I tried to extricate myself from him, the more mercilessly he dragged me along.

It was no longer just my food that was causing me pain, the Alpha King's bodyguard's tight hold on my wrist that he used to drag me along was crushing the delicate bones of my wrist together. As we walked that piece of stone finally dislodged itself from my foot, but the pain didn't ebb in any way. There was no other option left for me other than to accept my fate as I reached up and wiped away my tears. That was when I heard the sound of women giggling. The voices were still a good distance away but my wolf's advanced hearing had picked it up. As soon as I lifted my head and looked around me, I began to tremble. I realized that Zach was taking me in the same direction that the voices were coming from, the brothel!

"DID YOU EXPECT TO FIND A MATE?!! DON'T YOU KNOW THAT A WHORE'S JOB IS JUST TO SPREAD HER THIGHS FOR ANY MAN, JUST LIKE YOU MOTHER DID?!!! NOT TO FIND A MATE!!" "YOU'RE A WHORE! BORN ONLY TO BE FUCKED!" "THE ONLY PLACE FOR YOU IS IN A BROTHEL!" "YOU'LL BE MY PERSONAL WHORE" All the taunts and insults that I had received since I was a small child started repeating themselves in my mind.

Only one word has followed me throughout my existence coming to encompass everything that I was to those around me, I was a whore. Everyone had called me a whore since birth even though I was both a virgin and a slave. I've never lived in a brothel nor have I ever entertained a man in bed. The King's man was leading me towards my biggest nightmare just like the Alpha King had ordered.

"I won't go in there," I informed Zach even though he just continued to ignore me. I didn't matter, I refused to go into that place. I would rather die than actually become a whore. Far too quickly I found myself near the front door, I immediately bit his hand, running away the second that his grip on me had loosened enough to do so. I only managed to make it about five steps before he caught me, carried me inside, and unceremoniously tossed me into one of the rooms at the brothel. I hit the floor hard. I heard his footsteps approaching, I frantically tried to scramble away thinking that he would hit me because I had bitten his hand.

"You're lucky that I'm far more forgiving than the Alpha King. If you had dared to have bitten the Alpha King, your head would have already been removed," he calmly explained to me, but I could easily tell that he hated me over the crimes he thought that I committed, killing his Luna Queen.

"I know that you hate me, I can even see why no one believes me, but I don't want to marry Alpha King as some twisted sort of punishment for a crime that I didn't commit. Please help me," I clasped my hands together as I begged him for assistance in running away. I couldn't help but try one more time even though I knew it was a waste of time. This was due to the fact that he was the bodyguard of the Alpha King, A position that required the person in it to have unwavering loyalty to the point that they would never even think about betraying their King.

"After the unforgivable crime that you've committed, the Moon Goddess herself couldn't save you from what the Alpha King has in store for you. He is the one that is now responsible for writing your fate. If you try to escape from this place, you'll bear the brunt of his fury. Just know that the result of one mistake will cause every woman and guard that reside at this brothel to suffer. So don't even contemplate running away or else the Alpha King himself will hunt you down and you don't want to find out what he will do to you," he firmly warned before starting to walk away.

"You only have fifteen minutes. Get changed quickly because the Alpha King is about to arrive," he cautioned then closed the door behind him. I ran to the door as soon as it closed behind him to try and open it only to find that he had locked the door from the outside. I studied the window for a moment but it was obvious that the windows were also locked from the outside. It was official, I was stuck in this place. What was I going to do now? How could I possibly run away? The room I had been given was in a brothel, but it seemed like it was situated away from the other rooms, giving it more privacy. Almost as if it was a special room within the brothel. Suddenly a woman entered the room carrying a wedding gown in her arms.

I was going to try and plead my case with the woman to garner some help, but she ran out of the room immediately after placing the gown on the bed then closed the door firmly behind her. Two minutes passed, yet I still couldn't bring myself to touch that dress. I didn't want to get married. Never in my wildest dreams had thought that I would be forced to marry someone like this. I sat there on the floor in utter despair, yanking at my hair, as I cried over my situation. The door of the room opened again, only this time the bodyguard entered the room.

"Do you have a death wish girl? Don't force me to do something that I don't want to do. I'll only give you one more chance to listen. When I come back in here in five minutes you need to be wearing that wedding gown. If you still haven't changed then you will force me to inform the Alpha King of your disobedience, then he will come and help change your clothes himself," he sternly warned before stepping out of the room again, then closing the door behind him.

I became absolutely incensed with fear. The Alpha King himself would come and help me change my clothes? What did that mean exactly? I wiped the sweat from my forehead, remembering how mercilessly he had torn my clothes off. If he learned that I was disobeying his orders again then I didn't know what he would do to me. I immediately ran towards the wedding dress and quickly began putting it on.

My fear of him has turned me into a total crazy person. As soon as I put the wedding dress on I noticed that there was a comb and make-up on the dresser. Was I supposed to comb my hair and do my make-up too? The bodyguard never mentioned that. I didn't know how much time I had left, but I quickly did my hair. When I was done with my hair, the door of the room was flung open, the comb fell from my hand in surprise when I saw the Alpha King standing in the doorway. He was wearing a royal uniform and it gave me chills when he checked me out from head to toe. Only one thought echoed in my mind... I'm dead... I'm dead... Those two words, two simple words that ladened with so much fear came straight from my heart, but the moment that I saw him my heart stopped beating.

I had no clue as to why I felt as if I had gone back in time, yet it felt like the first day I had met him. He was wearing a similar uniform then, he looked just as handsome. There had been a smile on his face then that had made my heart beat just for him. Looking at him now, though there was only hatred and anger in his eyes, which was all thanks to me. His smile had disappeared because of me. Upon entering the room all of his attention was on me, he never took his eyes off of me as he drew closer. I lowered my gaze as a sign of respect, but also out of pure fear.

"It would be a blatant lie to say that you didn't look beautiful," he quietly admitted. I raised my eyes to his, in surprise. His voice seemed more normal than I've ever heard it. He seemed calmer than he had earlier in the day. Did that mean he really finds me beautiful? No one has ever called me that before, they all called me ugly or dirty. Unfortunately, his anger from earlier returned to his face when I looked up at him.

"You use this beauty to take advantage of men, so that you can play with their hearts. That way you can get whatever you want, fulfilling your every selfish desire," he growled accusingly. Now there was a change in his countenance to what I had expected to be facing to begin with. This was what he truly thought of me. It didn't matter that I was innocent, his mind had already been made up about me, I was a whore and a murderer.

"Only this time you made the mistake of choosing the wrong victim. You've killed my mate, your Alpha King's mate! So now I'll be making it my mission to ensure that you'll finally get everything that you deserve," he promised, roughly grabbing my wrist before dragging me out of the room. The Moon Goddess had given him a mate, a mate that he loved beyond words. Of course, this meant that he never loved me. I had always coveted his love, it had been the only thing that helped me through all of those years of torment in Opal Moon. Not that I had known that my hopes and dreams would be fulfilled in such a horribly twisted way, that he would force me to marry him as a form of revenge. Without saying a word I quickly stumbled after him while still being dragged by my wrist. I managed to hold up the bottom of the long train of the wedding gown a little with my other hand, so as not to fall or trip.

I was petrified, I just wanted to tell him over and over again that I didn't want to marry him, but I couldn't, not after what Zach had told me. If I stepped a single toe out of line or disobeyed him in any way, then the lives of all the women and guards in the brothel would be in danger because of me. When we exited the brothel, I saw four cars parked nearby. Upon seeing them I knew right away that they were cars belonging to the royal family. The man I now knew to be Beta Rex opened the back door to one of the cars, the Alpha King tightened his grip on my wrist before throwing me towards the open car door car and shoving me in before slamming the door closed behind me. I began to panic further when I looked back only to find that he was not there.

Why did he imprison me in this car? I was left alone with just the driver for company. He just stared at me as I began to frantically search for the Alpha King's location. Even though I was scared of him, I didn't want to be left alone with the driver, I didn't know what he would do to me. I had never sat in a car before today and tight enclosed spaces always made me feel like I was suffocating. I couldn't sit in this car alone. I looked around, the Alpha King was still nowhere to be found. I was starting to go insane in my panic. I jumped when the door beside me suddenly opened, when I looked over I saw the Alpha King getting into the car to sit next to me.

At least I wasn't alone with the driver anymore, not that the current situation did much to calm my racing heart either. The car started moving in an unknown direction, it felt like we were going way too fast. It was already evening, which turned the dense woods on the other side of the windows into an impenetrable black wall. I held onto the car seat in fear then glanced over at the Alpha King. I could still feel his dangerous aura. On top of that, I didn't know why but my gut was telling me that he had something awful for me planned. I was straining my eyes trying to catch a glimpse of something out of the window as I tried to figure out where I was, but the road was only getting darker and even more dangerous.

"What…what will you…do….with me?" I dared to ask, stammering out of fear. "Please, let me go…you are the Alpha King…why do you want to…marry me? I do….don't want to…marry yet. Leave me right here if you want, but please... don't make me marry you…" I pleaded again, only this time I had somehow gained more courage than before. Marriage was a big deal to me, in the library at the Opal Moon Pack I had read so many books. Those books had described marriage as a holy and unbreakable bond between two people. So, even if he pushed me away and tossed me out of his life I would never find it in me to leave him. Yes, I had always dreamed of marrying him, but not like this. I was well aware that this marriage was going forward for the sole purpose of his revenge. While marriage has always been something you do out of love in my mind. I want to marry him because we loved each other, not out of revenge. No matter what happened I wouldn't marry him.

He didn't acknowledge my pleas, but when he looked over at me I lowered my gaze in submission. My questions had only angered him further and his eyes were beginning to turn black again.

"NOT ONLY DO I HATE YOUR FACE, BUT I HATE YOUR VOICE TOO!! IF YOU DARE TO SPEAK ANOTHER WORD

TO ME, I WILL FUCK YOU RIGHT HERE IN THIS CAR!!" He roared as I flinched, sliding down in the seat. He was looking at my dress again. Maybe he was contemplating tearing it off of me right now in front of the driver. He grabbed my chin tightly, forcing me to meet his gaze.

"The more you say that you don't want to marry me, the more I want to chain you to me with this bond," he snarled, just as the car stopped.

"What do you mean?" I asked as he quickly got out of the car, but he didn't bother to answer me. He reached back into the car grabbing my wrist then using it to pull me out of the car after him, he was taking me somewhere. With no moon hanging in the sky there was only darkness around us, but it looked like we were by a small mountain. I then noticed the same river from earlier. I realized that he had brought me back to where I had almost drowned earlier that day but we were at a part of the river where no one was allowed to go because it was part of the King's private property.

This place was one of the most sacred places in our Kingdom. People have always said that if you were to make a wish here under the light of the moon, then it was bound to you forever, that it would become your destiny. I was still in his grasp as he dragged me along behind him, I couldn't stop thinking about what he said in the car. He would chain me in this bond. Without thinking about the consequences, I grasped his hand that was gripping my wrist like a shackle with my free hand which caused him to stop and look back at me with a confused expression on his face.

"What do you mean?" I asked, now that we were facing each other. We had reached the end of the path that we were following, it had stopped at the flowing river as I waited for his reply.

"I will bind you to me with an unbreakable bond that will be sustained for your next seven lives," he replied, his voice echoing eerily as it made my eyes widen.

"What?" I gasped, suddenly I saw the moon come out from behind a cloud, its light falling on the both of us.

"For what you have stolen from me, you will have to pay the price for your crimes for the next seven of your lives. When I am reborn, so too shall you be reborn. You will only be born to bond with me and in every birth you will neither forget me, nor I you. In every life you will pay for your crimes, this will be your punishment," he announced before grabbing my hand and sliding a ring on my finger. When I looked at the ring I understood what he had just done, he had bound our destinies together for our next seven lifetimes.

"NO!! NO…NO!!!" I screamed, trying to pull the ring off my finger, but it didn't work. It shouldn't be like this, I didn't want his hate to follow me into the next seven lifetimes. The ring was wrapping itself around my finger. The more I struggled to take it off the tighter it seemed to get.

"No!" I wailed, crying dejectedly until suddenly my body was roughly pulled back into him and he grabbed a fistful of my hair.

"Yes, yes, and yes," he taunted with a sinister grin as I shook my head in disbelief. He had done this in a sacred place under the light of the full moon so that it would become our destiny.

"Please break it. Take it all back. Please! I don't want this," I begged. That was when I saw his wolf's eyes emerge. What? What was happening to him? Why was he looking at me like that? Why was he growling? I saw his eyes focus on my neck, it seemed like he had lost control of his wolf. I grew scared and tried to run away from him. I pushed him away with whatever strength I had left and tried to run, but I stumbled on this absurdly long train of the wedding gown.

I was about to fall, I could tell that my head was going to make a direct hit with a large stone. Then I felt his arms around my waist as he pulled me back towards him again. My back slammed hard against his chest and I screamed out in fear. No, he had caught me. I failed to get away again. Why did the Moon Goddess hate me?

He turned me around to face him and pulled me even closer to him. The next thing I knew I felt were his canines sink into my neck. My eyes shot wide open as I screamed in pain because he was marking me against my will. My hands went to his chest as I tried to push him back, but I couldn't. He just dug his canines deeper and deeper into my neck as I struggled against him.

"AHHHHHHH!!!!" I shrieked, digging my nails into his arms in pain, as I felt his teeth deep inside my neck. I could feel my blood pumping out of my neck. He…he just…marked me. What kind of game was destiny playing that I was now forcefully bound to him, of all people? For seven lifetimes? How could he mark me? Why had he done it? I felt so dizzy due to the pain, so I closed my eyes though tears were still falling fast. Maybe, this awful pain would finally kill me. I couldn't believe that the Alpha King had marked me, even though we weren't mates…

15. She is My Slave!

Third Person

"What's going on? What's all of this commotion about at this time of night?" Emmett's step-mother, Luna Amanda asked incredulously, coming out of her room as soon as she began to hear strange noises caused by the erratic activity. At the same time, Ariel and Raymond came out of their bedroom. It was abnormal for so much activity to occur that close to midnight.

"What's happening?" Ariel asked Raymond in confusion that was when all of them noticed Zach entering the palace, but there's no sign of the Alpha King.

"What's the meaning of all of this?" Amanda asked.

"The Alpha King will be returning soon," Zach informed the trio with a respectful bow. After witnessing all the bloodshed of that morning, everyone's faces turned white as soon as they heard that the Alpha King was coming back. The mysterious disappearance of the Alpha King's mate that morning had quickly been brought to everyone that resided in the palace's attention. Anyone that was thought to be involved with her unknown whereabouts had been brutally punished.

Ariel had not stepped one foot out of her room during the entirety of the interrogation that morning out of fear, not that it had kept their screams from reaching her. Raymond had stood in the hall with Emmett during the whole ordeal never daring to say a word. The knowledge that Emmett was on his way home made them nervous. They didn't know what kind of havoc he was going to wreak next.

"Emmett's coming? Thank Goddess! I was looking forward to my son coming back home in the morning," Luna Amanda anxiously announced while staring at the door. After glancing at Luna Amanda, Ariel rolled her eyes in exasperation.

"Death himself is about to enter the palace and our Luna is eager to greet him," Ariel mind-linked Raymond with a dramatic shake of her head.

"What are you thinking?" Ariel asked Raymond.

"I'm not sure. I feel like something is wrong," Raymond muttered, causing Ariel to frown.

"What? Don't go talk shit now. My head is already filled with enough nonsense as it is. On top of this mysterious mate disappearance, my sister cried her eyes out last night because the Alpha King never actually joined the mating ball last night. All she's ever wanted was to become the Alpha King's chosen mate, but look at what's happened! The Alpha King's mate ran away without anyone seeing her which caused a great deal of blood to be spilled. I don't think I can handle any more bad news," Ariel complained to Raymond. She was quite angry with him too. It would've been the perfect outcome for them if Naomi had become the Alpha King's mate, but everything had been ruined. Ariel's frustration quickly turned to surprise when she saw her sister Naomi entering the palace.

"Naomi! What are you doing here?!!!" She almost shrieked in surprise. After being so heartbroken over last night's events, Ariel never would have thought that Naomi would come back to the palace so soon. Naomi ran towards her sister and hugged her with a big smile.

"I didn't come because I wanted to. I was summoned here. I was ordered by the Alpha King, himself," Naomi explained, overwhelmed with happiness. Naomi was unable to stand in one place and was going absolutely jittery with excitement.

"What? The Alpha King has summoned you here?" Ariel asked. She couldn't believe her ears, even Raymond was surprised to discover this. Ariel could tell that even Luna Amanda was paying close attention to everything being said.

"Yes, that is correct. I was summoned by the Alpha King. Tonight I'm going to get everything I've always dreamed of. I knew that he always loved me! Didn't I always say that Ariel? I'm sure that he's called me here to ask me to be his chosen mate!" Naomi replied, tightly hugging Ariel again in her excitement.

"That's wonderful news! That means you'll be our Luna Queen," Ariel said delightedly and looked up at Raymond.

"I still can't believe it," Raymond murmured, his mouth still wide open in surprise. He couldn't shake that feeling that something bad was going to happen, even when faced with good news.

"I sincerely apologize, Luna Amanda. I did not greet you as befits your station due to my excitement. Please forgive me" Naomi immediately asked for forgiveness, earning a smile from Amanda.

"It brings me great pleasure to know that Emmett has finally chosen a mate for himself. Nevermind that she is a woman from such a nobel family," Luna Amanda replied with a proud smile on her face. Naomi was the daughter of an Alpha of a powerful pack, it was one of the top five packs that were under Emmett's protection.

Meanwhile, Zach was quietly listening to their entire conversation. He knew exactly what was going to happen, which was completely different from what anyone was expecting.

"I still can't believe that this is happening, Ariel," Naomi squealed and hugged her again.

"Yes! Now my sister will be the Alpha King's mate, she'll be the Luna Queen. Now everyone will have to bow before me. I'll fulfill everything that I've ever dreamed of," Ariel mind-linked Raymond. They smiled at each other evilly because not only would Ariel benefit, but Raymond would also achieve his dreams. Naomi was the golden ticket the them had been waiting for.

"The Alpha King has returned," Zach suddenly announced as soon as he received a mind-link from Beta Rex. Everyone in the hall immediately bowed their heads as Emmett entered.

The sound of his footsteps echoed off the walls, everyone's excitement was building to a fever pitch for what they anticipated was about to happen. Everyone was curious to hear the Alpha King announce Naomi as his mate from the man himself, but instead they heard something unexpected. They heard a noise that sounded like a girl moaning in pain. The noise was accompanied by an unfamiliar fragrance. These unexpected events forced them to look up at the Alpha King.

Everyone's eyes widened in surprise. Naomi's mouth remained wide open when she saw an unknown woman in the Alpha King's grasp. She placed her hand over her mouth in disbelief when she saw Emmett's mark on the woman's neck. The unknown woman had been marked by him!

Elaine

He yanked me out of the car by my wrist, I stood outside the palace for the second time in my life. The first time I had come here of my own free will, well really I had been ordered by Natasha but I had willingly come. This time I had been brought to the palace by force. After he had marked me, I had nowhere else to go. He had made me his property, effectively blocking any other path of escape that I could have possibly taken in the future. Now I would never be able to leave him. I was bound to him forever in this life as well as my next seven.

Once he began to drag me inside the palace I was consumed by panic. The palace had once been the loftiest of my dreams, it had been turned into my living nightmare. I had been attacked by Lewis on my way here, I had been dragged here on more than one occasion, and I had lost my virginity at the hand of a stranger here. My whole life had been turned upside down the day I stepped foot in that building, yet I was back here again.

Despite everything that had happened and what he'd done to me, both my wolf and I, who had already been in love with him, were now falling even harder for him thanks to the forced bond. I had gone crazy over him, I loved him.

His grip on my wrist was starting to cause me a great deal of pain to the point that it was becoming unbearable. I continuously tried to free my wrist from his grip, but he wasn't paying any attention to me. While I was focused on trying to free myself from his grasp, we had already made our way into the main hall of the palace. There were so many unfamiliar people standing around watching me with surprise and confusion written clearly on their faces.

"Emmett!" A woman exclaimed. When I looked up I saw an older woman that closely resembled the Alpha King. She must have been his mother because only the woman that had given birth to him would have dared to call him by his given name.

Surprised she took me in from head to toe. Her eyes lingered on my neck where he had marked me. My eyes turned away from her scrutiny, scanning over the other people in the hall. I recognized one of the other people there as Prince Raymond, he was standing next to his mate Princess Ariel.

There were none more beautiful than the women present. She was standing right beside Princess Ariel, but I didn't know who she was. I had this feeling that I had seen her before but I was having a hard time placing where. Suddenly it hit me and I remembered her face. I had seen her only once before, when she attended a birthday party for Alpha Fabian the previous years. She was the younger sister of Princess Ariel, Princess Naomi. I was surrounded by Princes and Princesses. In other words, I was in imminent danger.

"Who is she?" Luna Amanda asked the Alpha King, I lowered my head in submission. She was the Dowager Luna Queen, I wasn't allowed to look at her. I could feel the loathing and indignation of every person in that hall and knew that it was all directed solely at me. They could sense that I wasn't from a nobel family. On top of that based on my thin frail body, they could easily assume that I was an Omega slave. My status alone as an Omega was bad enough but appearing with his mark on my neck I might as well have spit in their faces. No one dared to ask the Alpha King about it though. He looked towards his family before glancing down at me.

"This is my slave!" He announced as I looked up at his emotionless face. It would have been a lie if I had said that his words hadn't hurt me. They hurt me more than they should've to hear that he thought of me as merely his slave. I knew what he thought of me but there was a part of me that still clung to the wish that things were different. I was just a slave to him, nothing more yet he had married me. Why had he married and marked me if he only wanted a slave?

"What? A slave?" Princess Naomi asked. I watched as the Alpha King turned to look at her.

"Yes, just a slave," he repeated. I noticed that she blushed whenever he spared her a glance. She wore a smile that screamed 'Thank god that bitch was not the Alpha King's mate'. I also noticed Prince Raymond was studying with some interest, yet there was no hate. He just seemed surprised.

Suddenly Beta Rex appeared in front of the Alpha King with a silver tray. It looked like there were some kind of gloves on it. The Alpha King picked them up and quickly put them on, but they seemed to disappear once they were put on his hands as if he were wearing nothing. I was quite surprised to see that the rumors were true.

There were rumors amongst the surrounding packs, people say that the Alpha King never touches anyone. If he planned to touch someone then he always wore some kind of gloves on his hands to form a fabric barrier. No one knew the reason behind his actions. They said that when the Alpha King was born, his mother knew he suffered from some type of affliction, so she had some of her skin removed. She gave this removed skin to some witches who used it to make gloves for the Alpha King. Once these gloves were donned, their magic affected his entire body like a shield.

Seeing those gloves, I understood that those rumors were true, but why was he only putting them on now? What were they protecting him from? What was the point of them if he didn't wear them all of the time? He wasn't wearing them when he touched me earlier.

While putting them on he watched me out of the corner of his eyes. "Rex, get her out of my sight," the Alpha King ordered. He violently shoved me back until my back hit Beta Rex.

"Follow me," Beta Rex instructed. I noticed that once I had righted myself after being pushed, Beta Rex had not touched me. I was surprised that he wasn't dragging me away by my hair or wrist like everyone else always did, yet he let me leave the hall under my own power. It was incredibly unsettling. Were they trying to give me a false sense of comfort?

As I began following Beta Rex, I glanced over as Princess Naomi. She was still blushing at the Alpha King, whereas Luna Amanda, Princess Ariel, and Prince Raymond were all glaring at me with pure unadulterated hatred. How many enemies had I made by being forced into this marriage? All I knew was that I had more than just the Alpha King to worry about. I just couldn't bring myself to worry about them right now, not when I didn't even know what was going to happen to me next.

16. His Picture in My Heart

Elaine

I was being taken to another part of the palace by Beta Rex when he suddenly stopped. I looked up and it seemed as if he was talking to someone via mind-link, that was when I noticed another member of the pack coming towards us. He was in a rush.

"The Alpha King is going to the conference room. We should join him as soon as possible," the man informed and Beta Rex quickly nodded in agreement. Perhaps whatever information that he had received via mind-link was concerning the same issue. Beta Rex nodded again and the two of them left, leaving me standing in the hallway alone, unaware of where I should go or what I should do. I glanced around and every direction looked the same. There wasn't even anyone around that I could ask where I should go.

"Are you lost?" A voice came from behind me startling me so much that I jumped. She was dressed in casual clothes, just with more makeup and lipstick on her face. The woman in her thirties happened to be none other than Princess Naomi's personal maid. I knew this because she hadn't been alone when she visited the Opal Moon a year ago. She had many servants accompany her to my pack, one of them had been this woman.

"I don't know where I'm supposed to go," I replied. I wasn't sure why but I felt as if she was speaking to someone via mind-link, but she had a big smile on her face when she focused back on me. Why was she smiling at me? It all seemed more than slightly creepy. Even though she was a maid, she was a maid to a member of the nobel family. Even a gardener working for the royal or a noble family would see an Omega slave then dislike them immediately on principle.

"Alright, let me help you. You're going to go straight down this hallway, turn right, then you'll need to go into the last door on the left," the woman explained, but as soon as she finished speaking she turned around and left. I didn't even get a chance to thank her. It seemed as if she was in a hurry. She was looking back and forth quickly as if she wasn't supposed to be here or something.

While following her directions, I couldn't help admiring the beauty of the palace around me. Everything was beautiful. As soon as I turned right, I immediately noticed the last door on the left, the one I was supposed to go through. My mouth fell open in surprise. It was made of sandalwood; it had been carved into a magnificent piece of artwork that was priceless.

I questioned myself at least a thousand times before entering. Was I really allowed to enter this room? Surely that magnificent room wasn't meant for the likes of me? However, that maid had told me to go to this room specifically, I knew that I had followed her instructions correctly. If I didn't do as I was told, it would be a violation of the Alpha King's order. Had I been sent to this room to clean it? Or did the Alpha King plan on using this room to torture me? After struggling with this mental dilemma for three minutes straight, I finally decided to go inside the room before I ended up being beaten for disobeying an order.

I slowly took one step inside the room then immediately stopped. The room was breathtakingly beautiful! I could smell his scent in the room and I closed my eyes, inhaling his scent as much as I could. This room was full of his addictive scent. He must have been in this room before. I opened my eyes again, surprisingly, I couldn't even blink as I took in the beauty found within that room, it was similar to what I imagined would be found in a Luna Queen's room. Everything in the room was luxurious. There were precious paintings and artifacts adorning the walls and prized glass and ceramic vases decorating different tables. The room looked like it had been decorated as if to suit someone's particular tastes.

Ignoring all of the precious items in the room, my eyes were enraptured by one thing. It was the king sized bed in the middle of the room. I had never seen such a large bed before in my life. I had only ever slept on a pad on the floor with only a torn sheet that was never enough to protect me from the cold. The thought of sleeping on something that looked so incredibly soft was enough to bring tears to my eyes.

While looking at the bed, my gaze went to a very large picture hanging on the wall behind the bed, which made my heart beat even faster. It was a huge portrait of the Alpha King, the portrait made it seem as if the man himself was standing in front of me. The sharpness and gallantry of his face could be seen clearly in the portrait as well, it was enough to make me hold my breath. I stood staring up at the portrait for what felt like hours but was probably only minutes. The picture I had of him was quite old, small, and torn, but I'd looked at it so many times that it was engraved into my heart, no one could take that away from me.

BANG!!!

I jumped out of my skin when I registered the loud crash of the door being kicked open. I quickly looked at the door that was barely hanging on by its hinges and saw that the Alpha King was standing in the doorway fuming with rage.

Emmett

All of the other members were already waiting for me when I arrived in the conference room. I immediately took my place at the head of the table then glanced at my bodyguard Zach, which was the sign for him to start speaking. He began by bowing his head with respect.

"Alpha Fabian of the Opal Moon Pack urges you to please allow his daughter's body to remain buried in the territory of his pack. Alpha Fabian had no idea that his daughter was your mate at the time of her passing, he had already buried her on their lands. He pleads for you to not exhume her body and allow her to rest in peace," Zach notified me of what Alpha Fabian requested.

The moment that everyone learned that she was my mate, any right they had to her was removed, including the right to her corpse. They may have buried her before they knew she was my mate, but that would not stop me from making sure that she ended up in a proper final resting place like she deserved.

"Send a reply to Alpha Fabian that his request has been denied! My mate's body will be buried in the Royal Mausoleum, nowhere else! That is my final decision," I ordered, but just as I was about to rise from my seat, I saw Zach kneeling on the floor.

"I apologize for interrupting you like this Alpha. There is one last thing that I need to tell you and it might make you change your decision," Zach earnestly suggested. I sat back down and waved for him to continue.

"When I asked the pack members why the corpse was buried before the Royal Pack arrived, they said that it was the Luna Queen's dying wish to be buried in her pack," Zach explained, this forced me to rethink my decision. I was unaware that this was her dying wish.

"Okay, I accept my Luna Queen's dying wish, her corpse will continue to be buried in the Opal Moon Pack. However, it will be placed in a location of my choosing, that way her wish will be fulfilled," I replied. Many of the members present at the meeting didn't understand my point, but Rex and Zach understood perfectly.

Rising from my seat, I felt as if there was someone in the room that my mate and I had shared our one and only night together. I angrily exited the conference room, fisting my hands tightly at my sides as I proceeded towards our room. There was only one person who would dare go in there. The person was none other than the same woman that I hated the most!

Since my mate had disappeared no one had been allowed to enter. How dare she presume that she had been permitted inside such a sacred room? Using my wolf speed, I appeared in front of the door in just a few seconds and angrily kicked it in.

17. I Hate You...

Elaine

I was scared seeing him so furious and began to take a few steps backward, but he was too quick. Suddenly he was clutching a handful of my hair as my head was violently yanked back.

"HOW DARE YOU STEP FOOT IN MY MATE'S ROOM!!!" He roared as I cried out, but it wasn't just because of the pain. I was absolutely terrified over how he was going to react, I hadn't known that this was his mate's room and now I understood why it looked like the room belonged to a Queen.

"I'm...sorry. I didn't know," I tried to explain to him while attempting to unweave my hair from his grip.

"WHY THE FUCK DID YOU ENTER THIS ROOM IN THE FIRST PLACE?" He yelled, giving my hair another severe yank. I was sure that if I didn't give him a proper answer, he might actually strangle me to death.

"A woman, sh…she…she told me to come in here…" I stammered, but stopped. I didn't bother to complete my sentence when I realized that he wasn't going to believe me no matter what I said. He never did, plus I didn't have any evidence. After all, why would someone tell me to go into this room if they knew that it was forbidden for anyone to enter? I hadn't known that this room was special, that it was prohibited. He saw me closing my mouth and the defeated look of acceptance in my eyes as I gave up trying to defend myself.

He pulled me closer to his face as he said, "Lies, lies, lies!!!" in a low tone while tears rolled down my cheeks unchecked. I was in unbelievable pain.

"I have never met a woman like you. Someone who's a crafty liar. Someone who couldn't tell the truth even if their life depended on it," he sneered into my ear, gritting his teeth. I could only sob. I couldn't bring myself to say a word.

"Wait a minute. Why the hell did I not think about what you were trying to do…" he asked rhetorically gently letting go of my hair as I tried to control the sound of my sobs.

"You came here because you want to replace her, right?" He inquired, eyeing me suggestively. When he began to undress, I nearly had a heart attack.

"No, you're...wrong. I didn't come…here for this. Trust me…I…" I couldn't complete my sentence before he pulled me close to him, the next thing I knew his lips were crashing into mine. I panicked and tried to push him away. I could tell that he was getting angry with me struggling, that was when I felt him bite my lip.

The taste of blood flooded my mouth and I gasped in pain. He took that opportunity to insert his tongue and deepen the kiss. He was holding me now with only one hand, but he was still strong enough to keep me from getting away. I wasn't able to breathe properly and in a few seconds I was starting to get light headed. As soon as I felt him loosen his grip on my body, I immediately pulled myself away from him rather than trying to push him away. I noticed him licking his lips with an evil smile while I tried to steady my breathing. After taking a few steps backwards I placed a hand over my mouth in fear that he would try to kiss me again.

"Since you've entered this room, let's continue with what you have come here for," he suggested, stopping me in my tracks.

"What…what..do you..mean?" I stammered in fear.

"Strip!!!" He ordered coldly. I froze in shock, but clutched my clothes in the hopes of preventing him from ripping them off.

"No, please don't…" I pleaded, shaking my head. My feet seemed to unglue themselves from the floor and I managed to take a few more steps backwards. In my mind I was experiencing flashbacks of Lewis in the forest and the Alpha King in the hut, both of them tearing my clothes from me against my will. I was terrified thinking about what was about to happen.

"Strip right now or I will tear your fucking clothes off of your fucking body!" He yelled, hearing this warning I became so frightened that I ran towards the door to try and escape. Before I could manage, he grabbed me by the waist and threw me on top of the bed. I screamed out in fear as I watched him climb on top of the bed. I ran towards the door again, but he caught me once again. Only this time he turned me so that I faced him.

"Please…I don't want to…Please, forgive me for entering this room but…didn't do it…" I begged with my hands clasped together in front of me. I begged him for forgiveness, it seemed like that might be my last chance I had left to save myself. Nobody was coming to save me from his clutches. He's the Alpha King and no one would dare speak against him. My whole body trembled like a leaf in his grip. That was when I noticed a change in his eyes. His eyes changed to black which meant that he was utterly outraged. He violently shoved me away from himself, turning my body into a crumpled heap on the floor. I whimpered in pain.

"Did you really think that I would even touch your filthy and disgusting body? Who knows how many times you've been touched by other men?" He asked, his words like thorns piercing my heart. In his eyes I was just a whore, nothing more.

"You'll never get what you want! I'll never touch you, your body disgusts me. Why would I settle on you when I can get any woman I'd like to slack my needs?" He sneered, looking towards the door. When I followed his gaze I saw Princess Naomi standing there. She quickly entered the room with a bow of her head to the Alpha King.

"Come here baby," the Alpha King crooned, pulling her into his arms, the next thing I knew he was kissing her. My eyes widened in shock at witnessing such an intimate scene first hand. A split second later she had stripped herself of all clothing before the Alpha King threw her onto the bed. She was giggling and staring at him, but his eyes were on me as he threw his shirt on the floor right near my feet.

"Stay and watch!" He ordered as he climbed onto the bed. Princess Naomi pulled him down on top of her to kiss him. Watching them together like that was killing me, being forced to continue standing there and witness them have sex was psychological torture.

Just a few hours ago he had married me, bonded me to him for the next seven lifetimes, then marked me. This was supposed to be our first night together as a married couple, yet there he was with another woman in his arms. He was screwing another woman in his bed right in front of my eyes, while forcing me to watch. I could hear Princess Naomi' moans when he kissed her. She was touching what was mine.

I turned my face away and moved to leave the room. I couldn't stand being here another second listening to her moans. I didn't know where I was going, but I knew that I needed to just get away from here. I was going to go crazy if I had to stand there and listen to her moaning his name or the other disgusting sounds of them having sex. I just needed to not be there anymore.

I began to run, I ran as fast as I could. When I reached the hall I found Beta Rex. He seemed a little shocked to see me running and crying through the hallways of the palace, but I just continued on my way until I had made it to the garden. From there I followed a path that led to an exit at the back of the palace. Dodging the guards, I finally exited the palace sprinting through the unknown forest in the dead of night.

My feet were being pierced with debris and sharp stones, but the pain of the blow that he had just delivered to my heart was even more unbearable. Seeing the man that I loved being intimate with another woman had been the worst form of punishment. I hadn't known that I was destined to be punished in this way. I just wanted to kill myself. I had finally lost all reason to live, I had made my decision. I was going to end my life so that my suffering would end, then the fire of hate filled fury in his heart would subside. Everything would be over once I died.

I had been running for about ten minutes when I realized that there was a chasm nearby. It was huge and even with the aid of the moonlight I couldn't see across it. The bottom had to be far below, far enough that it would kill me.

I increased my speed so that when I reached the edge I could end everything with one final jump. I was only five meters from the edge now. I closed my eyes and used my remaining strength to jump as far out as I could knowing that everything would be over soon.

It was at that moment when my body collided with something hard for the side, I felt my body land on the ground by the edge of the chasm. Something had hit me, preventing me from jumping into the chasm, now I was rolling on the ground away from the edge. A few seconds later when my body stopped, I slowly opened my eyes and saw the Alpha King! He tackled me to keep me from going over the edge. He still had my body locked in his arms as he looked down at me. What was he doing here? Why had he stopped me? He had been busy with Princess Naomi in the palace, so why would he be here? Had he followed me? The idea seemed ludicrous in its improbability.

He stood up, roughly pulling me up towards his chest.

"WHAT THE FUCK DO YOU THINK YOU ARE DOING?!!" He barked in my face, boiling in rage.

"Why did you save me? Please just let me die," I begged and in return he pinched my chin hard.

"You're not going to die anytime soon. Your death will not be an easy one. Your future is going to be filled with sorrow and a great deal of pain and suffering!" He pontificated as more tears fell from my eyes.

"I will not be the only one to suffer for your crimes. I'm going to make sure you suffer until the last breath leaves your worthless body!" He promised, looking into my eyes.

"You belong to me now. Your life, your body, even your soul, every little part of you! Each one of your heartbeats is mine, you are not even allowed to breathe without my permission! If you try to do something like this again, not only will the Opal Moon Pack be destroyed, but each and every maid and palace guard as well as everyone in Marvin's pack too!" He declared. This threw me into a pit of despair that there was no return from. If I stepped one toe out of line then, then everyone would die.

"WHY? WHY ARE YOU DOING THIS?!!!" I screamed at him as he lifted my body and threw me over his shoulder to carry me back to prison, to my own personal hell.

"You killed my mate, because I hate you…" He replied in disgust, that was the last thing that I heard before I fainted again.

18. Why Won't He Believe Me?

Third Person

"Natasha, Lewis, come down, dinner is ready," Luna Wilma called out to her children. It was eleven o'clock at night and they were only just now having dinner due to the upheaval caused by the Royal Pack's arrival which had only calmed down an hour ago. To make matters worse, Lewis had only just returned home.

Alpha Fabian wasn't currently in the pack's territory as he had accompanied Alpha Alfred to his pack and has yet to return. Beta Dale said that there wasn't a definitive time of return for Alpha Fabian, so dinner was being served without him. Natasha was coming down the stairs, carrying a mirror in her hand, in which she was slowly applying night cream to her face. She stopped in front of the dining table wearing a short nightgown.

"Ohh...I'm so hungry!" Natasha said, immediately setting the mirror on the table and sitting down. On the other hand, Lewis came out of his room with an irritated look on his face, his eyes landing on the Omega that was serving the meal. She wasn't Elaine. Seeing her, he sat in his chair then studied the food that he was being served. He could tell that the food wouldn't be any good because Elaine hadn't cooked it. Natasha and Luna Wilma brgan eating, but Lewis just sat there, staring at the food in front of him.

"I won't eat this garbage!" He suddenly barked.

"Why? What's wrong with it?" Natasha asked while licking her fingers. She was trying to pretend that the awful food was actually quite tasty, but Lewis knew the truth.

"There's no need to pretend for my sake! I know you're both just acting like you're actually enjoying this crap!" Lewis snapped at Natasha, she promptly glared at him in return. He turned his piercing eyes on Luna Wilma meeting her angry glare.

"This tasteless disgusting slop shouldn't be eaten by a stray dog! I want the food that I always get, otherwise I would rather go hungry," Lewis commanded, shoving the plate of food away. Luna Wilma was appalled at his display of childish behavior.

"I know very well what you're trying to say, Lewis, but you need to grow up and act according to your station. Unfortunately circumstances have changed. This Omega will now be making our meals for us every day. Everyone will have to eat the food made by her or go hungry. You shouldn't even be thinking about that bitch Elaine because luckily that whore will never darken our doorstep again now!!!" Luna Wilma angrily sneered at Lewis. It was a thinly veiled warning aimed at him. Natasha chuckled and shook her head while eating dramatically.

"That bitch hasn't even been gone a day and Lewis already misses her. Is it just the food or ..." Natasha inquired, though didn't feel the need to complete her question as she smirked at Lewis who was boiling in anger.

"YOU!!!" Lewis yelled at Natasha, but before he could continue, Alpha Fabian entered the dining room and everyone went silent when they saw the furious look on his face. Natasha and Lewis were nervous because Alpha Fabian was staring solely at Luna Wilma who was eating quietly even though she knew that Fabian was glaring at her. Alpha Fabian charged towards Luna Wilma dragging her out of the dining room by her wrist and heading to his office. She didn't try to wriggle free or ask about his strange behavior, she just followed behind him silently. The door to Alpha Fabian's office slammed closed but he kept a tight grip on her arm.

"I NEED SOME CLARIFICATION WILMA!! YOU OWE ME A FUCKING EXPLANATION!!!" He screamed at her. She stood in front of him like a statue.

"An explanation for what? I don't know what you're talking about!" Luna Wilma innocently replied. Alpha Fabian's eyes turned red when he realized that she was still trying to play dumb. He slapped her across the face and the corner of her mouth began to bleed.

"DON'T YOU DARE LIE TO ME!! WHY THE HELL DID YOU TRY TO KILL ELAINE?" He continued to yell and slapped Luna Wilma again. She was taking deep heaving breaths as she walked up to him chuckling softly.

"REALLY?!! YOU DON'T KNOW WHY I DID IT?!! ARE YOU REALLY ASKING ME THAT?!!!!" She shrieked back at him in fury. She slammed a letter into his chest that she pulled out of her pocket. Alpha Fabian was shocked to see this piece of paper and looked back at Luna Wilma in surprise.

"How did you get this letter? I tore it to shreds. Did you go into my office behind my back?" He asked. He was furious, no one was allowed into his office without his permission.

"Does it really matter? You didn't even try to cover your tracks. Why didn't you tell me that you received that letter? I did everything in my power to secure a bright future for my children and for all of us, but you put all of that in danger with your actions. Your lust led us to this point. You just couldn't keep your dick in your pants!" She spat out, Alpha Fabian was taken aback by her words. Her anger was only fueling his fury.

"I still don't understand why you felt the need to kill Elaine? Was it out of anger, this situation has now reached the Alpha King. You don't even know what I've had to do to try and fix this mess," he explained as she crossed her arms over her chest.

"I did what I felt was right at the time. Anyway you were contemplating removing Elaine anyway. I just made your work easier. You should have done this years ago. I don't know why you never listened to me, today the results are that all of our lives are now in danger. This letter is an indication that there is someone else who knows about it," Wilma pointed out, gesturing to the letter in his hand. Listening to Luna Wilma, Alpha Fabian turned his face to the side and leaned forward, placing both hands on his desk and looked towards the window.

"Don't worry about it. I've taken care of the whole situation. Our pack members handled the woman who was on her way to ruining everything and now there should be nothing else to worry about," Alpha Fabian informed, assuring Luna Wilma.

"Hopefully everything has been handled and nothing else will come up because all of our lives are in your hands," Luna Wilma replied. After saying that, Luna Wilma stormed out of the office, still down right furious. Alpha Fabian picked up a file and some other papers that were sitting on top of his desk, tossing them to the floor. He screamed out in angry frustration at the same moment that Beta Dale entered the room. He saw the papers scattered all over the floor and got an idea of what happened in here as he had seen Luna Wilma coming out of the room seething.

"Alpha, I received a report from the palace," Beta Dale reported, giving the report to Alpha Fabian. Upon reading the report Alpha Fabian became even more angry and threw it on the floor in frustration.

"What's wrong Alpha?" Beta Dale asked Alpha Fabian, simultaneously reading the letter lying on the ground. According to this letter, the body of the second daughter of Alpha Fabian was not allowed to be buried in the Opal Moon Pack.

"FUCK!!!" Alpha Fabian roared in frustration as he slumped in his chair.

"Alpha, what'll happen now?" Beta Dale asked, panicking.

"Warn all the members of the pack. If anyone dares to open their mouth, they won't only be given the death penalty, but their entire family will be put to death as well. Make sure everyone is aware of this, tell them to forget that a girl named Elaine ever lived in our pack. I never want to hear that name again!" Alpha Fabian ordered, but what neither of them knew was that Natasha was standing on the stairs listening to their entire conversation.

"Oh dear, father. What have you gotten yourself into now?" Natasha whispered to herself while sporting a big smile on her face. She promptly turned around and headed down the hallway trying to figure out what her next steps would be.

Elaine

I felt as if someone was splattering water on my face. Keeping my hands over my eyes, I began to slowly open my eyes. After seeing only a blur at first, a woman's face appeared before me, she seemed to be around twenty-six years old.

"Are you alright?" She asked, looking at me with big eyes, wide in surprise, as she waved her hands in front of my face. I tried to sit up while nodding as she helped me up. I looked around, and I found myself in an unfamiliar room. I was terrified to be left alone with this unknown woman.

"There's no need to panic, I'm not going to hurt you. The Alpha King gave me the responsibility of waking you up," she explained and as soon as I heard her utter 'Alpha King', I remembered everything that had happened before I had fainted. He caught me at the perfect time. He refused to allow me to jump off the edge of the chasm. He refused to let me die. He threw me over his shoulder and brought me back to the palace, now I couldn't run away again without causing the death of way too many innocent people.

Every one of his bitter words had taken up residence in my mind like poison, I wasn't able to forget any of it. I just kept seeing the kiss between the Alpha King and Princess Naomi over and over again as if it were burned into my brain. I just wanted to cry, but the woman was watching me carefully so I turned my face away from her in hopes of hiding the tears that were threatening to fall.

"Excuse me but..." She began to speak. "The Alpha King ordered that as soon as you wake up, you must go to his room," upon learning this, I immediately stood up from the bed so I could be on my way in the hopes of not angering him. I paused by the door when I realized that I didn't know where I was going.

"Umm, can you tell me where the Alpha King's room is?" I asked her in a hurry.

"Yes of course, right now you're in my room which is part of the maids' corridor. After leaving here, you'll need to walk towards the north then the room in the center of the palace is the Alpha King's room," the woman kindly explained. It wasn't easy to trust this woman after Princess Naomi's maid tricked me into going to the wrong room, but I had no other choice. This woman didn't seem to be pretending to be nice to me. She wasn't faking a smile. She seemed sincere.

"Thank you," I told her and she smiled at me.

"Don't worry about it. My name is June by the way," the maid introduced herself. I reciprocated by telling her my name, but I needed to get to the Alpha King's room as quickly as possible so I immediately set out on my way. As I approached the door, I could tell that this was the Alpha King's room. His scent was coming from the room, but I didn't dare to enter fearing that I would see him with Princess Naomi again. No! I wouldn't be able to take that. I took a couple of steps back, when I heard him shout.

"GET IN HERE, RIGHT NOW!!!"

I jumped in fear. He knew I was here and I had upset him again. I cautiously opened the door to his room. As soon as I entered the room I saw that this room was even more beautiful than the room in which I had entered the previous night. I looked around, but he wasn't in the room. Suddenly the bathroom door opened and the Alpha King came out. His hair was wet and he was dressed casually, not in his royal garb. He had taken a shower and looked even more handsome. I immediately bowed my head as soon as he entered, he scanned me from head to toe.

"You called me here? How can I serve you?" I asked him as he threw the towel he was holding on the floor.

"I didn't call you here because I have work for you to do. I called you because you will be staying in this room. So that whenever I need you, you will be close by. If I have use for my slave in the middle of the night, then you will be readily available," he harshly clarified. I was surprised that he was allowing me to stay in his room. I thought I would be sleeping on the kitchen floor or worse, the dungeon.

"DON'T JUST STAND THERE GAWKING AT ME!! GO AND CLOSE THE DOOR!!" He snapped at me, I immediately ran to do his bidding. I then returned to stand in the same place to wait for the next command. When he glanced over at me, he studied me from top to bottom, my heart beat like a hummingbird in my chest out of terror. I was completely alone with him in his room. I had even closed the door with my own hands.

"STOP STARING AT ME WITH THAT WRETCHED FACE!! TURN OFF THE LIGHT AND GET LOST!!!" He yelled at me, I immediately followed his exact order. He laid down on the bed, but turned so that he was facing away from me. I kept standing in the same spot in confusion. I didn't understand what I was supposed to do now or where I should sleep.

Without making any noise, I ended up sitting in a corner of the room. I was still wearing my wedding gown. I ran my hand down it slowly. For the first time in my life, I was wearing a garment of impeccable quality and it was a wedding gown. I had never expected that. This would probably be the last decent garment I would ever be given.

After looking over at the Alpha King one last time, I laid down on the floor in the corner of the room. In this position he wouldn't have to see my face. Other than being married and marked against my will, nothing had changed in my life. I was still just a slave only now the pain I was expected to bear had now increased.

I used to sleep on the floor and I was still sleeping on the floor. The only difference was that I used to sleep with his photo in my hand, now I was actually in his room. While lying on the floor, I looked over at his bed where I could clearly make out the outline of his back. He wasn't facing me which was disappointing. I wish I could see him but he hated everything about me, even my shadow. I just didn't understand what happened... Why wouldn't he believe me? Those were the last thoughts circling my head before I fell asleep.

19. Treasure the Wedding Gown

Elaine

I slowly moved my body around on the floor, I knew it was time to wake up. I had the habit of waking up at six in the morning, it was something that had been ingrained in me since I was a small child and would probably never go away. The first rays of sunlight were filtering through the open window, I quickly closed my eyes trying to get them to adjust.

I quickly brought my hands up to shield my eyes from all of the light. As I started to sit up, the light was suddenly blocked by something big. Whatever it was, was so big that it blocked all of the light from reaching me. Slowly removing my hands from my eyes, I tried to see what was in front of me. When my eyes finally adjusted I saw that the face of the Alpha King was right in front of me.

His broad body had completely obstructed the light coming through the window leaving my body at the mercy of his shadow. I was sitting on the floor while he sat on the edge of the bed as we looked at each other. I never thought that I would wake up to him in the morning. Even though the day was just beginning he still looked just as handsome as ever. When I saw him, my mouth dropped open. It was a stark reminder that I was no longer in my room at the Opal Moon Pack but in the Alpha King's room!

My life had changed completely since yesterday and like an utter fool, I had somehow forgotten it in the haze of the early morning. After seeing his face, though, I remembered everything! His eyes were as cold as ice, making me realize that I had definitely done something wrong. That's when I realized that the Alpha King was in front of me and I was still just sitting on the floor like a lump before him. I immediately stood up and bowed my head in respect but his chocolate brown eyes continued to stare at me.

His eyes were blank and it was hard to tell what was going on in his mind but it was clear that there was plenty of loathing. Of course that was probably from seeing my face as soon as he woke up, he must have felt as if his whole day had been ruined because I had been the first thing he had seen that morning. The scary thing was that I had no knowledge of how long he had been sitting on the bed watching me.

"I'm sorry," I said quietly. I couldn't bear his hateful eyes on me any longer and instinctively apologized. He rose from the bed to come stand in front of me.

"What are you apologizing for?" He asked, his heavy frightening voice filling my ears as my body trembled. It seemed to me as if I was going to be beaten if I gave the wrong answer.

"You...you told me yesterday that you didn't want to see my wretched face, but you had to see it...early in the morning. I...I'm sorry." I replied, apologizing even before I could be sentenced to some Goddess-awful punishment. I knew that whatever punishment that would befall me here would be ten times worse than the punishment I would have received from my pack. When he didn't answer, I slowly looked up at him and found that he was glaring at me with an angry fire growing in his eyes.

That was when I noticed that he was raising his right hand, I immediately closed my eyes. I knew that I was going to receive a hard slap to the face. I had been beaten by Lewis and Alpha Fabian almost daily for my entire life. So I was familiar with how hard a man could hit, but this was the Alpha King, my death was certain. I squeezed my hands into fists and held my breath in preparation for my beating, only instead I felt his hand softly rest on my head which caused me to snap my eyes open. What was he doing? His fingers wove themselves through my hair as I stopped breathing from his sudden gentleness.

"I COULDN'T SLEEP THANKS TO YOUR PRESENCE IN MY ROOM. NOW I'M EVEN MORE FRUSTRATED THAN I WAS BEFORE!! YOU WERE SLEEPING SO PEACEFULLY, SO SHAMELESSLY IN FRONT OF MY EYES, ALL NIGHT!!! YOUR INNOCENT ACT IS DISGUSTING!!! YOU CONTINUE TO RUIN MY ENTIRE DAY BY SHOWING ME YOUR WRETCHED FACE!!!" He suddenly screamed while vigorously clutching my hair. I howled out in pain. He was once again taking out his anger on me.

"Oww, I'm…sorry," I cried out.

"I don't know how many hearts you have played with by using that innocent face of yours! I don't know how many lives you have ruined! I don't know how many people have lost their reason for living because of you!!!" He yelled, his gaze boring deep into mine. His last statements were related to his mate. I knew he was referring to his situation. Hearing him say that, fresh tears began running down my cheeks. I couldn't say anything to defend myself because no matter what I said I knew he wouldn't believe me.

"Never cry in front of me! Your crocodile tears will never have an effect on me! They will just make me hate you more!!!" He warned, shoving me away so that I hit the wall hard.

"REX!!!" He suddenly called as I quickly wiped my tears away before the Beta arrived. I didn't want him to see me so low. A few seconds later he entered the room, Beta Rex bowed his head to the Alpha King before turning his attention to me. Wrapping my arms around my waist, I cowered in the corner trying to make myself as small as possible.

"Get this woman out of my sight. Oh, and don't let her forget that she's my slave! From today forward, she will take care of everything for me. It will be your responsibility to keep an eye on her. Make sure she knows what she should be doing and when. I won't tolerate a single mistake from her. If she causes even an ounce of trouble or makes a single mistake, I am to be the first to know about it," he commanded. I was frightened by this. I needed to know what would happen to me if I made a mistake or if I tried to do something suspicious.

As if he could read my thoughts, the Alpha King stalked up to me and said, "The punishment for any mistake you make won't be administered to you but to every servant here, even if they're just a small child!" My heart dropped when I heard this. Many people could get hurt because of me.

I quickly followed Beta Rex as he headed out of the room. The servants of the palace that we passed all looked at me strangely because I was still wearing my wedding dress.

"Come in here quickly and put this dress on," Beta Rex said, handing me some clothes. I entered the room, and took a look at what he had given me. I quickly realized that he had handed me a dress made for a slave. I had no objections to wearing this, it was what I had always worn in the Opal Moon Pack. I wasn't destined to wear such a beautiful dress as my wedding gown. This new dress had no holes or tears in it at all, and the fabric was much softer than I had ever imagined.

After changing into this slave dress, I held my wedding gown in my hand, with a sad smile on my face. I knew this would be the last time that I would ever have a chance to wear such a beautiful article of clothing, I would likely never get to see it again after today. Opening the door of the room to exit, I froze when I saw Beta Rex standing a short distance away talking to someone.

"Why is this Omega slave bitch still in the palace?! Get her out of here," the woman demanded, it was none other than Princess Naomi.

"I'm sorry Princess, but I can't do that without the permission from the Alpha King," Beta Rex told her politely. She folded her arms over her chest, looking out right furious. This was obviously not what she wanted to hear.

"It would have been better if she had just jumped into that chasm and died. All of our troubles would have disappeared, but instead she came back to ruin our lives like the worthless Omega that she is. What I do know is that her 'suicide' attempt was just a dramatic way for her to get the attention of the Alpha King! It seems that what people are saying about her is true! She's just like her mother...a whore!" Princess Naomi's shrill voice carried.

I had never gotten the chance to meet my mother, but I had always heard others ruthlessly insult her. I don't know why, but my heart was never convinced that my mother was a bad person and even if she was, she was still my mother. It had never been easy for me to listen to the insults about my mother in the past, nor was it easy now. After wiping my tears away and taking a long deep breath, I exited the room. Princess Naomi was nowhere to be found now, only Beta Rex was left in the hall. The way he looked at me, though, I could tell that he knew that I had heard their little exchange.

"Let's go," He said before he started quickly walking down the hall.

"I wanted to ask you something, even though I'm in no position to ask you for anything, " I quietly began, stopping him as he turned around to look at me.

"Would it be possible for me to keep this wedding gown?" I asked, hugging the wedding gown close to my chest. I knew that once it left my hands, I would never see it again. It would probably be burned or destroyed in some way. I didn't want to lose it. He looked down at my hands while I stared up at him expectantly.

"Okay," He replied, answering me with that one simple word. It brought a huge smile to my face.

"Thank you! Thank you very much!" I exclaimed, bowing to him and he started walking again without acknowledging me. I was allowed to keep it! I quickly turned around to leave the gown in the room that I had just changed in because it didn't seem like it was currently being used. It was a storage room that no one had used in years. I decided that after I was done working that day I would come back to get my wedding gown. It would get dirty if I took it with me and I wanted to keep it as pristine as possible. I planned to treasure it for as long as I lived.

20. Unwanted?

Elaine

"As you heard, you'll be taking care of all of the Alpha King's needs from now on. The Alpha King gets up promptly at six in the morning, so you'll need to be up before then so that you'll have enough time to prepare in advance. By half past six, his majesty's morning coffee should be in the Alpha King's hands. Remember that small mistakes of any kind will result in a huge punishment. Normally he doesn't eat breakfast. He prefers to have coffee in his room, but today he will be joining the Luna in the dining room as she has requested, so you'll need to bring his coffee to him there instead. Remember to refrain from touching the Alpha King at all..." Beta Rex advised, before he suddenly stopped and turned around, carefully studying at me.

I don't know why, but he seemed to be paying special attention to my hands. Could it be that because the Alpha King had touched me, my hands would be cut off? That thought in itself was quite scary. I immediately hid my hands behind my back fearfully, ignoring my reaction, he started speaking again as we continued walking towards our destination.

"There should be no delay in any kind of the services that you provide. Keep in mind that everything regarding the Alpha King is different from serving anyone else, from his coffee cup to every book in his room. If there is even the slightest bit of damage to any of his belongings, then his anger may double and the one responsible will be punished severely," he warned as they stopped near the kitchen door. I nodded to show that I understood what he was telling me. Looking at me expressionlessly, he stood in front of me to the side of the door. I didn't know what he expected me to say or do, so I just bowed my head for a lack of anything else to do.

"There are only fifteen minutes left, until half past six," he circumspectly reminded me about the coffee that I need to deliver to the Alpha King. When I heard him, I quickly ran inside the kitchen. My jaw dropped when I saw the beauty of the kitchen. It was magnificent. The kitchen counter was so shiny and clean that I wondered if it was brand new. It was full of luxurious appliances that I had never seen before. Working here would be easy, but I didn't know how to use any of these fancy gadgets so would have to learn. Apart from me, there were four other women who were busy making breakfast.

Everyone looked at me as soon as I entered the kitchen. Their eyes turned to me, I could read the anger and disgust in all but one pair of eyes. June was amongst the women and she was the only one that smiled at me. I gave her a small smile in return, at least someone was happy that I was here. It was nice that there was at least one person that I wasn't making uncomfortable with my presence. I quickly went over to the coffee machine and started preparing it, doing my best to ignore the women sending me hateful glares. I knew I needed to hurry as I was running short on time.

"Murderer!" Suddenly one of the women proclaimed. I looked towards the woman who had spoken and realized that she was Princess Naomi's maid. There was anger in her eyes. Why couldn't I be allowed to have one moment of peace?!

"Why did you lie about the room? You knew it was the wrong room yet you still sent me there anyway?" I asked accusingly, she rolled her eyes in disgust.

"Isn't it obvious? You're the stupidest woman I have ever met. I did it because I was under the orders of my mistress. Though honestly, I did it gladly," she sneered, shoving me out of her way as she walked past me. It was unbelievable to me that Princess Naomi would do something like that to me. I was no one to her, just an Omega slave. Why would she waste her time having her maid send me to a forbidden room? Thanks to her low handed actions, the Alpha King thought that I willingly entered that room.

"What a shameless woman! After killing our Luna Queen, you should be put to death, perhaps even by consuming poison. You deserve the most painful death possible!" Another woman snickered.

"I don't even understand how she is still breathing!" A third woman exclaimed, now all three of the women were taunting me. June gave me sympathetic looks but remained quiet. She didn't say anything bad about me but neither did she come to my aid.

I made the Alpha King's coffee and exited the kitchen as quickly as possible. When I entered the dining room I realized that the Alpha King wasn't alone. Luna Amanda, Princess Naomi, Princess Ariel, and Prince Raymond were also attending breakfast.

Everyone's eyes turned to me as soon as they smelled me, everyone's faces changed from normal to pure loathing. Princess Naomi sat beside the Alpha King which was much too close for my liking. Lowering my head, I began to walk towards the Alpha

King while carefully carrying his cup of hot coffee. He knew I was there, but he refused to acknowledge me.

Slowly lifting my eyes, I looked at him through my lashes and saw that he was dressed as if he was going somewhere, maybe to a morning meeting. He looked handsome in a nice suit. Maintaining sufficient distance from him, I placed the cup of coffee before him. I was happy that at least he was willing to drink coffee made by me.

"My King," Princess Naomi began to speak, gaining his attention. "Please don't drink that coffee prepared by that disgusting slave. I'm afraid that she mixed something awful into it," she continued, causing the Alpha King's eyes to go to the coffee. What she was implying terrified me. What if he really thought that I had poisoned it? In a split second she had moved the coffee away from him to prevent him from even considering drinking it.

"Well? Why are you just standing there? Quickly throw the coffee away!" She ordered, raising her eyebrows. I heard a chuckle from Princess Ariel. She shook her head dramatically while eating her toast. I caught a movement out of the corner of my eye and when I glanced over I saw Prince Raymond. He was running his hand through his hair, but when he saw me looking he smiled at me with a wink. I immediately lowered my gaze in panic and started to take the coffee away from the table. Why would he wink at me? As I was picking up the cup, Princess Naomi's elbow bumped into my arm which caused some of the piping hot coffee to spill over the lip of the cup onto my hand.

"Ahh!" I yelped when I felt my hand getting burned by the hot liquid. On instinct I let go of the cup and it fell to the ground where it broke into pieces.

"WHAT THE HELL DID YOU DO?! YOU JUST BROKE THE ALPHA KING'S CUP!!!" Luna Amanda screamed at me. I remembered what Beta Rex had told me before dropping me off at the kitchen: everything that belongs to the Alpha King was special and the person responsible for any damage would be punished. I looked over at the Alpha King in fear, only to see that he was furious.

"I…I'm…so sorry," I quickly said, apologizing to him. I bent down and started to pick up the broken pieces of the cup with my trembling hands. It was proving to be a little difficult because my hands were shaking so badly. Especially when the one that was burned felt like it was on fire and I could already see that it was beginning to blister.

"Oh…please Luna. You shouldn't have to waste your energy on this Omega slave. She isn't worth your time. Please give me the honor of handling her," Princess Naomi crooned as Luna Amanda glared at me. My wolf flinched away from her anger. I bit my lip to keep in the sobs, my hand was throbbing.

"Well, Emmett?" Luna asked the Alpha King, who turned his attention towards her. I hadn't heard him utter a single word since I entered the dining room. He was the Alpha King, but he hadn't spoken or given orders very often. He only spoke when it was necessary. Beta Rex placed another cup of coffee in front of the Alpha King. It seemed like he was ready with another cup for him as if he knew that the one I had brought was going to be rejected.

"You didn't choose a mate at the mating ball, so why don't you announce it right now? Princess Naomi is here so accept her as your chosen mate, son. She already loves you," Luna Amanda suggested with a big smile on her face. My heart almost stopped in my chest upon hearing her words. What? Would Princess Naomi become the chosen mate of the Alpha King? I glanced up at the Alpha King to find that he was already looking at me. If he chose her then what would become of me? What was I to him? Why had he marked me if he was just going to choose another mate? Tears gathered in my eyes and I immediately lowered my gaze as I resumed picking up the broken pieces. Why was I so hurt by her question?

He was the Alpha King, he should be mated and marked to a Princess not an Omega slave like me. He had already made it clear to me that I was just a slave to him, but...but I still had hope. I still hoped that he would grow to love me someday, but hearing this destroyed even that small distant glimmer of hope. He had been with her on our wedding night because she loved him and he loved her. She would become his mate...his chosen mate.

I was still working at picking the broken pieces up, but I wasn't being very quick about it. I wanted to hear what his response would be. Was he really going to announce Princess Naomi as his mate?

"Let's talk about this matter on another day. I have a lot of work to get done," the Alpha King replied as he got up from his chair, leaving the dining room. I watched him go out. He didn't look back, but he suddenly stopped and I quickly turned my face away. I didn't know if he was looking back at me or not, but I didn't want to get into any more trouble so I avoided his gaze.

My eyes flickered over to Princess Naomi finding that she was smiling at the Alpha King. He had turned to look at her, not at me.

"Slave! Are you spacing out?" Princess Ariel yelled, jolting me out of my thoughts. I quickly got up from the floor with the shards of broken cup in my hands.

"Get out of our sight and don't come back. I want to eat in peace, your presence only makes me want to vomit," Princess Ariel commented and I nodded my head. After bowing my head to the Luna, both Princesses and the Prince I exited. I didn't look back at Prince Raymond as I already knew he was studying me. He was scary, I didn't know what he was wanting from me.

After I left the dining room, I disposed of the pieces of the broken cup then just walked around aimlessly because I didn't know where I was supposed to go. I wasn't welcomed in the kitchen as all the maids hated me. So I was stuck without a clear purpose as to what I was supposed to be doing. Suddenly I felt as if someone was walking behind me, before I could turn around, my burned hand was violently grabbed. I screamed out in pain. Princess Naomi dragged me to the other side of the palace.

"Aaaahhh...Princess...please....Let me go. It... it hurts..." I tried to say, but after listening to my pleas, her only response was to dig her nails into the burned part of my hand. I felt like my hand was going to fall off. I was screaming in pain, but she didn't let go. Suddenly she threw me to the floor, I got dirt all over my dress as well as my face. I quickly looked around and realized that we were in a garden.

"YOU SLAVE BITCH!! HOW DARE YOU SEDUCE THE ALPHA KING?!" She shrieked as I stared up at her in terror.

"I didn't seduce the Alpha King, your Highness," I quietly replied.

"I know that's a lie! You did more than seduce him apparently, since there has to be some reason he didn't announce me as his chosen mate. It's all thanks to you!" She yelled as she stomped the heel of her sandal down onto my burned hand. I screamed louder than I thought was even possible as I tried to pull my hand away but she again slammed her sandal down on the same place. She was taking her anger and frustration out on me. The problem was that I didn't know why he had refused to proclaim her as his chosen mate. Why wouldn't he choose a Princess as his mate? Why would he settle for a slave?

"Remember this always. The next time I see you seductively eyeing the Alpha King I'll pluck your eyes out with a dull rusted spoon. That way you'll never be able to seduce a man again! You shouldn't dare to even dream about the Alpha King! Do you understand me?" She asked threateningly, I quickly nodded my head hoping she would leave me alone.

"Now for the punishment of breaking the Alpha King's cup, ruining our breakfast, and daring to touch me..." She started and I looked at her in surprise. Touch her? Her elbow had hit me. I never touched her.

"You have to clean this entire garden. I don't want to see even a single weed when I return. Those are just like you! Unwanted!" She said flatly before she finally left.

Just like me? Unwanted? I thought to myself as I lay on the ground cradling my severely injured hand, sobbing from the agony. Well, she was right. I was unwanted and rejected by everybody.

Slowly getting up from the ground I started to clean the garden. It was a royal garden, so it was pretty big. It was probably going to take me the whole day to clean it up properly, plus my hand being injured definitely wasn't going to be helpful.

21. Stealing Food

Elaine

Working under the scorching sun, it was starting to feel like it was raining fire down on me. I didn't expect it to be so hot during the rainy season, but it seemed as if the sun was taking this opportunity to punish me as well. It was 4:00 in the afternoon and I was currently weeding the garden. Sweat was pouring from every pore in my body. My clothes clung to me, causing my skin to chaff. All I wanted to do was go and take a bath, but I wasn't allowed to leave before making the garden look pristine. Thinking about it I realized that Princess Naomi had never mentioned when she would come back to check on me.

No one was in the garden except me, probably because no one else was stupid enough to stand under the punishing sun. There was no one around to keep an eye on me, but the scent of the flowers was enough to calm my mind. I was trying hard not to think about Princess Naomi and the Alpha King, but it was proving impossible. Even though he hadn't announced it today, I knew that he was probably going to announce that Princess Naomi was his chosen mate in the near future. She loved him. Whenever I thought about that very possible future, my goose bumps broke out on my arms. I already knew that my future was as dark as the deepest pit in hell , it would only get worse if they became mates. I wasn't sure what I would do on the day that they stood in front of me as mates, kissing each other or even worse, forcing me to watch.

I could feel myself starting to slip into a depressed state, but what really worried me was that my wolf seemed especially melancholy. I didn't understand why she seemed to be so sad. The Alpha King wasn't our mate, so why was she so miserable and restless? What reason did she possibly have for being depressed? So many questions were running through my mind that I was starting to go absolutely crazy.

The burning pain in my hand had doubled as the blistered skin had peeled off after being abused by Princess Naomi's sandals. Even though I was a werewolf, I was smaller and weaker than a typical werewolf due to being malnourished all of my life. I had never been trained to fight, it was also very rarely that I had the opportunity to shift. I was really only a werewolf in species, I had next to no knowledge about my own kind. Nobody had taught me anything at all, everything that I've learned had been picked up from listening to others' conversations. All of this had combined to lead to my body being unable to heal itself quickly from any injury. In essence I healed at the same speed as a human, which was tortuous.

I was trying to work as fast as I could while weeding the garden when something came to me and I immediately stopped and looked around. This was the same garden that I had lost that wooden box in the night of the Mating Ball! How could I have been so irresponsible? How had I forgotten about that? That lady had given me the responsibility of safely handing over the box, but I had lost less than two hours after it had come into my possession.

Taking advantage of being out in the garden alone, I instantly began moving towards the fountain that I had fallen into. I was determined to find that wooden box as soon as possible, I still needed to finish my work in the garden otherwise I would be punished. When I reached the area around the fountain, I noticed that the grass had grown quite a bit, which meant that no one had tended to the garden in a while. Maybe, that meant that no one had found the box, that it was still out here somewhere. A ray of hope kindled in my heart, I immediately started searching for the box by uprooting the grass nearest me. I needed to do this quickly, if anyone caught me I wouldn't have a proper excuse to give them.

Despite thoroughly searching for about an hour, I wasn't able to find that wooden box anywhere I was starting to worry. I even looked in the fountain because I had fallen into it, so I thought that maybe it had sunk to the bottom but it wasn't there either.

If that woman somehow found me again and asked about it I didn't know what I would tell her. She must have thought that I handed over that box to the Alpha Prince like she begged me to, but I failed. I was ashamed of myself. She said that the box held the future of a Princess. I didn't understand how that box could have just vanished, or what had she meant about it holding the future of a Princess in it. I did know that it couldn't have just disappeared unless someone else had found it. I needed more time to search the garden, but I needed to finish cleaning it up first. Hopefully I could sneak back here later and continue searching.

It was now 5:45pm but I wasn't even a quarter of the way done with the garden. This garden was too big for just one person to take care of, I was already terribly exhausted on top of it. I hadn't even had the chance to drink so much as a drop of water since this morning. Now that I thought about it I realized that I hadn't eaten or drank anything significant in the last 2 days since I was at the Opal Moon Pack , I hadn't been fed since I had been at the palace. My stomach felt like it had shriveled up into a dried husk from lack of nourishment. Despite feeling weak from hunger and my injured hand, I continued to work on the garden as time slowly passed.

I had always been a constant victim of misfortune, the Goddess loved to remind me of that. It began raining heavily about 2 hours ago. The water was as cold as ice, the wet chill led to my entire body shaking but I never stopped working. I could leave the garden as soon as I was finished but I hadn't made much progress in this humongous space.

From where I was kneeling on the muddy ground, I could see the window of the Alpha King's room but it was dark. It was almost 11:00pm at this point, so he was probably asleep. The one positive note was that he didn't have to see my face before going to bed. So he would hopefully get a peaceful night's sleep. I, on the other hand, was upset over the fact that I hadn't gotten to see him. I wanted to see him one more time before the day was over. Moving my gaze away from the window, I resumed my weeding while I uselessly tried to wipe the pouring rain off of my face. Water kept falling into my eyes which just added another annoyance to deal with.

The rain was accompanied by lightning followed quickly by the roar of thunder from the clouds. I was outside weeding a garden in the middle of a thunderstorm. A scream escaped me, but I immediately put my hands over my mouth to try and stifle the noise. It felt as if the lightning was going to strike me because it seemed to have struck so close. The lightning streaked across the sky and the thunder boomed loudly in my ears causing my hands to tremble.

After a few minutes, I could barely hear the sounds of someone approaching me over the thunder. I looked to my right and saw that it was Zach coming up to me. Getting up from the ground, I bowed my head to him. Why was he out here in this storm?

"Staying out in the garden or out on palace grounds at night is strictly prohibited for security reasons. You need to get inside immediately," Zach ordered, at the same moment lightning struck again. I jumped from the resulting thunder, quickly nodded my head in assent.

I entered the palace, grateful to be out of that terrible storm. I walked towards the Alpha King's room and thanked Goddess that I was given the opportunity to come inside, instead of staying outside in the soaking in the rain like an animal all night. Did a bodyguard have the authority to overrule an order given to me by a Princess? I didn't want him to get in trouble for my sake, but also was not permitted to remain outside until finished. I just decided to do as he ordered, I definitely didn't want to stay outside even if it meant that I would be punished more later for not finishing my chore.

The door to the Alpha King's room was closed. I was pretty sure that he was sleeping, so I was having a hard time deciding whether or not I should enter. If I didn't go inside then he would most likely be angry. He was the one that had ordered me to stay in his room, that was the thought that gave me the courage to enter.

Slowly opening the door, I entered the room as silently as possible. I closed the door behind me without a sound. The lights were off so I could barely see him lying in bed, utilizing the little bit of light that was coming in through the window. I was shivering from the cold due to my wet clothes but I didn't have anything to change into, something to help dry me off, or keep me warm. I sat on the ground in the same corner I had occupied last night and placed my hand over my stomach. I was beginning to feel unbearable hunger pains. Today had been my third day without food. While basking in my despair, I smelled a delicious aroma.

My eyes eagerly snapped open as they began frantically searching the room, looking for the source of the delicious smell. A plate of food sat on the table nearby quickly caught my attention. The table was next to the Alpha King's bed. Maybe it was leftovers from his dinner?

My stomach cramped even worse thanks to the tantalizing smell that had even made my mouth start to salivate. Knowing that I was about to do something that was definitely going to get me into trouble, I cautiously crawled over as quietly as possible, my eyes widened when I saw the plate. He hadn't eaten all the food, actually it didn't look like he had eaten much of anything. Instead he had just left it on the table. Why hadn't he eaten any of it? I had never seen such delectable food in my entire life. My throat and tongue went completely dry, I knew that I was on the verge of starvation. I glanced over at the Alpha King, he was still sleeping soundly. I moved my hands slowly towards the plate, constantly trying to talk myself out of what I was about to do.

I was stealing, what made it even worse was that I was stealing from the Alpha King but I couldn't bear to be hungry any longer. All this food was just going to be thrown away in the morning anyway, so surely I could eat a little, right? He wouldn't notice that a bite was missing.

Finally convincing myself, I put the plate on the floor and just picked up a single pea. I have never eaten peas before. What did they taste like I wondered? I would just eat this one tiny morsel then put the plate back right where I had found it. Just as I was about to put the pea in my mouth, my hands trembling from the cold, the lights were suddenly turned on and I saw the Alpha King sitting up in bed. He was staring at me with a blank expression. He caught me. He caught me stealing from his plate. The pea fell from my hand out of fear, dropping to the carpet. I scrambled from him, pushing myself backwards along the floor towards my corner. He was going to punish me. Stealing was something that was never tolerated. Luna Wilma had thrown a glass at me once, she had nearly blinded me because she caught me stealing some food out of the trash.

"Forgive me...I know...I've...stolen. I will never do that again...I'm sorry...So sorry..."

22 Getting Hard

Emmett

After what happened in the dining room, I spent the rest of the morning in meetings and before I knew it it was afternoon. Solving issues in the surrounding packs was never a quick and easy matter. I was still in my office when Zach informed me that Elaine was weeding the garden as punishment, given to her by Princess Naomi. I glanced out a nearby window that looked out onto the garden to see if I could spot her. The sun was high in the sky, it must've been pretty hot outside. If one was not careful they could suffer from heat exhaustion in this weather. She was out working in this harsh heat but I decided to ignore her. She could handle herself! She deserved to be harshly punished!

Rex was showing me a few important documents and I was trying to read through them, but I couldn't concentrate on anything other than her. I angrily threw the papers down onto my desk and went over to the window. I instinctively looked down and there she was. Her entire body was covered in a sheen of sweat and her skin had become red due to the harsh sunlight. She seemed so small and fragile. I was afraid that she would break if I touched her. She was vigorously shaking her head as if she was thinking about something and trying to shove it out of her mind so that she could focus on her task. I heard Rex's footsteps approaching, when I glanced over he was standing next to me looking down at her as well.

"She's been out there working since morning," Rex informed. I immediately turned my gaze away and went back to my desk.

"I didn't ask," I told him sternly.

"I'm sorry but I thought you would be interested to know," Rex replied and I angrily glared at him. He had never informed me of anyone else before, so why did this woman's condition concern him? He lowered his eyes in submission and I turned and stormed out of my office. He quickly followed me as I continued on with my work for the day.

In the evening, Rex came up to my bedroom with some coffee. I was sitting on the sofa taking a few sips as I listened to the rain. It was raining heavily outside and she was still working out in that damn garden while I was trying to enjoy my coffee and attempting to forget about her. It took only two sips, though, for me to realize that I couldn't enjoy my coffee because my focus kept being drawn to the woman who was working outside in this ridiculous weather. I was becoming extremely frustrated. I just threw the coffee away and pulled the curtains shut over the window so I wouldn't be tempted to look out at her any longer.

Most evenings, I ate dinner in my room as I finished my work for the day. When Rex entered with my meal I realized that it was already 10:45pm. I relieved him of any more duties for the day and started to eat. The rain continued to get worse , now it was thundering and lightning.

Suddenly I heard her scream, I jumped up, leaving the food on the table, and quickly went over to the window. She was biting her lip to try and prevent any more screams from escaping. It seemed like she was afraid of lightning. More than half an hour had passed by with me standing at the window, watching her work. As if sensing my stare, she raised her head and looked at my window. I was taken aback when I saw her innocent eyes looking straight back into mine. Well, it seemed like she was looking back at me, but I knew that her weaker eyes wouldn't be able to make me out through the storm. After a brief moment, she turned her eyes back to the ground and continued on with her work.

"Zach, get that woman back inside the palace in the next five minutes. She can't die so soon. Being wet, cold, and tired will be great excuses for her," I mind-linked Zach before moving away from the window.

Turning off the lights, I laid down in bed to go to sleep. I no longer felt like eating. Only five to ten minutes later, just as I was about to slip into unconsciousness the sound of someone's footsteps accompanied by a beautiful fragrance woke me up instantly, Elaine. I always tried to ignore it, but her fragrance was very attractive and had proven to be impossible to disregard. It made me want to grab hold of her and eat her. This absurd thought had crossed my mind many times but I always chose to try and ignore it.

Even though I didn't open my eyes, I could feel her every move. She slowly entered the room and sat down in a corner. I could hear her chattering teeth from her shivering. She was trying to warm herself by rubbing her hands together. All of a sudden I felt as if her fragrance was getting stronger, as if she was getting closer. Why was she approaching me while I was 'asleep'? Her actions seemed very suspicious. She was coming closer to me even though she knew what the consequences would be if she were to touch me. I didn't want to be touched by this woman ever again.

Instead of her continuing her approach, however, I heard the sound of the plate being lifted off of the table then placed on the carpet. This had me opening my eyes in curiosity, when I looked at her I saw that she was unaware that I was awake.

Even though the room was dark, I could clearly see her. She was in the process of picking up a pea from the plate and putting it in her mouth when I turned the lights on. Seeing me awake and looking at her, she began to tremble and the pea fell from her hand. She started pushing herself backwards in fear.

"Forgive me...I know...I've...stolen. I will never do that again...I'm sorry...So sorry..." She begged for forgiveness. Her fear was at a peak and her eyes filled with tears. It seemed as if she had been through a similar type of situation before in which she must've received a harsh punishment. Her long silky hair was wet from the rain and dripping water. My eyes went to the floor then back up to her.

"Do you realize that you're making my floor dirty?" I blatantly asked, ignoring all of her fucking begging. She immediately got up from the floor but now water was dripping off of her entire body in rivulets. Her wet clothes clung tightly to her form, so that I could clearly see all of her curves. I looked her over slowly from head to toe. My eyes stopped on her lips which were soft, beautiful, purple, and still trembling from the cold.

A drop of water trailing down her neck to her chest and my eyes followed it almost hungrily. The dress she was wearing had a somewhat deep neckline. Looking down a little further, my eyes stopped on her breasts. Due to the thinness of the cloth, I could see her nipples, which were hard and showing through the fabric, taunting me. I didn't know why but the thought of my mate when I took her pink soft nipple into my mouth popped into my head. My dick twitched and I instantly grew hard. Fuck!!! How could I get a hard-on looking at this woman's body?

"Get out!" I ordered. I needed this awful temptation out of my sight before I did something I would regret.

"W... what?" She asked, panicked and confused.

"I SAID GET OUT!!!" I yelled at her in anger. The longer that she just stood there ignoring my orders, the more my wolf grew more out of control. I was a few seconds away from grabbing her and fucking her until she screamed.

"But...where should I go?" She was holding one hand behind her back as if she was hiding something.

"I don't fucking care. Just get out," I said, gritting my teeth in frustration and she nodded her head. As she turned to leave, walking towards the door I could see her fucking wet back. Her round ass looked so deliciously wet. If she walked out of this room in this condition then any other male would see her like that. Then they…I hated the thought of any other man witnessing the sight of her hardened nipples and plump ass.

"Stop!" I snapped. When she turned back around in surprise I tossed a blanket over to her.

"Hurry up, take off your dress. You're still ruining the carpet and floor. I hate a mess almost as much as I hate you!" With the blanket in her hand, her face was full of fear and confusion. She was clearly baffled by the mixed signals my instructions contained, I was still trying to figure out whether she was supposed to stay or leave. She was testing my patience.

"DON'T MAKE THE MISTAKE OF STEPPING OUTSIDE THIS ROOM!!! NOW HURRY TO THE BATHROOM AND DON'T DIRTY MY FLOOR!!!" I barked at her. When she ran inside the bathroom, she closed the door in a flash. I closed my eyes in frustration. I didn't understand how I could lose control so easily. Why did my body react after seeing her? She had killed my mate! Even my wolf was having lustful thoughts towards that slave.

I settled back into bed and turned off the light. I was lying down but my eyes remained on the bathroom door which still hadn't opened after ten minutes. Was she planning to sleep in the bathroom?

That would be great! Then I wouldn't have to see her wretched appearance. I closed my eyes again and tried to sleep but after another five minutes had passed I sat and suspiciously looked at the bathroom door. Why hasn't she come out yet? I wanted to know! Has she tried to commit suicide again? At that thought, my mind exploded with anger. She couldn't escape from me that easily!

Getting out of bed, I rushed to the bathroom. When I opened the door I saw her sleeping on the floor with her back against the wall. Her wet clothes were hung up to dry on the shower rod. She had wrapped the blanket completely around her trembling body in a desperate attempt to warm herself. She was asleep but still shivering from the cold. I decided to close the bathroom door and leave her there for the night but stopped and glanced back at her.

'She might try to escape out of the window in here if she were to wake up in the middle of the night.' I thought to myself, so I bent over to scoop her up into my arms, I took her back out to the bedroom so that I could better keep an eye on her. I placed her back down on the floor in the same corner where she slept last night. I went back to my bed but I couldn't seem to look away from her face. The moonlight was coming in through the window and landed on her face, making her appear innocent. How could someone so evil look so innocent? She moved a little as if to get more comfortable and wrapped the blanket more tightly around her.

Her legs now stuck out a bit from the blanket, they were so thin and long. Her wrists were too thin and her collar bone seemed to be sticking out of her body. It seemed like she was only skin and bones, not an ounce of fat on her. She must be starving. If she was so hungry then why had she only stolen a measly pea when there were other, more delicious options for her to choose from?

When she shifted again the part of the blanket that was covering her breasts began sliding down. As it was about to reveal a full view of her breast and nipple, I immediately averted my gaze as I didn't want my body to react to seeing her again. Throwing another blanket over her, one that completely covered her, I went back to bed so that I could finally get some sleep. For the rest of the night, I never glanced over at her but I listened to her breathing… breathing that was weak, breathing that was empty, breathing that snatched sleep away from me.

23 A Whorish Bitch?

Elaine

I woke up as the first ray of light hit my face, when I looked over at the clock I saw that it was already 6am. Wait! What? 6AM!!! My eyes snapped open as I sat up in a panic. I had been ordered to wake up before the Alpha King so that I could get his morning coffee prepared for him. I quickly glanced over at the bed, thankfully he was still asleep. I thanked the Goddess a million times over that he hadn't woken up yet.

When I began to stand up, I curiously pulled the sheet away from myself. Upon seeing my nakedness, I immediately used it to cover my chest again. What in the world? Oh my Goddess! Where were my clothes? Why was I naked? Had…had he…done something to me?

I placed a hand over my mouth, trying to force down the sobs. Had he done something to me? Slowly I began to remember everything that had happened last night. I remembered that I hung my clothes up in the bathroom to dry, but I also knew that I had fallen asleep in there. I hadn't come back out as far as I could recall, so how was it possible that I had woken up here in the bedroom? Had the Alpha King brought me out? No, that was not possible. He would never willingly touch me. Was it possible that I walked out in my sleep?

Upon further inspection I realized that I now had two blankets, but last night he had only given me one. None of this was making any sense, but I didn't have time for further contemplation. Quickly getting up from the floor I ran to the bathroom but without receiving significant nourishment over the past few days, my body was becoming very weak. I feared that I was close to starving to death.

After taking a quick shower and putting on my one and only dress that was thankfully completely dry, I sped-walked out of the Alpha King's quarters. I entered the kitchen, swiftly beginning my tasks with the understanding that I was running short on time. Like yesterday, there were four to five maids working on preparing breakfast. I didn't have time to take notice of them or see if they were all throwing me hateful looks. I just focused on preparing the Alpha King's coffee when June approached me.

"You weren't in the kitchen when Beta Rex came in here a little bit ago," she quietly informed me. I was terrified to hear that the Beta was looking for me when I wasn't here.

"Oh my Goddess! I woke up at 6am, it's totally my fault. What did he say that he wanted?" I hastily asked.

"He commanded that you needed to make breakfast along with coffee for the Alpha King this morning then take it up to the Alpha King's room," June replied.

I felt as if a huge weight had just been placed on my shoulders. It was nearly 6:30am and now I had to prepare breakfast in just fifteen minutes then serve it to the Alpha King. With the little time I had, I could only think of one thing to make and that was a sandwich, but I needed some tomatoes and lettuce. I hurriedly sliced the tomatoes and any other veggies I needed. I took out two slices of bread. There were so many types of bread to choose from: white, wheat, sourdough, there were even more that I couldn't identify. I decided to go with wheat as it seemed like a safe choice. I was looking for some condiments to add to the sandwich. I decided on some mayo and spread some on each slice of bread. Placing meat and cheese on it I added the toppings before placing the last slice of bread on the top.

I poured the coffee into the Alpha King's new cup as soon as it was done brewing. Everything was ready to deliver the Alpha King's breakfast. Quickly walking back to his room, my breathing was rapid. I just prayed to the Goddess that I wouldn't be late in serving him his breakfast.

The door to his room was open, when I entered I saw that the Alpha King had already taken a shower and changed clothes. The good thing was that I wasn't late. He glanced over at me and I bowed my head in submission. I placed the coffee and sandwich on the table, which he looked at with a narrowed eyed gaze as if suspicious.

"Here's your coffee and breakfast my King," I informed him. He leaned closer to me and just stared at me. I stood in front of him, frozen like a statue, trying to figure out what was going on. Was he going to scold me again for what happened last night?

"Drink," he ordered, jolting me out of my thoughts.

"What?" I was confused and wasn't sure if I'd heard him correctly or not.

"Did I stutter? I said drink it," he repeated sternly, now I understood why he was asking this of me. He must have thought that I might try to poison him after Princess Naomi's accusations yesterday. He wanted to know whether anything that I'd prepared contained poison. The thought of poisoning him has never even crossed my mind, but I could easily prove to him that the beverage was safe. I picked up the coffee and took a small sip while he watched me closely. When the coffee hit my tongue, my mouth was flooded with a bitter taste. I could not help the grossed-out face I made as I felt the coffee travel down to my empty stomach. I had never had coffee before, it didn't taste very good. I had only been allowed to drink water before.

Placing the coffee cup back on the table, I looked at him then he pointed at the sandwich. He was asking me to taste test the sandwich as well. I picked up the sandwich feeling humiliated. Having to prove yourself not guilty to someone that always thinks the worst of you was an awful feeling. He was still waiting for me to take a bite. I once again was able to prove my innocence by eating a small piece of the sandwich. I placed it back onto the plate and stepped back so that he could enjoy his poison-free breakfast.

"I don't want it now," he scoffed, walking towards the door fixing his clothes as he walked.

"What? I've proven that the food is safe. There's no poison mixed in it," I said in alarm. I just couldn't understand why he wasn't willing to eat it when I had proven that it wasn't poisoned. What was wrong with it now? He turned back to look at me with a surprised affronted look. That was the moment that I realized that I was speaking to him very casually. I immediately bowed my head, fixing my eyes on the floor, not daring to look back up at him. He walked towards me, completely towering over me.

"If I say I won't eat something, then that means that I won't eat it!" He barked in my face and I nodded my head quickly.

What came over me? Why did I think that I could talk to him like that?

"Do you really think that I would eat something that you took a bite of? Me? A King?" He scoffed, now I understood. He found me dirty and disgusting, so of course he wouldn't want to eat something that I had taken a bite from. Yes, he was right. How could I offer him compromised food?

I began to remove the breakfast from the table when he asked, "What the hell are you doing?" I looked up at him, still holding the tray.

"You said that you aren't going to eat this," I replied.

"So?" He questioned again, raising his brows.

"So I'm taking it back to the kitchen," I responded and he frowned.

"How dare you throw that food away," he snapped, causing me to flinch.

"I...I wasn't..." I couldn't finish my response before he interrupted me.

"Do you have any idea how much this food would mean to a person who's starving!" He accused. In his arrogance, he had no idea that he was talking to someone who knew what it felt like to starve more times than not. If anyone knew this food's value, it would be me.

"I'm sorry, my King," I replied. I don't know why I was apologizing except that I didn't want him to shout at me, ruining his morning further.

"Eat!" He ordered and I looked up in surprise.

"What?" I asked, blinking my eyes up at him in shock.

"Eat that and finish the coffee too. I don't want to see you even try to throw that food away. If I catch you trying to sneak out, trust me, you'll be thrown in a cell for one week without food or water," he warned, glaring at me then went over to the mirror. I just continued to stand there holding the tray too shocked to move.

"Why are you just standing there? Are you daring to disobey an order?" He asked with a raised brow, looking at me through the mirror. I quickly sat on the floor with the tray in my lap and started eating. The sandwich was so delicious, I never thought I would get the chance to eat something so yummy. I drank the coffee too even though I found it very bitter because I needed something to wash down the sandwich with.

Tears gathered in my eyes as I ate. I wasn't sure if I would get the opportunity to eat anything again anytime soon and after surviving three days without food I had thought I was going to die. Suddenly I felt the Alpha King's finger lifting my chin as he forced me to look up at him. Like before, when I had first met him in the hut, he was sitting on the sofa while I was sitting between his legs. His gaze bore deep into my eyes.

"Why are you crying?" He asked, seeming genuinely concerned. I felt as if he was actually worried about me. It was nice to see him appear to care, even if it was fake or short lived. No one had ever cared about me before.

"I was so hungry. I hadn't had anything to eat in three da…" I was about to explain to him, but he chuckled and I stopped.

"After all, you are such a whorish bitch," he sneered contemptuously.

"A whorish bitch?" I asked, stunned as he moved his face closer to mine, looking deep into my eyes.

"Yes…a whore…a bitch…someone that's happy eating other's leftovers like a stray mutt," he spat out as what was left of the sandwich fell from my hand.

"What did you do before coming to the palace to get food?" He asked and I couldn't answer.

"Answer me! I already know the truth but I want to hear you say it. Did you serve them in bed? How? Did you suck them off or go so far as to actually fuck them? It must not have been easy, right?" He inquired as tears ran from my eyes at his words. He thought so little of me... too little. I scrambled to quickly get up from the floor, placed the plate back on the table, then bowed my head to try and hide my tears.

"Please let me know if you need anything else," I quietly offered before turning to leave. I felt him grab my wrist in a punishing grip as he pulled me back and the tray fell from my hand, falling to the floor with a clatter.

"YOU WILL FUCKING ANSWER ME NOW!!!" He barked as I closed my eyes in fear.

"WHAT DID YOU DO?!" He yelled again, grabbing my arms tightly, causing me unbearable pain. The pain forced me to open my eyes as I stared into his red ones that were full of hate filled rage.

"Would you believe me if I told you that I never did any of the things that you just accused me of?" I quietly asked, trying to find some semblance of trust in his eyes, but was unable to.

"Never! I'll never believe anything that comes from a woman like you. I would believe it if someone came in and told me that it was night time right now, but I will never believe anything you say!" He spat at me, shoving me away and causing me to fall to the floor. He left the room in a rage, and I was left sitting on the floor. I shouldn't have been surprised to hear that he would never believe me, but it still hurt.

24 Alive or Dead

Elaine

My mind was out of sorts after everything that had just happened. Whenever he accused me of doing something awful it always caught me by surprise and made me feel incredibly sad. That sorrow eventually turned into a pain that was almost impossible to bear. I was trying to distract myself from this bleaky pain through work. From morning until noon, I silently did all the kitchen work alone. June was surprised to find me doing it alone, but I let her know that I had received the job as punishment seeing as I hadn't finished weeding the garden yesterday.

This punishment had of course been issued by Princess Naomi, she vehemently instructed me not to leave the kitchen and specifically told me to not enter the dining room. She must have specified that because the Alpha King could be in there and see me. She didn't want the Alpha King to see me at all or she would beat me to death.

My hand was still pretty raw. I healed slowly for a wolf so my burn was still painful. I hadn't even considered asking for anyone's help since that would go against Princess Naomi's orders. Not that anyone in the palace was aware, but I had done all the kitchen work alone since I was a small child. This was a piece of cake in comparison, I didn't need anyone's assistance. There was even a bright side: I was so busy that I had forgotten about everything that had happened this morning. It was time for lunch, all the maids had taken the food that I had prepared into the dining table to be served.

I was the only one who remained in the kitchen since I wasn't allowed to leave without Princess Naomi's permission. Despite being in the kitchen, I could clearly hear what people were saying in the dining room. I learned that the Alpha King wasn't present and Princess Naomi was highly disappointed that he hadn't joined them. Her planned course of punishment, making me stay in the kitchen, had been ruined by his absence. I also heard a maid say that the Alpha King never dines with everyone. He only dined with the family on special occasions or at Luna Amanda's insistence. I was worried for him, recalling that he hadn't eaten his dinner last night, his breakfast this morning, and now he was skipping lunch. It seemed that I couldn't be the only one that was hungry. He had to be getting pretty ravenous by now.

I wasn't sure how I had come to this conclusion but I felt as if he was holding a deep well of sadness inside him. There seemed to be an untold pain that he was masking behind that strong front that he constantly had on display. Was his depression due to his dead mate? I didn't know why, but I felt like I was the reason for his pain. Things shouldn't have started the way they had with us. I felt like our relationship had gone down the wrong path. The relationship had started with a lie, the seeds of which I had sown with my own two hands.

An hour passed with me consumed in these thoughts. The other maids came back into the kitchen to take a plate of food then left. I was also allowed to take a plate of food, I sat on the floor in the corner to begin eating as I still hadn't been granted permission to leave. Even if I was allowed to leave, I didn't have my own room to retreat to. The maids were all lucky enough to have their own rooms.

The food looked even better than the Alpha King's leftovers from his room last night. I thought that, like in the Opal Moon, I would only receive food every two days, but I was glad to be proven wrong. For the first time in my life, I was in possession of a full plate of food. I made a bowl of gumbo with rice like I had for the other maids. This was also the first time that I got to eat any of the food that I had prepared for others. My hands were trembling and I was worried that a glass might suddenly fly at me, but I was still alone.

I picked up a spoonful and was about to put it in my mouth when I remembered the harsh words the Alpha King had spoken that morning. What had I done to deserve this food? His words made me wonder how I had been able to survive in that hell for so long. I thought about how hard it was to get food and water after two days. How had I been able to save myself from Lewis' evil eyes and cruelty while being so malnourished and weak?

Now the sight of this delicious food made my stomach twist up into knots. I covered the bowl with a plate, I didn't think I'd be able to eat it now. I knew that there was a possibility that I would not get any food tonight, so I really needed to eat this. Maybe I would be able to eat it in a little while, when my stomach had settled.

I looked around the kitchen realizing that there was still a lot of work to get done. I was thinking about where I should start, when I heard the rhythmic clicking of high heels approaching. Glancing over my shoulder, I saw a furious Princess Naom. I immediately scrambled back a few steps in an attempt to prevent her from hitting me. My hand was still suffering from her abuse yesterday.

"IT'S ALL YOUR FAULT!!!" She shrieked at me, but I didn't react. I couldn't even ask her what I had done as I knew that it would cause her to grow even angrier. I couldn't talk back to a Princess. Her personal maid was also standing behind her, glaring at me.

"He didn't come down for lunch because of you, and you'll be punished for it!" Saying this she stormed out of the kitchen boiling with fury. I just couldn't understand these rich, snobby, royal people. Natasha used to blame me for everything that went wrong in her life. Now Princess Naomi seemed to be doing the same thing. When in reality he was most likely too busy to come down. There was no way that a slave would have kept him from eating. He was the Alpha King, after all, he had an entire Kingdom to worry about. Plus there weren't always enough hours in a day to solve all of the issues that came up.

Just because you were born with a beautiful face and a powerful name didn't mean that everything in life was handed to you on a silver platter, I sneered to myself. I wish I could've said all of this to her face, but I was well aware of the aftermath that would ensue, so I just kept my mouth shut. What punishment was she speaking of? She never elaborated on that part, which worried me. I decided to put this interaction in the back of my mind as I continued on with cleaning the kitchen.

Lewis

I quietly left my living quarters and headed out to my car. It was easy to avoid the eyes of most of the pack members, except Natasha and my mom. They had been keeping an extra close eye on me for the last twenty-four hours while almost everyone else had gone to Alpha Marvin's pack, the Shine Moon Pack. It seemed like the perfect opportunity for me to leave. I immediately pulled my car out of the garage, driving at full speed, and only stopped when I arrived at a dense section of forest which was my destination. Jumping out of the car, I walked towards the man that was waiting for me.

"Alpha," he greeted with a bow of his head in a sign of respect. I didn't have time for all of these formalities.

"Has my Beta already explained the situation to you?" I asked him and quickly he nodded. I had my Beta assist me seeing as he could leave the pack whenever he wished, whereas my every move was now being watched. Even my father has been keeping an eye on me, but this was my chance. I wanted to personally speak with this man, he was our pack's spy and he knew a lot of valuable information.

"Unfortunately, there is a problem, Alpha. Your Beta didn't give me any kind of photo of the woman that you're searching for and I've never seen her. How will I be able to recognize her?" The spy asked, concerned.

"You'll definitely recognize her. Elaine is the most beautiful woman that you've ever seen. Her beauty shames that of any Princess or Queen. If you see a woman that fits the description that I've given you, then it can't be anyone other than Elaine. Understand?" I asked and he nodded in surprise. He must have thought that there couldn't possibly be a woman as beautiful as I had just described, but there was. Elaine was the most beautiful woman that I had ever seen. Father and Uncle said that Elaine had been taken by the Alpha King so that he could execute her, but I refused to believe them. My father and uncle were a couple of sly men, no one could see through their tricks better than me.

They had to be hiding something. It wasn't just them though, Natasha and my mother were keeping something from me as well. How had Elaine fallen into the river? That's one of the biggest mysteries for me. She was somehow able to escape me the night of the Mating Ball, but she still returned to the pack. So how had she ended up in the hands of the Alpha King? It was eating me up inside. I couldn't believe that she was going to be executed if she hadn't already. She had survived in our pack for eighteen years in awful conditions. I shouldn't have let her get away from me that night. If I had been able to have her that night then things might have turned out differently. She would have been marked by me and been mine for forever, but now that wasn't an option. The Alpha King had taken custody of her because she had supposedly murdered his mate. She was probably dead by now, but I had to know for sure whether she was alive or dead. If she was still alive then I would do everything within my power to get her back!

25. If This Was Going to Be My End Then So Be It...

Elaine

I pulled my hair up into a bun to keep it out of my face while I worked. About an hour had passed when I felt a sense of peace fall over the palace which was very unexpected. That was when I realized that none of the other maids had come into the kitchen during the last hour. Where were they all? Just as this thought crossed my mind, June walked in.

"Are you still working? I wish I could help you," she said and I smiled softly when I heard the sadness and regret tingeing her voice.

"No need to be sad. I'm almost done, but can you tell me why I feel such a sense of peace has over the palace all of a sudden?" I asked her while I simultaneously continued to clean the kitchen counter.

"Hmmm, I'm not sure, but I saw Luna Amanda and Princess Ariel leaving the palace. Their cars just left. Only Princess Naomi is still here because I saw Prince Raymond leave the palace too a little while ago," June replied and I just nodded as I continued to work.

"Your clothes are getting dirty from all the cleaning you're doing," June said. I looked down and saw that she was right, but that reminded me of something else. I quickly washed my hands and ran out of the kitchen.

"Elaine! What's going on? What's wrong?"June called after me but I didn't look back, instead I increased my speed. My wedding gown! I had forgotten to pick it up from the storage room. It had completely slipped my mind because I had worked in the garden until late last night then had gone straight to the Alpha King's bedroom. How could I have forgotten such an important thing?

When I approached the room, I found the door ajar. A sense of dread settled in the pit of my stomach. I remembered vividly that I had locked the door when I left and it seemed as if no one ever really used that closet so it was weird that the door would be open.

My heart skipped a beat as I entered the room, my eyes went straight to the table that I had left my wedding gown on. It was missing! How was this possible? Had my gown been stolen? Why would anyone want it? It wasn't of any value to anyone other than me. After all, who would steal the dress of an Omega slave and wear it? I knew it wasn't a normal dress, that it was a wedding gown but still. I started rummaging through the closet and when I still couldn't find it, I left to ask June. Maybe she had seen it. When I had returned to the kitchen, she wasn't there. She must have left to begin working in another part of the palace.

I didn't get it. No one liked me here, so even if I did ask someone, no one would help me. It had taken everything in me to gather up the courage to ask Beta Rex for permission to keep the wedding gown in the first place. Why was the world so set against me?

I laid my face on the kitchen counter, clenching my eyes shut. I didn't want to cry even though I could feel the tears threatening to escape. I would keep searching. I would search every corner of the palace until I found my wedding gown. It has my...As the thoughts were racing through my mind, I felt someone's hand grab my waist. I could tell that it wasn't the Alpha King because I was well aware of his touch, this was a stranger.

My eyes snapped open in bewilderment. I immediately took both of the unwanted hands off of my waist and pushed them away from me without looking at the man. When I scornfully lifted my gaze, I found Prince Raymond was the one standing behind me. My eyes widened in fear. I had pushed a prince, but he'd touched me inappropriately and against my will.

"Your Highness, what are you doing here in the kitchen? I thought you had left the palace," I asked, trying to suppress the nervousness in my voice. June had told me that he had left, so why was he here? In the kitchen no less? Why had he touched me in such a provocative way?

"This is my palace, I can come and go whenever I wish. I don't think I need to answer to an Omega slave," Prince Raymond replied, moving towards me. I couldn't move any farther away as my back was already against the kitchen counter.

"What are you doing? Why are you getting so close to me?" I asked, my voice trembling slightly. He winked while moving towards me with a sly smile on his lips. My whole body shivered when I saw his lust-filled gaze on my breasts. I immediately raised my hands up to cover my chest and he chuckled.

"No need to act innocent in front of me. I know what you are. You're a whore. An Omega slave whore. I couldn't help but overhear your and the Alpha King's conversation this morning as I was passing by. You suck cock and f*** people, right?" He asked as he reached out, dragging a finger across my cheekbone. I shoved his hand away again, not caring about the punishment that I would receive from offending a Prince.

"Don't touch me! And whatever you've heard is a lie. I am not a whore!" I sternly told him. All of a sudden he had my hair clenched tightly in a fist.

"HOW DARE YOU RAISE YOUR VOICE TO ME!! HOW DARE YOU SHOVE MY HAND AWAY!!" He yelled in my face as I struggled to free myself from his grasp.

"LET ME GO!!!" I screamed in defiance but he just laughed at me.

"Don't you worry. I'll let you go, but before I do you'll need to warm my bed like you do for the Alpha King. After all, it's your job as a slave to please your master," he whispered into my ear, making my eyes widened. I didn't know that I was a slave to everyone in this palace. I thought that I was only the slave of the Alpha King. Had the Alpha King planned to share me with others without letting me know?

"No! I refuse! Let me go!" I argued and scratched his hand that was still holding onto my hair, but instead of letting me go he started to drag me out of the kitchen. I was screaming for help, but no one was in the palace to hear me. Even if they were, they wouldn't stop Prince Raymond. He was going to rape me. No, I can't let that happen! I pushed him away using all of my strength then tried to get away from him, but he instantly caught me and threw me against the wall. Groaning in pain, the next thing I knew was that he tore my sleeve.

"NO!!! HELP!!!" I screamed again, but I just got a slap to my face for my efforts. He forcefully tried to kiss me, but I was frantically moving my head from side-to-side to evade him. I was calling out for June, but she didn't seem to be anywhere nearby. Why was no one coming? Could no one hear my screams? When he delivered another slap I felt as if I was going to faint, but I couldn't pass out and leave myself so vulnerable to him. I needed to stay awake so that I could protect myself. He finally got tired of my shrieks and covered my mouth with his hand, stifling my calls for help.

"Why the hell are you yelling? Do you expect someone to come help you? Who would risk their lives to help a slave?" He asked condescendingly. Upon hearing this, tears began to roll down my cheeks and onto his hand. He was right. Who would be willing to help me?

"I'm a Prince, even if you were to tell someone that I raped you, no one would believe you nor would they even care. No one would come after me. Instead you would be killed for spreading such a scandalous rumor about your Prince. And if you're hoping that the Alpha King will believe you then you're even dumber than I thought. He will never believe the woman who killed his mate..." he whispered with an evil smirk as I sobbed in despair. Everything he said was true. The Alpha King hasn't believed anything that I've told him so far. He would believe his step-brother long before he would believe me.

He removed his hand from my mouth and tried to kiss me again, but I just continued to push him away. This time I succeeded in getting away from him then was able to escape the kitchen. Even though no one would believe me, I still refused to give in to being raped by him, or anyone else for that matter. I heard his footsteps getting closer and closer. He was going to catch me. I had nowhere to go, so I ran out of the palace. I had a better chance evading him out there than in this maze of a palace that he knew like the back of his hand.

As I crossed the threshold, I heard a car door slam shut, I glanced over, and saw that it was the Alpha King's car. He had returned. I ran out of the palace as fast as I could, crying hysterically. I ran towards the Alpha King in hopes that he would protect me.

Beta Rex, Bodyguard Zach, and the rest of the Alpha King's usual entourage were shocked at the sight of me. My sleeve was torn, my cheeks were probably red from the series of slaps that I received, and I was sobbing uncontrollably. I grew nervous when I noticed the men's eyes turn lustful at the sight of my exposed skin. Their looks were just like Prince Raymond's. It was only the Alpha King's eyes that weren't scaring me.

Despite my distraught mind, something caught my attention that took my breath away. Princess Naomi, she was…she was standing in front of a big fire and she was holding my wedding gown. She met my gaze with a smirk and I frantically shook my head as she threw my wedding gown into the fire.

"NO!!!" I screamed at the top of my lungs and ran towards the fire. The fire was so large that the flames were taller than me and as wide as a car. The issue was what was burning in that fire, was not just my hopes and dreams it was my whole world. My prized possession, the picture of the Alpha King was tucked within the folds of that dress. That was also burning in the fire. At that moment, I was willing to die for that photo. I was ready to suffer the pain of being severely burned in that fire, even if there was only a small chance that I could save it. When I got close to the fire, I was about to reach into the flames to retrieve my prized possessions but before I could I felt hands on my waist pulling me back. These hands belonged to none other than the Alpha King himself.

"MY DRESS IS BURNING!! LET ME GO!! I HAVE TO GET IT OUT!!!" I yelled, trying to struggle out of his tight hold. I was continuously screaming as I desperately watched the fire burning everything that mattered to me. He wouldn't let me go, instead he turned me around to make me look him in the eyes.

"It's just a wedding dress! Let it burn! It's not worth dying over since you'll never wear it again anyway. You were lucky that you got the chance to wear it at all. You're a slave and you always will be. You didn't even deserve that kindness!" He snapped peevishly, his words breaking me. I knew that I had never been a bride to him, but that didn't change the fact that I was his bride and I wanted to treasure that dress for the rest of my life. He was my husband. He was the one who bonded me to him.

"Remember when you asked me this morning about what I would do to get food? How low did you think I would sink to earn a meal?" I asked, voice filled with despair while gazing into his eyes.

"You asked the wrong question. You should have asked, why I was still alive even though I was continuously starving. What kept me from succumbing to death?" I told him, he just stared at me blankly. He didn't believe me, just like Prince Raymond promised.

"What's burning in that fire is my reason for living. There's a picture of my first and only love burning in that fire. That photo contains my hopes and dreams for a better future. It was what kept me going all of those years. For that photo, I would willingly walk through fire," I frantically explained before shoving away from him. I saw that the fire had grown during our quick exchange, I glanced back over my shoulder at him for what was possibly going to be the last time before I turned back and leapt into the fire. If this was going to be my end then so be it...

26. A New Friend

Elaine

I could hear some movement going on around me and the conversations of several men and women but they weren't clear enough for me to make out what they were saying. They sounded like they were far away from me. All of the noise was echoing in the ears. My eyes were closed and seemed heavy, but I wanted to open them and figure out where I was. Taking a long exhausting breath, I slowly opened my eyes. The smell of medicine hit my nose as I quickly surveyed my surroundings. Green curtains were around the bed where I was laying.

"Am I in the hospital?" I mumbled in confusion and suddenly the curtains flew open causing me to startle a little. It was like they were waiting for me to wake up! A tall, broad-shouldered man with an alluring aura was standing at the end of my bed. This man had a big smile on his face that wasn't only strange but also terrifying. When someone laughed or smiled at me, I knew that they meant nothing good towards me. Princess Naomi's maid did the same thing and I ended up on the wrong end of the Alpha King's wrath. I was trying to sit up in bed while looking suspiciously at everything around me.

"Easy there," The handsome man said as he helped me to sit up. His hands were soft as if he had never worked a hard day in his life, but they were firm and confident. It was clear from his dress and manner of speaking that he belonged to a rich family. This man gazing at me was just smiling in what seemed to be a friendly way. His continued staring started to make me feel awkward and embarrassed. In response to this, I just bowed my head respectfully to him and decided to break the silence.

"Where am I?" I asked him in a quiet voice, unsure of what his reaction to me speaking out of turn would be.

"Ah... so you can speak. I was beginning to think that you were dumb!" He exclaimed while laughing. So did that mean that he was waiting for me to speak? Is that why he was staring at me?

"Who are you?" I asked him as he gently grabbed my hand and started examining the vein of my wrist.

"I'm the Doctor of the Royal Pack. You can call me Dean." He replied. Doctor? I was shocked. No one would think that he was a doctor. Maybe a thug, a member of a gang, or a criminal, but definitely not a doctor.

"I'm also the one who has been taking care of you. I haven't been able to sleep a wink these past three days, you know?" He said, raising an eyebrow. This expression showed off how handsome Dean was, but what he had just said completely diverted my attention from his charm.

"WHAT? THREE DAYS!!!" I almost shouted in surprise and my eyes widened. I looked at the window and saw that it was morning.

"Yes, three days. You have been lying here in this bed for the last three days. You never opened your eyes once until now and for a moment everyone thought that you were dead or in a coma. Eventually, though, my medicines started working and now you've woken up. Are you crazy or did you want to die? How can you be so stupid to jump into a fire?" He scolded me, crossing his arms over his chest and narrowing his eyes at me. He seemed to be pretty angry and disappointed in me. I just looked down at my hands and didn't reply to him.

I remembered now that I had jumped into the fire to save my wedding dress and the photo I had put in it, but I don't remember what happened after that. The surprising thing was that I was sitting here, alive, despite jumping into the fire. What does that matter though when I've now lost both my dress and my photo.

"Hey now. Why the long face? Honestly it does not suit you at all." He said and now I was confused. Why does he care if I'm sad or happy? Why is the pack doctor even caring for a slave in the first place? He chuckled at my expression and I smiled when I realized that he was just trying to get me to smile.

"Now there's that beautiful smile! I knew it was there somewhere." He said with a laugh. "If you could tell me that you regret jumping into the fire then I would be happy to reward you." He said while waving his hand towards a bag that was placed on the side table.

"I don't want anything." I replied sadly and declined his offer because I don't regret it. I regret that I wasn't able to save my precious items. I regret that I was still alive despite my efforts.

He took a deep breath dramatically, "So this means that you don't want your wedding gown back?" He asked and picked the bag up. He was about to throw it in the dustbin next to the bed.

"NO WAIT!!!" I shouted and immediately snatched the bag from him and looked inside. My jaw dropped and eyes widened in complete surprise when I saw my wedding gown. It was in pristine condition and didn't seem like even a thread of it was burned. It was in the same exact condition that I had left it in in that storage room. I immediately reached my hand into the folds of the dress to dig out the photo. I was shocked to see that the photo was perfectly fine and it wasn't burned either. I hugged both the wedding gown and the photo tightly and closed my eyes trying to hold back my tears. It was like I had just woken up from a nightmare and none of those dreadful events had happened at all. I felt his gaze on me and I looked over at him.

"It was burned. Princess Naomi threw it into the fire right in front of me. I saw her do it! How is it possible that they're not burned at all?" I asked in confusion.

"You're right. She did throw it into the fire, but the person who followed you into the fire to save you is more dangerous than some pesky flames." He chuckled.

"What do you mean? Someone came after me? Who?" I asked.

"The Alpha King was who. As you were about to jump into the flames he pulled you back, not letting a single hair on your head burn. He saved not only you, but your wedding dress too." He replied and upon hearing him my heart nearly stopped beating and the wedding gown fell from my hands.

"The Alpha King…? He followed me…? He jumped into the fire too? Is he…is he hurt? Did he get burned at all?" I asked in a panic. He put his hand over my knee in an effort to get me to calm down.

"No need to panic. He's fine. After all, he is an Alpha, I would never allow him to stay injured for long." His explanation was a huge relief. I couldn't even imagine how I would continue to live this horrible life if he got severely hurt because of me. I never thought that he would pull me back out of the flames. I know for damn sure that he didn't save me because he cares about me. The only motive I can fathom is that he couldn't let me die because my punishment wasn't over. He bound our destinies together so he

208

couldn't let me die so easily. I looked back up at Dean and it seemed as if he was closely studying my face. I quickly diverted my attention away from him and tried to get up from the bed.

"Where are you going? You are still pretty weak." He said, but I still got up and put my slippers on.

"I am always weak, but I'll manage like I've done for my whole life." I said. He also got up and was standing beside me acting like he was ready to catch me if I fell. I glanced down and finally noticed that my hand, which was burned by the coffee, was healed.

"How did my hand heal so fast?" I asked in surprise. I looked up at Doctor Dean and he had a sly smile on his face. Man was I stupid! He's a doctor. He must have treated that injury too while I was out of it.

"Thank you." I said while I bowed my head to him in respect.

"You're welcome! Though it is my job to take care of the injured, I'm thankful that I'll be able to sleep peacefully tonight." He gave me a playful wink while sporting a proud smile on his face. I giggled at his antics as he passed me some clothes that I could change into.

"I think you should take a bath before changing." He suggested and I discreetly smelled myself. I had been sleeping for three days and, as such, I couldn't get up to bathe myself so I was starting to smell a little funky. It was embarrassing to have someone telling me to go and take a bath. I immediately ran inside the bathroom without looking back so I couldn't see his expression, but I could hear him laughing which just added to my embarrassment. I peeled off what seemed to be a hospital gown before sinking into the bathtub. The feeling of the hot water on my body was heavenly.

I always had to use cold water for my baths so I wanted to enjoy this. While washing my hair with the shampoo that was provided, I smiled. The shampoo smelled so good and I couldn't even remember the last time I got to use shampoo. Without realizing it, I spent more than an hour soaking in that tub, relishing in the warmth. While I was drying myself with a white, cozy towel, I took a closer look at my hand. It wasn't just healed. It was as if it had never been injured. It was so strange. There was no scar or anything that showed that it was ever burned. Whatever type of medicine he applied to it made it like my wound was never even there. I quickly got dressed in the clothes that he gave me and I came out of the bathroom. He was casually sitting on the bed, waiting for me.

"Wow. Done already?." He asked sarcastically.

"I am so sorry. I lost track of time." I apologized. I knew that, as a doctor, his time was precious.

"That's quite alright. I actually had something that I wanted to ask you." He said gently. When he shifted to the side, I saw my old dress, the one that had been torn by Prince Raymond, was sitting beside him. He put his hand on top of that dress.

"Who did this to you?" He asked. I noticed that his tone and demeanor was different now. He was no longer smiling. He was using his authority. What do I tell him? If I say that Prince Raymond was behind this he won't believe me. No one ever believes me.

"No one did." I said simply while staring at the floor.

"So why is your dress torn as if someone forcefully tore it? Why was your skin scratched?" He interrogated me and I was trying to come up with a plausible explanation that wouldn't get me into trouble.

"When I was working, my sleeve got snagged on a sharp edge and it scratched me as well as tearing my sleeve. The room was dark so I couldn't see much and it all happened so fast." I quickly replied with a bow and tried to leave the room before he inquired any further. I could tell that he wasn't buying my story and I just wanted to get out of this conversation.

"I know you're lying. I can guess who's behind this." He said gently as my eyes widened. I quickly schooled my expression but didn't meet his eyes. He knows? No, he couldn't possibly know. I heard him getting up from the bed and approaching me.

"You're lucky that I was the one who interrogated you because you can lie to me, but you can't lie to the Alpha King." He said softly. This made me finally meet his sincere gaze.

"What do you mean? Is the Alpha King going to interrogate me?" I asked frantically, nearly having a heart attack because if he asked then I knew that I wouldn't be able to lie to him.

"Luckily for you he's not because I asked him if I could interrogate you myself. I still have to report your response to him. Seeing as he saw the condition you were in before jumping into the fire, he's very curious to know what happened to you. I know that you're not naming your attacker because of fear which is understandable. I'll inform the Alpha King of your explanation, but remember that you can't lie to him. Someday he's going to find out that you lied to him, and when that day comes you're going to be in even worse trouble. He hates liars. He even had his own uncle beheaded because he dared to lie to him." Doctor Dean said, sending chills up my spine. He hates lies. He hates liars. I have a huge problem. I can't tell him about Prince Raymond. Even if I do, he'd never believe me. I'll be condemned as a liar either way. I just prayed that Doctor Dean would do everything in his power to help me.

"No need to worry. I'll help you because I consider you my friend." He said with a gentle smile and the word friend attracted my attention.

"You consider me your friend? You know who I am, right?" I asked in disbelief. I didn't want to begin this newfound friendship with lies. We were just walking out of the hospital at this point.

"Yes. I know who you are, Elaine. You are the Omega slave who killed our Luna queen and now you are a slave to the Alpha King himself." He said, rolling his eyes and I chuckled.

"So, knowing all of that, you still want to be friends with me?" I asked skeptically.

"Yes." He definitively said. This was so weird. Why didn't he hate me like all of the others? He would be my first friend in my whole life and he seems to actually care about me.

we exited the room that I had been treated in and entered the main part of the hospital. I looked around me in amazement, everything was so grand and expensive. The Royal Pack had everything a person could hope to have at their disposal when it came to hospital care, the latest top of the line equipment, a specialist for every department, and medication to treat any disease you could think of.

People said that even if every pack stood together against the Royal Pack, that the might of the Royal Pack would still be able to defeat them. No one knew exactly how many pack members were a part of the Royal Pack. Maybe it's for everyone's safety that they didn't disclose it. I knew there had to be a lot of members because there were more than one hundred and fifty members of the hospital staff moving through the building in front of my eyes. Who knew how many staff were hidden behind closed doors or in restricted areas and this was just the hospital. We kept walking until we exited the hospital and ventured out into the pack itself.

"You haven't had a chance to explore the pack yet, right? Let me give you a tour," he suggested as I nodded my head in excitement. I wanted to see more.

"You've already seen the hospital, so now let me show you the library. It's only two minutes away," he said. I didn't think that I would be allowed to go inside the library. I didn't want to disturb the people that were in there, but I peered up at the outside of the building. It was pretty big. I wish I could go inside. I've always loved to read, but I knew that I wouldn't be given the chance to relax with a book for a long time. From there he showed me the stables, which I was already familiar with.

"Well, why don't you show me that photo? People said that you went crazy, trying to rescue it from a fire. That he was your special friend," he said with a wink. Looking down at my hand, I quickly tucked the photo back into my pocket.

"He's just someone…" I shrugged with a little smile, he narrowed his eyes at me.

"I should have just snuck a peek when I had the opportunity. I want to see who this guy is!" He exclaimed, I could tell that he really did regret that he hadn't taken his chance earlier. The positive thing was that he had given me the chance to hide it before he saw that the picture was of our Alpha King. When he realized that I wasn't going to give in, he took me to the cafeteria located in the packhouse where the staff working in the palace and the hospital were eating lunch.

"Let's eat something. I'm starving and I'm sure you are too!" He offered, but I didn't dare to step one foot inside the cafeteria.

"What's wrong?" He asked in confusion.

"Am I allowed to go inside? I mean my presence will surely spoil the appetite of everyone inside. No one wants to be bothered by a slave and I don't want to ruin their meals," I quietly answered as he looked over at them. Everyone eating in the cafeteria was already throwing daggers at me with hostile glares, it was definitely a warning not to step inside.

"Don't worry about them. Right now, you're my patient and I need to make sure that you are healthy. Part of that is making sure that you have been fed. I was told to take care of you by the Alpha King himself so I can't neglect my duties," he stated confidently, pulling me inside the cafeteria, forcing me to follow him. I quickly lowered my head. Everyone in the cavernous room bowed respectfully to Doctor Dean.

"What would you like to eat?" He asked as I anxiously rubbed my face.

"Anything is fine," I replied, not telling him that pretty much everything that was available, I hadn't tried before. He quickly piled two plates with a variety of food then headed outside where there were seats available. I was quite comfortable here because there weren't as many eyes on me. I scanned the area around us, my eyes went to a nurse that was out here having lunch then I looked back at Doctor Dean. He was wearing a loose shirt, khaki pants, and boots. He has an earring, red lips, and messy hair that somehow made him look even more handsome. His large figure must have been sporting a six pack. I seriously questioned that he was even a doctor.

"What? Why are you looking at me so skeptically?" He asked, raising his eyebrows as I quickly lowered my gaze in embarrassment. Thank Goddess that he hadn't thought that I was checking him out.

"No, I'm not," I lied. He just picked up his drink to lazily take a sip.

"Don't lie, you are pretty easy to read. Just tell me what's going on in that head of yours," he quietly inquired.

"Are you actually a doctor? I mean you seem like..." I trailed off while looking deep into his eyes so I was able to see any changes going on in them.

He looked at me with interest as he put his glass down on the table. "Please continue... my peach," he said. Had he just called me his peach? His voice sounded deep and I had noticed far too many things hidden in the depths of his eyes.

"You seem like...like you're an Alpha," I finished, seeing the truth reflected in his eyes.

His lips turned up into a smirk. "You know, talking to me so carelessly could get you into trouble," he sternly replied with raised eyebrows.

"You were the one who said that we were friends. So I'm just talking to you and expressing my thoughts as a friend. Would you punish a friend for speaking freely?" I countered. The two of us stared at each other for a few seconds before he broke out into a fit of laughter, even I left out a little huff of laughter too.

"I chose correctly. From now on, you're my best friend. You've passed the test," he smiled and shook my hand. I liked his company. He seemed like a great person to have as a friend.

We finally settled down and started eating. It seemed like most of the food on my plate was vegetables, which was a little odd. Maybe he chose them for me to help with my health or something. I started to eat, it was all very delicious. My cooking couldn't hold a candle to this.

"Eat some meat. You could use the protein," he advised, putting some of the meat from his plate on my own.

"I already have enough Dean," I tried to stop him, but he just plopped a bite of steak in my mouth instead. I didn't have any idea how he was fast enough to do it.

"Just eat as much as you can and stop talking," he ordered. It wasn't fair because I couldn't even argue with him because my mouth was full. We continued on with our meal. He continued talking but anytime I tried to contribute to the conversation he would just shove another bite of food into my mouth until I just stopped trying. He told me so many things about working in the hospital and the pack as we laughed together. This went on for a little while until, suddenly, the area outside the cafeteria became eerily silent. I looked up to see Dr. Dean was staring behind me. He quickly got up from his seat, I got up as well and when I turned around I realized that the Alpha King was behind me! I was so scared when I saw the fury in his eyes that I took a few steps back until my back hit Dr. Dean's chest.

"Come here!" The Alpha King yelled as he roughly pulled me towards him, yanking me away from Dr. Dean. My breasts slammed into his hard chest, I was startled by his actions. He was enraged.

"What are you doing here?" He asked, gritting his teeth in anger.

"I…I was…eating," I replied as he glanced down at the plate of food then the meat that was still unchewed in my mouth.

"Spit it out now!" He ordered.

"What? Spit it out? But why?" I asked as he just clutched my jaw and plucked the piece of meat out himself and threw it down onto the table.

"Because I can't hear you clearly with your mouth full of food," he snapped, which I found strange. Why couldn't he at least let me finish that bite? I know that I could speak clearly even if I had food in my mouth. He was getting angry over nothing.

"Was there no food left in the palace? Why did you need to come here to eat?" He inquired; I heard a chuckle from Dr. Dean which attracted the Alpha King's attention.

"I was just feeding my patient, my King," Dr. Dean pointed out. I shivered when I noticed the Alpha King frowning. He tightened his grip on me again as if he thought that I was going to try and get away.

"Go and bring some coffee to my room!" He ordered thrusting me away as I quickly nodded my head. I turned to head back into the palace.

"WHY ARE YOU GOING BACK TO HIM?!!" The Alpha King suddenly yelled, making me jump. Going to whom? Dr. Dean?

"I was just heading to the palace," I answered quietly, but he just grabbed my hand and tugged me behind him until we passed Dr. Dean.

He then pushed me before ordering, "Now go!" and quickly walked away. What's wrong with him? Why was he acting so weird?

27. Mine!

Elaine

I quickly returned to the palace, and headed towards the kitchen. I felt like he had been waiting for me to wake up, but the moment I had he ordered me to make coffee? Why was he so angry at me for eating in the cafeteria? Eating in the cafeteria and the palace were the same, right? I just didn't understand why he had yelled at me in the first place. I had done nothing wrong. I was eating with Dr. Dean. Now what would happen to Dean? Would he be punished? I had noticed that he wasn't afraid of the Alpha King. The Alpha King also hadn't said a word to him. Was I missing something?

I entered the kitchen and, as always, there were several maids diligently working to prepare lunch. June turned around when she caught my scent and her eyes widened. "Oh my Goddess! You're finally awake!!!" June exclaimed, running towards me with a shocked look as she hugged me tightly.

"I was so worried. I thought that you were going to die," she whispered. I pulled myself away a little to find tears shining in her eyes.

"I'm completely fine. I'm sorry that you were so worried about me," I reassured her with a smile and she nodded her head while pulling me into another hug.

"I'm so happy. It's like a miracle," she said, handing me a glass of water. I only took two sips before I remembered why I had come to the kitchen in the first place. Immediately putting the glass down on the counter, so that I could start to make some coffee. Only wait a minute! It was time for lunch. Was he really going to want coffee? Shouldn't he eat something? Why did he seem to eat less than everyone else? However, I knew that if I didn't follow his orders he would only grow angrier with me so I just decided to do as he commanded. I put the bag that was holding my wedding dress on the floor to the side. I could hear the distinctive chatter of people beginning to arrive in the dining room for lunch.

I could hear Luna Amanda talking to someone. When I was pouring the coffee into a mug, I noticed that one by one all of the maids were exiting the kitchen while giving me bitchy looks. June was leaving as well, but just before she left she gestured to my right. At the same time, a familiar scent hit my nose, I knew who it was. Following June's gesture, I found Princess Ariel heading straight towards me. I quickly bowed my head to her. She gave me a once over with another bitchy look similar to what the maids gave me.

"So, you're alive," she stated, sounding irritated because I wasn't dead. I silently nodded.

"Please explain to me what exactly happened that day," she demanded as she poked a finger into my chest. It sounded like she was interrogating me.

"What do you mean Princess?" I asked, looking up at her, I noticed that one of the maids had closed the door to the kitchen so I was with Princess Ariel. Why had they locked me in here? What was she planning to do?

"You will tell me exactly what happened," she reiterated, shortening the distance between us even more. I felt her dangerous and evil aura as she approached me.

"On that day…Who was in the kitchen? Who tried to rape you?" She asked. What? Rape? How had she known that I was going to be raped?

"Was it Raymond?" She inquired and all I could do was just stand in shock. How had she known? The way she was pushing me made it seem like she was sure about her information, and just wanted me to confirm it. I nodded because there was no use in trying to hide the truth from Prince Raymond's mate. She knew her mate best. She was the only hope that I had of being saved from any future attacks from him.

"Please save me. He touched me without my permission. He was going to force me to sleep with him. He…" I suddenly stopped talking when I felt a burning sensation on my cheeks. She had delivered several hard consecutive slaps across my face. I placed my hands over my sore cheeks in surprise. Why had she slapped me? What had I done to deserve that?

"You better watch yourself slut! If you try to tell anyone about that day or if you dare open your mouth, then I swear, no one will ever find your body," she threatened from between teeth gnashed in anger. I was surprised by the venom in her voice. Despite being aware of all the transgressions committed by her mate, she was threatening me not to tell anyone. I used to think that rich members of the royal family would be honest and would have some dignity, but it had been an illusion of my own creation that was slowly beginning to crack then shatter. This Princess was more than willing to cover up her mate's crimes! All of these people were the same. Each one was more evil and sinister than the last.

"Especially the Alpha King. He can never know about what Raymond is doing! Do you understand me, slave?" She commanded me, but I didn't answer as I was still thinking about how evil these people were when suddenly she twisted my hand sharply then repeated her question. Once I nodded, she shoved me to the floor and walked out of the kitchen after washing her hands of my filth. I sat on the floor as not only the sound of her sandals echoed in my ears, but every word she spoke. The kitchen door opened again as all the maids returned. They all busied themselves with their work, trying to catch back up, while ignoring the fact that I was on the floor.

June walked over to me as soon as she came in. "Are you alright? What happened?" she asked worriedly, but I just remained silent.

I got up off of the floor and started heading out of the kitchen with the coffee. One thing I knew for certain, everyone here was evil and I had to protect myself from them. With the cup of coffee in hand, I entered the Alpha King's bedroom but he was nowhere to be found. He told me to bring the coffee to his room, so where was he? There was no sound of water coming from the bathroom, so he probably wasn't in there. When I turned to take the coffee back, I found him standing behind me. With great difficulty I managed to keep the coffee from spilling onto his clothes. How did he move so quietly? I was very nervous and scared, especially when Prince Raymond popped up in my mind. He had also snuck up behind me that day.

"Here's your coffee, your Majesty," I said, offering the cup of coffee to him. He looked at it for a few seconds before he took it from me. He lifted it up to take a sip, his lips touched the rim and I was happy. Finally he was willing to drink the coffee that I had prepared for him. He glanced down at my face only to throw the coffee on a plant before he had consumed any of it!

"What are you doing?" I asked in alarm. Even though he was pouring the coffee into the pot, his eagle-like gaze was trained on me.

"Are you useful for things besides flirting with other males? Or do you only know how to take advantage of handsome rich men?" He scornfully asked, cold irritation filling his eyes. I was extremely confused by his questions. When did I flirt with other men? I'd never even pursued a man in a romantic fashion before. What did he mean by the rich handsome men that I'd taken advantage of? He seemed to be very frustrated with me, even more than usual.

"I asked you a question. Do you know how to do anything other than luring in males with your looks?" He pointedly asked again. Who were these other males that he was referring to?

"I can work in the kitchen, garden, clean, as well as do all of the house work," I quietly answered him. Instead of lashing out again, he pulled a key out of his pocket and tossed it to me. I somehow managed to catch it then looked down at it in shock. It was a big key that looked quite beautiful. It was made of a rare metal and had a beautiful design on it. It seemed to even have diamonds embedded into it.

"Then put yourself to good use. Go to my office and retrieve a file for me. Bring the file to me at the Red Moon Pack within the next hour. Do as you're told as this meeting is very important. Don't even think about wasting time or there will be consequences!" He commanded, then left the room with a warning glare. Picking the mug up from the table, I started to follow him out of the room. When he crossed the threshold and took a few steps he suddenly stopped and turned back around. Unfortunately for me, my head ended up bumping into his chest because I was walking so closely behind him. I quickly backed away from him before he could shove me away to keep me from touching him.

"What the fuck did you think you were doing that day? You jumped into that fire just because of that fucking photo of your first and only love?" He barked in my face until I flinched. I had

ALPHA KING'S INNOCENT BRIDE

hoped that he had forgotten about what I had said, but apparently he hadn't.

"WHERE'S THAT FUCKING PHOTO?!! WHO'S YOUR FUCKING LOVER?!! YOUR FIRST AND ONLY LOVE?!! SHOW IT TO ME!!!" He yelled. Upon hearing him, I lowered my head as I tightly clutched the pocket that held the photo. I never want him to see the photo that I carried of him. I could never show it to him because he would kill me for deceiving him. I would either die a brutal death or maybe even be tortured to death. I couldn't take that risk. I had to lie to him once again.

"Did you not hear me? Show. Me. The. Fucking. Photo," he napped, spitting each word out between his teeth. Why was he so obsessed with seeing the photo?

"I…I lost it. Maybe it fell from my dress and burned in the fire," I lied and suddenly his expression changed back to normal. Did he actually believe me for once? And so easily?

"So it did burn?" He inquired, raising an eyebrow skeptically. I nodded. He was definitely going to kill me when he found out that I lied to him. A satisfied look came over his face when he accepted the fact that the photo had indeed been destroyed.

"Forget him!" he ordered randomly.

"What?" I asked in confusion.

"Forget him. He's no longer a part of your life. Even if the photo has been destroyed I know that he still has a special place in your heart. You're not allowed to dream about other males," he stated matter of factly.

"But why? I have the right to love whomever I please and I love him," I simply pointed out, suddenly he tightly grabbed my arms in anger.

"NO!! YOU DON'T HAVE ANY RIGHTS!! YOU'RE NOT FREE TO LOVE ANYONE!! YOU KILLED MY MATE, MADE

ME MATELESS, AND NOW YOU CRAVE THE LOVE OF THIS MAN?!! HOW DARE YOU!!!" He growled and yanked my body towards him. I was scared. What was he going to do? If he gripped me any tighter, he might just tear my clothes.

"Please let me go," I begged but this just caused him to tighten his grip on me even more.

"After ruining my life, I refuse to let you live a happy peaceful one! I would rather pull out your heart so there is no place for that man to live. I will tear your heart apart. I marked you and as such you are my fucking property. Mine! No one else's! I will make sure that there aren't any misunderstandings. Be ready to be fucked tonight!" The Alpha King sternly warned.

28. Come Back

Marvin

"Alpha...your father, Alpha Alfred, has ordered you to appear at the dining table. Alpha Fabian and Luna Wilma have arrived with Natasha. Everyone has been waiting for you in the dining room for a while now. Please go or the Alpha will grow angry," My Beta, Eric urged, knocking on the door again. I swore that he had knocked on my door a hundred times over the last forty-eight hours. Ever since my father had brought me back alive from the Royal Pack, I had locked myself away in this dark room. Anger, hatred, and sadness gripped my heart and mind in such a way that I was having a hard time controlling my wolf.

I wanted to destroy the Opal Moon with my bare hands, using this fire that was building higher inside me every second. It felt like the fire might actually burn me alive if I didn't find a way to release it. I hated myself the most because I hadn't been able to save Elaine and now she was married to the Alpha King. She has gone somewhere that was absolutely impossible for me to follow. She had become something that could no longer be touched. She had become the Alpha King's property.

Just thinking about taking something from the Alpha King was like willing taking the Devil's hand as he led you straight to hell. On the day of the Mating Ball, Elaine had disappeared for twelve hours. After searching for her the whole night, I decided to wait for her at the main access of the territory, thinking that she would be back soon seeing she had nowhere else to go. She hadn't come back though, in the morning I had received the news from Beta Eric that she had committed suicide by jumping into the river.

I immediately returned to the Opal Moon Pack, but everything appeared to be normal. Watching Luna Wilma and Natasha, it hadn't seemed like someone from their pack had committed suicide. They hadn't appeared shocked or distressed in the slightest. Despite asking Natasha a thousand times, she would only tell me that Elaine hadn't come back yet. I had more faith in my Beta's words. The river that ran through the territory was quite dangerous. The rapid current of the water made it almost impossible for anyone to escape. So if Elaine had in fact jumped into the river then she had committed suicide.

That thought had taken away a majority of the hope I had of getting her back, but I had still followed the bank of the river in hopes of finding her. Maybe, I would be able to save her, I had thought. About two hours later, I finally found her surrounded by members of the Royal Pack. I was taken prisoner as soon as I called out Elaine's name. I didn't know the reason why. I didn't even know why the Alpha King had taken her captive! After my father came to rescue me, I learned that Elaine had been accused of killing the mate of the Alpha King. The ground slipped out from under my feet, I had been about to tell the Alpha King that there was no way that Elaine had murdered someone as well as the fact that Alpha Fabian only had one daughter made this whole situation even more fishy. Before I could my father forced me back to our pack using his Alpha tone. I was so angry and confused that I began taking my emotions out on my mother. She ended up telling me the truth: that Luna Wilma and Natasha had tried to kill Elaine. Natasha had thrown her in the river in order to kill her.

Reliving those memories was causing my emotions to eat me up from inside until there was nothing left but a hollow shell. In the end, I had to lose the person that I had always loved. I tried to do everything possible to keep her safe, but everything had been ruined.

After about five more knocks on my door, I still didn't respond and Eric left like every other time. I stopped talking after my father had slapped me. He wasn't speaking to me, nor was I to him.

My mother came to call on me several times a day, but I was determined at this point to not only destroy the Opal Moon Pack, but my father as well. I would play with all of their lives in the same way in which the two evil brothers had played with Elaine's and mine. My father had been well aware that I was in love with her. It was time to take advantage of being an only child and son. I would raze all of my father's dreams to the ground. He blindly believed in the rights of nobles, blood, and family, he wanted me to become the next Alpha of Shine Moon. I had decided that I wouldn't become Alpha! With this move, the Shine Moon Pack would move towards its imminent destruction. I would destroy my own pack along with the Opal Moon. What had been done to Elaine couldn't have been justified.

Still standing by the same window, I stared outside at the same place where I used to watch Elaine work. I used to stand here and watch her for hours on end. She never knew about that. I yearned for a glimpse of her. Her innocent face and eyes refused to allow me a wink of sleep, but the picture I held in my hand calmed my heart for a while, it brought some relief. That was when I heard the tinkling of a key and looked towards my door. Someone was unlocking it from the outside. The door opened wide, revealing Eric standing there with his head bowed.

"I'm sorry for entering without your permission, Alpha. All I request is that you please listen to me, after hearing me out, you can make your decision about becoming the Alpha. I won't keep pestering you, if you just listen first," Eric pleaded. Besides me, only Beta Eric knew of my desire to shed the Alpha position. Without saying a word to him I just glanced down at the photo of Elaine again. He closed the door and looked at me, hesitating, unsure whether he should speak up or not.

"Well spit it out," I flippantly waved him on.

"Alpha... I... I'm here to convince you to not give up the position of the Alpha," Eric began then hesitated, causing me to look at him.

"I'm not going to change my mind no matter what you say. I'm more than willing to give up my position for Elaine. If I can't have her as my Luna this whole world is wasted on me," I lamented as I started walking towards the balcony with a glass of scotch in hand.

"You're doing all of this for Elaine, right? Then you need to become Alpha!" He advised, his words making me stop. I put my glass down on the table.

"What do you mean? What's the connection between becoming Alpha and saving Elaine back?" I asked, turning around and walking towards him in confusion. Eric grew excited as he saw me express interest in his comment.

"If you become Alpha, then you can find a way to get Elaine back from the Alpha King," he pointed out. His words hit my mind so hard that my veins felt like it was going to burst from the sudden influx of hope running through my veins.

"What do you mean? How?" I asked, with a big smile he took my hand and placed a key in it. The key belonged to our pack library.

"You'll find your answers in there," Eric suggested with an evil smile, I understood what he was trying to say.

Elaine…I would save you…

29. Shopping

Elaine

The Alpha King left the palace shortly after he commanded me to deliver the file to him. I was sure that he was going to beat me as I had talked about the love that I still held for the man in the photo. He was furious. Well, that was understandable. I shouldn't have said all of that when I knew that he had lost his mate recently, but what he had ordered me to do was impossible. I can't just forget someone I loved. I could never forget him.

I finally had the chance to eat some lunch in the kitchen even though I was in a hurry. According to the prescription that Dr. Dean had given me, I needed to take it with food. I finished my meal in less than ten minutes then quickly got up from the floor. It was a wonderful feeling when your stomach was full.

Now I had to figure out where the Alpha King's office was. I needed to ask June as she was the only one that I could trust. I didn't want to accidentally enter another forbidden room. When I tracked her down, she told me that it was in an isolated area of the palace that not many people ventured to.

When I got near his office, there were so many plants in the hallway which I found so peaceful. I closed my eyes and inhaled the scents of the greenier and damp soil, it was refreshing. Now I understood why he had selected this location for his office. Werewolves preferred nature, we find it very calming.

Once I entered the office I began searching for the locked filing cabinet that the key the Alpha King had given me belongs to . The room was big and there was a sweet smell to it. My greedy hands couldn't stop themselves from running over the chair behind the desk where the Alpha King always sat. Every object in the room was soaked in his scent. I felt a sense of calm settle over me as I inhaled his addictive scent. It wasn't just me, my wolf also appreciated his smell. I had to move away from the chair otherwise he would know that I had touched his things.

I quickly found the locked filing cabinet, opened it using the key, and pulled out the only file that it contained. It seemed to be highly important seeing it was being kept separate from everything else. Written across the outside of the file was the statement that 'this file held important information related to the Red Moon Pack.' Carefully locking the filing cabinet, I placed the key back in my pocket. Just as I was about to leave the room, I longingly looked back at his seat before leaving. When I exited the palace I made my way to the parking lot where I happened to have found the Gamma of the Royal Pack.

"Sorry to disturb you, but can you please tell me the way to the Red Moon Pack?" I asked him with a small smile, in return he just gave me glare.

"Why do you want to know?" He rudely asked. It's obvious that he was just like all of the others.

"I was ordered by the Alpha King to deliver this important file for him, but I don't know the way to the Red Moon Pack," I explained. When he heard that I had been commanded by the Alpha King, he suddenly changed his attitude and he sincerely told me the way. I was surprised to learn that it wasn't that far and I could easily make my way there in half an hour.

"Thank you so much," I told him with a smile. This time he didn't return it with a rude look, instead he just ignored me as if I wasn't there. Well, it was better than a hate filled glare. I was walking out of the parking area when I realized that the Alpha King had gathered a group of loyal people around him; his Beta, bodyguard, and Gamma, all of them were faithful and honest. They also mirrored the Alpha King's feelings towards me; they hated me, but they were never 'appropriate' like Prince Raymond was. Luckily I hadn't encountered him since that day. I never wanted to see that man's face again.

As these thoughts were flying through my head, I looked up and saw a car that was coming straight towards me at full speed. It looked like it was going to hit me. I shrieked in fear, clenched my eyes shut, as the file fell from my hand and landed on the ground. I opened my eyes after a while when I didn't get hit, realizing that the car had stopped incredibly close to my body. They were only a few inches away from hitting me. When the car door opened, Princess Naomi stepped out.

"Still alive?" She snapped with an evil smirk. I didn't respond as I bent to pick up the file that I had dropped. I hoped that it hadn't gotten dirty or I was dead!

"Well, I guess I shouldn't be surprised. People like you don't tend to die easily, only kill," she quipped while I continued to ignore her. I loathed her. When she threw my wedding gown into that fire, she became the one person in the world that I despised above all others. Of course, if I was being honest with myself it wasn't just her, it was her elder sister Princess Ariel and Prince Raymond too. With a bow I started to continue on my way, but she grabbed my wrist and snatched the file from my hand.

"WHERE ARE YOU GOING WITH THIS IMPORTANT FILE? ARE YOU STEALING OR SPYING?!!" She accused me in a scream. I looked around in fear. If someone really thought that I stole the file then they would beat me to death.

"No, I didn't steal it. I'm going to deliver this file to the Alpha King in the Red Moon Pack. He needs it," I explained as she examined it like it was suspicious.

"Please give it back to me. I'm going to be late," I said. I tried snatching it back from her but she moved it out of my reach.

"If it's that important, then it shouldn't be in your hands. I find it hard to believe that the Alpha King gave you such an important task. You're a murderer, an evil bitch. You should be removed from this earth. So now I will be the one who will deliver this file to the Alpha King. Everything related to him belongs to me," she haughtily stated before putting it in her car. She glanced back at me as if she was waiting for me to argue with her about this matter.

"Okay, thank you," I replied, not showing how disappointed I was that I wouldn't be able to see the Alpha King or see how he ruled over the pack. I didn't want to give her the satisfaction. When she saw that I was unaffected, she realized that she was now doing the work of a slave even though she was a Princess.

"DON'T THINK THAT YOU WILL JUST BE WANDERING AROUND THE PALACE LIKE A QUEEN! GO AND FETCH THE SHOPPING LIST FROM MY MAID. WHEN I GET BACK FROM DELIVERING THIS IMPORTANT FILE TO THE ALPHA KING, I WANT MY DRESSES IN MY ROOM OTHERWISE YOU WILL BE HARSHLY PUNISHED!!!" She yelled. She was unbelievably angry and humiliated because she wasn't able to get to me. I bowed my head to her again then walked away from her. I could hear her frustrated screams and the slamming of her sandals on the ground as she vented her anger.

I made it back to the palace and with great difficulty I was able to get the shopping list from Princess Naomi's maid. I couldn't understand her deal. She acted like I had personally wronged her somehow. I mean, the hate was mutual because she got me into trouble by sending me to the wrong room. She was just like her mistress. A Bitch! I didn't even waste my time asking her the way to the market, instead I just left and found the way on my own. About fifteen minutes later I arrived, that was when I finally read the shopping list that made my jaw drop. What the hell was wrong with this Princess? Why did she need so many dresses?

I used to think that Natasha was very materialistic seeing as every week she would buy something new, but this Princess has really crossed the line into madness. It seems like she donned a different dress every hour. For the first time in my life I got flustered because I needed to be quick about this. It was soon going to be evening. It was already 5 pm and I needed to head back to the palace soon.

"Hey Peach!!!" Dr. Dean appeared out of nowhere, I jumped in shock.

"Oh my Goddess! You scared me to death!!!" I exclaimed, he chuckled. I just shook my head in exasperation.

"What are you doing here? Shopping? I never expected a slave like you to have so much money," he said as he pointed towards the money in my hand. At the same time I noticed that he had some snacks with him that he was enjoying. Hmmm, he openly called me a slave. He was very straight forward which is refreshing.

"I'm not shopping for myself. This is for Princess Naomi and the money is for her clothes," I explained, continuing to shop.

"Does that beautiful yet utterly brainless woman want to buy the whole market?" He asked, I couldn't contain the bark of laughter that escaped me. We both laughed together as I stepped into the most expensive shop in the market, where I decided to buy everything that she wanted.

"I'm surprised that you would speak so brazenly. Aren't you afraid that you'll get punished for speaking so freely? My experience is that you have to keep your mouth shut, even if you're speaking the truth or just want to explain yourself. You have to hold your tongue in front of these noble and royals because they'll punish you for it either way. They don't have any dignity, kindness, or mercy in their hearts," I told him seriously. He sat there studying me silently as if he was reading my soul. I just smiled at him, I felt nervous with his eyes focused on me for so long. I turned and asked the shopkeeper to pack up the dresses that I'd selected.

"It seems like you have gone through abuse in the past," he murmured. I took the shopping bags from the shopkeeper and handed them the money owed.

"Yes, you're right. After all I am a slave, don't forget that fact," I said matter of factly.

"Give those to me," he gestured, taking the shopping bags from my hand. All of that clothes was a bit too heavy for me.

"Well, what are you doing in the market? Shouldn't you be in the pack hospital?" I asked because it was surprising. It was 6 pm and he was wandering in the market like a stray cat with nothing to do.

"I...." He began to answer while rubbing his chin. His mouth was so full of food that I wasn't able to understand what he was trying to say.

"I can't understand what you're saying when your mouth is that full," I said with a giggle. I waited for him to finish chewing what was in his mouth so that I could hear the answer to my question

"I'm a senior doctor so I'm allowed to take breaks. Plus most of my work can be handled by juniors. Actually I like to use my juniors to my advantage!" He said with a laugh and I nervously laughed with him. He was so strange! Openly telling me that he took advantage of his juniors!

"Okay Peach, I think I should leave. I had hoped I could accompany you back to the palace, but I have some work that I have to get done," he lamented, handing me the shopping bags. He walked away so fast it was like he was flying. He appeared out of nowhere and now he's vanished into nothing. At least I enjoyed the time I spent with him. He left before I could even ask him what he had to do or thank him for his help carrying the bags. I realized that he really was my friend. Who would've thought that I'd have a friend who was so handsome and helpful. I didn't know why but he reminded me slightly of Marvin. I wonder what he was up to now.

I hope that when I accepted the fate that the Alpha King had decided for me, that he wouldn't harm Marvin. I always got a little sad thinking about him. I hoped that Marvin would be able to move on with his life, I knew he loved me. I hoped that he realized that his feelings for me were based solely on physical attraction. It wasn't love or anything serious. I also wished that he would find his mate so that he could fully move on. I was lost in thought while walking through the crowd and heading back to the palace. I had no idea what was going on around me. I was so tired that I just wanted to sleep.

"WHAT THE FUCK ARE YOU DOING HERE?!!!" I heard someone roar. I flinched and squeaked in fear when I realized that it was the Alpha King, it caused me to drop all the bags on the ground. I was shocked to see him standing in front of me. What was he doing here? He was the Alpha King! It was all so shocking. I wasn't the only one terrified, the people all around me that had been shopping ran away from us in fear, leaving me standing alone with him in the street. I had a chance to flee with everyone else, but my stupid heart faltered when I thought that he had come there for me…

30. Fire!

Elaine

I saw Beta Rex, the bodyguard Zach, and the Gamma whose name I was still unaware of, were standing near the Alpha King's car studying their surroundings in order to maintain the Alpha King's safety. So he hadn't come here alone, wait a second that meant he had come straight here from the Red Moon Pack meeting?

"I asked you something," the Alpha King reiterated. His voice was grave and filled with anger as he walked towards me. I shook my head a little in fear as well as confusion.

"I came here to buy dresses for Princess Naomi," I replied, gesturing to the shopping bags that were laying on the ground in front of me. I bent down to quickly pick them up. I didn't want to think about what would happen if any of the dresses got dirty then I would definitely be punished by her, but there were so many shopping bags that I was unable to carry them all at once.

"LEAVE THAT FUCKING SHIT ON THE GROUND!!" He barked at me, I immediately dropped the bags and stood up. I watched him in fear as he kicked each bag out of his way and nearly crushed one dress. He was irritated over the fact that I was more worried about the dresses than I was worried about him.

"I told you to get your ass to the Red Moon Pack with that file in an hour! How dare you come here to market instead, imposing your work onto others," he angrily spat out through clenched teeth. I shouldn't even be surprised at this point. Obviously the Princess had deliberately lied to the Alpha King by telling him that I had gone to the market while giving her my work. She was the one that had snatched the file from my hand and wanted to go to the Red Moon Pack!

"It was not like that..." I began to argue until he narrowed the distance between us even further. My heart pounded in my chest. His face was a few inches from mine, his red lips were mere inches away, and his hot breath fanned my face driving me crazy.

"What?" I managed to say, I couldn't bear to be under the unyielding pressure of his hot sexy aura any longer. I didn't know why but my wolf was getting out of control. One thing was still unclear, why was my wolf attracted to the Alpha King?

He gently wrapped his arms around my waist, pulling me close, and getting rid of what little space was left between my breasts and his chest. "Were you trying to run away for fear of being fucked tonight?" He whispered in my ear and my knees felt weak, they trembled as soon as his words registered.

"No, it's not like that," I quietly answered with great difficulty because both my wolf and my heart were now out of control. I closed my eyes, sucking in a few deep breaths, my body ignited at his words.

"Then you want to be fucked?" He asked and my eyes widened.

"No, I don't want to," I immediately corrected him. Suddenly his usual face changed into that of a devil. The arm around my waist grew painfully tight, he was once again back to his angry domineering self.

"It wasn't a question. I was telling you. Every word that comes out of my mouth to you is an order. You will be fucked tonight and you will be ready for it. I also want to taste you. I want to find out what made other males go crazy over you. Tonight you will provide me with your services," he stated point blankly. It was at that point that the warmth that I was feeling inside my body turned cold with fear. It shouldn't be like this. He wanted to fuck me as a punishment. I hoped that he would make love to me, but he wanted to use me like a whore. The fate that I had worked so hard to avoid in my old pack was to be my destiny nonetheless. It hurt. It hurt too much.

"Why are there tears in your eyes? Are you pretending to be innocent? You know that won't work on me," he said as his fingers gripped my chin with an evil smirk as I looked up at him.

"No, I'm not pretending to be innocent. I can't pretend to be innocent because I'm not innocent anymore. I'm not a virgin," I told him honestly. The smirk on his face disappeared, I saw there was a change going on behind his eyes. It seemed like he wanted to fuck a virgin, not a dirty woman like me. There was no use in trying to hide that fact, he would find out when he fucked me later anyway. I knew it wouldn't help my cause to tell him, seeing he already thought that I was a whore, but my heart wanted me to be honest with him.

"I also wasn't trying to run away from you. There's nowhere for me to run to, you've bound us together. I have nowhere to go but to you. If you want to fuck me, then there's nothing I can do to stop you. After all, you are the Alpha King. You can force me, so I'll be forced to bend otherwise I'll crushed under you. Your orders will be followed. I'll be ready tonight," I explained while picking up the bags of clothes that didn't appear to be too badly soiled by their rough treatment.

The Alpha King Emmett

After saying all of that shit, she began to pick up the dresses that I had kicked away. I clenched my fists in anger. How dare she talk to me like that? I didn't know why, but after listening to her it seemed like she would be a victim and I would be her rapist! How could she give in so easily? Was she trying to play the innocent victim in the hopes that I would let her off the hook for tonight? She was my slave and had to give her body, soul, and life to me! Everything that belonged to her was now mine so when she said that she would be ready to be fucked tonight why didn't it feel right? She picked up the bags and began to head back into the palace. She couldn't just leave after talking shit to me like that!

"STOP!!!" I barked in anger. I decided to teach her a lesson right here in front of everyone, to teach her that she was to hold her tongue in front of me. When she turned, I took a few steps towards her, suddenly there was a loud bang like something had blown up. The bags slipped out of her hands as she screamed out in fear, eyes searching in the direction that the noise had come from.

"Alpha..." Rex, Zach, and my Gamma Seth came up beside me, standing at full attention and scanning the area around us for danger.

"What's going on? It sounded like something blew up and it's starting to smell like smoke. There must be a fire!" Rex hazard to guess. His point was proven when the sounds of people screaming and moaning in pain began echoing around us. There was a stir throughout the market as people noticed the fire starting to intensify as it came from the opposite direction.

"Alpha, we can take care of this, take shelter in the palace," Rex suggested.

"No! I can't just stand by while my people are hurt. These people are my responsibility, their safety rests on my shoulders. It's not in my nature to sit comfortably in the palace, turning away from trouble like a coward. Get everyone safely out of the market. Mind-link all of our pack members, warn them of the fire and tell them to get a safe distance from the flames. I don't want anyone getting injured. Get everyone out of their shops and homes safe and alive!" I told them and upon receiving my order, Zach and Seth immediately ran to protect the people, but Rex stayed with me.

"Alpha, please allow me to stay with you. I can't leave you alone," Rex pleaded. When I noticed that Elaine wasn't where she had previously been standing.

"FUCK! WHERE IS THAT WOMAN?!!!" I angrily barked as I quickly looked around to see if I could catch a glimpse of her. The bags that she had been carrying were laying on the ground. That meant she…Fuck…

"I think she went to try and save people," Rex advised, completing my train of thought. My eyes went to the fire that was spreading throughout the market. In the short time since it had started, it had already doubled in size and she had gone into the thick of it to save people? I gritted my teeth in anger. How could she be so stupid?

"Rex! Search for her everywhere and drag her back to me. Don't let her get burned or allow any harm to come to her. I want her alive!" I ordered Rex. This time I would show her what happened when someone ignored me and didn't follow my orders.

"Zach! Seth! If you see my slave anywhere, drag her back to me immediately!" I mind-linked both of them. Members of my pack were beginning to arrive.

"Go and help everyone you can!" I ordered. Upon receiving my order, everyone spread out to cover every corner of the market, saving children, the elderly, and women, along with anyone else that needed help. The smell of things burning was so strong that it would burn the hair in your nose off, but I somehow managed to catch a whiff of a lovely fragrance that happened to belong to none other than Elaine. I turned in the direction of her scent, realizing that was the direction that she had headed. Following her scent, I covered the ten minute route in only a few seconds as the place was quickly being engulfed in flames. Behind a tree that was safe from fire for now, I spotted her scarf. She was sitting behind the tree! What the hell?!

"WHY ARE YOU SITTING HERE?!"

31. Need...

Alpha King Emmett

"WHY ARE YOU SITTING HERE?!" I roared, yanking the scarf off that she was wearing. When I removed the scarf I saw that it wasn't her sitting there but a little girl. Upon seeing me she started sobbing. I mind-linked one of my pack members, calling them there so that they could take the girl to safety. I smelled the scarf. It was her fragrance, but it seemed that after saving the girl, she had wrapped her scarf around the girl then went on to save other people.

As I continued looking for her, I helped every person that I encountered along the way whether they were trapped by the fire or were hiding somewhere, getting them to safety. I heard from some pack members that the cause of the fire had been the careless use of matches in a kerosene shop. The shopkeeper, who was trying to escape in order to save his life, was dragged in front of me. I slit his throat for being so careless, and as an attempt to quell my mounting anger. How dare he ask for mercy after ruining the living of so many people?

"Seize all of his assets. We'll use them to help cover the losses that our people suffered in the market!" I told my people while ordering his body to be taken away. That greedy evil bastard's body disgusted me. He was the most prominent trader in this market, he'd been accused of corruption in the past. He had more property and money than most people would know what to do with. He earned all of it through greed and exploitation. Today his pot of sin was full, it was time for him to pay for his crimes. Almost two hours passed, the market was beginning to clear, but the fire had now spread to the other side of the street.

That was when I received a mind-link from Rex, "We've found Elaine." After saving one last child, I started to head back towards my car where I knew he had been standing. Now she would be back in my grasp, so I could teach her a lesson! Apart from the Royal Pack, members from nearby packs had also arrived to help in extinguishing the fire because if it were not taken care of the fire could reach their packs as well. Of course, they were helping for selfish reasons, but for the moment I could ignore it as long as they were saving people's lives.

"Where is she?" I growled. As I approached the car, I noticed that Rex was alone even though he had said that he had found Elaine...

"How are you here? Someone just raised the alarm. They said that you had gone to the grain warehouse that just caught fire. As soon as Elaine heard this, she ripped free of my grasp and ran away. She was crying while she ran too. I tried to stop her, but there were more people trapped in the fire. I worked on saving them as per your orders. But if you're here, who is spreading the fake rumor that you are in the warehouse?" Rex panicked when he told me this due to its strangeness.

"BUT WHY DID SHE GO INTO THE WAREHOUSE WHEN SHE KNEW THERE WAS A HUGE FIRE?!!!" I yelled. I was furious at Rex, he immediately dropped down to a kneel in an attempt to placate me.

"I'm sorry Alpha. I couldn't keep control of her, but I feel like she went there to try and save you," Rex quietly explained.

"What? That small, fragile woman went there to save me?" I asked in confusion while at the same time I saw Zach running towards me.

"Alpha, I saw Elaine run into a warehouse that was engulfed in flames. I tried to chase after her, but the door somehow got locked behind her and I couldn't enter. It seemed as if someone might have locked her in there. I think..." Zach reported, but he didn't complete his final thought as he lowered his head.

"YOU THINK WHAT?!!! TELL ME!!!" I snapped, losing my patience as I had so many awful scenarios playing out in my head.

"I think she has probably been burned alive and is dead," Zach quickly replied. I was taken aback by his comment. I wasn't sure why but my hands were trembling and my wolf wanted to take over in a pure rage. I closed my eyes for a few seconds to regain control of my wolf as I ran towards the warehouse. Zach and Rex followed close behind me, when I arrived at the warehouse Seth was already trying to break the doors down so that he could make an attempt at saving Elaine. At this point not only was the warehouse on fire, but the door was too! My wolf was on the surface, we were sure that she must have died if she was inside that building! An angry growl escaped from my lips as I sucked in deep heaving breaths that made everyone move out of my way.

"MOVE..." I ordered, Seth stepped aside. I ran up to the door, gathering my strength, I kicked the door and it fell apart into two pieces. As soon as the barrier of the door was removed a wave of flames came rolling out, I could see that everything inside was badly burned.

"Alpha...please don't go inside," my whole pack was kneeling behind me, begging me not to go into the warehouse, but my wolf and I knew what had to be done. I could no longer hear the people around me. I could only hear the beating of my heart. I had to bring her out alive! She hadn't been sufficiently punished yet for the crimes she had committed against me. So if she died, then the vow though bound our souls together for the next seven lifetimes would also be rejected.

I couldn't let that happen. She couldn't die without my permission! As soon as I entered the flames, I could tell that all of the grain that was stored here was burned beyond salvage and nothing could be seen through all of the smoke. I was able to see more by using my wolf's eyes, moving quickly through the warehouse, a figure appeared in a corner in the middle of the raging inferno. I just knew that it was Elaine. I could even smell her, despite all of the smoke. She was glued to the far wall, I could tell that her clothes seemed to be singed in several places.

Part of her sleeve was currently on fire. I watched as she quickly tore it off and threw it away. She was coughing pretty hard from smoke inhalation.

"MY KING!!!" WHERE ARE YOU?!!" I stopped in my tracks when I heard her calling for me which was immediately followed by a bout of coughing. Interesting, she really had jumped into the fire to save me. I could see her, but she obviously couldn't see me. I watched her manic state as she constantly screamed for me, but she stopped when she saw me coming out of the flames towards her. Her eyes were filled with tears as she gazed up at me in amazement.

"My King..." she called me softly under her breath, I could clearly read the fearlessness in her face. Completely forgetting about her burning dress, she ran towards me. Suddenly I felt her breasts collide with my chest. She was hugging me.

"You're safe...thank Goddess...nothing happened to you..." she muttered, still tightly hugging me. I was just standing there like a statue.

"So it's true. You're impervious to fire. It can't burn you. I'm so glad that it's true..." She said and her words shocked me. No one knew that fire didn't hurt me because of the curse. There was so much anger burning inside my blood that external fire didn't harm me. The thing was only a few people, the ones that were closest to me knew about it, so how did she know?

"How did you...?" I was about to ask, but before I had the chance to finish my question she began to breathe heavily as if she wasn't able to do it properly. A big piece of wood, which was the only support for the balcony above us, looked like it was mere seconds from buckling. This place was about to collapse. Right before the beam failed, she pushed me with all of her strength. I was now on one side of the fire while she was on the other with the huge chunk of wood between us.

"You have to get out of here. This warehouse is about to collapse," she urged, unable to breathe as her dress caught fire again.

"What about you?" I asked. She just smiled softly, causing my heart to stutter.

"No one cares about me. As long as you're alive everything will be fine. No one needs this Omega slave..." she assured, taking a few steps back. She backed away into the fire, until I couldn't even hear her coughing anymore. It drove me crazy that I could no longer hear her. I picked up the huge piece of wood to throw it out of the way, but there was another that was going to fall soon so I needed to be quick. I wanted to get out before the building collapsed on top of us.

Tossing the wood and crossing the fire, I saw her semi-conscious body lying on the floor. Her clothes were burnt and torn so badly that they barely covered her body. Wrapping my coat around her, I scooped her up into my arms. As I walked towards the exit, I looked down at her and noticed that she was trying to open her eyes. Maybe she knew that she was in my arms.

"What…why…are…y…you…?" She tried to stutter out but immediately started coughing. All of my pack members were standing outside looking at me, at us. I looked down at her.

"Because…I need my slave…forever…" I whispered into her ear.

32. Conspiracy

Alpha King Emmett

"Alpha..." Rex said, as I exited the warehouse with Elaine. Everyone except Zach, Rex, and Seth stared at me in wonder. Some of them were ordinary residents, while others were pack members. They all marveled at me as they watched me walk out of the fire with Elaine completely unscathed. Not a single part of my body was burned which surprised them. Part of my secret had been revealed. People were whispering, confused as they tried to figure out what I was since I obviously wasn't a normal werewolf. Their eyes were focused on me and on an unconscious Elaine. My coat covered almost seventy percent of her body, but it left her legs bare. As soon as I noticed that some of their eyes were landing on her legs, my anger boiled over out of control as I roared at them. They all ran away in fear which was wise because I was only a short breath away from beheading them.

"Alpha..." Rex called again, the three of men were the only ones left to stare worriedly at me, even knowing that I wouldn't be harmed by the fire, they had still worried. I had given them strict instructions not to enter the building, so that they wouldn't get hurt trying to follow me.

"I'll go get the car," Seth suggested as he ran away. Within minutes he had brought the car to a street that was close to the warehouse. I sat in the back seat with Elaine still in my arms. I instructed Seth to drive as fast as possible, her breathing had slowed down. It was now so slow that it seemed as if she was mere minutes from death. Seth drove the car as fast as he could towards the palace, while Rex, who was in the passenger seat, kept glancing back at me. Zach sat beside me in the back, with his eyes trained on me.

"Alpha, I'm sorry, but I don't think she'll be alive when we finally make it to the palace. Her heartbeat is already on the verge of stopping and her breathing is extremely shallow," Zach softly pointed out. I was well aware of all of that, I had my hand resting above her heart alerting me to the fact that it was pumping fewer and fewer times every passing minute. Seth, who was driving, kept looking back at me through the rearview mirror. I wasn't sure what else to do, so I did the only thing I could think of. Pressing Elaine's cheeks together with my fingers, her little mouth opened, and I began to give Elaine mouth to mouth. I didn't know whether it would work or not, but I was determined to bring her out of the throes of death once again.

When I rescued her from the river she hadn't been breathing, but after giving her mouth to mouth she came back to life which had been such a strange thing to witness. If it had been possible then, it was possible now. At the same time, I could hear everyone's rapid heartbeats. Everyone was nervous because I wanted to save this woman no matter what it took. My passion was centered around taking revenge on this woman, and if she died then my passion would turn into madness. As soon as the thought of her death crossed my mind my wolf began going crazy.

"Just a couple more minutes," Seth assured, but I couldn't lift my head to acknowledge him because I was too busy pressing my lips against her soft ones and constantly breathing for her. The moment the car stopped, Rex opened my car door for me and I immediately climbed out with Elaine in my arms. The car was in the drop off area right in front of the Royal Pack Hospital entrance. There were doctors running around inside, working on patients that had been injured in the fire. One of them saw me and immediately called for the chief doctor. As soon as I laid her on the nearest empty bed, Doctor Dean came running up.

"My King," he said, bowing his head as he stood before me. He seemed to be waiting for further instructions, which only doubled my anger.

"THERE'S NO TIME FOR THIS!! CHECK THIS WOMAN OUT QUICKLY!!" I barked at him, he immediately ran over to check her pulse while his nurse started setting up equipment. The curtain around the bed was drawn, but I was only a few inches away from it. Rex, Seth, and Zach stood some distance behind me. When the curtain opened about two minutes later, the doctor came out looking terrified.

"My King..." the doctor stood before me, panic was evident in his eyes and voice.

"The smoke has gotten into her lungs which is why she's having so much difficulty breathing, it's also why her heart has begun to slow down," he explained. He was having a hard time maintaining eye contact with me and his heart seemed to be trying to beat its way out of his chest due to his anxiety.

"I don't want to know whether her heartbeat is slowing or whether she can breathe properly. I don't fucking care. All I want is for you to keep that woman alive using whatever means necessary! If she stops breathing, then so will you!" I replied sinisterly. All the doctors and nurses that were listening to me got down on their knees to beg for mercy. Ignoring all of them, I simply exited the hospital.

"Zach, you need to be kept informed of what's happening every minute in that hospital room. That's your responsibility," I commanded. I needed to know what her condition was and when she would eventually open her eyes. "Rex, you're to investigate this fire incident at the market," I ordered. "This whole matter isn't as straightforward as it appears. There has never been a fire in the market before today. If someone is a kerosene dealer, then they wouldn't use matches so carelessly. He definitely seemed ready to escape. It's clear that he knew that there was going to be a fire and that he would be the first one to be blamed. None of this is normal, there seems to be some type of conspiracy going on," I had so many thoughts swirling through my mind as I tried to figure out what was going on.

"Alpha, do you think that someone was trying to trap Elaine in that warehouse?" Seth asked. I stopped in my tracks at his words and looked back at him. I had been contemplating this possibility too.

"What do you mean? Why do you think that?" Rex asked.

"I saw her run inside the warehouse, at the time the door was open but when I reached it to follow her the door had closed and I couldn't break it down. Elaine wouldn't be stupid enough to lock herself inside of a burning building, so that only leaves the possibility that someone tried to trap her in there. If I had to bet, I'd say that whoever tried to trap her was probably the same person that orchestrated the market fire. Maybe it was all a conspiracy to kill Elaine," Seth replied. I was taken aback by this revelation, but the more I thought about it the more it made sense.

"Do you have any suspects?" Zach asked Seth but he didn't answer. I turned back and looked at Seth who seemed to be carefully considering his answer.

"Tell me the names of anyone you suspect." I sternly asked.

"I'm not sure, but I saw Princess Naomi while I was putting out the fire." Seth replied. I was surprised by this.

"What is a Princess doing at the market?" Rex asked.

"Order both of the sisters to appear in my office within the next two minutes," I told my men then proceeded to the palace. It was time to get to the bottom of this.

33. Testimony

Alpha King Emmett

A couple of minutes later...

"What's going on here? How dare you treat my mate like this?!!!" The commotion was coming from right outside of my office. Raymond was arguing with Rex.

"I apologize, but I'm not touching or dragging Princess Ariel or Princess Naomi. I asked them to come to the Alpha's office by the order of the Alpha King. He urgently wishes to speak with them. If you have an issue with that then I suggest that you speak to the Alpha King yourself," Rex respectfully replied to Raymond. Ariel, Naomi, and Raymond entered with Rex. Everyone seemed terrified seeing as before today I had never allowed anyone to enter my office.

"My King, what is the meaning of this? What has my mate done? Why is she being called upon like this?" Raymond asked while

Ariel trembled in his arms as if she was about to be on the receiving end of the death penalty. Naomi was looking down at the floor, unable to meet my gaze.

"You're not involved with this matter, Raymond. I'm sure your mate has enough brains to answer any questions I have for her. You better leave while you still have the chance," I told him sternly. When he saw that I was serious, he turned and hugged Ariel.

"I'm so sorry, but I can't leave my mate alone," Raymond answered. As soon as those possessive words left his big mouth, I rose from my chair and walked up to him. Both my hands were now stuffed in my pockets as I carefully inspected the two of them.

"Then why haven't you marked your mate yet?" I asked and he looked up at me in surprise. "Listen to me: mark her, leave the palace now, and go far away from here. If you are willing to do this, then I won't question your mate at all," I laid the gauntlet at both Raymond and Ariel's feet as their faces turned white.

"I… I…" Raymond stumbled over his words, he couldn't seem to form a reply.

"RAYMOND!!!" Suddenly Luna Amanda yelled, appearing at the door.

"HOW DARE YOU QUESTION OR DISOBEY THE WORDS OF OUR ALPHA KING!!!" She shrieked, her eyes full of burning rage directed at her son. He lowered his head in shame as she seethed.

"Get out of there! The Alpha King is holding himself back because I have begged him to not pay attention to your childish antics! Don't test him!" She scolded her son like a small child. He quickly left the room after apologizing to me. He was only nineteen, around ten years younger than me, Amanda always asked me to go easy on him.

"I'm sorry, my King. I promise that it won't happen again. Thank you for your patience," Amanda said with an apologetic expression. She knew that if she had been just five seconds later, Raymond would be standing outside the main gate of the palace with his newly marked mate. Now it was just the two Princesses, Rex, Seth, and I in my office, Zach was at the hospital waiting on any updates on Elaine's health.

"Alpha King, why have we been called here?" Naomi softly asked. Her body language was as casual as ever, she didn't seem nervous at all. She was looking at me with a slight smile on her face as a blush creeped across her cheeks.

"Both of you have been called here because you may have a connection with the accidental fire that occurred in the market," Rex explained as Ariel frowned in confusion.

"If there was a fire in the market, how is it related to us? I never go to the market myself. I always send a maid to get what I need," Ariel argued, maintaining a proud posture and attitude.

"You two are connected because both of you were seen in the market when the fire was raging," Rex stated. An expert in diplomacy and conversation, Rex was interrogating both of them, while I was able to watch their expressions and body language.

"What evidence is there that I was in the market?" Naomi immediately asked, looking arrogant.

"Seth saw you in the market," Rex replied. Upon hearing this, there was a noticeable change in Naomi's features as well as in Ariel's.

"You can't accuse me based on the words of a single Gamma's statement. I am a Princess, if you are accusing me then you need to have actual evidence. It would be embarrassing for anyone, especially our Gamma, if I were to be accused to only later be found innocent," Naomi scoffed. She definitely knew how to use her position to her advantage. After listening to Naomi's comment, Seth couldn't say a word. By accusing a Princess, from one of the top five packs no less, if he was later proven to be a liar, he would be severely punished. Seth had to back down even though I could read the disagreement clear as day on his face. He believed in what his eyes were telling him, it just wasn't an easy feat to accuse a Princess.

"I'm sure we can go now. Please excuse us," Princess Ariel flippantly commented, sporting a victorious smile on her face.

"You might not believe the word of a Gamma, but if an Alpha Prince says the same then maybe the Alpha King will believe it," Vincent countered, storming through the office door. My best friend, Alpha Prince Vincent, entered with a big smile. I checked him over, seeing as it was the first time that today that we had seen each other. I was glad to see that he came dressed appropriately, so that people didn't mistake him for a goon. Ariel and Naomi bowed their heads in his direction but his sly eyes were fixed on me.

"Long time no see, huh?" He raised his arms up then proceeded to hug me, before I pushed him off in annoyance.

"Stop being ridiculous. We just saw each other yesterday," I replied to him coldly.

"Yeah, you are right, it seems like forever ago though..." Saying this Vincent turned to Ariel and Naomi.

"I remember quite clearly seeing two cars at the market. One of those cars belonged to Princess Ariel, while the other car belonged to Princess Naomi. The two of you might not be willing to believe Seth's word because he's a Gamma, but I have also given testimony against you. I hope the Alpha King will take this into consideration while he's making his decision," Vincent said, looking at the two sisters with a careful grin while they looked bewildered.

"I also seem to remember that the punishment for lying to the Alpha King is beheading or having their tongue cut out. So keep that in mind while he's questioning you," Vincent thoughtfully pointed out to both Naomi and Ariel as they began trembling in fear.

"Okay, I confess that I was at the market," Ariel admitted, taking a step forward. Ariel knew when to accept defeat. Vicent sent a sly smile in my direction as his trick worked.

"But I don't know how the fire started or who was responsible for anything that happened there," Ariel continued bowing her head.

"So can you tell us why you were there? You told us yourself that you never go to the market, that you always send a maid to fetch the things you need," Rex reminded Ariel about the lie she had just told a few minutes earlier and I could tell that she was terrified.

"I...I," her voice was stumbling. "I went there to get an abortion," I raised my eyebrows skeptically. She went to get an abortion? Vincent seemed to be thinking the same thing as our eyes met from across the room.

"Raymond doesn't know about it. I wanted to keep it a secret that was why I decided to not go to the pack hospital. Instead I went to a normal hospital that was located in the market. Shortly after the procedure was finished the fire broke out, so I quickly came back here. I lied about being at the market because I didn't want anyone to know about what I had done," Ariel admitted as she explained further. Her pregnancy and abortion issues weren't related to me. Those were issues that should stay between her and her mate. So I turned my attention to Naomi. I charged towards her as she took a few steps back in fear. Was she the one who had orchestrated this whole scheme, in an attempt to kill Elaine?

"IF YOU DARE TO LIE TO ME AGAIN, THE NEXT PLACE YOU'LL FIND YOURSELF IN IS A BROTHEL!!" I roared. I hate liars and she had dared to lie and say that she hadn't been in the market. On top of that, she accused my Gamma of lying just because he's of a lower rank than her. She had to be held responsible for her actions.

"I…I'm sorry that I lied…" She began to explain as her eyes began to fill with tears.

"Then tell us. What was the reason for you being at the market Princess? Actually I have too much work left to do so, unfortunately, I can't stay here and listen to your dram….I mean your tears. I'm quite busy, you know. I also wish to have some of the Alpha King's precious time," Vincent inquired while absent-mindedly playing with his rings like he always did. Naomi looked at him from out of the corner of her eye.

"SPEAK!!!" I barked at her. I didn't have time for her games.

"I...I came to see you," she replied as tears started pouring out of her eyes.

"You went there to see me, why?" I asked her as she wiped away her tears.

"You were so angry when I brought you that important file at the Red Moon Pack because I had come instead of Elaine. You left so quickly that I didn't even get a chance to talk to you. I hated that and I was jealous of that Omega slave since you went looking for her. I was afraid that she would steal you away from me so I went to the market, but then the fire started so I wasn't able to find you in all of the chaos," she conceded, spitting out the whole story in one breath without stopping, expressing her jealousy, insanity, and insecurity. After listening to her, Vincent immediately left the room acting like he hadn't heard or seen a thing.

"I was worried about you, my King…" Naomi said, getting closer to me. She gazed up at me with her puppy dog eyes and now I was in trouble. Rex cleared his throat and quickly excused himself along with Seth. Those jerks!!!

"You fucker, get back in here and help me out!!" I mind-linked Vincent, but he just ignored me. I took a few steps back, not wanting to let her touch me even though I was wearing my gloves. Her lustful eyes revealed her desire for me.

"Now that you've explained yourself, please allow me to have some precious time with our Alpha King," Vincent interrupted, suddenly coming back into the room. Naomi jerked in surprise, looking up at me to find out what my decision would be. I could tell that she was angry and disappointed with the interruption, but she couldn't argue because he was an Alpha Prince after all.

"Okay, I'll be waiting for you at coffee time," Naomi murmured as she left following Ariel. When she was gone, I could finally sigh in relief.

"You need to reward me with a treat, seeing as how I saved you from her," Vincent said with a bright smile.

"Actually, you don't deserve anything since you are the one who was responsible for that shit," I told him coldly.

"But how would I know that she would suddenly confess her feelings for you then admit to her jealousy towards Elaine to boot? She has lusted after you since she was thirteen and now she wants to become your chosen mate, which I'm sure will happen soon. She could even be jealous of me for all I know given all the time that we spend together. Women's jealousy is the scariest thing in this world," Vincent replied seriously, taking a deep breath he sat across from me. I just shook my head in exhaustion. He was not wrong.

"Well we've learned a little bit more at least. They were both at the market, but there's no proof that they were the ones who orchestrated the fire or locked Elaine in that warehouse," Rex pointed out. He and Seth had snuck back into my office after the Princesses had left.

"I think we can all concur that at least one of them is lying," Vincent flatly stated as we nodded in agreement.

"The day I discover that either one of them was involved in that incident, that will be the day that that person will be severely punished. The punishment will be so horrific that even their souls will tremble!" I declared, going over to the window from which I could see the hospital.

"So you saved the life of the woman who killed your mate? Why would you do that?" Vincent asked. I was taken aback by his words. He was watching as a small smile crept across his face.

"Because she'll only die by my hands. Her life and death are in my hands now. She can't die without my permission…" I answered.

34. Illusion?

Elaine

"My King..." I murmured. All I could see was the fire that was surrounding me. Even if I had wanted to, I couldn't have left because I had an important reason for entering the fire. I had to save the Alpha King who had been trapped inside. Someone had locked me in here, but I couldn't even think about escaping without the Alpha King. I was so happy when I saw him alive in front of me, a happiness that I had never experienced before in my entire life. He wasn't hurt. So what he had told me when I was a child was true? He had said that there were many mysteries in his life and one of them was that his body wasn't affected by fire. At that time I had thought that he was joking, but watching him step out of the flames unharmed like a god, I was completely shocked but thrilled too.

I remembered collapsing from all of the smoke then all of a sudden he was there, lifting me up, and carrying me out of the fire even though the entire warehouse was about to collapse. No! He should have left me, before it was too late. I was going crazy thinking about this because I couldn't remember what had happened after that. Had the Alpha King gotten stuck in the warehouse with me? Had the building collapsed? Had he gotten hurt because of me? I was turning my head from side-to-side trying to open my eyes.

"Calm down... Calm down…" A very kind voice softly whispered in my ear. I felt a warm hand cover my forehead, preventing me from moving my head. It was a male voice. "Yes, very good...calm down...quieter…nothing has happened. You're safe," that sweet, gentle voice entered my ears again and I could feel his warm breath brushing my ear. I stopped shaking my head and I heard him chuckling softly, as if I had amused him by listening to his instructions.

"Now slowly, try to open your eyes," the same voice calmed the fear of the fire from my mind before I slowly opened my eyes. I blinked a few times to try and get my eyes to focus, when they finally did I turned my head in the direction of the voice. I found a tall man standing there.

"Hey there, glad to see your eyes open," the man said. He seemed young, about 17 years old, and was quite handsome and wore a big smile. He had big eyes and a sharp nose situated over beautiful lips that were enough to make him the center of attention. He had crossed his arms over his chest and was wearing a white coat which told me that he was a doctor.

"Can you see me?" He asked, I slowly nodded my head in affirmation.

"Good," he then went to check my pulse and listen to my heart and lungs. I just lay there and let him examine me. This was the second time I had been a patient of this hospital, but me being here must have meant that the Alpha King got me out of the burning warehouse. That meant that he was safe! That thought alone released so much pent up anxiety that I hadn't even realized I was carrying.

"Water..." My throat and tongue felt as dry as dust. I could desperately use some rehydration.

"Of course, please wait for just a moment while we fetch some for you," he advised. I saw that a woman was now standing next to him. She was probably his assistant, she quickly left hopefully to get me some water. My back was a little stiff, most likely from lying down for so long. So I tried to sit up, which the doctor helped me with.

"Take it easy there, you're still weak," he suggested. I saw his nametag, his name was Lax. Why was he here? Where was Dr. Dean? The woman came back carrying a tray in her hand. When she set the tray down, I immediately reached for the water. I gulped it down and realized that for some reason this water was lukewarm instead of cold. I slowly drank it all, I felt so much better afterwards.

"Thank you," I said to the doctor and he smiled at me.

"You don't need to thank me, it is our job. You were brought here by the Alpha King. When your breathing and heart rate became so low that you were on the verge of death, the Alpha King made it clear that if you died then all of our lives would be in danger too. Before you, all of the doctors have never had to work so hard in order to save the life of a patient. We worked day and night, constantly monitoring your health. We were waiting for your eyes to open even more impatiently than the Alpha King. We knew that if you didn't recover, then we wouldn't be around for much longer either," he chuckled. I could still hear the panic and fear in his voice over the Alpha King's threat. It seems that he was desperate for me to live, probably because he hasn't taken his revenge out on me yet and if I were to die, his vow would have gone unfulfilled.

"I'm sorry for all of the trouble I've caused," I apologetically bowed my head.

"No, no, there is no need for all that though maybe Doctor Dean would appreciate an apology due to the fact that when you were brought here Alpha had yelled at him a great deal. He even threatened to kill him. That poor man cried," I was surprised to learn everything that Lax was saying. The last time I saw Doctor Dean and the Alpha King face-to-face was in the canteen, it didn't look like there was an issue between them.

"Can you please call Doctor Dean here? I would like to apologize to him," I asked as soon as the words left my mouth, the curtain around my bed was drawn back and there was a man of about 35 years standing there.

"You wanted to see me?" A man with a cold expression asked.

"What? I think there's some sort of misunderstanding, I asked to see Doctor Dean," I told the man as an irritated smile crossed his face.

"I am Doctor Dean," he pointed a finger to his name tag. I was shocked. This was Doctor Dean?!

"But...how is that possible? I've met Dr. Dean before, he is someone different. Is it possible that there's another doctor by that name that works here?" I asked and everyone looked confused. Then the man who was calling himself Doctor Dean came up to me and began checking my pulse while looking at me cautiously.

"You seem to be a bit confused. It's probably due to the smoke inhalation, you are in dire need of some rest. I'm the only Doctor Dean in this entire pack, I'm the senior doctor here." He told me the same information that the previous Doctor Dean had. I could tell that he didn't like me much. It all seemed quite strange. If this man was Doctor Dean then who was the person I had met the first time I was here? I hadn't only seen him once, I had spent time with him at the market, and I ate food with him at the cafeteria. Was it all just an illusion? But how was that possible?

"Please don't take offense to anything he says or does. Not sleeping for four days will make even the nicest person grumpy," Lax whispered so quietly that only I could hear him.

"What? You guys haven't slept for four days?" I was surprised, but when I looked at his face more carefully, I noticed that he had bags under his eyes.

"Yes, you weren't regaining consciousness and the Alpha King's bodyguard was here the whole time to keep an eye on your condition. His presence here made it clear to us that we couldn't relax or even take a moment to sleep. We had to dedicate every moment to your care. Any information regarding your condition or what we were doing to help was being relayed back to the Alpha King. Just when you were about to regain consciousness, the bodyguard went back to the palace to inform the Alpha King that you were about to awake," Listening to him, I felt a strange feeling in my heart. It was as if someone had placed a heavy burden on me. So many people had been inconvenienced by me. I felt so ashamed because I couldn't even thank them properly.

"I'm really...really sorry..." I apologized to Doctor Lax over and over again. I hoped that apologizing would help lessen this feeling in my heart.

"Well, I guess if you're really sorry then I'm ready to forgive you on one condition. You have to eat this soup, then the eggs, and take your medicine so that you can regain some strength and recover," he said with a laugh. A delicious breakfast was placed in front of me which I immediately dug into. I ate in silence; I was so hungry. Even though it was food for patients, it was actually quite tasty.

When I was done eating, I picked up the pills that I needed to take. I never liked taking pills so I was gathering some courage before consuming them but it was better than an injection. I had a glass of water in my hand, just before I was about to take the medication Doctor Lax stopped me.

"You have food on your mouth," he chuckled softly. Just as I was about to wipe my mouth, he stopped my hand and ran his thumb over the corners of my lips. I flinched a little as I never let men touch me but I shouldn't be afraid because he was a doctor. He was not trying to flirt or do anything wrong, but still my heart was beating fast in fear from this man's touch.

"What's going on here?"

35. Deceiver!

Elaine

"**W**hat is going on here?"

It was at that moment that a dangerously deep voice echoed through the room. Dr. Lax and I followed the sound of the voice and found it was none other than the Alpha King whose eyes were red with anger. His eyes were focused on Dr. Lax's thumb that was touching my lips. Why was he here?

"Alpha," Doctor Lax immediately pulled his hand away, stepped away from the bed, and bowed his head. I also tried to get out of the bed to greet him properly, but was stopped by the doctor when he told me that I shouldn't get up from the bed.

"Looks like she's doing quite well if she's flirting with a man younger than her. She's acting as if nothing happened to her, instead she is living a comfortable life. I already told you my King, there was no point in leaving such an important meeting to come here," Princess Naomi's voice came seemingly from out of nowhere. Upon further inspection, I noticed that she was standing behind the big body of the Alpha King. She wasn't alone, Zach and Beta Rex were there as well.

What did she mean that I was flirting with Doctor Lax? She definitely had the wrong idea about what was going on.Wait a second! Had she said that the Alpha King left an important meeting to come and visit me? I was up on cloud nine in my excitement. I was about to ask him how he was, but he just glared at me then turned around to leave the room. I panicked because it seemed like he had thought that I was flirting with Dr. Lax. I just didn't understand why he would believe her word and not even consider my side of what was happening. I didn't know what to do. I was about to call out to him since I couldn't get up and follow him when Princess Naomi was suddenly standing next to me.

"Why can't you just die?" Princess Naomi quietly spat out so that only I could hear. What she didn't know was that Doctor Lax was listening to her every word. He was quite shocked but did his best to not react.

"You can fool everyone else into believing that you're good. You ran out into the burning market to save people then ran into a burning warehouse to save the Alpha King. Of course, you never fooled me for a second," she let out a short laugh, seeming rather proud over the fact that she hadn't fallen for my 'innocent act'. What was she trying to prove? Why was she even here in the first place?

"It will be better for you in the end if you just stay away from the Alpha King or else…" I didn't stay to listen to her nonsense. I got out of bed and ran out of the room without even sparing a moment to put on some shoes.

"What the fuck? I was speaking to that slave and she just ignored me like I was beneath her then she ran after the Alpha King like a bitch in heat! How dare she ignore me?!!!" I could hear her frustrated screams as I left my hospital room behind. I was standing in the hallway looking for the Alpha King. I knew there would be consequences for me walking away when a Princess was speaking to me but right now I needed to find the Alpha King. I had to tell him that I wasn't flirting with that doctor. I found him just about to exit the hospital.

"My King!" I called out, surprisingly he stopped and looked back. I didn't have a lot of strength but I was still trying to move as fast as I could, which caused me to trip over my own two feet. I closed my eyes with a little scream, I knew that I was going to slam face first into the hard floor. This was going to hurt. I could see everyone panicking, including the Alpha King who watched everything happen as he ran towards me. I closed my eyes preparing for the impact.

"Got you," I felt someone's large hands cradling my waist to help steady me. My eyes were closed but I knew that they weren't the Alpha King's. I opened my eyes and looked at the person that was holding me, it was none other than the man that lied to me and said that he was Dr. Dean!

"Dr. Dean!!!" I almost squealed in surprise. This proved that this man was not just a figment of my imagination, I wasn't going crazy. This handsome hunk of a man was real.

"Aaah, I think it's time that I properly introduce myself," he said with a big smile that seemed to be mixed with an apology.

"I lied when I told you that I was Dr. Dean," he confessed. I narrowed my eyes at him. He really had played me! What a liar!

"I'm actually Alpha Prince Vincent," he introduced himself, making my jaw drop in shock. My throat instantly went bone dry and my knees felt like they were going to give out. This handsome man, whom I had considered my friend for so long, with whom I had dinner with, and even roamed the market with was Alpha Prince Vincent?

After carefully looking him over, seeing him in royal attire, I was convinced that he wasn't lying. This time he was telling the truth and what he told me was very dangerous. He wore a big smile but I panicked. His name reminded me of the lady that had given me the important task of handing that wooden box to Alpha Prince Vincent which I hadn't completed.

Was it possible that he knew that I had been given that box and never gave it to him? If he came here to ask me about it or if he came to get it from me, what would I tell him? I asked myself then immediately moved away from him. My life was now in danger! I immediately bowed my head to him, as an Alpha Prince he couldn't be my friend. At the market, I had told him some very bad things about some very rich people. The whole time that he had been with me, he had never told me that he was the Alpha Prince. I barely even recognized him in his royal attire. He looked so different from what he did in his more casual clothes.

"Why are you so nervous, Peach?" He asked and I immediately cleared my face of any expression. It seemed like he was acting the same towards me as he had when he was pretending to be Dr. Dean. Maybe he wasn't aware that I had been given that box? Yes, He probably thought that the woman would bring him the box, so he didn't even know about my involvement. I needed to just pretend that I didn't know anything about it until I had the chance to find that wooden box.

Once I calmed down, I shook my head and acted normal again. At the same time my eyes went to the Alpha King who was standing only a few inches away from us. How had he gotten so close to me so quickly? The way he was standing made it seem like he had planned to catch me when I was about to fall but I knew that was just in my head. He would have loved to see my blood oozing out of a head wound, he probably would have wanted some popcorn to snack on while he watched.

The Alpha Prince bowed his head to the Alpha King. "Are you here to see Elaine, my King?" He asked.

I watched as the Alpha King's face changed. "I don't have time to waste on her. She seems to be busy flirting with all of the men in this hospital!" He snapped with an angry fire blazing in his eyes.

"Oooh... I just assumed seeing the moment that she opened her eyes you booked it over here. So I thought that you were worried about her," Alpha Prince Vincent pointed out which annoyed the Alpha King to no end. My eyes widened at his words. I couldn't believe that he would speak so boldly to the Alpha King.

"Why would I come here to see that wretched being? Don't I have other more urgent matters to attend to? I just came here to see whether she was still fuckable or not, or whether she was just a useless piece of shit. If she loses a few body parts, then she'll have to be beheaded!" He yelled while continuing to glare at me with fury in his eyes. I just couldn't understand why he was getting so angry. I hadn't done anything wrong. I hadn't even asked him to come here. I was also glad that I hadn't lost any body parts in the fire, but I was still worried that he was going to kill me because I hadn't obeyed him in the market and had run away to save anyone that needed help.

"I didn't mean to offend you. I'm sorry that I wrongly assumed, it seems, as you are just passing by. I would like to spend some time with my Peach here, as she's still a little weak. I want to take her to the garden, with your permission of course," he asked with a respectful bow of his head. I knew that he was asking for a scolding, but the Alpha King only seemed to enjoy rebuking me. He was always yelling and getting on me about different things. After listening to his request, the Alpha King looked at me for a few seconds. I wasn't sure what he was looking at me for or what he saw, but he eventually turned around and walked away without saying a word. I could hear his angry heaving breaths as he walked away from us. I took a deep breath and felt myself relax as he left.

36. Benevolent And Flirting

Elaine

"**S**o are you ready to go?" Alpha Prince Vincent asked me.

"But the King didn't grant his permission," I objected but he just rolled his eyes.

"Maybe not, but he didn't say no either. Plus I've learned to read him, I know what his silence meant," he countered, wiggling his eyebrows in a silly manner.

"Really? What did it mean then?" I was curious.

"His silence meant do whatever you want!" he told me with a wicked laugh, upon hearing that I calmed down but at the same time chills went down my spine. This Alpha Prince was not only handsome, he was a little devious too.

"Let's go!" He suggested, grabbing my hand that I politely pulled away from him.

"Please don't hold my hand, everyone's watching," I requested with an apologetic smile. I hoped that he understood, because he did not force me as we kept walking. If he had tried to hold my hand before I knew who he really was, then I probably would have let him, but now I knew that he was the Alpha Prince. If he was seen in public holding my hand, it might start rumors of us being together. Plus everyone's anger always seemed to be focused on me, I didn't want any more jealous or hateful looks aimed my way. I could see that unmated she-wolves were drooling over him as he walked by. It was obvious due to the fact that he was equally handsome as the Alpha King.

"Are you friends with the Alpha King?" I couldn't control my curiosity.

"Finally you speak. I thought that my title had turned you into a scared little kitten which is why I didn't tell you when we first met," he explained and I laughed a little. "Yes, we've been friends since we were small children," he finally answered my question, looking happy. "He's just a little aggressive and has a temper but he also has a kind side. He just doesn't like to show it very often," he continued. I couldn't keep my shock from showing on my face. The Alpha King, kind?! That seemed absolutely impossible, I had only seen his violent and brutal nature.

"You're thinking I'm insane right?" He asked me with a smirk. I quickly adjusted my expression, but didn't reply. He just laughed.

"You're easy to read, Peach," he said as I gave him a small smile. Now I understood why everyone in the cafeteria had given him so much respect.

"Didn't I tell you not to do anything stupid? Why did you jump into the fire when you knew you could die?" He scolded me.

"I went in there to save the Alpha King. I thought he needed help, there was no one else so I…" I began to explain to him but he was focused on my facial features. He could tell that I loved the Alpha King.

"As his slave I had to protect the Alpha King," I quickly changed my answer, not that he bought it for a second he was just nice enough to let the matter go. "You see my assumption was correct, you are an Alpha," he stopped when I said that and looked at me with a blank expression.

"Yes, it's quite shocking actually. We had never met before, so how was it possible that you knew? How did you know that I'm an Alpha?" He asked seriously while I just wrung my hands in nervousness.

"Please don't take my question too seriously, I was just thinking out loud," a nervous smile played on my lips but he was still staring as he seemed to think about something. We started to walk again. We had been in the garden for awhile now as we talked about a variety of things.

"Seriously though, I'm happy that you woke up. If you hadn't, I knew that Emmett was going to be extremely angry. The entire time that you were in the coma, he was keeping an eye on the hospital through his window even though he had Zach to keep an eye on you inside. At the same time Rex has been investigating the matter related to the fire," he told me.

"Do you remember who locked you in that building?" He suddenly asked.

"No, I don't have a clue," I replied.

"Are you trying to protect the guilty party, like you did last time?" He accused, raising an eyebrow.

"No! I'm not, I'm telling you the truth. I don't know who did it," my answer made him sigh in relief.

"I really hope that you're not lying because the last time I covered for you so that the Alpha King didn't ask you any questions. Your clothes were torn and there were scratches on your arms, it was clear that someone tried to hurt you. Even though you're his slave, he's practically the father of justice. He hates this kind of thing. He didn't interrogate you because of what I told him. If he had, you would have gotten into trouble," he explained.

"I'll always be grateful for your help," I bowed my hand respectfully to him.

"Don't worry about it. Just think of me as a benevolent friend. Though if you're feeling up to it, can you make me a cup of coffee?" I laughed at his request.

"Yes absolutely! It's evening anyways, that means it's time to serve coffee to the Alpha King. I don't feel as weak as I did earlier so I will definitely make coffee for the both of you," I told him as we both started walking towards the palace.

After preparing the coffee and giving a cup to the Alpha Prince, I went up to the Alpha King's room with his cup. The door was half closed but I still knocked before I entered. I saw that he was standing by the window, he was looking down at a book that he was holding and didn't seem to notice me enter. My plan was to discreetly put coffee down without him noticing me then I would leave the room. So I quietly headed towards the table then turned to leave after putting the cup down on it.

"Where do you think you're going?" His voice was sharp and cold like a blade. I stopped in my tracks and looked back at him. When I turned around I saw that he was very close to me, so close that I just about fell backwards in panic. Before I could he wrapped his arm around my waist, saving me from falling.

"My King…" I murmured quietly under my breath.

"How did you know that I don't get burned by fire? That fire doesn't affect me?" He looked at me suspiciously, his words were firm. My face turned white when my brain registered what he had asked. He remembered what I had said so carelessly to him. I had hoped that he would have forgotten.

"Alpha Prince Vincent had told me when he explained to me how you had pulled my wedding gown out of the fire," I quickly lied but I could tell that he didn't completely believe me. Apparently the use of Vincent's name held some weight as he didn't question me any further. It seemed that their friendship was a strong one.

"Vincent?" He raised his eyebrows in surprise and I quickly nodded, holding my breath as I also knew that he could feel people's emotions.

"Why did Vincent hold your hand?" He was angrily glaring at me now. I thought that he had left before that had happened? Was he keeping an eye on me?

"He…he calls me his friend, so…" I replied and he frowned.

"So you would let any male hold your hand just because he called you a friend? Are you so hungry for friendship that you would do anything?" Gritting his teeth in anger, he barked in my face.

"And why was that other guy touching your lips?" He suddenly asked. I knew that he was talking about Doctor Lax. I think that he took Princess Naomi's comment seriously and thought that I was flirting with Dr. Lax.

"I swear that I wasn't flirting with him. He was just wiping food from my mouth. He was just helping me, seriously. Please don't misunderstand it," I told him and his eyes were fixed on me as he was reading something there.

"I don't believe you," he shook his head. I could see that he was speaking the truth.

"Then what can I do to make you believe me?" I asked desperately, he was quiet for a few seconds before he responded.

"Don't talk to him ever again. Not just him, but any other male. If I see you with any other male, then trust me you'll regret testing my patience," he commanded, sending chills down my spine. I just couldn't understand why he was behaving like this, but he had a crazy dangerous look about him and I didn't dare disobey him. But…why in the hell did I find this side of him so hot and sexy?

37. Insecurity

Lewis

A week had passed since our pack's spy went missing and never returned. I feared that my probing would reach the Alpha King if the Royal Pack questioned the spy, but I was sure that even if he got caught that he would never reveal who had hired him seeing as such spies were given special training for this very situation. They would die before ever giving up the name of the pack or individual that had hired them, but if he was dead then I wouldn't be able to learn whether Elaine was still alive or not.

I expected him to return two days after our last meeting, but a week had now passed and I didn't know why he hadn't returned. This whole week I hadn't been able to breathe freely for a single moment because I just felt so anxious all of the time. I had no idea what he might have discovered. At the same time, there was a rumor going around that there had been a fire in the market and a beautiful woman had been trapped in a burning warehouse.

I wasn't sure if it was Elaine or not, but the way that they had described the woman made me feel like it was her. All of this information was fucking with my mind until nothing made sense to me anymore. Could that woman really have been Elaine?

"Lewis! Lewis!" Natasha yelled from the other side of my bedroom door, but I was so immersed in thoughts of Elaine that I didn't move from my bed. When I didn't respond to her, Natasha entered my room without knocking. Even though I had tried to ignore her over and over again, she refused to listen to me. She wasn't letting me sleep with all of her high pitched shrieking.

"YOU FUCKING JERK!! AREN'T YOU LISTENING??!!" Natasha yelled at me, though I still hadn't opened my eyes. Suddenly I felt the splash of water on my face then, the next thing I knew, I was completely soaked. Startled, I opened my eyes furious to find Natahsa standing there with an empty pitcher in her hand. She had a proud smirk lingering on her lips, it just pissed me off even more.

"I should've used this method earlier," she snidely remarked. Without bothering to wipe my face I sprang from my bed, throwing the blanket off me, and grabbed her by the throat. She tried to protect herself, but I didn't give her the chance.

"YOU BITCH!! HOW MANY TIMES HAVE I TOLD YOU NOT TO PLAY WITH ME?!!!" I growled, pinning her against the wall. I yelled in her face as she kept struggling in my grasp, trying to free herself. She was about to knee me in my groin, but before she could I used my legs to trap hers, totally caging her in.

"WHY CAN ONLY THAT BITCH ELAINE PLAY WITH YOU?!! DID I DISTURB YOU WHEN YOU WERE DREAMING ABOUT YOUR PRECIOUS WHORE?!!!" She screamed back at me. I nearly strangled her right then and there when she called Elaine a whore.

"DON'T YOU DARE CALL HER A WHORE!! YOU ARE NOTHING BUT TRASH COMPARED TO HER!! SHE IS AS PURE AS HOLY WATER!! YOU KNOW QUITE WELL THAT SHE WAS A VIRGIN AND SHE HID IT FROM ALL OF US, FEARING THAT WE WOULD MAKE HER THE PACK'S WHORE!!! I KNEW THAT SHE WAS A VIRGIN, BUT I ALWAYS CALLED HER A SLUT. I THOUGHT THAT SHE WOULD GIVE IT UP TO ME, BUT SHE NEVER DID!! NOW SHE HAS DISAPPEARED FROM MY LIFE WITHOUT A TRACE AND I DON'T WANT TO HEAR ANY KIND OF SHIT SAID ABOUT HER!! I'M WARNING YOU!! DO IT AGAIN AND I WILL KILL YOU!!!" I yelled in a dark and foreboding voice, watching as she struggled to breathe. Her face was turning red and it seemed like she was moments away from passing out.

"LEWIS!! WHAT THE FUCK ARE YOU DOING?!!!!" My mom screeched, entering my room and shoving me off of Natasha. She slid down the wall, holding her throat and gasping for oxygen. My wolf was out of control, I took deep heaving breaths in my fury. Mother was worried as she inspected Natasha's neck which was now red and covered in my fingerprints.

"WHAT THE HELL ARE YOU DOING?!! YOU WERE GOING TO KILL YOUR OWN SISTER?!!" My mom screamed at me, her eyes turning red in anger at seeing Natasha in this condition. I charged towards my mother with the same anger. I didn't care that she was my mother or the Luna right now.

"I DID IT BECAUSE YOUR BITCH OF A DAUGHTER DESERVED IT!! YOU'RE BOTH RESPONSIBLE FOR MY CURRENT CONDITION!! YOU WERE BOTH WELL AWARE THAT I LOVED ELAINE AND THAT I WANTED TO MAKE

HER MY MATE, BUT THE BOTH OF YOU SNATCHED HER AWAY FROM ME!! NOW I FEEL LIKE I'M GOING CRAZY!! I'LL BREAK EVERY SINGLE RULE, EVERY LAW, AND EVERY FAMILY TIE IF SHE HAS DIED!! MARK MY WORDS, THE DAY I DISCOVER THAT SHE HAS LEFT THIS WORLD, LEAVING ME ALONE. THAT DAY WILL BE THE DAY THAT YOU'LL LOSE YOUR ONLY SON!! I'LL LEAVE THIS PACK , CHOOSING TO LIVE THE REST OF MY LIFE AS A ROGUE. I'LL REFUSE TO STAY HERE!!!" I yelled back and tried to walk away, but my mother grabbed my arm stopping me.

"NO!! YOU ARE NOT GOING TO DO ANY OF THAT!!! My mother screamed at the top of her lungs, afraid that I was really going to go through with it. Only she was unaware that I had already made up my mind.

"I'll do it. I see Elaine everywhere I look here. If she is dead I don't want to stay here a second longer. Just pray that she isn't because you'll lose everything that you've worked for, starting with your son," I pointed out. My mothers eyes widened as all the color drained from her face in fear. I violently shoved her hand away as I walked out of my room, grabbing my coat along the way.

Raymond

Two Days Later...

Having parked my car outside the palace, I entered quickly, and proceeded towards my room. My mind was bursting with anger. I had learned that Ariel had an abortion without even telling me. I had been asking her for several days now why the Alpha King had invited her and her sister to his office. She had just said that it was to inquire about the fire in the market because she had been there, but she hadn't told me the reason that she had visited the market in the first place.

I hadn't gotten any answers from her so I went to the market to find out for myself. It was there that I discovered that she had gone to the hospital and had gotten an abortion. My mind exploded with anger as I immediately returned to the palace. I opened the door to my room with a kick while simultaneously trying to calm myself but to no avail.

"Oh my Goddess, Raymond! You kicked the door so hard that you scared me!" Ariel cried while glaring at me. She was combing her hair in front of the dressing table. Grabbing a hold of her arm, I angrily dragged her up and the comb fell from her hand.

"WHAT THE HELL ARE YOU DOING?!!" She shrieked.

"How dare you get an abortion," I exclaimed, gnashing my teeth as I clutched her arms painfully tight. Her face turned pale as her eyes widened, proving that what I had heard was true.

"How... how did you find out?" She asked, stumbling over her words. I couldn't believe she had the nerve to ask me this. I slapped her across the face and she collapsed to the floor.

"HOW DARE YOU ASK ME THAT!! WHY SHOULD YOU CARE WHO TOLD ME?! YOU HAD AN ABORTION WITHOUT TALKING TO ME, WITHOUT CARING ABOUT MY FEELINGS, WITHOUT CARING ABOUT HOW LONG I'VE BEEN CRAVING FOR YOU TO HAVE OUR BABY!!!" I shouted. She hELD her hand to her cheek where I had slapped her. She wasn't looking at me. It didn't seem to me that she was at all regretful about what she had done. I violently yanked her up from the floor.

"FUCKING ANSWER ME RIGHT NOW!!! WHY DID YOU KILL OUR BABY?!!!!" I barked.

"YOU DON'T DESERVE TO HAVE ONE!!" She yelled back as she pushed me away, with a world of anger in her eyes.

"What do you mean?" I asked, confused.

"YOU TRIED TO FORCE ELAINE IN THE KITCHEN THAT DAY!! SHE TOLD ME THAT YOU WANTED TO SLEEP WITH HER!! YOU TRIED TO RAPE HER!! WHY DO YOU WANT A CHILD FROM ME WHEN YOU HAVE YOUR MIND FIXED ON ANOTHER WOMAN?!! IT DOESN'T SEEM LIKE I CAN FULFILL YOUR NEEDS IF YOU CRAVE ANOTHER WOMAN'S BODY, IF YOU HUNGER FOR ANOTHER WOMAN'S BODY!! I DON'T THINK THAT YOU HAVE THE RIGHT TO CARE ABOUT WHAT I DO WITH MY CHILD!! YOU CHEATED ON ME, I WILL DECIDE WHETHER I WANT TO GIVE YOU A BABY OR NOT!!!" Ariel screamed at the top of her lungs. I was shocked that she knew what had happened in the kitchen. I thought that Elaine would be too fearful to tell anyone.

"What are you saying baby? That is complete bullshit!" I replied, walking over to her to pull her into a hug.

"Don't touch me, Raymond! I hate you!" She warned, trying to push me away.

"How can you believe the words of a slave? She told you that I tried to rape her and you believed her so easily?" I asked, holding her tightly in my arms as she stopped wriggling.

"What do you mean?" She asked in confusion.

"Yes, I admit that I was in the kitchen that day. I just wanted to get a drink, she was the only one in the kitchen who could make me one. She took advantage of the situation and tried to seduce me. I told her that I have a beautiful mate and that I only love her. When she realized that she wasn't going to get what she wanted, she acted like I tried to rape her. She pretended to be the innocent victim like always. She's doing everything she can to try and snatch me away from you, baby. You have to believe me," I

284

explained while lying through my teeth. I cupped her face, giving her my puppy eyes.

"What? So she lied? She's trying to steal you away from me?" She repeated, becoming insecure which was exactly what I wanted.

"Yes," I told her, kissing her cheek.

"I'll kill that slave bitch! How dare she touch you! I doubted you because of her and thought that you were cheating on me. I'm really sorry Raymond," Ariel lamented, hugging me tightly. I could tell that she was upset with herself. I hugged her back, mentally sighing in relief. I never thought that she would find out or that Elaine would dare to tell Ariel about what had transpired in the kitchen that day.

I had barely made it through that. I knew that if I didn't convince her then she was going to do something horrific. I had an evil smile on my face because now I was going to teach that whorish Omega slave a lesson! She would regret the day that she decided to mess with me!

38. Seduced!

Marvin

I opened the door to my room as soon as I took a step out, my Beta, Eric welcomed me.

"Thank Goddess you came out of your room and are in as good of shape as you are. I was worried that you'd have dark circles under your eyes," he said. I just rolled my eyes and began walking down the stairs towards the dining room. He followed behind me. I finished buttoning my shirt as I entered the dining room, where my parents were already seated. They were surprised to see me, no one expected me to make an appearance at the dining table today. Not paying attention to anyone, I took my usual seat as my mother happily began serving me food since I had finally left my room.

"So you finally set your pride aside and decided to come out?" My father sneered. I wasn't surprised by his snide question, I had expected this from him. Though a part of me did wonder why I couldn't just have a peaceful breakfast?

"I never said that I wouldn't, but since you brought up my not leaving my room it must have bruised your ego. Now that I have come out, though, you've decided to treat me like this to help make you feel like the big, bad Alpha again. If you want, I'll apologize for speaking the truth," I smugly replied with a smirk. The entire time my mother had been trying to advise me with her frantic gaze to keep my mouth shut. Upon hearing my words, my father's eyes turned red with anger.

"Watch what you say to me boy!" He snapped, gritting his teeth in anger as he slammed his hands down on the table, making my mom panic.

"Please calm down. He's finally come out of his room. If you keep badgering him, he may isolate himself again or do something far worse," my mom warned as she put her hand on Dad's shoulder in an attempt to calm him down. Ignoring everyone, I started eating when my dad's Beta entered the dining room.

"Alpha, we have received an invitation from the palace," he announced while handing the envelope to my father. I wanted to know what this invitation was for. The mention of the palace had gotten my full attention.

"Do you know anything about this?" I mind-linked Eric in the hopes of getting some more information.

"No, I don't. It seems like some kind of event at the palace," Eric replied. There was a smile on my face. I clenched my fists under the table to try and get my emotions under control.

"I know what you're thinking, Alpha," Eric said. Mentally smirking as father put the invitation down on the table, I immediately grabbed it and read. As expected, it was an invitation for a birthday celebration for Luna Amanda. Our pack was invited!

"Please send our response to the palace saying that we'll gladly accept their invitation and will be happy to join the festivities celebrating Luna Amanda. Oh, and don't forget to thank them for giving us the honor," my father dictated. I immediately got up from the dining table and walked out of the pack house. Yes! I howled in my head and heard Eric laugh. He was following me.

"The Moon Goddess gave you a big break, Alpha," Eric said. I placed my hands on the tree where I had carved Elaine and my names. It had been years yet it was still the same as the day that I had carved it.

The day that I went to the library, I figured out how to get Elaine back into my life. In the ancient books there, I found guidance on how to obtain the property of the Alpha King whether it was a person or thing that was in his possession. I knew it would take some time if I took that approach, but it would be worth it if I could have Elaine. I didn't think that Moon Goddess would give me a chance to see her so soon. I wouldn't let it go to waste.

"I'm coming for you Elaine..." I said, gently touching the carving.

Elaine

I had to get up at about half past five this morning because it was Luna Amanda's birthday and all of the servants that worked in the palace had been given strict instructions to not be late, myself included. When I arrived, Princess Naomi's maid was dividing the responsibilities and tasks to everyone there.

288

There were more people working in the palace than I ever could have imagined. She divided all of the people up into groups of ten. The largest undertaking was going to be decoration, so several groups were entrusted to decorate different areas of the palace. To my surprise, she didn't put me into any group and now I was the only one left standing in the kitchen. She inspected me from head to toe then rolled her eyes as if she was tired of seeing my face.

"You'll cook all the food for the guests who come to the palace today," she said with a demonic expression on her face. I realized that she was speaking to someone through mind-link and it was that person that had ordered her to give me this task. She had to be acting on the orders of Princess Naomi, but there were a lot of people coming for this birthday celebration!

"I won't have time to prepare all of the food, the celebration begins at nine this evening. Even if I start on it now, I won't have everything ready by tonight if I'm by myself," I explained to the maid, she just rolled her eyes at me.

"If that's so, then I'll send June to help you. If you still can't accomplish the task, then you'll have to face Luna Amanda and the Alpha King. Remember that the Alpha has great respect for Luna Amanda, he won't tolerate any mistakes during her birthday celebrations. You are going to fucking die today," she smugly pointed out before walking away with a big laugh.

I clenched my fists in anger, this was all because of Princess Naomi. She wanted me killed by the Alpha King and now she had found the perfect way of manifesting it into being. The maid hadn't even told me how many guests were attending the party!

I quickly made coffee for the Alpha King then went back to his room. He was putting his shirt on , seeming to be unaware of my arrival. I quietly put the cup on the table and snuck out of the room without bothering him. When I entered the kitchen again June was waiting for me.

"Hey, I'm here to help," she said and I was glad to see her. At least she would be here to help and I wouldn't have to do it all alone.

"Let's get started then," I said as we both started to arrange the raw materials that we needed on the counters.

"I don't think that we're going to be able to finish all of this in time. They're so incredibly mean and awful! Do you know that Luna Amanda and Princess Ariel have gone shopping? While Princess Naomi is busy getting a full spa treatment in her room. I'm sure she won't be coming out for a while. When she finally does emerge we'll find that her face is covered in makeup and that she's wearing a beautiful dress that'll tightly hug her body. We servants really do get the short end of the stick. Here we're making food for them like diligent worker bees without stopping and they'll just eat it in a few minutes without considering how much time we invested in it. We at least deserve a 'thank you' but no one cares about the people working behind the scenes," June begrudgingly grumbled. I had to agree with her.

"You're right, but it's foolish of us to have any kind of expectations or hopes when it comes to these people. I've spent almost all the years of my life working like an animal day-in and day-out at the Opal Moon Pack. There was never a time when I served them their food late. I always respected everyone and never talked back. Even the leftovers of the food that I had prepared for them were just thrown away. I wasn't given so much as a crumb of it to eat," I told June. She understood my point, she had told me that she used to work at another pack like me. She had also faced torture and abuse in life, but not quite as bad as I had. I glanced over at her, she seemed to be lost in some bad memories.

"Let's just forget about everything for now, that way we can try to finish our work as soon as possible. The one positive thing about this situation is that there's no one here to bother us," I said with a laugh and she joined in. About five hours had passed while both of us worked and now it was time for lunch, but there was no one in the palace for us to serve food to. I was cooking food for the celebration that night only, but I had already finished with all of the sweets as well as some of the appetizers.

"It would have been nice to know how many guests were coming," I grumbled.

"You're right. Don't worry, I'll go and find out!" June suggested with such confidence that made me laugh. I watched her walk behind me then all of my attention was focused on the pot in front of me.

"Could you please taste these for me and tell me what you think?" I asked as I put some sweets on a plate for her to try. I was still stirring the contents of the pot, when I realized that she hadn't tried any sweets yet.

"Please, could you tell me how they taste?" I asked her again. She picked up the plate of sweets without saying a word. When she didn't answer I began to worry that they were awful. I had made all of the sweets already and we didn't have any time to waste on remaking them.

"What's wrong? Why aren't you saying anything?" I asked as I turned around to look at her, but when I did the spoon that I was holding fell out of my hand in shock.

"My King..." I said as the Alpha King was standing right behind me with the sweets in his mouth. He was the one who had taken the plate to sample them. June wasn't here so I was the only one with him in the kitchen. She must have left to go to try to find out how many guests would be attending the event that night. I was so busy cooking that I hadn't realized that June had left and that the Alpha King had come in. It seemed that I had inadvertently forced the Alpha King to eat the sweets.

"Did you ask me something?" His hot, sexy voice entered my ears, but his jaw was still moving as he continued to eat one of the sweets I had made. It was like a dream. He was standing so close to me that my eyes couldn't seem to stray from his lips.

"I asked how they were," I quietly repeated as I licked my own lips. I didn't know why but my wolf was getting excited by our close proximity. She wanted me to attack his lips with mine. It wasn't just her though, I also wanted to kiss him.

"Why don't you taste them yourself?" He asked, putting a piece of a sweet in my mouth, I felt his thumb rub against my lips. I swore that I lost control right there. I closed my eyes and held my breath. He needed to move away before I embarrassed myself. I was so distracted that I couldn't even chew it.

"What? You don't want it?" He asked as I opened my eyes, not understanding what he meant.

"Then give it back to me," he said, making me even more confused. How would he take it back? He quickly snatched the sweet that was still not fully in my mouth. He then proceeded to toss it into his mouth and eat it then he walked out of the kitchen without saying another word.

My mouth still hung wide open in disbelief. He had just snatched the food from my mouth, his lips had been only an inch away from mine! I sat down on the ground and put my hand over my heart, I could feel it beating out of control. What the hell was that? Why had he come in here? What was he planning? With all of those questions running through my mind, I was sure of one thing. He had seduced me!!!

39. A Promise

Seth

After inspecting the decorations in the garden and completing other pack matters that had been assigned to me by the Alpha, I was now only a short distance away from the main entrance of the palace. I saw Beta Rex and Zach coming towards me.

"How's everything going?" Zach asked.

"Everything's fine. All of the pack members are working together like usual so that everything is going smoothly. After all, no one wants to anger our Alpha," I replied with a chuckle.

"I hope there won't be any disturbances during the celebration and that the entire event goes off without an issue," Rex stated. We had been busy with different aspects of the preparations since four in the morning. I nodded while taking in the decorations around me, the responsibility for which had been handled by Beta Rex. They had come out nicely. The sun had set and it was now early evening.

"Where's the Alpha King?" I asked because Rex was always with him no matter what the situation was. Of course, he was looking after the preparations today instead, which was strange.

"He's still working in his office. You know how he is. No matter how big the celebration is, he won't ignore the work that needs to be done. At least today he let me have a bit of a break from the usual paperwork. Since I have a hard time sitting around not doing anything, I decided to help out here. So I'm keeping an eye on security with Zach. We have men stationed all over the palace. Even though the guests that are visiting are familiar to us, security can't be ignored," Rex offered by way of explanation. Suddenly Zach was scanning his eyes over the crowd.

"I can't explain why but that woman over there seems like she might be a security threat," Zach grumbled in a gravelly voice. Rex and I followed his gaze finding a suspicious looking woman whose eyes were darting around like she was trying to discover something.

"Who is she?" I asked, raising my eyebrows. I'd never seen her before. She reminded me of a little rabbit in a white dress.

"She's a maid that works in the royal kitchen, though I'm not sure why she's acting like that," Rex replied as Zach continued to frown, not fully convinced of her innocence. He was taking her strange behavior as a challenge. He charged towards her as if he would execute her if she couldn't answer for her actions within five seconds of being interrogated by him.

"Hold on brother," I said, grabbing a hold of Zach's arm to stop him.

"She's acting suspicious!" He muttered, sounding serious. It made me roll my eyes. Once again his bodyguard instincts were coming through. He was going to kill this woman with the death glare he was sending her way, she didn't even know that she was in great danger.

"If she is up to something then she'll recognize your face and lie to you. I'm sure she hasn't seen me since I've been away from the palace for the last two months and only returned to the pack two days ago. Let me handle this," I suggested after studying the women for a few seconds, he agreed. His expression made Rex and I chuckle. I left the two of them behind as I walked towards the suspicious woman.

I was sure that she was new. She must have arrived at the palace while I was away. She seemed to be hiding behind a wall while trying to peek around it. This woman seemed rather young, maybe eighteen or nineteen. I snuck up next to her and began to imitate her movement. My head was next to hers as she was moving her head right and left, so I did the same. It was quite fun, I was trying to figure out what she was trying to see. When she moved her head again, her eyes finally met mine, and she screamed in surprise.

"OH MY GODDESS!! WHO ARE YOU?!" She shrieked in fear, placing her hand on her chest to try and calm herself down. She was startled to see me and didn't seem to recognize me. I knew it, she didn't know that I was the Gamma.

"That's the same thing that I wanted to ask you. You're over here acting quite suspicious. So who are you?" I inquired, raising an eyebrow as she looked at me from head to toe with her big, round eyes.

"Even if I look suspicious, how do you not know who I am if you're from this pack? How do you not know that I'm June and I work in the royal kitchen? I'm not going to tell you who I am because I don't know who you are!!" She exclaimed, crossing her arms over her chest. It made me laugh because she had inadvertently told me exactly what I had wanted to know without even realizing it. This game had turned out to be highly entertaining, I wanted to keep it going.

"Why are you laughing?" She asked. She was quite annoyed now, she was throwing daggers at me with her eyes.

"I just remembered something," I lied.

"Well what are you trying to look at?" I probed again.

"Oh!", she gasped. "I need to..." She trailed off as she once again assumed the same position and started looking around. Oh, why was she acting so suspicious? If she continued on like this, then Zach would come over to interrogate her.

"Maybe I can help you?" I offered. She seemed to contemplate my offer for a few seconds before replying.

"Really?" She skeptically asked while raising a brow.

"Yes," I replied, attempting to win her trust.

"Can I trust you?" She questioned, still doubting me as I stepped closer to her.

"Absolutely," I replied, looking deep into her eyes. She got close to my ear.

"I'm here because I need to find out how many guests will be here for the party. I'm helping Elaine with the cooking in the kitchen, but we weren't told how many guests are expected to attend so we're having trouble deciding on how much food to prepare. So I decided to discreetly try and find out. Don't tell anyone," she quickly whispered. She pulled away from me slightly after explaining everything.

"Ohhhh..." I muttered in surprise as she nodded.

"Yes, now you understand my predicament. You promised that you would help me. Do you have any idea how many guests will be coming tonight?" She asked with hopeful eyes. It made me smile to see her childish ploy. I quickly told her how many guests were expected to attend, she was overjoyed that I was able to provide the information.

"Thank you so much!" She sincerely exclaimed as she bowed her head in respect.

"Don't worry, it was just a little information," I assured her as she studied me suspiciously.

"But how do you come by that information? Who are you?" She asked again. I thought about what I should tell her. If she knew who I really was, then this little rabbit would act differently around me.

"I'm just someone who knows a few things," I hedged. She suddenly took a few steps back and put both of her hands over her mouth in surprise.

"Oh my Goddess! Don't tell me that you're a spy!" She yelped in fear.

"A spy?" I sputtered in disbelief. I, the Gamma of the Royal Pack never thought that someone would accuse me of being a spy. I couldn't tell if it was supposed to be a compliment or an insult.

"Don't worry, I won't tell anyone that you helped me. Your secret is safe with me," she quietly promised. So that only I would hear her, it made me chuckle that she was ready to hide this secret for my benefit.

"Really? Do you promise?" I asked in an equally quiet voice, like I was trying to hide from everyone that I'm a spy.

"Yes, I promise," she answered me with confidence. I wiped fake sweat off of my forehead to show her that I had been worried.

"Thank you!" I replied and she gave me a knowing look that seemed to tell me that my secret was safe in the deepest part of her heart.

"You're welcome, but I have to leave. I've left Elaine alone in the kitchen for too long as it is. I need to go and help her," she explained, running back to the palace. Her speed was unbelievable. I was right! She was like a little rabbit, quickly vanishing out of sight. I laughed out loud. Who was that woman? Was she stupid or something? At least she was entertaining.

40. He Hates Me...

Elaine

Sometime later, June returned to the kitchen out of breath as if she'd been running. Just like she had promised, she came back with the number of guests that would be visiting. I laughed at the giddiness caused by her success, but now that we knew how many people we had to cook for, the task had become slightly easier. Before we knew it, the clock chimed eight pm and the guests slowly began arriving, the activity increased with their arrival. Even though I was in the kitchen, I could hear the low hum of all of those people chatting and laughing.

The entire palace smelled different with all of the different wolf scents, that wasn't even taking into consideration the perfumes that some she-wolves had applied so strongly that I felt suffocated. They must all be beautiful since they were all from noble families, some were even Princes and Princesses. Another forty five minutes passed in a flash. After so many hours with it just being June and I, a figure appeared in the kitchen doorway. It was none other than Beta Rex. Had he come to take stock of our progress? The food was one of the most important parts in any celebration. June and I bowed our heads when we saw him.

"Is the food ready?" He asked. I wasn't sure why, but I always felt that in comparison to Zach and Gamma Seth, Beta Rex hated me almost as much as the Alpha King. I figured that was why he always spoke to me using the fewest number of words possible, without showing any expression.

"Yes, the food is ready..." I answered, but couldn't even get the full sentence out before he left the kitchen.

"He's quite arrogant," I heard June whisper into my ear so that he wouldn't hear her.

"Maybe, but his behavior towards me is understandable, after all he thinks I killed his Luna Queen. To him, I'm just a murderer that doesn't have the right to live. I can understand how some people might want to kill me the second they lay eyes on me," I countered as I thought about the incident in the warehouse. I knew that the only purpose behind locking that exterior door was so that I would die in that fire. Somebody had wanted to kill me but the Alpha King had saved me again. I shook my head, shoving all of those thoughts out of my mind so that I could focus my attention on the servants who were now entering the kitchen to take all of the food. It looked like a parade, there were so many. I was finally able to take a breath since our task was finally done. I leaned against the kitchen counter, wiping the sweat off my brow with my elbow. I had been working nonstop all day, I never had a chance to take a break.

"Hey! Don't put your dirty hands on the kitchen counter and don't dare lean on it! It'll get dirty!" Suddenly Princess Naomi's maid entered the kitchen. Did she not realize that I had made all of the food so I had touched everything in this kitchen? Had she forgotten already? I quietly moved away from the counter and sat on the floor to rest. I didn't even know her name and I had no interest in learning it, so I'll call her The Witch in my mind!

"What are you doing?" She barked at me again. Was I not even allowed to sit on the floor now?

"I'm taking a break since the food has all been prepared. I'm exhausted," I explained since she was being ridiculous now.

"A slave like you doesn't have the right to a break. Quickly, go and help the others with serving everything," she ordered, before walking out of the kitchen.

June and I just looked at each other. I groaned as I got up from the floor then armed with a tray of drinks I went out with the other servants, June following behind me. As we walked out of the kitchen the noise intensified as we entered the party hall, everyone's curious voices could be heard. About twenty servants were walking in front of me, I was at the back of the line.

Suddenly we stopped in our tracks, before we could enter the hall. Why were we stopping? When I tried to peek around everyone, I saw that Luna Amanda was standing in front of a huge cake in the middle of the hall and the Alpha King was sitting comfortably nearby.

The cake was being cut while people were clapping, but my eyes were fixed on the Alpha King who seemed to be looking around for something or someone but whom? First the Alpha King congratulated Luna Amanda then after that everyone else started congratulating Luna Amanda one by one. This went on for a little while, after that the servants began to slowly enter the hall one by one. After what seemed like forever, I finally entered. This hall, even more beautiful than I could have imagined, shone like it had been cast in moonlight. It was so captivating and alluring that I couldn't even take it all in. When a man looked at me strangely from head to toe, while taking a glass off my tray, I realized that I was wearing the same clothes that I'd been cooking in and there were oil and spice stains all over it.

Ignoring his gaze, I bowed my head, and continued serving. After handing out drinks to three or four people, I moved on to the next lady who was wearing a gorgeous pink gown. She was the Luna of one of the top five packs under the Alpha King's protection. While talking to a man, she took a glass from my tray without sparing me a glance, but she looked over at me as soon as the man pointed. Moving away, she stared at me with utter disgust in her eyes.
"Hey! This drink is as bad as your dirty dress and ugly face! Who hired you? I don't want anything from you. Just go away!" She exclaimed, insulting me as she put the glass back on the tray. People around her laughed as she fanned herself with her hand.

"I'm sorry, ma'am," I apologized then tried to leave the hall so that I wouldn't ruin anyone else's night.

"You can't leave! Do the work assigned to you or face the consequences," the Witch snapped as she appeared in front of me. I was getting really annoyed by her bossiness. Was she keeping an eye on me?

"Hey! I would like a drink!" Someone called to me, when I turned I saw that it was Princess Naomi, and she wasn't alone. She was standing with the Alpha King in the middle of the crowd as if they were a couple. The Alpha King looked unbelievably handsome and very sexy. All of the women were eyeing him, but Princess Naomi was acting like she was his mate. I walked towards them, my eyes inadvertently went to her hands which were locked on the Alpha King's. I stood in front of the two of them with my tray, but neither of them took a drink. I chanced a peek at the Alpha King through my lashes and was surprised to see that he was already looking at me.

"My King, would you like a drink?" Princess Naomi asked, crushing her large breasts against his arm intentionally while her right hand was slowly sliding up his chest. I noticed that he didn't stop her. I wanted to shove her away so badly. My wolf was provoking me to do something but I needed to be careful so I didn't do something that I'd regret. Still looking into my eyes he took a drink and gave it to the Princess.

"Ladies first," the Alpha King replied as he passed her the glass of wine that she grabbed quickly as if she were desperate for the drink.

"Oh my Goddess! Thank you, my King!" She preened, suddenly kissing his cheek. I clutched the tray tightly in shock. He...he let her kiss him. Something was going on inside me that made me sad, angry, and disappointed. I peered into his eyes while all of these emotions swirled inside me, I knew that he was aware of everything that I was feeling due to our bond.

"A kiss should be in the right place, not on the cheek," he said, looking at me while pulling her into his arms. She grabbed the back of his head, with her lustful eyes, totally jumped on him. I wanted to turn away, not wanting to watch the both of them, but I couldn't. I saw their lips touching as they passionately kissed each other.

She wrapped her arms around his neck, shoving her tongue into his mouth. My heart broke into infinite pieces at the sight of him in another woman's arms. He opened his eyes and watched me. My eyes were full of tears as he placed his hand on her hip pulling her even closer.

I would have given almost anything for this to stop. He knew that he was hurting me. Didn't he? Couldn't he feel my pain? I wanted to get down on my knees and ask him but I couldn't find my voice. I wished I could say the words, but...did I have the right to? I was his, but he was not mine. Why was I the only one that had to bear this pain? I had so many questions but I already knew the answer. He hated me...

He hated me...

41. Threatened

Elaine

He hated me…

Eventually I tore my gaze away from them and quickly turned around, moving in the opposite direction so that I could try to calm my heart and mind. I could normally control my wolf, but it seemed an impossible task when I could still hear Naomi's giggling, their lips smacking as they kissed, and remembered how she moaned his name against his lips while they kissed.

I increased the speed of my steps, all I wanted was to get out of here as quickly as possible until suddenly someone was standing right in front of me. I almost fell backwards when I stopped abruptly to avoid running into them. If I hadn't been able to stop myself in time then the last two glasses of wine on my tray would have spilled all over his royal uniform. Wait a minute, royal uniform? Who was this?

I looked up to find that the person I had nearly bumping into was Prince Raymond, he was standing in front of me with an evil grin plastered across his face. The hair on the back of my neck stood on end as I quickly backed away while I trembled in fear. I hadn't seen him since the incident in the kitchen because I never went into the dining room anymore.

I tried to avoid being in his presence, but now I was in a predicament from which there was no escape from him. If I even attempted to, it would be viewed as an offense to leave without being dismissed. If I were to disobey him, then he would have to punish me, especially with all of the eyes that are around us at the moment. He stepped towards me like a hunter stalking his prey that had frozen in fear. The whole place was so crowded that I couldn't get any farther away from him without bumping into a guest, and if I touched any of them the consequences were going to be dire.

"What is the name of this wine?" He asked, taking a glass of wine from the tray I was still carrying. My mind automatically went back to that day in the kitchen and all the nasty things he had said to me there when he spoke to me.

"W….white….wine…" I managed to stutter out my reply, trying to control my nervousness and fear. He could sense it though and a soft chuckle escaped his lips.

"While speaking to me, why are you stumbling over your words? Why are you stuttering? Are you scared of me, my slave?" He asked with all due seriousness. He wasn't ridiculing me, his intention was dirty when he referred to me as a slave.

"I'm not your slave. I'm the Alpha King's slave and his alone. I'm not afraid of you," I quietly replied hoping it would disguise my uneasiness. I couldn't show him any weakness or else he would try to take advantage of me again.

"Yes, I can see that you aren't afraid of me and are, in fact, quite courageous. I must admit that I made a big mistake when I considered you weak and naive. I thought that you wouldn't mention our little incident to anyone, yet you spilled the beans to Ariel the first chance that you got. How dare you! Thanks to you she had an abortion and I lost my baby. Thanks to you I almost lost my mate. You've made a huge mistake by screwing with me. I'll fucking make your life a living hell," he growled in anger. My eyes flicked down to his claws that had unsheathed themselves, I knew that he wanted to rip my throat out for the face that he had lost with his mate.

"I just told her the truth. If you really love your mate and care about her, then you'd never even think about touching another woman. You wouldn't even look at me with anything but the purest of intentions. As far as the abortion is concerned, that was her decision. You're only angry because your plan failed, now you're putting the blame for the fallout on me. You want me to pay the consequences of your actions," I calmly pointed out.

"You!" He growled, coming closer to me because he was offended by the truth. I grew scared, thinking that he was going to slap me, but then he stopped and studied our surroundings as if he just remembered where we were. I was lucky that he couldn't do anything to me because there were so many people around us.

"You'll regret this!" He threatened me.

"You're probably right, you have all the power. You can misuse it to harm me in whatever way you deem fit, but I'm not afraid of you. It would be better for both of us if you'd stop chasing me," I retorted as my hands and feet turned to ice, my heart was beating as fast as if I had run a race, but I refused to let my fear show. The moment I let my fear conquer me I knew it would be the day that he would destroy me.

"I don't know why but I'm enjoying our little game even more now. I accept your challenge, just know that in the end you'll be the one to lose. Do you know what? The reward I'll receive for winning will be? Your body. All of your soft, juicy, fuckable holes," he whispered, leaning down closer to me. He was acting as if he was merely talking to me about the wine, but his disgusting comments scared me so much that I was shaking. My hands trembled to the point that I was about to drop the tray when he quickly placed his hand under it, supporting it so that it wouldn't fall and draw attention to what was actually going on.

"Well, well, well, I see that your courage has finally disappeared. What will happen when you're in my bed, where I can do anything that I want with you?" He asked, smirking evilly when he saw how terrified I was. I took two steps away from him , trying to leave, but he blocked my way again.

"Don't tell me you're imagining my length and getting excited? Trust me, my member is bigger than anything you can imagine. You'll enjoy every fucking moment of it. If you want, I can give you a demo," he quietly suggested so no one could hear. I was so disgusted with his comment that I just wanted to slap him hard across the face and tell how much I hated him.

"Raymond," suddenly Princess Ariel stopped next to us with a glass of wine in her hand.

"Hey baby," Raymond replied, changing his entire demeanor from an evil pervert into a polite school boy. It was as if there was a totally different person standing in front of me now.

"What were you talking to this slave about?" She inquired as she angrily glared at me.

"Nothing baby, she was trying to serve me this wine but when I refused she kept insisting that I have one. I was trying to explain that I just wanted to have a drink with my mate," he quickly lied to her as easily as others breathed. My eyes widened in shock at witnessing first hand how quickly he made up that lie to cover himself and portray me as the one that was trying to snatch away her mate. It was wrong, but if she really believed him then it would only mean more trouble for me later. Werewolves were extremely possessive of their mates. Her eyes turned red as she walked up to me.

"How dare you try to seduce my mate?" She snarled, baring her teeth in anger.

"He's lying. I didn't try to seduce him," I tried to explain to her, but she just slapped me.

"You're lucky that we're in a crowded party or else I would show you what happens when you try to touch another woman's mate. If you're so hungry for some dick and want to satisfy your heat then why don't you go and find your own mate? If that won't suffice, then there are plenty of man whores out there for you to choose from. The next time I see you anywhere near my Raymond, trust me when I say that I'll strangle you to death!" She threatened her wolf coming forward in her eyes.

"Come on Raymond," Princess Ariel cooed after staring me down one last time and turned to him.

"Yes baby," he smirked and turned to leave with her, his arm wrapped around her waist as he kissed her cheek. Of course, as expected he turned back and winked at me. My whole body burned with the fury of my rage. He was an evil, wicked man, it was not just him though it was Princess Ariel too. I didn't think that she would be quite that stupid that she would turn a blind eye to the evil actions of her mate.

She had to know everything and understand that he was lying to her, but she didn't want to believe it because he was her mate. So instead, she chose to believe in the beautiful lies that he spun for her. They were desecrating the sacred mate bond by covering for each other's mistakes. That was not love, Princess Ariel had only given herself a false sense of comfort. She didn't even know that when all of this came to an end, she would be the one that would be hurt the most.

42. Mine!!

Elaine

An hour passed while I worked, observing the spectacular celebration. I also noticed that some of the men and women that were in attendance had found their mates, but no one dared to mark each other here. As people said, marked wolves were prohibited inside the palace.

My hand subconsciously went to my mark. The Alpha King had marked me... I thought with a smile on my face. I had always wanted to be marked by him, but not in the way that he had done it. He had not been marked by me so he was not tied to me. I was glad to see the happiness in all of their faces. The positive thing was that the Alpha King and Princess Naomi weren't visible to me anymore thanks to the crowd.

At the same time, I was trying my best not to appear anywhere near them. So I asked June to serve drinks to that side of the hall. Suddenly there was an uproar and everyone was bowing their heads in respect to whomever it was that had walked through the door. I tried to see who it was and I immediately regretted it.

The Opal Moon Pack had arrived. How could I have forgotten about them? When all of the big packs had been invited to the celebration. So obviously the Opal Moon Pack and Shine Moon Pack would also be attending. Though I didn't think that the Shine Moon Pack had arrived yet because I hadn't seen Marvin.

Alpha Fabian and Luna Wilma were the first to enter the hall, holding each other's hands. He had his hand locked possessively around hers while she wore a big smile on her face. She showed off her looks preening over all the attention. People were showering her with compliments. After all, who wanted to be their enemy? Behind them, Natasha entered. She wore a beautiful pink and black gown and had an excessive amount of make-up on her face.

This was the first time that I hadn't done her hair for an event. I wonder who had dressed her and done her hair and makeup for this celebration? As soon as she entered, her eagle eyes began scanning the room for handsome unmated men. When she found a victim that interested her, she went up to them and threw herself into their arms, crushing her breasts against their chest. She didn't waste time flirting instead she just went straight to shoving her tongue down their throat, she always chose younger men.

Perhaps she thought that if she was with younger men, then she could keep them under her control more easily. Even back at the pack, she would take a young man up to her room every night to perform sexual favors. I just shook my head as her display was nothing new, but my hands and feet turned to ice when I saw Lewis walk through the door next. I had forgotten that if the Opal Moon Pack was here, then Lewis would definitely follow shortly behind. I wasn't sure how, but he was able to quickly pick me out of the crowd of wolves and our eyes met. Oh… how could I have forgotten that he could smell me?

"Elaine…" Lewis mouthed. I couldn't hear him over the music but I could easily read his lips. He had an astonished look on his face while a huge smile spread across his face as if he had just conquered the world. I immediately turned away from him. After what he had done to me in the forest that night I couldn't even bear to look at him, my soul trembled even at the mention of his name. Why had he smiled at me? Why was he calling for me? I immediately started walking faster, putting the tray I was carrying down onto a table. I needed to leave the hall as quickly as possible.

"Elaine, what happened? Why are you so nervous?" June asked when I ran into her, but all of my attention was on Lewis. I just hoped that he wouldn't follow me.

"I can't stay here. I'm getting sick. Please tell whoever asks, that I went back to my room to rest," I told June. She agreed that I looked a little pale and told me to take a break, that she would handle the rest of the night without me.

"Thank you," I said in appreciation with a small smile. I was about to exit the hall when someone suddenly grabbed my wrist. I screamed in fear because I knew that it was Lewis that had grabbed a hold of me, but the music was so loud that no one heard me.

"Elaine, I've finally found you," he said with a gleam in his eyes, but upon seeing that smile, I grew even more scared. I jerked my arm away from him to create some distance between us.

"What are you doing? Let me go," I finally managed to jerk away from his tight grip. When I said that, the smile disappeared from his face. The anger in his eyes and that devilish air I had always known instantly returned.

"You've only been living in the palace for a few days and you dare speak to me like that? While living here, have you forgotten whose bitch you really are?" He barked while gritting his teeth. I thought

I had been saved from dealing with him, but my hopes had been dashed. The fear I had lived with for the last eighteen years came flooding back with renewed strength. My fear of Lewis. My fear of becoming his personal whore.

"It's about time that you found this bitch," Natasha's voice interrupted us. We looked back at her in surprise. She walked up to us, holding a glass of wine in her hand as she intentionally exaggerated the movements of her hips in a manner to lure males. It was clear that she was quite drunk already. She winked and blew kisses at men to show them that she was interested in them.

"I wondered why you were so eager to come to the palace! Your only objective was to find this bitch," Natasha remarked, completely draining the glass of wine before picking up a new wine glass.

"Get out of here Natasha! I don't have anything to say to you in front of everyone here. If you don't leave us alone, then I'll do something that we'll both regret!" Lewis warned her. He was down right furious with her, it was clear that something must have happened between them. Usually the evil twins would never dream of speaking to each other like this. Ignoring his threats, she just smiled at him as if she were trying to say that it was time for her revenge. She just wanted to give him some kind of pay back. Taking her eyes off of him, she turned to me. She leaned down to my ear then began to speak.

"I already told you not to get in my way, but somehow even though you're no longer a part of our pack you're still ruining my love's life. You're no longer there, but I'm still unable to gain his attention. I thought that after getting rid of the thorn in my side I would finally get to be with him, but I was wrong. I've come to realize that as long as you are alive, he won't be able to forget you. So now you must die. We all know that you're a leech, so you'll never commit suicide otherwise you would have done it years ago. Looks like I'll have to do the dirty work and get you killed somehow," Natasha rambled. I didn't understand what she was talking about. Who was she in love with? I wasn't even living in the pack anymore, so who was Natasha still unable to sink her claws into? I remembered that she had accused me of sleeping with the man that she loved on the night of the mating ball, but I didn't remember anything about him. Who was he? Wait…Did she just threaten to kill me?

"Aren't you ashamed of what you've done?" Natasha suddenly accused loudly, pulling me out of my thoughts. I noticed that the music that was playing had slowed down, so the people nearby could hear her over it. All eyes had focused on me, I was very nervous because I wasn't sure what Natasha's plan was.

"What do you mean? Please let me go," I pleaded, taking a few steps backward.

"Are you trying to run away because of the shame you feel after killing the Alpha King's mate?" She asked, violently yanking me back by my dress. I was about to fall onto the floor, but I managed to catch myself. Everyone around us heard her and started to whisper. Now they knew that I had been the one that was accused of killing the Alpha King's mate. They were talking about me as they glared with hate in their eyes.

"Wait? She's the one?" One woman asked accusingly.

"No… I'm not…" I tried to explain, but she slapped me across the face before I had the chance. A sharp pain exploded through my head as someone pulled at my hair. I glanced over my shoulder and saw that it was Natasha, she still clutched my hair in her fist.

"Yes, she's the one. She was the whore of the Opal Moon Pack. See how shamelessly she's walking around even after committing such a horrendous crime," Natasha egged on the crowd before pushing me into them. I fell to the floor, my head knocking hard against it. A cry of pain escaped my lips.

"She's a whore?" A Princess asked. None of them knew that Natasha was feeding them lies, calling me a slut, a whore, and a murderer. This was what she meant when she'd threatened to get me killed. She was succeeding too. Everyone had crowded around me to deliver their own punches and kicks to my body all the while saying awful things to me. I didn't look at anyone when I finally managed to get up from the floor. I could feel the blood dripping down my face. I was in so much pain from the blows I had sustained, but it had been their words that had been the most painful. I wanted to scream at them that I wasn't a murderer. I hadn't been the one to deliver that unbearable pain onto him. I loved him.

"YOU FUCKING WHORE!! JUST DIE!!!" A woman shrieked as she threw her glass of wine in my face along followed shortly by the glass itself. It hit me hard, but I was relieved that the glass hadn't hit my eyes.

"KILL HER!!!" Suddenly Princess Naomi yelled, urging them on from the crowd. She was alone, the Alpha King was no longer here to aid her. It was better that he wasn't here otherwise he would believe that I was Opal Moon's whore. I never wanted that rumor to reach him because it wasn't true and he already despised me enough as it was. It hurt me every time that he called me a whore. Princess Naomi made her way over to me while Princess Ariel was enjoying the show from the corner of the hall.

"Wait! Instead of killing her we should ruin her beauty, so that she can no longer seduce men," Naomi suggested as Natasha shared a smile with the Princess. They were obviously working together. That was when I noticed Princess Naomi's maid coming to her with a pair of scissors.

"Cut all of her hair off!" She ordered the maid as I slid back along the floor in fear. Everyone began laughing, I noticed that Luna Wilma tightly held Lewis's arm. Refusing to let him get involved in the matter I guessed. She smiled at him before meeting my gaze, I cried when I registered what she mouthed at me.

"This is your destiny, just like your mother," she mouthed and I froze right there. What? This was my destiny? Why? I hadn't chosen any of this so why was it mine? And what had she meant about my mother? I felt the maid grabbing a hold of my hair, but I didn't stop her. I knew that I wouldn't be able to.

"Now you'll finally look like the ugly bitch that we know you are. Let's see who will look your way then," the maid sneered between laughs. I closed my eyes letting my tears flow. Natasha, Naomi, and the laughter of everyone else in the hall echoed in my ears. She yanked my head back and was going to cut my hair as close to the scalp as possible. When an angry growl broke over the hall, making me open my eyes. The growl came from none other than the Alpha King himself.

In a split second, Princess Naomi's maid had been thrown off of me by the Alpha King. her head to a hard bounce off of the wall. I noticed that her head was bleeding as her lifeless body collapsed to the floor. I started to cry hysterically when I saw the Alpha King, but suddenly a woman, who looked like a Princess, ran over and hugged me tightly which only made me cry harder as I returned the hug. Everyone grew scared and began begging for mercy. Everyone in the hall fell to their knees, lowering their heads in response to the Alpha King's rage.

"WHO THE HELL GAVE YOU ANY OF YOU PERMISSION TO PUNISH OR KILL HER?!!!" The Alpha King roared as everyone buried their heads into the floor, even Alpha Fabian and Luna Wilma were on their knees.

"EVERY SINGLE HAIR ON THIS WOMAN'S HEAD BELONGS TO ME!! SHE IS MINE TO PUNISH!! MINE TO KILL!!" The Alpha King loudly growled. I lifted my head to find that Marvin was here, he stood near the entrance of the hall. He had seen and heard everything. The Alpha King looked over at me then followed my gaze to see that my eyes were fixed on Marvin and that his eyes were fixed on me.

"MINE!!" The Alpha King thundered as he glared angrily at
Marvin. Their eyes met, both of them refusing to look away, it
was like they were in a standoff.

43. Beautiful Scourge

Third Person

The Alpha King Emmett had left the hall for a few minutes as there was a suspicious matter involving rogues that he needed his immediate attention. Gamma Seth and Zach had left with him, while Beta Rex had stayed behind in the hall per Emmett's order. When Beta Rex had witnessed everything the Princesses and noble women were doing to Elaine, he immediately mind-linked the Alpha King. Emmett was already angry thanks to the rogues and it didn't help that his wolf Emil was acting rather odd.

Emmett was unable to leave the palace grounds because his wolf felt restless, Emmett's eyes automatically went to the hall that was far away from where he was. When Beta Rex informed him about what was happening with Elaine, it just added more fuel to the fire, making Emmett charge straight into the hall using his wolf speed.

Marvin had just arrived when he saw Elaine sobbing on the floor, he had clenched his fists in anger. He came here hoping to catch a glimpse of her beautiful smiling face, but what he found was her crying instead while surrounded by evil women.

When Marvin arrived, Princess Naomi's maid had just been about to cut Elaine's hair and just as he was about to run over and stop her the Alpha King entered the hall, running right passed him through the main entrance. He struck the maid's chest with one large hand knocking her away from Elaine. The Alpha King's speed was so incredible, it was like watching lightning strike. Marvin didn't even know that it was him until he stopped to stand in front of everyone. As soon as the maid was removed from the scene a woman wearing a beautiful gown that looked like a goddess ran behind the Alpha King heading straight to Elaine.

There was no doubt that the beautiful woman was a Princess, when Beta Rex noticed her running by he almost forgot to blink. The woman glanced at Rex but quickly diverted her attention to Elaine, making him clench his fists in frustration as he watched her. The woman took in Elaine's condition as she hugged her tightly, trying to comfort her. THe problem was that Elaine's sobs echoed off the walls and the Princess that was hugging her was tirelessly trying to pacify her. Beta Rex, Gamma Seth, and Zach were all standing behind the Alpha King, waiting to receive his orders.

"Please calm down my dear," the woman softly urged while stroking her back trying to calm down the fear that had overtaken Elaine's trembling body. Everyone was shocked to see a Princess hugging Elaine as none of them had anticipated her arrival. Zach's eyes immediately went to Beta Rex, who took a deep breath before looking at Emmett.

"WHO THE HELL GAVE YOU ANY OF YOU PERMISSION TO PUNISH OR KILL HER?!!!" The Alpha King barked as everyone bowed their heads to the floor.

"EVERY SINGLE HAIR ON THIS WOMAN'S HEAD BELONGS TO ME!! SHE IS MINE TO PUNISH!! MINE TO KILL!!" The Alpha King continued to growl loudly. Marvin recognized the crazed look in Emmett's eye, his wolf's eyes had come forward and his claws were extended ready to tear apart anyone that attempted to touch what was his, Elaine. The security Elaine began to feel made Emmett's fury grow to new heights. He wanted to know why she felt so secure, was Emmett the reason for it? Was his presence making her feel secure? He couldn't help but glance back at her, but when he did he noticed that she was looking towards the door. Emmett followed her line of sight and found that Marvin was watching her with no small amount of worry, care, and love, which just made Emmett's wolf furious.

This meant that she only felt secure because of him. Marvin and Emmett's eyes met neither of them blinked. They stared at each other for almost a full minute as Emmett's wolf's eyes grew darker and he roared in Marvin's direction.

"MINE!!" The Alpha King growled as he angrily glared at Marvin. They both refused to be the first one to look away, they were in a standoff. When Emmett's possessive growl entered Marvin's ears his wolf submitted, he dropped down to his knees and bowed his head. Marvin was scared to see the Alpha King's crazed possessiveness as he stared down the crowd because of Elaine. There was no anger in his eyes, there was only hate as the Alpha King looked back at Elaine he glared at her too, making her take her eyes off of Marvin. This made her realize that the Alpha King didn't want her to look at Marvin.

"Oh my Goddess! What's going on here?" Luna Amanda asked when she returned to the hall with Prince Raymond. She was confused to find everyone's heads were bowed so low that they touched the floor, they were acting like they were going to be beheaded any second. Luna Amanda had left the magnificent hall for a mere ten minutes with Prince Raymond, when she returned the atmosphere in the hall had turned into something more akin to a funeral rather than a birthday celebration. Everyone's hearts beat loudly with fear and guilt in the hall. There was pin drop silence opposite from where the Alpha King was standing in a burning rage. Luna Amanda panicked and walked towards Emmett.

"Please calm down, my King. They'll die of fright, you know they can't bear your wrath. Please have mercy on them," Luna Amanda begged, bowing her head as she tried to calm him down, but it was no use.

"THERE WILL BE NO MERCY!! THEY TRIED TO TOUCH WHAT BELONGS TO ME!! EVERYONE IN THIS HALL WILL BE BEHEADED!!" Emmett screamed as everyone's heart started beating erratically. Elaine panicked when she looked up at his face. The statement he had made was clear, there was no room for interpretation. The problem was that there were innocent people in the hall that didn't deserve to be punished. That was when Luna Amanda grew alarmed as did Prince Raymond as Princess Ariel was there. She was going to be beheaded if the Alpha King followed through with his order.

"But my King... My mate..." Raymond started to protest, but quickly shut his mouth when his Alpha King's furious gaze landed on him. Raymond was only going to beg for his mate's life.

"Every word that comes out of your mouth should be sensible, selfless, and worth of my time otherwise you will be standing in line with the rest of these people to be beheaded," Emmett cautioned through gritted teeth. Raymond felt his legs grow weak as he sent a pleading look to his mother, who was now even more alarmed as her son's life was being threatened too. Luna Amanda glared at Raymond, nearly killing him with her eyes before she focused back on the Alpha King.

"Please, listen to me, my King," Luna Amanda said, getting down on her knees and asking for permission which he granted her.

"I won't deny that they're guilty, but they're all Princes, Princesses, nobles, Alphas and Lunas from different packs. If they're all killed then there will be a lot more issues that will arise due to their vacant positions. I don't know what they did, but I think that whatever mistake they have committed may not have been done intentionally. I beg of you to forgive them, consider this their first and last mistake. With me being Luna to all of them as well as being your mother, I beg you to please have mercy on them.To give them one last chance," Luna Amanda pleaded while kneeling before him then lifted her head up to look at him.

"Please," Luna Amanda added, then after her request the hall fell silent. There was not a single sound, not even of someone breathing. They were all holding their breath while they waited for the Alpha King's reply. The only noise that could be heard was that of Elaine's soft sobbing. Emmett turned his back on Luna Amanda to look at Elaine, who was desperately trying to get control of herself so that she would stop crying. Elaine had heard everything that Luna Amanda had said while begging on her knees, but all of this had made her feel guilty.

Elaine looked up at Emmett to find his eyes already on her. Beta Rex, Gamma Seth, Zach, and the beautiful woman gazes flickered back and forth between Emmett and Elaine, who seemed to be communicating with each other using only their eyes. It was as if Elaine and Emmett were alone in the hall while time stood still for the two of them as they looked at each other. Elaine just shook her head as if she were asking him not to punish them, to just let them go instead. Emmett's heart skipped a beat when he saw the raw innocence in her eyes, then she blinked and looked down at the floor taking her eyes off him. Emmett didn't know why, but seeing Elaine with her gaze lowered gave him a strange feeling that words were unable to describe. He hated it when she took her eyes off of him, it only added fuel to the fire. He wasn't able to go against her will. She didn't want him to punish them, so he wouldn't. It was as if he would hurt her if he punished them. His wolf only grew more agitated seeing her in this condition. Emmett turned his gaze on everyone's bowed heads as he made his final decision.

"The bitch that made the mistake of touching this woman's hair, the woman who is in my possession, shall be the one who is punished. Cut off the hand that she used to hold the scissors and cut out her tongue that she used to verbally abuse what's mine," Emmett announced, making everyone's eyes widen. The hair on the back of Elaine's neck stood on end in her shock. He had stolen everything from Princess Naomi's maid, he had made her life worthless. The Alpha King cleared his throat again making it clear that he wasn't finished with his sentencing.

"The most important thing you all need to keep in mind is that if this maid ever commits suicide, then upon her death every individual that is in this hall...all of you will receive the same punishment that she has, with the addition of having your heads removed as well. That is my final judgment!" Emmett announced, making his ruling final. Elaine's jaw dropped, her eyes were still fixed on him as Emmett walked out of the hall he glanced at Elaine out of the corner of his eye.

Zach, Beta Rex, and Gamma Seth followed closely behind the Alpha King, while the Princess lifted her eyes to look at Rex, who turned his gaze to meet hers. All four men left the hall, once they were gone everyone else raised their heads in disbelief. Not a single one of them was without fear. The verdict that Emmett had delivered was a death sentence for everyone there due to the fact that once that woman's right hand and tongue were removed then her life would basically be over then she would definitely try to commit suicide to relieve her suffering. That woman held the lives of every person in the hall, now their lives balanced on the edge of a cliff that they could be pushed into at any time. Everyone stood up from the floor together and thanked Luna Amanda for getting the Alpha King to spare their lives.

She just smiled at them. Prince Raymond who was standing in the corner of the room was stunned to hear the punishment that had been handed down. This had all been because someone had dared to touch Elaine's hair? So if the punishment for that crime was to have the tongue and hand cut off, then the day that Emmett learned that it was Raymond in the kitchen who tried to rape Elaine. Raymond wouldn't just receive the death penalty, he would be severely tortured by Emmett, which would be a hell of a lot worse than the death penalty. Elaine glanced over at Raymond, but quickly ignored him, causing him to clench his fists in panicked fear.

"No matter what happens, I won't let the truth come out. I'll take my revenge on the beautiful scourge," Raymond vowed under his breath, but the fear and panic he felt turned into curiosity. He looked at Elaine with a sly smile as his passion for conquering her ceased his mind.

44. Dream And Kiss...

Third Person

"There's no need to say thank you. Please, rise and continue to enjoy the party," Luna Amanda announced as everyone got up and returned to having fun and behaving normally. As they tried to forget what had just happened, but it wasn't that easy to just drop all of that fear.

Elaine got up from the floor with the help of that mysterious Princess. "Thank you," Elaine said, but the Princess just shook her head offering a small smile.

"There's no need to thank me," she replied politely.

"Elaine!" June called as she came running up to her and pulled her into a tight hug. Elaine returned the hug with all of her strength.

"I'm sorry…I'm so sorry." June cried like a baby in her arms, Elaine smiled while trying to calm her down.

"Why are you sorry? It wasn't your fault. You couldn't have done anything that wouldn't have put you in danger too, so please stop blaming yourself," Elaine assured and June nodded her head. She wiped her tears, finally noticing the Princess that was listening to their conversation.

"I'm so sorry, your highness," June apologized with a bow.

"There's no need for an apology. Elaine is a friend of my brother, so she's also a friend of mine," the princess replied.

Elaine was confused. "Your brother? Who? Who are you?" She asked. June was curious as well.

"I'm the sister of Alpha Prince Vincent. I'm Alpha Princess Rosaline," she introduced herself and both of them immediately bowed to her again. Elaine couldn't believe that a Princess had helped and comforted her. It was only now that she had noticed everyone in the hall was giving her fearful glances and bowing with respect when in her presence.

"Why don't you go and wash your face? And change clothes too?" She offered, Elaine looked down at her dress while touching a hand to her cheek. She looked like a beggar.

"Let's get to work," Elaine said enthusiastically, grabbing a tray again and getting back into the work. Everyone was watching her out of the corner of their eyes, she could feel that the whole atmosphere had changed. There was no longer any abuse, taunting, or hate filled glares.

Natasha slammed her wine glass down onto the table while staring daggers at Elaine, Naomi just dug her nails into her palms in frustration. Her plan had taken a u-turn, she had been close to dying thanks to that slave. It was unbelievable that women of their status had been at the mercy of a slave.

"What's wrong with your brother?" Naomi asked, Natasha glanced over at her mother and brother who were engrossed in an argument. Lewis was angry because Luna Wilma hadn't let him save Elaine.

"That fucker wanted to help that Omega whore! He's become my enemy when it comes to her," Natasha replied, gritting her teeth in annoyance before taking another sip of wine.

"So, after facing that much disrespect, I don't want to stay here any longer. I want to go home," Natasha grumbled in frustration, but Naomi looked at her with an evil smile.

"Why don't you stay and accompany me in some revenge?" Naomi slyly suggested, confusing Natasha.

"How? Don't forget what the Alpha King said. I can't afford to take any more risks otherwise my father will behead me long before the Alpha King has the chance," Natasha pointed out and Naomi glanced back over at a working Elaine with her eagle like eyes that were tinged red.

"Just wait and watch then!" Naomi advised with an evil grin. She gestured to her friend that had thrown the glass of wine at Elaine's head earlier. She smiled back with an evil smile and proceeded towards Elaine.

"Ummm…" She awkwardly cleared her throat and Elaine looked up at her. She recognized her bitchy face, but still bowed in respect due to her status as a Princess.

"I just wanted to apologize to you for what happened. I don't want any hostility between us going forward. So I would love it if you would join us for a few drinks," the Princess proposed, gesturing towards her friends. At the table she gestured to were Naomi and Natasha as well as a collection of other Princesses. Elaine looked over at the table and had the feeling that whatever was going on was a bit fishy. They were all acting normal, especially Princess Naomi and Natasha which was a huge red flag.

"There's no need to apologize, your highness. I hold no ill will towards you so there's no need for me to join you ladies. I do, however, need to continue serving these drinks. My apologies, but I can't accept your humble invitation," Elaine politely replied, declining her request in a way so as not to offend her, but the Princess' friendly mask slipped for a second after hearing the polite refusal.

"See here, you! I'm not asking! I'm ordering you. You are to have a drink with my friends and I and that's final. Do you want to embarrass me in front of my friends? Do you want to disrespect a Princess?" She asked, gritting her teeth in anger while fake tears glistened in her eyes as she tried to make Elaine feel guilty. Elaine looked around the hall and saw that everyone was watching her again, she thought that the Princess was making a scene on purpose to try to cause more trouble.

"Please stop crying, your highness. People will get the wrong idea," Elaine said in a panic and the Princess sent a sly smile in Natasha and Naomi's direction.

"I will if you come and have a drink with us, show everyone that you have forgiven my friends and I," she added, wiping away her crocodile tears. She had intentionally said it loud enough that everyone around could hear, showing that she was the bigger person because she was apologizing to a slave. She smiled as she turned to walk back to her table, towards her friends, and gestured for Elaine to follow her.

Elaine sucked in a deep breath while looking at Natasha and Naomi as she walked over to their table. She was terrified of what would happen when she got there but she couldn't afford to stir up any more trouble during this celebration. It didn't help that she knew that Princess Naomi and Natasha were furious at her.

"Come and have a seat," the Princess recommended. Elaine's gaze shot over to Naomi who didn't object. They were asking a slave to sit with them? She really didn't have a good feeling about any of this, but she sat down anyway.

"Let's toast," She said, offering Elaine a glass of wine that she obediently took. It was strange that Natasha and Naomi were toasting with them. What were they playing at? Everyone began to sip from their glasses but Elaine just looked down into her glass of red wine. The last time she drank wine in the palace, she had lost her virginity. If she drinks again and becomes incapacitated, then she was afraid of what would happen to her this time seeing she was surrounded by enemies.

"What's wrong bitch... I mean Elaine? Drink up, it's not poisoned," Naomi promised, toasting again. Elaine nodded as she took a sip then made a strange face when it hit her tongue. It was awful and had a bitter taste. She wondered if it was because she never drank this type of wine before? She coughed as she finished the glass. She quickly wiped her mouth then noticed that there was a smirk on Naomi's face.

"Wow, I didn't know that you were such an avid drinker. Now it's my turn to apologize. Please, forgive me Elaine and join us in having another drink," Naomi suggested, pouring her another glass.

"No, please I can't drink any more. It tastes awful," Elaine replied, refusing the offer.

Naomi frowned, but she kept herself under control. "Please give me this honor Elaine," she prompted, placing the glass in Elaine's hand. Elaine's face was already red. Naomi gave her a big smile and Elaine knew that she had to drink it.

"Why are you honoring this Omega bitch? Is this part of your revenge? It's so humiliating to sit with her," Natasha whispered to Naomi.

"Just wait and watch. I'm going to get her drunk but I've also added something to her drink. That way she'll embarrass herself in front of everyone," Naomi whispered back. A big smile grew on Natasha's face upon hearing this, now she was having fun.

"This is a fun game," she said, quieting down as she didn't want to interrupt the game. Naomi and her friends politely continued to offer Elaine drinks as a form of apology, until her stomach was full of alcohol. Elaine put her glass down on the table and tried to focus her eyes on them. She was seeing two of everything which wasn't helping. She blinked her eyes a few times and slapped herself on the cheek too, but she still couldn't see anything clearly. She finally decided that it was time to leave.

"Where are you going Elaine?" Naomi asked intentionally only to laugh along with Natasha. Elaine didn't answer them, she just got up. She bumped into someone, but didn't stop. She just wanted to go back to her room, but quickly lost track of where she was going or how to get there. Her fingers played with her hair while her feet moved to the music as she stood in the middle of the hall.

"Hey, I want that bitch to undress herself in front of everyone in the hall.Then they'll see how innocent she truly is!" Natasha crowed and Naomi smiled. Her plan had succeeded.

June's jaw dropped when she saw Elaine's condition. "Oh my Goddess! She's drunk!" She muttered under her breath and decided to help her. Just as she was about to run over to Elaine, it was already too late. Elaine bumped into the Alpha King and didn't even realize it. Elaine looked up at the person but their face wasn't blurry. That didn't seem to matter, what did was that she liked his touch on her waist. It was so smooth. She ran a hand over his chest and looked up at him with a confused expression. Emmett watched her blink rapidly as she tried to get them to focus on his face. His heart fluttered because she was acting so cute. It was a side of her that he had never experienced before.

"Why have you been drinking? How dare you?! You are here to work, not to enjoy yourself. Do you understand?!" He sternly scolded, but she ignored every word he said because she was lost in her own world.

"I asked you a question! Do you understand? Answer me!" He coldly ordered but the only answer he received was her touch. He looked down at her. She was touching him like she owned him. She was doing something that no one else had the audacity to do. He forgot what he had asked and peered deeply into her confused eyes.

"Why..." She began to ask as she blinked her eyes a few more times. "Why do you smell like the Alpha King?" She inquired. He pulled her towards him, crushing her breasts into his hard chest, not even letting air get between them. He leaned down towards her face, only a few inches away from her lips, and inhaled her alcoholic breath.

"Because I am your King..." He softly whispered with an evil smirk. Even though she was drunk, he wanted her to remember that she belonged to him. His smirk disappeared when her small hands came to rest on his cheeks.

"My King..." She murmured with a small beautiful smile playing on her lips.

"I wish this dream was real," she said.

Emmett was about to explain to her that this wasn't a dream, and that he really was there, but before he got the chance he noticed that her eyes were closing and she was touching his lips with her own. His eyes widened in shock because she was kissing him! Naomi, Natash, and everyone else's jaw dropped in shock as they watched their plan go up in smoke.

Princess Naomi became furious and stood up from the table. She planned to go over there and stop Elaine, but she stopped in her tracks when she saw what Emmett did next. Eliane had just touched his lips with hers and he hadn't moved at all. His heart began beating out of control as he lost his mind. This woman did something to him. His hand traveled to the back of her head as he deepened the kiss.

"Yes.... This is all a dream. Forget this ever happened," he whispered into her mouth.

45. Secret and Destruction

Third Person

"Yes... This is all a dream. Forget this ever happened," the Alpha King whispered into her mouth.

Everyone in the hall had their mouths hanging open in shock. None of them had seen the Alpha King kiss someone publicly before. Nevermind an Omega slave and the Alpha King it was scandalous! Some of the couples in the hall found the display so hot that their sexual desire began to rise and their lust wanted to take over.

Emmett's display showed how good of a kisser he was, so good in fact that just witnessing it was enough to seduce any woman in the hall. The way he clutched Elaine's waist, his fingers roaming, softly digging his nails into her soft curves of her waist all while kissing her pink lips made Naomi wet between her legs. She hadn't realized that she was drooling.

Natasha looked at Naomi in shock. "I can't believe that you're aroused by watching him kiss that bitch!" Natasha spat out. Her words drew Naomi's attention, making her both embarrassed and upset with herself. She immediately crossed her legs, but it was no use. Natasha rolled her eyes and grabbed her purse.

"That's enough! Enough is enough! I can't bear it anymore. I'm leaving. My father already left after sending me a mind-link to get my ass back to our pack as soon as possible. I don't know what's wrong with him," Natasha grumbled, sending a last hateful glare in Elaine's direction.

The glare was lost on Elaine of course because she couldn't even see Natasha when she had her eyes closed as she enjoyed the King's attention. She didn't even know that the person whom she was kissing was none other than the Alpha King. Elaine still thought that it was all just a dream.

Naomi couldn't believe what she was witnessing, but she noticed Natasha leaving. She didn't have that option however. She was stuck watching this disgusting display. Her eyes were full of anger. Ariel approached her and placed her hand on Naomi's shoulder.

"Naomi, stop watching them and come with me. Let's get out of here," Ariel suggested, but Naomi wasn't willing to leave.

"Can't you see what that slave is doing? How dare she kiss the Alpha King? He's mine. How could he even let her touch him?" Naomi asked, spitting out questions one after the other, Ariel reached out to grab her hand.

"Don't pay attention to them. Did you forget that you mixed something into her drink? She's lost her mind and doesn't know what she's doing. That's all this is," Ariel explained and Naomi shook her head in denial.

"She may be drunk, but the Alpha King isn't. He's in full control of himself. He knows what he's doing. Plus, I've kissed him many times before, but what they're doing in front of me now, is different from all of the kisses that we've shared. There's emotion in this kiss. So much so that it's bringing lust to the forefront of every wolf's mind that is in this hall. I feel like I'm going to lose the Alpha King..." Naomi replied in a broken voice. Ariel turned her sister so that she faced her to keep her from watching the Alpha King.

"Listen to me very carefully. She is a slave! She is the Alpha King's property which he can use whenever and however he wishes! You are not his soulmate so you have to make him want you. If you keep feeling insecure about all of these little things then you'll lose him forever. At most he just wants her body. That's all. Men are always hungry for a woman's body, they are never satisfied with just one woman. That's men for you. The more you try to control him, the more he'll want to go to another woman. But if you don't try to control him, he'll end up coming back to you in the end. So listen to me and don't take your eyes off the prize. You will be the Alpha King's chosen mate. You should focus on that and not on the trivial matter that this slave poses. Let that drunken whore enjoy these few moments of happiness. You need to focus on the bigger picture," Ariel advised as she tried to remind her disoriented and estranged sister of her purpose. Naomi had lost sight of her childhood dream of her and Emmett being together due to one kiss.

"Are you listening to me?" Ariel asked while looking into Naomi's still confused eyes and tightly clasping her hands.

"Y…yes…yes I understand," Naomi answered with a nod, as she tried to clear her mind.

"Okay, now let's go and have a few drinks. Raymond is waiting for us," Ariel said then tried to lead her to the other side of the hall.

"Okay, I'll join you soon. Just give me a few minutes," Naomi requested, pulling her hand back gently. Ariel decided to give her the few minutes that she asked for so that she could clear her mind and get her thoughts together.

"Alright, we'll be waiting," Ariel softly replied then left, but none of the words Ariel had said stuck in Naomi's mind for long. Her eagle-like, demonic gaze darted to the charmingly beautiful and innocent Elaine, whose lips were still glued to the Alpha King's.

"No matter what happens, I won't give up. The Alpha King was always meant to be mine and he will remain mine. I won't let this little snag steer me away from my goal," Naomi muttered to herself, taking a vow.

Meanwhile back in the Opal Moon Pack…

When Alpha Fabian's car stopped in front of the pack house, Beta Dale, who was driving the car, immediately jumped out of it and ran to open the car door for him but he was too late because Alpha Fabian was already out and he was furious. He stormed into the packhouse with Luna Wilma following behind him. Seeing his Alpha's anger, Beta Dale began biting his nails in nervousness. He could never have foreseen this outcome and was worried about the fallout as he followed the Alpha couple inside. He couldn't believe that Elaine was still alive. They'd been worried about the Alpha King wanting to claim the body of his dead mate, the second daughter of Alpha Fabian who didn't even exist. So much so that they had all thought that Elaine had died in the river, but when they saw her at the party they had all been taken by surprise.

Alpha Fabian went straight up to his room and slammed the door closed, using it as an outlet for his anger. He was furiously searching around the room needing something to break to help him release more of the frustration after what he had witnessed in the palace.

"My dear, please calm down," Luna Wilma softly cooed, following him into the room and walking towards him.

"CALM DOWN?!!" Alpha Fabian whipped around and snapped at her. She was so startled by his reaction that she didn't dare get any closer to him.

"DIDN'T YOU SEE WHAT HAPPENED?!!!" Alpha Fabian asked, closing the distance between them, but Luna Wilma didn't answer.

"DID YOU SEE IT OR NOT?!!" Alpha Fabian screamed at the top of his lungs. Beta Dale was standing just outside the room, listening to every word with a lowered head, but he didn't dare interrupt an argument between his Alpha and Luna.

"Y...yes...I saw..." Luna Wilma quietly replied, her voice faltering. She lowered her gaze as he gritted his teeth in anger. He wanted to strangle her, but instead he just turned away from her, taking a deep breath before turning back.

"I TOLD YOU!!!" Alpha Fabian yelled in her face. "I TOLD YOU NOT TO KILL ELAINE!! I WAS GOING TO HANDLE HER MY WAY, BUT YOU WOULDN'T LISTEN TO ME!! YOU NEVER BELIEVED IN ME. NOW YOU'VE SEEN WHAT HAPPENED!! YOU TRIED TO KILL HER BY THROWING HER IN THE RIVER AND NOW SHE'S THE POSSESSION OF THE ALPHA KING!!!!" Alpha Fabian roared, but she still couldn't meet his eye.

"What were you thinking? What was going on in your head when you tried to kill her? You wanted to remove her so that you could

336

bury that secret forever, right? The problem is you can see the results of your hasty actions now can't you? You've fucked everything up royally now! She's still breathing, she's still very much alive, and the worst part is that she's now under the PROTECTION of the Alpha King. She's now LIVING in the palace, the very place that you hoped to keep her away from when you attempt to kill her. She's living where our end begins. We are going to reap what you've sown with your hasty actions. Tonight I saw the first signs of our ruin at the palace. We will be destroyed once the truth finally comes to light," Alpha Fabian warned, recalling what happened to Princess Naomi's maid when she was about to cut Elaine's hair, Emmett had punished her harshly for such a small transgression.

He recognized the madness in the Alpha King's eyes, the intoxication, the craze that had arisen in the Alpha King only for Elaine. That terrifying scene wasn't just running through Alpha Fabian's mind, but Luna Wilma also trembled at the thought of what had happened. She shook her head in disbelief and wiped the sweat off of her forehead.

"No, that won't happen. I never thought that she would survive being thrown in the river. It never even crossed my mind as a possibility. You know that when someone drowns in that river, their body is never recovered. It was the perfect way to get rid of her. Someone must have saved her," Luna Wilma countered, frantically waving her hands in the air.

"DOES IT REALLY MATTER WHO SAVED HER?!!!" Alpha Fabian spat as he grabbed both of her arms tightly.

"The real issue is thanks to your jealousy, anger, and insecurity she's alive and under the Alpha King's protection. Now he's the only one with the right to kill her, but instead he decided to make her his slave. I think he did that in order to exact his revenge on her for a crime that she didn't even commit! His perverse need for revenge is going to doom us all! As long as she remains alive, our lives are threatened and it all happened because of your direct actions," he accused, violently pushing her away, making her back hit the nearest wall. She was trembling badly as she thought about the future that Alpha Fabian had just spoken about.

No one in their pack knew that Elaine was still alive and living in the palace serving the Alpha King. They had all been living peacefully thinking that they had handled the situation by successfully lying to the Royal Pack. The problem was as long as Elaine was alive there was a chance that one of their lies could be uncovered and the truth could be brought to light. Luna Wilma took a deep breath trying to gain control of her emotions as she moved away from the wall and walked up to Alpha Fabian.

"No matter what you say, I still believe that what I did was right. You're still only thinking about your position as Alpha, that's it. While I'm thinking about the pack, my children, and our future. I believe that some secrets should remain buried no matter the consequences," Luna Wilma said, but Alpha Fabian was barely listening, he was still far too angry. With those final words, she turned and left the room.

46. Regret And Kiss

Third Person

Lewis had been sitting inside his car outside of the packhouse for the last five minutes, he didn't want to go inside, instead he waited for Natasha to come home. After about fifteen more minutes, Natasha's car arrived and he exited his car to head towards her's before the car had even come to a stop. He dragged her out as soon as the car came to a halt.

"WHAT THE HELL ARE YOU DOING?!!!" Natasha shrieked as she struggled in his hold. Her continuous squealing was stopped by a slap to the face. She put her hand over her cheek and stared at him in disbelief.

"You...you slapped me..." She mumbled in astonishment. "YOU FUCKING SLAPPED ME!!!" Natasha barked, rage blazing in her eyes. Lewis grabbed her tightly by the jaw making her swollen cheek even redder.

"I'M SORRY!! I'M SORRY THAT I JUST SLAPPED YOU WHEN IN TRUTH I SHOULD STRANGLE YOU THEN RIP YOU APART!!!" Lewis screamed, peering into her eyes with a murderous rage.

"WHY?! BECAUSE YOU COULD NOT SAVE HER?!! BECAUSE IT MADE YOU FEEL WEAK, PATHETIC, AND USELESS WHEN YOU HAD TO OBEY THE COMMANDS OF OUR PARENTS?!! OR IS IT THAT YOU COULDN'T GO TO ELAINE WHEN THE ALPHA KING WAS STANDING IN FRONT OF HER, ABOUT TO TAKE OUR LIVES OVER THAT STUPID FUCKING WHORE OF AN OMEGA?!!" Natasha screamed at the top of her lungs, peeling Lewis' hands off of her before shoving him away.

"Yes, you're right. I do feel like a weak, pathetic, useless piece of shit because today I realized the truth. I've been holding onto the dream of somehow being able to bring her back into my life, but I finally understand that this is absolutely impossible. She's the sky and I'm the earth, doomed to desire her from afar with the knowledge that we can never truly be together. *She* belongs to someone else. She's become someone else's possession, property, and passion. Today I realized that I had the last eighteen years to spend loving her. I could've given her the respect that she always deserved, but instead I insulted her, forced her to do horrible things, and even tried to rape her. I thought that there would be a day when she would obey and bow down before me, but that day never came nor will it ever come. I've realized that I made a huge mistake. I've lost the one person that I've always wanted, now I'll never have her. I wanted to be loved by her," Lewis admitted with a sad laugh while looking up at the sky then suddenly stopped. Natasha was scared by his psychotic behavior.

"Le…Lewis…" Natasha stuttered as she took a few steps in his direction before he grabbed her by the throat. She struggled for breath while staring into his eyes which had gone completely dark.

"And now I'll never get another chance thanks to you and mother!" Lewis growled in a low, deep, and threatening voice. For the first time in her life, Natasha was scared of Lewis. He seemed to be exposing a part of himself that he had kept hidden, it was only being revealed now that the possibility of Elaine being part of his life was beyond the realm of impossibility.

"Wha…what are you saying? Let me go!" She managed to get out as she continued to struggle against his grip.

"LEWIS!!!" Alpha Fabien barked as he came out of the packhouse having been attracted by the noise of their shouting match. Luna Wilma ran out behind Alpha Fabien when she saw what Lewis was doing.

"LET YOUR SISTER GO THIS INSTANT!!!" Alpha Fabien commanded in his Alpha tone so that Lewis had to follow his order, but he just shoved her down to the ground. His gaze went to both of his parents. Luna Wilma appeared concerned while Alpha Fabien was down right enraged. Without saying a word Lewis just climbed back into his car and drove out of the pack. Natasha coughed badly and her face was flushed as she tried to get her breathing regulated. Luna Wilma stood next to Alpha Fabien.

"This all happened because of you. I told you to give Elaine to him, to make her his personal whore, but you refused to listen to me. Now look! He's gone crazy in her absence. I've lost my son due to your actions," Luna Wilma sneered, going back to pack house.

Meanwhile back at the palace…

Princess Rosaline was enjoying a glass of her favorite white wine while sitting comfortably near the counter. As she was appreciating the subtle hints of melon the wine was known for she also enjoyed the scene in front of her. She was glad that her decision to come to this party hadn't been a fruitless endeavor.

Rex, Seth, Zach, and even June were all watching Elaine and the Alpha King out of the corner of their eyes, pretending as if they weren't enjoying the show. When suddenly a man entered the hall who found the scene quite interesting. Everyone noticed Alpha Prince Vincent's arrival with his extraordinarily handsome appearance which was hard for any woman to resist. They bowed respectfully at his approach, but didn't get any reaction as he moved with a devilish smile plastered on his face towards a spectacle that was a rare sight.

"Ooh... if I had known that everyone was going to have a chance to kiss the beautiful Elaine, I would've been here since first light this morning waiting in line. Instead of being fashionably late," Vincent remarked, forcing Emmett to break the kiss, but more than that, what Vincent said irritated the Alpha King to no end. He wanted a chance to kiss her? Emmett thought. Did he mean for her to be kissed by other men? His wolf growled in a show of aggression and Emmett couldn't agree with him more!

"Now it's my turn," Vincent suggested as his sly hands slipped around Elaine's waist, but Emmett shoved his hands away as he pulled her closer to his chest.

"Fuck off!" Emmett snapped in irritation. No one but him would kiss her! Elaine's head was buried against his chest but she didn't seem to have any idea what was going on around her.

"What? Fuck off? Where? I'm your guest. How can you be so rude? It's as if you want to keep all of her kisses to yourself," Vincent expressed his displeasure and Emmett's mind was stabbed by his words. Did he really want to keep all of Elaine's kisses for himself?

"No, it's not like that," Emmett argued, pushing her head away from his chest and giving her a weathering glare even as she was closing her eyes. "She's the one who kissed me. I don't want anything to do with this woman," the Alpha King countered, planning to push her to the floor.

"That's perfect! So let me try my luck. Let me taste her," Vincent replied with a big smile. Vincent was about to make a grab for her again now that his friend had pushed Elaine away. Until Emmett quickly collected her and held her tightly against him again causing her breasts to crush into him. He could feel her round breasts and hard nipples in this position.

"NO!" He barked at Vincent at the top of his lungs even though he didn't even know why.

"WHY?!!" Vincent shouted back and everyone rolled their eyes as they watched the two of them fight over an Omega slave.

"Oh my Goddess! I can't believe how they are speaking to each other in such a familiar way in public. I can't tell who is the King and who is the Prince," June murmured quietly but Seth heard her. He quickly slipped in beside her seeing as she wasn't standing that far away from him.

"Yeah, I also wonder why they are acting like that! It feels like I'm wasting my time spying in this place," Seth said, sighing dramatically.

"Hey, I don't think that you're wasting your time. Don't give up just because they're arguing. I heard that this is a common occurrence between them as they're best friends. I'm sure that you'll be able to complete whatever mission has been assigned to you," June assured as she tried to motivate him to not give up while placing a hand on his broad shoulder in comfort. Seth was surprised by her response. How did she still not get that he was joking? Was she that gullible?

"Yes, thank you," he replied, holding in his laughter and dragged his attention back to the Alpha King.

Vincent crossed his arms over his chest and glared at Emmett. Why did I shout at him? Why didn't I just let Vincent kiss her? Emmett wondered. His gaze roamed over the hall. Rex, Seth, Zach, June, and Rosaline were all watching them closely, everyone was eager to understand what was going on.

"I mean, this woman belongs to me as she's my slave, my property. Don't you dare touch her. Plus, she also smells so bad that you wouldn't be able to stand it. Her hair is dirty and greasy. Her figure is chubby rather than curvy. She tastes bad, not sweet. You won't like her. She isn't your type," Emmett spat out every excuse he could think of in one breath. Listening to all of this, everyone watched the couple in confusion. They were standing close, even though she smelled? He seemed to be enjoying her warmth and curves even though he said that she was chubby? He wasn't even allowing air to pass between them and he had been kissing her only a few minutes ago even though she didn't taste sweet?

"Really?" Vincent inquired with a raised eyebrow and an antagonizing smile. Emmett noticed everyone was circumspectly doing the same.

"YES!! SO WHAT?!" Emmett snappled while pushing Elaine into June's arms.

"Take this drunken woman out of my sight. Don't let her step foot back into this hall for the rest of the evening. There are plenty of maids, so there is no need for her to be here. Just get her out of here," he Alpha King ordered and June nodded. She held onto Elaine as she led her out of the hall with a bit of difficulty as she wasn't able to walk in a straight line. Vincent smirked at Emmett, getting an angry glare in return. Emmett just walked away from him.

"Hey, wait. Are you angry with me?" Vincent asked, following him.

"Did you not hear me the first time? Fuck off!" Emmett repeated.

"Oh please! I know you're joking!" Vincent said with a laugh as they both started drinking together.

47. Gossiping Bitched!

Third person

"**B**e careful. Hold onto me tightly and try not to wobble too much otherwise we'll both fall," June told Elaine even though she wasn't able to concentrate enough to understand a word that she had said. June continued to hold a tight grip on Elaine's faltering body as she received no help from her drunk friend. She was taking Elaine straight to the servant's quarters, not to the Alpha King's room seeing as no one was allowed to go there. They only made it part of the way down the hall before they had to stop, Elaine had gone unconscious due to whatever drug Naomi had put in her drink.

From the time Marvin had entered the palace, his eyes had been glued to Elaine. Standing hidden in a shadowed corner, trying to avoid the Alpha King's possessive gaze, he kept an eye on her movements about the hall. That was also the reason that he had witnessed the full extent of their passionate kiss. The scene had made him feel so consumed with anger and jealousy that he hadn't realized that he was gripping his glass tightly until the glass shattered and a shard of glass pierced his palm. He had hoped to get Elaine alone so he took advantage of the opportunity that presented itself when he saw June helping her out of the hall.

His father, Alpha Alfred was talking to the other Alpha's while Marvin stood by his side, but only his body was present his soul and mind were completely focused on Elaine. With a fake smile to prove his sincerity he excused himself then followed June out of the hall, remaining about a 30 meters distance from the two women. When suddenly he saw Alpha Prince Vincent walk up to them. He halted his steps and quickly hid behind a wall.

"Alpha Prince…" June said, shocked to see him there after he was given an explicit warning from the Alpha King to stay away from Elaine. She tried to bow her head to him, but was unable to do so due to trying to keep Elaine from falling to the floor.

"Don't worry about it. I can see that you're a bit encumbered so don't move or else you'll both fall. It looked like you could use some help so here I am! Come on, I'll carry her," Vincent suggested then immediately scooped Elaine up into his arms, taking her to June's room. He had already gotten permission from Emmett to help. If he hadn't then he knew that he would create even more of a ruckus.

Marvin angrily clenched his fists, he knew that he couldn't approach her with Vincent around. At the same time, his father was bothering him via mind-link to come back to the hall so that he could join the Alphas' conversation. All of this was just fucking with his head and making him unbelievably irritated. This had been his golden chance. If he couldn't get to her today, then he didn't know when he would be able to get another chance to gain entrance to the palace again. He had to head back to his father quickly before someone spotted him acting suspiciously, but he had memorized the way to June's room.

Upon entering the bedroom Vincent looked for a place to lay Elaine down. June was fixing the bed, pillow, and sheets which she hadn't done before leaving this morning because she had been called to help Elaine in the kitchen. June was rather ashamed that the Alpha Prince was seeing the condition of her meek room. Vincent was heading towards the bed when Elaine seemed to regain consciousness and started to panic and wriggle in his arms. He didn't understand what was wrong, but Elaine opened her eyes and placed a hand over her mouth in alarm.

She kept wiggling in a more frantic state which caused Vincent to hastily place her feet first on the floor and she ran into the bathroom. Listening to the sound of her vomiting, Vincent started laughing. He had expected after she had drank so much that she would definitely feel the need to vomit, especially because she'd never drank alcohol before.

"My job here is done. I should go. You take care of Elaine," Vincent advised. June nodded in agreement as she ran inside the bathroom to check on her. Still chuckling, Vincent left the room and headed back to the hall.

The Alpha King was barely able to tolerate this boring birthday party with all its happy couples dancing, kissing, and flirting. Honestly, the entire event was fucking with his head due to the fact that most of the couples were mated and marked. Marked werewolves were typically not allowed in the palace, but today being Luna Amanda's birthday party happened to be one the few exceptions a year that all of the werewolves were allowed to attend.

After finishing discussing important matters with some of the other Alphas, Emmett was sitting at a table with a glass of wine in his hand, totally frustrated. Rex, Seth, and Zach were sitting with him and were just as frustrated at seeing all of the couples in love. They tended to not like the things that Emmett hated and one of those things was mated couples. Vincent rejoined the group and quickly noticed all of the frustrated men which caused him to roll his eyes. He took a seat beside Emmett and poured himself a whiskey.

"She's just throwing up, but don't worry she's fine," Vincent informed Emmett only to end up attracting everyone else's attention except for Emmett's. Rex, Zach, and Seth were shocked to learn this unexpected information. Vincent gave them a smirk like he was saying 'now do you see my game?'.

"I didn't ask you a thing," the Alpha King coldly pointed out.

"I know, but I thought that you would be worried," Vincent remarked while adding ice cubes to his whisky and was waiting for the consequences of his comment.

"WHY THE FUCK WOULD I BE WORRIED ABOUT THAT WOMAN?!! STOP TALKING ABOUT HER!! MY MOOD IS ALREADY RUINED ENOUGH AS IT IS!!!" The Alpha King barked, Vincent just nodded while sending a look to Rex, Seth, and Zach.

"So what's wrong with you three? I get that Emmett's angry, that's his permanent state of being. But why are you guys annoyed? Why do you three hate these beautifully adorable couples? I'm not sure why, but I feel like I'm at a funeral instead of a birthday party! Is it really too much to ask for you to laugh a little and smile?" Vincent teased, rolling his eyes at the other men at the table, the three only nodded in response. Vincent knew it would be of no use trying to convince the three of them to change their minds.

"Did you hear? Elaine tried to seduce Prince Raymond?" From afar, the Alpha King's ears picked up the voices of two maidservants gossiping. The conversation was overheard by not just the Alpha King, but Vincent, Rex, Seth, and Zach. Emmett lifted his gaze immediately in interest, but didn't look at them or they were going to figure out that he was listening and stop talking.

All of them sat there pretending like they were just relaxing while everyone's ears were perked and their eyes focused on any minute change in Emmett's expression. To his inner circle the Alpha King looked like the human embodiment of the calm before the storm. He was facing the opposite direction of the maids but Zach could see them from his seat.

"Oh my Goddess! Really? How do you know?" One of the women asked as she tried to get to the bottom of the matter. Maids were always eager to get the latest gossip.

"Princess Ariel and Prince Raymond were overheard by Princess Naomi's maid while they were quarreling. Prince Raymond told Princess Ariel that Elaine tried to seduce him. First, she had the audacity to kill the Alpha King's mate, but apparently that wasn't enough. Now she's tried to get in between Prince Raymond and Princess Ariel. It looks like she has her eyes set on Prince Raymond. She really is a witch!" The woman finished in a whisper, but it was clear that Emmett and everyone else at his table had heard every word.

After hearing all of that, Emmett's head felt like it was about to explode. He clenched his fist, trying to get control of his anger. Finally Emmett got up from his seat and looked over at them. The maids weren't aware of the reaction their gossiping had caused. Rex, Seth, Zach, and Vincent got up to see what was going to happen next as well as to reel in Emmett if the need arose.

"Wait Emmett, what's wrong? Don't tell me you..." Vincent began to say, but Emmett didn't listen to him.

"Rex, announce to everyone that the party is over!" The Alpha King ordered and Vincent buried his head in his hand.

"Oh… shit…" He mumbled as he watched Emmet exit the hall with large heavy strides.

"What do you think he's doing? Where's he going?" Vincent asked Zach in a broken voice as his plan to enjoy the night with Emmett was now ruined. Normally Emmet never drank at this type of function, instead he just opted to stay in his room, this time everything had been ruined by those gossiping maids.

"I think he's going to get Elaine," Zach stated the obvious. Vincent yanked at his hair in frustration as he glared back at the maids who were still laughing and gossiping.

"Zach, go and bring those gossiping bitches to me. I'll fucking kill both of them!" Vincent ordered. Like a robot Zach bowed, went to follow his orders, in just a matter of seconds they were thrown at Vincent's feet.

48. Worthless Dignity

Third Person

Elaine came out of the bathroom a while later to find June waiting for her with a damp towel. She gently wiped her face and noticed that Elaine was able to open her eyes and seemed to recognize where she was.

"How are you feeling?" June asked.

"Better, thank you so much for bringing me here," Elaine replied. "I'm glad that the Alpha King didn't see me in this sorry state. I don't think I'd be able to get over the embarrassment if he had," Elaine continued, giving June a hug to sincerely thank her.

"Ummm… Elaine…" June began, but her throat went dry when she realized that Elaine honestly didn't remember a thing. She wanted to tell her the truth, but before she had the chance Elaine started talking again.

"Would it be possible for you to go get me something to eat? I think getting some food in me would make me feel a lot better. Anything will do. I just want to get rid of this weird taste in my mouth from all the vomiting," Elaine asked, holding her head as if she was in a lot of pain. June immediately started to search for the chocolates that she then offered to Elaine.

After eating them, Elaine felt better and smiled at June. "Those were really tasty, thank you. I've never eaten chocolate before," Elaine thanked her as she ate more. Her mouth was full of chocolate when June decided to reveal the truth of what happened.

"Elaine, I need to tell you something," June nervously began.

"Okay, please go ahead," Elaine replied, her voice remaining casual.

"Actually, the thing is…" She began to explain, but got nervous and closed her mouth again.

"What?" Elaine asked, shoving more chocolate into her mouth.

"YOU KISSED THE ALPHA KING!!" June blurted out, freeing herself of the stress. Elaine's mouth dropped wide enough for a bug to fly into and her eyes were so wide that they looked like they were going to pop out. She immediately ran back into the bathroom and spit all of the chocolates out because she wouldn't be able to swallow it now. Then she returned to the room and stared at June with disbelief.

"I did, what?" Elaine asked again.

"You kissed the Alpha King in front of everyone in the hall," June repeated only this time more slowly.

"OH MY GODDESS!! WHAT HAVE I DONE?!!" Elaine shrieked, jumping around in the room in a mixture of angry frustration with a healthy dose of very added in.

"Oh my Goddess! Oh my Goddess! Oh my Goddess! Why am I still alive? I should be dead! What the hell have I done?" She was unbelievably upset and was on the verge of crying.

"Elaine, please calm down…" June tried to console her friend. She made her sit down on the bed as she sat beside her.

"How is this possible? I can't even imagine kissing the Alpha King," Elaine sputtered, her whole body trembling in fear. She couldn't remember standing in front of the Alpha King and daring to kiss him in front of everyone.

"I embarrassed myself, didn't I?" Elaine asked, wanting her friend's honest opinion.

"Not really…" June replied, not daring to look her in the eyes.

"I get it. I embarrassed myself so badly that I'll never be able to look him in the eyes again," Elaine muttered dejectedly and June sighed as she nodded her head in agreement.

"AAAAHHHH!!!" Elaine screamed in frustration, while rolling around on the bed like a cat. She had no room of her own that she could hide in. No matter what had happened in the hall, she had no other choice but to return to the Alpha King's room at the end of the day. She had no idea how she was going to face him from then on. He hated her and it was already clear that he didn't want anything to do with her, yet she had kissed him like a tramp that was looking for the perfect opportunity to take action. She had thought that it was all a dream as it had been her childhood dream to kiss him, to be able to kiss him like he was hers, but it had actually happened. She was slowly beginning to piece together the events of the evening though they were all still pretty blurry.

"Elaine, it's okay. You just need to try to forget what happened," June suggested in a worried tone. That's when Elaine stood up from the bed, startling June.

"Oh my Goddess! What's wrong? What are you doing now?" She nearly screamed in her panic.

"I've decided that I'm going to apologize to him," Elaine stated with all the confidence that she could muster. Shocked to hear that, June approached her.

"Do you even know what you're saying? Are you still drunk? You're talking about going to the Alpha King to apologize! Please come to your senses, he's beyond furious with you. Maybe you should wait until at the very earliest tomorrow? That way he has a chance to calm down a little," June advised, shaking Elaine as if to get her out of her drunken haze.

"I'm fully aware of my actions, June. Don't worry about me. I have to apologize or else I won't be able to breathe comfortably with all of this guilt," Elaine explained to her. Eventually, June understood her point.

"Okay…okay go. I know you want to give him an explanation for what happened tonight. Best of luck," June said, giving her one final hug.

"Thank you so much, you're a true friend," Elaine replied, returning her hug. "Okay, I'm leaving. Take care," Elaine said, pulling herself away and leaving the room. June lay on her bed thinking about what would happen to Elaine. She didn't have to go back to work for the evening because the Alpha King had given her the rest of the evening off to take care of Elaine.

Elaine left the room and was trying to walk quickly, even though she had a terrible headache due to all of the alcohol she had consumed. She already suspected that the ladies at that table had spiked her drinks with something but there was no way that she could've denied them without being severely punished.Though at the moment she fully regretted listening to them at all. She was also planning what she would say to the Alpha King when she found him. She couldn't help but wonder what hateful things he would spit at her this time as she attempted to gather her courage.

"The King must be very angry," she mumbled, unable to keep her body from trembling. "He must think that I did it all intentionally or that I would've kissed any man that I stumbled upon," she continued mumbling to herself. This entire situation was causing her to go crazy with fear. She wasn't focused on her surroundings when a big hand pulled her in the opposite direction and her back hit the wall. A scream was about to leave her mouth but before it had a chance a hand covered her mouth.

"Elaine, it's me, Marvin," he whispered softly with a big smile on his face. He had finally gotten to talk to her! Elaine's eyes widened in surprise at seeing him here. She immediately removed his hand from her mouth.

"Marvin! What are you doing here?" She asked in disbelief while frantically looking around to check if anyone else was watching them. He was in a part of the palace that was prohibited for outsiders to freely venture into. If someone saw him here then he was going to be in a lot of trouble.

"I would go to the very depths of hell to find you," he said lovingly while cupping her small innocent face in his big hand.

"You've no idea how I've spent my days without you. The past few days have been hell," Marvin murmured, kissing her forehead. Elaine flinched slightly at the touch. It wasn't the kiss itself that

356

bothered her seeing as he had done the same thing many times in the past, but after being marked by the Alpha King Elaine didn't want whatever this was to continue.

"Please, you need to go and never come," Elaine urged Marvin in a panic.

"What are you talking about? The only reason I came here was to see you. I came to tell you that I'm going to get you out of this hell hole soon. We'll be together again soon," Marvin tried to reassure her with a big smile, but Elaine frantically shook her head.

"That's not possible. You'll never be able to do that," she softly argued.

"Why? I can do it and I will. I have a plan," he eagerly pointed out.

"No, you can't. I've been accused of murdering the Alpha King's mate. I may be standing here breathing in front of you, but I'm not truly alive. I'm basically dead. I'm slowly dying a little more every moment that I'm here. Be that as it may, on the day that I attempt to escape or commit suicide that will be the day that the lives of every member of the Shine Moon and Opal Moon Packs will come to an end as well. Too many lives hang in the balance, a lot of them are innocent just like you. I can't risk your life for the sake of my selfishness. I wouldn't be able to live with the burden of your death. I would die the day you died because of me. So please stop, leave this place and forget about me," Elaine implored with tears in her eyes. She didn't want to face all of the pain and sadness that she was holding in her heart, just wanted him to go.

"What are you saying? You're sacrificing your life for mine? Why? I don't deserve it, Elaine. No one in those packs deserves it. Every person that belongs to either Opal Moon or Shine Moon Pack is responsible for your current predicament, even myself. I want you to be able to live the life that you deserve. I promise that I can help you," he argued, but Elaine helplessly shook her head.

"No! You don't understand. You'll never be able to save me, I'm no longer my own person. I belong to the Alpha King now. No matter where I run, he'll always find me. He's bound me to him. I'm his forever," Elaine explained and Marvin frowned.

"What do you mean, Elaine? You are no one's! I love you, you're mine!" He asserted, grabbing her arms as he stared into her eyes with disbelief. How could she say that she was owned by another man? She knew that he had loved her since they were children. He had always made his feelings for her known. Elaine's trembling hand went to her hair that was covering her neck. Marvin's eyes followed her hand.

"He..." Elaine began to say before glancing up at Marvin.

"He marked me," she explained, showing him the mark on her neck. Marvin's mind went completely blank, he felt as if someone had stabbed him in the gut. His eyes focused back on Elaine's which were full of tears. She felt like she had cheated him.

"No... it's impossible," Marvin stammered as his heart broke in his chest. Elaine's tears escaped when she saw how upset he was.

"Marvin... please..." She pleaded as she reached out to touch his arm to explain the situation to him, only he had suddenly pinned her against the wall.

"I said...it's impossible!" He repeated, now Elaine was scared as she looked up into his eyes, that weren't just hurt but shone with a crazed light.

"You're still mine," he growled and the next thing Elaine knew, her lips were being crushed by Marvin's. She closed her eyes against the attack but opened them again when she realized what he was doing. She struggled and moved her head from side to side making any attempt she could to get away.

"Marvin…What are you doing? No!" She exclaimed, looking at him with fear.

"Please, let me…." Marvin stumbled over his words with red pleading eyes and messy hair. He truly had completely lost his mind.

"Please…let me kiss you," he begged, then without waiting for a response kissed her again. She tried to push him away, but she wasn't strong enough. She forced herself to stop struggling because she didn't want to attract any attention. Marvin wasn't even supposed to be in this area of the palace and she didn't want to get him into trouble. She was holding back both her tears and fear.

Suddenly she felt a dangerous aura fill the hallway. She used all of her strength to push Marvin away when she realized that the Alpha King was there. She looked to her left and found him standing a little ways down the hall. Marvin also saw the Alpha King, his wolf quivered in fear at the sight of him there. The Alpha King's growl from earlier in the hall echoed in his mind. Elaine felt like dying when she saw the King's wolf's eyes focus solely on Marvin. His claws had come out too. He was going to kill Marvin.

"My K…king…" she stuttered, trying to explain the situation to him but it was too late. Emmett was already charging towards Marvin. Marvin took a few steps back in fear, he knew that his death was approaching him swiftly. Just as Emmett's claws were about to tear open his throat, Elaine jumped in front of Marvin with her eyes tightly closed as she knew that it would be her throat that was going to be torn out. However, the Alpha King immediately pulled his hand back when she got in his way though he wasn't quite quick enough. A scratch was left on her neck, just deep enough to make her bleed. The Alpha King couldn't believe that she jumped in between him and Marvin, saving him. She slowly opened her eyes with a whimper. Her eyes met with the Alpha King's furious, possessive, and crazed one's.

"Move!" He ordered but she shook her head weakly.

"I'm sorry but I can't," she argued, continuing to protect Marvin.

"I said move! I won't repeat myself again!" He growled, she glanced down at his claws that were elongated and bloodthirsty.

"Please forgive him. I beg of you," she pleaded with him, but it was no use. He was just going to yank Marvin out from behind her if she continued to refuse to move.

"I WAS THE ONE WHO SEDUCED HIM!!" Elaine falsely admitted which made the Alpha King stop. Marvin was shocked to hear her say that.

"I'm the one who called him here. He wasn't willing but I..." She explained only to have the words get stuck in her throat, she couldn't believe that she was lying and to prove to the King that she was a whore.

"I seduced him. I kissed him first. He's the victim here. This isn't his fault. I should be the one that's punished. Please let him go," she said all of this without looking him in the eye. Marvin had been about to confess that head been the one who had kissed her. That she hadn't seduced him. Elaine was just lying to save him, but before he could Rex appeared.

"Alpha," he said with a bow.

"Remove Alpha Marvin from the palace. From now on he is strictly prohibited from my home. He'll also never be able to step foot in the Royal Pack again. If he decides that he is above the commands that I've outlined for him, then he'll be beheaded!" The Alpha King announced. Marvin's jaw dropped. He was never going to be able to see Elaine again..

Rex dragged Marvin down the hallway then out of sight. Elaine watched intently before Marvin's hurt face disappeared. She had lost her one and only well-wisher, forever. He was the first person in her life that had loved her and cared for her. She continued to stare at the spot that he had been with pain in her heart. That was when the Alpha King moved to block her view of the spot where Marvin had been, taking the last few moments that she'd ever be able to see Marvin from her. She looked up at him ready to face the consequences of her 'actions'.

He grabbed her hand tightly then dragged her down the hallway, she didn't try to protest. After confirming in his mind that she was a whore, there was nothing else left for her to say. His bedroom door closed firmly behind them then he pushed her away from him. She saw that there was a long, thick whip already laid out on the bed, Elaine knew that it was meant for her. She was already familiar with the sting of a whip and how it felt as it pulled at your skin and made you bleed. The pain of it was almost unbearable. Her tears began to run uncontrollably down her cheeks when she watched him pick it up.

"Come here," he ordered, positioning her to stand in the middle of the room for her to receive her punishment. She followed his every command with her stumbling feet.

"Remove your clothes," the Alpha King said, making her eyes widened in fear.

"W… what?" She asked.

"I said remove your clothes. A whore like you doesn't deserve to wear clothes to shield your worthless dignity. Now that you've confessed that you're a whore, there's no need to keep up the pretense. Undress yourself otherwise you can wander the palace with torn clothes, for all I care. It makes no difference to me. It's your job to strip for men, so this shouldn't be a big deal for you," he directed. After listening to him, more tears fell that she hadn't even realized that she was still holding on to.

Everything was ruined. She'd lost everything. She would never be able to prove to the Alpha King that she was innocent. She had ruined everything with that one sentence. Her hand went to her top and slowly she started to lift it. He stood in front of her and watched as each curve of her body was slowly revealed. She let her top fall to the floor until she was only standing in a long skirt. His eyes travel up to her round breasts that weren't covered with a bra because she never received one from Princess Naomi's maid. She immediately used her arms to cover herself in embarrassment.

She flinched when he lashed the whip against the floor. He was telling her without words to drop her hands otherwise the next lash of the whip would be to her body. She sobbed in fear, but couldn't bring herself to move her arms. Suddenly, the Alpha King charged towards her, dropping the whip onto the floor. She closed her eyes in fear thinking that he was going to beat her using his hands instead when she opened her eyes she heard him moan.

Emmey pulled her towards him and kissed her neck. It was like she had cast some type of spell on him. His mind suddenly switched from anger to lust. She threw her head back from the heat that hit her body making her crave for him more. Even though he had been ready to kill her, his wolf was getting horny and the way that Elaine's body was responding only added more fuel to the fire. His lips sucked on the side of her neck that wasn't marked. Her wolf was growing excited, thinking that he was going to mark them again then they would finally mate. She bit her lip trying to hold in a moan that was gathering in her chest that would let Emmett's wolf know that she was ready. This was the best feeling that she had ever experienced. She forgot her state of undress and dropped her arms leaving her breasts exposed to his gaze.

"Oh… fuck," Emmett whispered then he suck his canines deep her neck, marking her for a second time, as he ran a hand over one of her breasts. She grabbed his arms for balance as a loud breathy moan of pleasure escaped Elaine. The feeling was making her crazy. She couldn't understand how her situation had changed that abruptly but she fucking loved it. He pulled her slender body to him then licked playfully her blood, making her moan.

He couldn't believe what he was doing! It was as if she was ready to mate him. His wolf was yearning to be marked by her at that moment. But no! He wasn't ready to let this woman dominate him! He only felt like this because he was mateless and a mateless wolf was always trying to find their mate. His wolf was trying to turn him into a man whore.

Her blood oozed out of the bite on her neck as she started to feel dizzy. His name emerged on her neck in bold capital letters, showing his claim on her after he marked her for the second time. She closed her eyes, embracing the darkness. What was happening to her?

49. Erotic Dream

Third Person

Emmett squeezed his eyes shut when he realized the full extent of his horniness, essentially he was seconds away from ravaging Elaine. Her wolf was tantilizing his wolf by sending signals that she wanted him to fuck her. He could smell her arousal.

"Control your wolf otherwise I won't be able to control mine for much longer if she continues on like this. I want to fuck you so bad..." He whispered into her ear and Elaine swallowed hard. She knew very well what her wolf wanted. She was provoking his wolf, but in all of the wrong ways. She felt his hardness pressing against her stomach.

"I'm sorry. If you leave me alone, then maybe I'll..." She began, but got distracted when she felt him kiss her throat. She moaned loudly, completely losing her train of thought while he drove her crazy. His hand traveled down to her thighs, but she closed them tightly before he could touch her private area. Emmett stopped to study her face which was red with embarrassment.

"I... I'm sorry," was all she said before she ran out of the room at full speed. Emmett watched as she ran away then looked down at his hand. Bringing his hand to his nose, he inhaled her scent then growled as his dick twitched and hardened further.

"Let's go and fuck her!" Emil suggested getting desperate, seeing Emmett was slowly losing control.

"No! She doesn't want it. Didn't you just see? She ran away from us!" Emmett snapped as Emil growled at him.

"She ran away because you didn't grab her in time!" He barked. Emmett regretted letting her go so easily, after all hadn't she been the one that seduced him?

"Give me control, I'll go correct your screwup," Emil suggested.

"No! I know what you'll do. Don't you dare forget that we don't touch a woman without her permission," Emmett reminded him sternly, Emil glared at him in his mind.

"But she's your fucking wife! No matter what you think, she's ours. Go and fuck her. Her wolf... she wants me... " Emil almost howled, sounding desperate.

"Why do you think that?" Emmett asked as his heart began beating faster. He also felt that there was something special going on between their wolves. Her wolf was as strong as his and they had both been desperately trying to connect with each other.

"I don't know and I don't fucking care. I want her, that's all that matters. We need her!" Emil snapped, gaining control over Emmett.

"What! No! Emil!" Emmett yelled as Emil overpowered him, taking charge. He exited the room with an excited smile.

"Emil! What are you planning to do?" Emmett shouted as the wolf could be a merciless monster. The way he took charge, it seemed like he had plans for Elaine and was dead set on executing them after her wolf had seduced him.

"I'm going to give her what her wolf wanted," Emil answered simply with a sly grin on his face.

*****

Elaine felt dizzy when she fell to the floor.

"What just happened? Why was my wolf trying to seduce the King's wolf?" After she confessed all of those lies, he hadn't even wanted to see her face. He hated her so much that he wanted to whip her as punishment, but everything changed the moment she started to undress. All of a sudden he kissed her mark, marked her again, then tried to touch her down there.

She looked back towards his room and knew that after the scandal with Marvin, he wouldn't let her sleep in his room. She hadn't meant to seduce him but the moans had just slipped passed her lips, she hadn't been able to help that she'd gotten so aroused. She knew that he wouldn't want her scent around him after the lies that she told him. She glanced at his door that was probably closed to her forever now. She had to get out of this hallway and away from him, but she didn't know where she could go.

She thought about June, hoping that maybe she would let her stay in her room, but if Elaine did that then June could be punished for letting her sleep there. Without any other options, she decided that she would just sleep on the floor in the hall. When she got there, she saw that the maids were gathering all of the decorations and other scattered items left over from the party. Upon her entrance, everyone's eyes went straight to her neck where Emmett's name was embossed in capital letters.

They began talking about her amongst themselves. Elaine immediately placed her hand on her neck to cover his name while lowering her gaze then continued to walk out of the hall towards the garden. The longer she stayed around people, the faster the rumors would spread. When she entered the palace gardens she was glad to see that it hadn't rained today and that Zach wasn't anywhere to be found to shoe her out. She sat down in the grass and traced her fingers across her neck where his name was.

It would be impossible to hide from him now that she belonged to him. Everyone was going to know that little piece of information by morning. Elaine didn't know what to do. The palace had become extremely dangerous for her, she didn't have any allies to protect her from those that were surely going to be enraged by her new mark. She also felt insecure over everything that had happened with Raymond and all the advances he had made in the past. That worm of a man was waiting for the first opportunity to get her alone so that he could take advantage of her. She raised her head to stare up at Emmett's window that was closed and the light in his room was off.

Maybe he went to sleep after she left. Even though she was away from him, she felt safe whenever she looked at his window. She laid down on the grass facing the window, but tears started flowing from her eyes again. She never thought that something like this would happen. After proving herself to be a whore he couldn't even look at her. Nevermind, be willing to share the same air as her, he'd probably feel like he was being poisoned. She brought her knees up to her chest as her gaze never wavered from the window. She knew that she was being stupid. It was foolish to expect something that had always been closed to her to suddenly open. Despite that she still wanted to see him, even if it was for the last time. Those thoughts plagued her as she drifted off to sleep.

*****

"Aaahhh…." Elaine arched her chest with a seductive moan when she felt a hot mouth on her breast. She had closed her eyes for just a moment, and now someone's tongue was playing with her nipple. She felt so good as her whole body was flooded with pleasure. She couldn't believe that a dream could feel so real!

"Ahh… It feels so good. Don't… stop!" She cried out in excitement, enjoying her dream. Emmett looked up at her face as his mouth continued pleasuring her breast.

"See! Didn't I say that she wants it?" Emil asked proudly while Emmett was lost in a pool of lust when he heard her moan. What he was doing to her felt so good that he didn't want to stop. The problem was that he needed to get control of Emil before Elaine woke up and realized that she wasn't dreaming and that a lusty wolf was licking her, sucking her, and would soon be fucking her.

"Stop, you bastard! She thinks that she's dreaming. She's not aware of what's actually going on," Emmett tried to explain to his wolf, wanting him to move away from her, but Emil just ignored him.

"So what? Don't be stupid. Her wolf wants me and I want her too. That's it. Once we fuck her, then she'll crave more," Emil argued making Emmett frowned.

"You fucking jerk. Don't cross that line. You're talking about forcing her into having sex!" Emmett yelled and Emil didn't like what Emmett said.

"It's not force. It's a need. We need her. If I don't do this, then you'll be the one who ends up doing it," Emil said as he lifted Elaine's skirt up.

"Fuck… she looks so delicious. Don't you want to eat her?" He asked, Emmett's mouth watered at the sight of all her smooth skin. Emil's lust added fuel to his desire. He was going to devour her violently and she wouldn't be able to stop him.

"Let's do it. I can't wait any longer!" Emil said excitedly as he pulled his monster out of their pants. He was going to hurt her with his massive length by ramming it into her without letting her adjust first.

"No!" Emmett growled, finally taking control back as his eyes turned back to normal and his wolf's eyes vanished. He sucked in deep breaths as he looked at his length that was too close to Elaine's dripping pussy. He was totally turned on even though she was sleeping. He couldn't believe that her wolf had gotten out of control like his.

"What the fuck? Let me out!" Emil was frustrated since he couldn't finish what he had started. Emmett ignored him and just buried his nose in her exposed chest.

"So sweet," he mumbled, still feeling uncomfortable from his hard on that he was rubbing against Elaine's pussy. It was hard for him to keep himself from fucking her when she was giving him full access, but she was sleeping. He cursed himself for losing control over his wolf.

"Ahh…" She moaned in need, Emmett noticed when she started to open her eyes. She was going to realize that this wasn't a dream!

When she finally opened her eyes, everything was blurry. As she blinked to get her eyes to focus, Emmett immediately put his hand over her eyes so that she couldn't see him.

"Mmmmm..." She tried to move her head so that she could see, but he kissed her lips to stop her. Elaine stopped wiggling, but she knew that this kiss was real. She was enjoying it, Emmett was shocked when he felt her return the kiss. He tightly closed his eyes as it triggered him further. He couldn't even tell her that it wasn't a dream. She would have yelled and fought him if she knew the state that she was in. She deepened the kiss as Emmett's heavy body laid on top of hers, touching her hardened nipples.

Why was this woman such a good kisser? Emmett asked himself, kissing her neck, and decided to wake her up so that he could have sex with her if she agreed. He was on edge when Emil suddenly snapped at his internal question.

"I don't think I need to tell you the reason for that! She told us that she seduced Marvin. That fucking bastard was kissing our woman!" Emmett's eyes shot open at his wolf's reminder. He pulled himself away from Elaine as everything came rushing back to him. She kissed Marvin! He felt disgusted again as his anger came back at full force.

He zipped up his pants then pulled her skirt and top back down. After he fixed her clothes so that they were back in place, he stormed out of the garden. He wasn't going to forget what she had done.

"I've lost my mind because of you! Don't lust after that woman again," Emmett snapped at Emil.

*****

Elaine jumped up from the ground as the feeling of freezing cold water hit her square in the face, soaking her and startling her awake at the same time. Someone had thrown a bucket of water on her while she was sleeping. She wiped the water from her face and looked around. It was five in the morning and a woman stood in front of her that she'd never met before but her face seemed quite familiar. She resembled Princess Naomi's maid as if she were her sister or another close relative.

"The time to rest is over, bitch!" Elaine heard Princess Naomi's say as she walked up to her. She had a huge smile on her face as if she had just finished conquering the world. Elaine got up from the ground and bowed her head.

"Hurry up and put these clothes on, so you can get ready for a job that was made just for you," Princess Naomi remarked then threw a piece of clothing at Elaine that was quite transparent.

"I...why would I wear this dress? These clothes are for..." Elaine stopped speaking as she was unable to get the words out.

"What? Are you ashamed to say the word? If so, then I'll do it for you," Princess Naomi snidely cooed as she came closer. "This is a dress for a slut which I have specially ordered just for you," Naomi replied, laughing with her maid alongside her. "From this day forward, you'll have to wear these clothes," Princess Naomi commanded before she turned away to leave.

"But why? I'm more than satisfied with the clothes that I'm wearing now. I don't need different clothes. I could spend the rest of my life in the dress that I'm currently wearing. I don't want to wear this," Elaine told her. After listening to her Naomi stopped and glanced back.

"Does this mean you're disobeying the Alpha King's mate?" Princess Naomi asked with a cocked eyebrow. When Naomi's words registered, Elaine's hands and feet became ice cold. She had just referred to herself as the Alpha King's mate. What did that mean? Last night Elaine had dreamed about the Alpha King touching, kissing, and licking her. She had a sneaking suspicion that it hadn't actually been a dream but now...

"The Alpha King's mate?" Elaine asked.

"Ohhh...Sorry I forgot to tell you. I spent the whole night in the Alpha King's room. I eased his stress with the help of my body and love...all night. At the same time, he declared that within a week's time he was going to choose me as his mate. I'm the Alpha King's future mate. That means I'll be your Luna Queen," Naomi revealed with a shit eating grin. The ground crumbled from under Elaine's feet. She looked up at the window that was still closed. Tears rolled down her cheeks when hearing this. After everything that she'd been through, he had chosen Naomi. Last night had all been a dream, none of it was real. He hadn't come to her in the garden.

She wasn't sure why, but she felt like he was watching her. She couldn't see him, but she sensed that he could see her somehow. At last, the day that she had feared had arrived. Naomi was about to become his mate and Elaine was to become a...

"A whore!" Princess Naomi exclaimed, finishing Elaine's thought.

"I'll be his mate and you'll be his whore," Naomi said pointedly and Elaine examined the transparent cloth that she was holding in her hands. Now she understood why she had been given such a ridiculous dress to wear, something that was only for women who worked in brothels.

"The Alpha King has given you the title of his whore. You are his personal whore!" Princess Naomi squealed, emphasizing the word whore.

"From now on, I'm your mistress and you'll have to obey everything I say. You'll be wearing this type of dress, that's an order. If you disobey my orders, you won't be allowed to wear any clothes at all. You will be left naked. So, from this day forward you'll come to the palace only to work then you will leave immediately after you've finished working. There will be no need to enter a spare room to change clothes, you'll change clothes in this garden," Princess Naomi ordered then left, her new maid threw Elaine's bag in her face which contained her wedding gown, towels, and a few other essentials. She was taking revenge on Elaine for what had happened to her sister.

"If I had any control over this situation, I'd have you killed right here. Thanks to you, my sister's hand and tongue were cut off. Her whole life has been ruined. Now Princess Naomi has imprisoned her in the basement of our packhouse so that she doesn't commit suicide. All this happened because of you! I hope that the same fate befalls you!" Princess Naomi's new maid spat out, cursing Elaine. She left, Elaine remained standing in the same spot. There was nothing good left in her life now. What was there left to live for?

She lifted her eyes up to that closed window again. She hadn't known that Emmett was with Naomi all night. The thought of it pierced her heart like a thorn. She hoped that it wasn't true, but it seemed like he had chosen Naomi while she was being pushed from slavery to life as a prostitute. She had run away from Lewis to escape the life of becoming his personal whore, yet in the end she couldn't run away from her fate. Now she was to become Emmett's whore. Staring at his closed window for the last time she picked up her bag from the ground and went to the nearby pond.

From that onwards, she would have to bathe here. She quickly took a bath and changed into her new clothes behind a tree, but after putting them on she realized that they were terrible. The top was completely transparent. Such dresses had been given to Nora to wear in the Opal Moon Pack. Elaine took off the clothes while panicking. She couldn't wear these clothes. She hadn't even been given a bra to wear and due to the transparency of the cloth, her breasts and nipples were clearly visible.

It was better to die than to wear a dress like that, but death wasn't an option. It was already quarter past five, she had absolutely no more time to waste. She had to start working in the palace as Princess Naomi had ordered. She picked up her white towel and tore it in two. It was quite easy to tear as the towel that had given to her was very thin. She wrapped half of it around her breasts then pulled the top over it. Her waist and chest were still visible, but her breasts were covered. She was satisfied with this. She left her bag near a big tree near the pond and returned to the palace.

50. Feeling Her?

Third Person

When she entered, she was told that a special breakfast had been organized to celebrate the arrival of Princess Rosalie or Rose for short in which Emmett was also going to attend. She was the only one in the kitchen and had to prepare everyone's breakfast by herself. June had been sent to work in another part of the palace, so she couldn't help her. She quickly prepared breakfast and everyone was waiting in the dining room when she finished. June arrived just in time to help her serve the food.

Luna Amanda, Princess Ariel, and Prince Raymond weren't attending the breakfast. According to June, they had all gone to visit Princess Ariel's old pack last night after the party. In addition to Emmett, there was Princess Naomi, who sat next to him, Vincent was sitting next to his sister Rose, Rex was also at the dining table, and Zach was standing behind Emmett.

"I didn't expect you to come, but I'm glad that you accepted my invitation. How long will you be staying?" Emmett asked before taking a sip of coffee. Rex's eyes were fixed on his empty plate, though he listened intently to every word spoken.

"I'm sorry, but I won't be staying long. I need to return home," Princess Rose replied. Rex clenched his fist under the table. His ears were dying to listen to her voice. He felt like he had gone to heaven.

"But why? You've only just visited after being away for almost two years! Why do you want to leave so soon?" Emmett inquired, glancing at Vincent. He gestured for him to try to convince her to stay.

"I agree with Emmett. There's no need to hurry back home so quickly, you could stay here to complete your training," Vincent suggested, placing his hand over Rose's as he tried to persuade her.

"Absolutely!" Emmett said, studying Rose's face which appeared to be in deep contemplation.

"I'm glad you both want me to stay, but I still need to go back home," she argued with a small smile as she denied the two of them.

"But why?" Emmett asked again. Rose was seven years younger than him, he'd watched her grow up in front of his eyes. He used to treat her like a younger sister, but for the last two years she refused to come to the palace. Now that she'd finally come to celebrate Luna Amanda's birthday, she insisted on returning home right away. Everyone at the table wanted to know why she needed to leave so soon. Everyone waited for her answer. She lifted her eyes and looked at Rex.

"Maybe, I just have no reason to stay," was her soft reply, meeting Rex's gaze until his heart hurt over what she had said but he refused to look away from her.

Seth entered the dining room during this conversation and listened to the whole exchange. All eyes were on Rex and Rose and after hearing this answer from Rose, no one had anything else to say. Emmett and Vincent shared a look. Elaine saw the hurt look in Rose's eyes. Yes, she had been hurt deeply.

"Muhm…" Emmett began speaking, clearing his throat.

"No matter what you say, you can't leave so soon, that's an order. Vincent and I have decided that you'll complete your training here in the palace. Vincent will talk to your father. I'm sure he'll listen to Vincent," Emmett announced. After that Rose couldn't refuse. She just nodded her head, now everyone was happy over the fact that Rose was going to stay.

Naomi gave her a fake smile, but there was a lot of anger in her heart because she couldn't bear that Rose was prettier than her. She couldn't tolerate any female that was beautiful being around Emmett and now he had ordered Rose to stay in the palace. She wanted to kick all of the beautiful women out of the palace. Then again at that moment the most beautiful woman in the palace entered the dining room attracting the attention of everyone.

Emmett was still smiling at Rose as he drank his coffee when the intoxicating scent of Elaine entered his nostrils and forced him to look at her. She was wearing a pink colored nightie whose top was completely transparent. Her smooth milky waist was incredibly provocative.

"What the hell?! Why is she wearing that?! All of the males are looking at her!" Emil was furious even though he still admired her curves like a pervert along with Emmett. Why was she wearing that?

It was clear that the cloth she had wrapped around her breasts wasn't a part of the outfit, but the way she had wrapped the fabric still looked attractive. Naomi's jaw dropped when she saw her. She looked even more gorgeous than she did in normal clothes. Princess Naomi had intentionally chosen that type of outfit for her. No one in the dining room was able to take their eyes off her. Naomi was furious, but unable to do anything about it.

"Ummm…" Rose cleared her throat with a slight smile, trying to bring all the men back to their senses. Emmett immediately took his eyes off of Elaine and began drinking his coffee again. He remembered what had happened between them last night. He really had crossed the line.

June and Elaine were the only ones serving breakfast. Elaine gestured to June to serve Emmett because she couldn't bear to be near him after what had happened. She couldn't even raise her gaze to look at him.

"Peach, you look so beautiful," Vincent complimented her in front of everyone with a smile on his face. That made her nervous. He was calling her beautiful? Wearing this dress? She thought people would insult her. She just nodded with a small smile.

"What do you think, Rex?" Vincent suddenly asked. Rex panicked at this unexpected question. He glanced at Emmett from the corner of his eye.

"Yeah…she's beau…" Rex started to say, but he didn't manage to complete his sentence before he noticed Emmett's palm balling up into a fist. He hadn't said anything to Rex, but his expression and his body language were clearly expressing his displeasure at them talking about her beauty. Vincent had a conspiratorial grin on his face when he saw Emmett's changing expression.

"What about you, Seth? Do you think that she's beautiful?" Vincent loudly inquired.

"I…I don't…know, Alpha Prince. I'm not good when it comes to women," Seth replied, wisely saving his ass as he had felt Emmett's fury growing rapidly.

"Oh please! Look at her thoroughly, like I did!" Vincent egg him on with a wink, adding fuel to Emmett's irritation that he was barely holding in check.

"Why the fuck do you need to look at her?" Emmett growled along with Emil, making everyone jump out of their skin. Why was his wolf also furious? Rex immediately got up from his chair and took his place behind Emmett beside Zach. Zach had a smirk on his face when Rex had moved to try and keep himself out of harm's way.

Seth was just as terrified and as Vincent had suggested, he looked her over thoroughly. Emmett's wolf was furious to think that all of the males in the room were olging her body, lusting after her. He never thought that she would dare wear something like that. Vincent just smiled at him then began to eat his breakfast. Emmett glared at everyone. His eyes went to Elaine who still wouldn't look at him. She wouldn't even approach him to serve him. She was currently serving Vincent. His wolf was growing restless at seeing her so close to another male.

"You look very beautiful. I've never seen this kind of dress in my home before," Princess Rose commented to Elaine while touching her pink dress. Elaine smiled at her. She was being very friendly, she wasn't looking down on her like the other Princess was.

"It looks like she's from outside of the palace, perhaps from a brothel. Whores wear that kind of dress. She's a whore," Princess Naomi announced and Elaine grew scared. She had said all of this in front of Vincent and Rose.

"What? A whore?" Both Vincent and Rose exclaimed in unison, this was news to them.

"Yes, the Alpha King has appointed her his personal whore," Princess Naomi informed them all. June was shocked to learn this as well. Everything had changed overnight. Vincent looked at Elaine and she lowered her gaze. He used to call her his friend, but she knew that once he found out the truth he would turn his back on her. No one wanted to be friends with a whore. Elaine looked at Emmett who wore a cold expression. His hate was visible in his eyes. Naomi cackled with glee as she placed her hand on Emmett's. Elaine looked at their hands. Emmett touched Naomi softly. She looked away from the two of them. She couldn't bear to watch them interact.

"Alpha Prince, you didn't know whom you have befriended," Naomi remarked with fake sympathy as she smiled at Vincent. Vincent returned her smile.

"That garment wasn't made for any particular person. The wearer doesn't necessarily have to be a whore. The beauty of this dress comes from the wearer. Her title won't affect our friendship in any way," Vincent replied and Naomi frowned.

"But she is a whore, Alpha Prince. If you remain friends with her, it will ruin your reputation and no one will respect you," she protested. Vincent's smiling face changed into a knowing look.

"Whether she is a whore or a slave, her title doesn't matter. She's still the Alpha King's woman! I'm not friends with her because of her title. The bottom line is that she is Emmett's woman, Princess Naomi. Don't forget that or I'll have to keep reminding you," Vincent pointed out sternly which got Naomi to shut her mouth.

She couldn't argue with an Alpha Prince. Elaine's heart was beating fast listening to all of this. She looked over at Emmett and saw that he was watching her intently without hate in his eyes. He hadn't denied any of what Vincent had said. He seemed to acknowledge that she was his woman.

"She isn't the Alpha King's woman," Naomi repeated in anger, but held back a little because she didn't dare offend him. "Anyone can have her…" Naomi added as Emmett slammed his fist down on the dining table with a ferocious growl.

"She is MY woman! No one else can have her!" He growled in her face, she turned white in fear. Her wolf submitted, lowering her head after nearly giving her a heart attack. Everyone in the room went silent. Emmett's eyes went back to Elaine when he noticed that her heartbeat had sped up. Wait! Has she remembered? Did she know what happened last night? Why was her heart beating so quickly? Her feelings must have changed. She seemed to feel safe and secure, but there was something else. Something Else there, it was pure and untouched. He was trying to figure out what it was that she was hiding. She lowered her gaze again and it caused his heart to skip a beat when he realized what it was.

Love… She had love in her heart, but for whom? He felt her, he felt her emotions, but how? Why? He couldn't understand why he could feel her emotions all of a sudden.

51. My Woman

Elaine

"She's my woman! No one else can have her!" The Alpha King growled in Princess Naomi's face. As soon as I heard those words leave his mouth, the panic in my heart completely disappeared. My wolf was so gleeful that she was jumping with joy. Those simple two words 'My woman' were like a beautiful and lovely song that I was willing to listen to for the rest of my life. My heart leapt with joy and beat loudly, but as soon as I saw the Alpha King gaze at me it was as if I knew that he could hear my heartbeat. I was not sure why but I felt as if he were able to feel me and suddenly I was able to feel him too. What was this?

I immediately looked away before he was able to feel the love I had for him in my heart. I tried to rein in my emotions, there was no way that I could ever reveal this secret to him. The strange thing was that I didn't understand why but I was able to feel his emotions now. How was this possible? I wasn't his mate so how was this didn't make sense? Why did last night's dream seem so real? Had he really....? My face turned red when I thought about my erotic dream.

"Elaine," suddenly the Alpha Prince called me, attracting my attention. Not just mine but the Alpha King's too.

"If you have time, let me take you out for a bit of horseback riding. I'll even take you to the market afterwards," Vincent suggested while finishing his breakfast. A big smile spread across my face as soon as I heard the mention of horseback riding. It had been a dream of mine since I was a child to go horseback riding, but I'd never gotten the chance to go. I couldn't bring myself to meet anyone's gaze.

"Yes, I have time... I..." I began to say, but couldn't complete the sentence before the Alpha King interrupted.

"No! I don't think she has time to waste wandering around with other males. She has a lot of work to do. She won't be able to go with you," the Alpha King remarked, drawing everyone's attention. I frowned to myself in confusion. I had already finished all of the kitchen work and had not been assigned any other tasks. Also when had I ever wandered around with another male? He must've been talking about the time I had eaten and talked with the Alpha Prince in the pack hospital's cafeteria.

"Really?" Vincent asked, raising his eyebrow skeptically at the Alpha King. The Alpha King just gave him an irritated look in return.

"Do you really have work to do?" Vincent asked me directly this time.

"Ummm.... I don't know... perhaps," I hedged, in a dilemma because I didn't even know what my work for the day entailed.

"Yes, she has to work. Today she must clean my office and bedroom. So she will be busy with that. Therefore, she can't go with you," The Alpha King told Vincent, but I was sad. I wanted to go horseback riding, but he was deliberately not letting me go. Princess Naomi smirked at me. She was thrilled to see me so upset.

"Are you really going to allow this slave to enter your office and bedroom? Everyone is forbidden from entering those rooms, isn't that correct?" Princess Naomi suddenly asked, hearing this from her ignited anger deep inside of me. What did she mean? I slept in his room every night, well except for last night and so far I hadn't touched anything in his room. From the way she was speaking, it seemed as if she was calling me a thief.

"Oh Goddess! I guess I'll have to remind you once again that she is the Alpha King's woman!" Vincent reminded Princess Naomi with a smirk as Princess Rose laughed lightly, adding fuel to Naomi's anger. She looked furious. She glared at me with fury in her eyes, I turned away from her. If looks could kill, then I'd surely be dead already.

"Looks like I won't be able to take you horseback riding today. Don't worry though, I'll take you next week," Vincent promised. I nodded my head not only in sadness, but while also clinging on to some hope. I knew he could tell that I was sad as he smiled at me kindly and held my hand. At that moment the Alpha King got up from his chair and came over to us, roughly pulling me away from Vincent.

"Why are you still standing here? Get out! I want both my office and my bedroom to be cleaned immediately. After that I expect you to clean every corner of this palace from top to bottom. I better not find so much as a speck of dust otherwise you'll be spending the next week in a jail cell!" The Alpha King announced as he had moved so close to me that I could no longer see Vincent.

"Okay," I replied.He waved his hand in a gesture for me to leave the dining room. I left immediately without saying a word to anyone. I didn't even say goodbye to Vincent. I entered the kitchen and noticed that June was already there. She now knew that I was a whore. All of the maids were making fun of me, yet she just hugged me. I knew that she found my position in the palace rather tragic, but she advised me to have courage and to never give up. I felt better after talking to her, though I didn't have much time with her before I had to run out of the kitchen while quickly putting my hair up into a bun. I didn't know how I was going to clean the entire palace in such a short amount of time! As I walked through the hall to the Alpha King's room, I passed Princess Rose's room and heard voices.

"Vincent, are you still waiting for Katrina to arrive?" Princess Rose asked, there was concern in her voice. I refrained from stopping to listen to the conversation and kept on walking.

"Yes, I came here to meet up with Katrina and have stayed on because she has yet to arrive. She promised me that she would bring that wooden box to me at the mating ball. That was the only reason that I came to this palace," Vincent replied. The moment that he mentioned the wooden box, my feet stopped of their own accord and I grew very nervous. Now I had to listen to their conversation in the hopes of finding out more about that wooden box.

"I don't understand how she could just disappear like this? She's never done this before. She's the most reliable woman I've ever met," Rose pointed out to Vincent.

"I don't know, but I've sent some of our pack members out to look for her. I'm sure that something must have gone wrong during her journey here otherwise she would never have shied away from her responsibilities. They're looking for her everywhere, but it's like she's just vanished. I'm just looking forward to hearing what good news she has," Vincent replied.

"But what if we never find her? What will happen then?" Rose asked frantically. Hearing the worry in her voice, I peeked around the door.

"That won't happen! I'll never let that happen!" Vincent answered passionately. Upon seeing his face, I became very nervous. Until now, I'd only ever seen him smile and laugh, but the man that was in that room right now was quite scary.

"I've devoted the past fifteen years of my life to looking for that wooden box. I've searched for that thing like a mad dog and now that I know that it's in Katrina's possession, I refuse to let it escape my grasp. I will find her! I will retrieve that wooden box by whatever means necessary!" Vincent grumbled, taking deep angry breaths. Rose tried to calm him down, but he was inconsolable. I left and hurriedly started running towards the Alpha King's room. I didn't know what could have been in that wooden box that would have caused him to be so desperate to retrieve it. He seemed to be obsessed with that box.

So the woman that I met while I was on my way to the mating ball had been Katrina? Vincent hadn't known that the lady, Katrina, had handed the wooden box off to me so that I could give it to him, but I had lost it. I couldn't breathe just thinking about it. If he knew that I was responsible for the missing box, he wouldn't think twice about killing me. It would only compound the issue if he told the Alpha King about it. I was really scared but at the same time I was curious about the situation too. Where had Katrina suddenly disappeared too?

I clearly remembered how the Opal Moon Pack had been following her. When we met she had been running away from them. Had my old pack members harmed her? I didn't understand anything about what was going on. I wasn't in a position to confess anything to the Alpha Prince nor was I in a position to hide anything. With all of these swirling around in my head, I entered the Alpha King's room.

52. His Secret Revealed

Elaine

I'd never entered his room in his absence before, so I took the time to carefully look around. I found everything in the room incredibly beautiful. His intoxicating scent had soaked into every crevice of the entire room. His scent wasn't just driving me crazy, but my wolf was also going nuts for some reason. It was a strange feeling that I had always wanted to experience. Walking further into his room, I gently ran my hand over his bed. This was where he slept every night. After what happened in this room last night I thought that he would never allow me to enter his room again, but he had suddenly ordered me to clean it.

I picked up the blanket to change out the bedding. A moan escaped my lips at how delicious his scent was. I wanted to eat it. I wanted to eat him. I knew that if anyone saw me doing this, they would think that I was mad, but I couldn't stop myself. I'd been crazy about him since I was a child, since the very first moment I saw him. I walked towards his bookshelf. It was pretty large. There were so many books in it that it seemed as if it were a mini library. I loved reading books. When I couldn't sleep at night due to hunger, I only had books to keep me distracted. I've spent many nights just reading books. They were my greatest escape from a dreadful existence. I saw that there were a variety of books on his shelf, I even spotted quite a few romance novels.

I eagerly picked up a book because there was no one there to watch me, especially not Princess Naomi. No one was allowed to enter the Alpha King's room without his permission. The book had been written by an unknown author but when I read the first page I realized that, in every word of the text the author clearly displayed their love in such a beautiful way. It seemed like they were very sad, their heart had been waiting for the one who would complete them. They were impatient, but were willing to wait for that person forever. I wanted to sit there and read the whole thing, but I knew that I didn't have the privilege of time. I wished I had the time to read this. I put the book back as I remembered that Rex had said to never touch any of the Alpha King's belongings.

He was very possessive about his things. I put it back in a hurry because if he found out, then he would be very angry with me. I might even receive some new type of punishment for a new type of transgression. As soon as I turned to put the book back on the shelf, there was the sound of another book falling. Turning back, I looked down at the floor and saw that another book had indeed fallen. When I picked it up, I realized that it wasn't a typical book but a diary. It looked worn, but was very well kept. Just as I was about to put it back on the shelf, a picture fell out of it. I immediately bent over to pick up the photo, discovering that it was of a very beautiful woman with a small child. A smile spread across my lips when I saw the Alpha King sitting in his mother's lap. He seemed to be around two years old and very happy to be with his mother. He still looked the same now, even though I hadn't seen him smile yet. I wish I could see him with the same smile that was caught in this photo on his lips now.

The pages that photo had been tucked between were spread open in front of me, I quickly realized that the diary had belonged to the mother of the Alpha King. She had written his name on the page in bold letters. My fingers traced over his name. It was clear that his mother had started this diary around the time that he was born. I knew that I was reading someone else's diary without permission and that it was wrong, but I still wanted to know what his childhood had been like. I wanted to read about what the time he had spent with his mother was like while I had been washing dishes and clothes in the Opal Moon. I wanted to catch a glimpse of how much his mother loved him while I had been on the receiving beatings from the Alpha and Luna. I wanted to know about the moments in life when he had been happy.

Leaning against the wall, I slid down until I was sitting down on the floor, and read the first page of the diary. The entry was written about the day on which the Alpha King was born. It was a golden day in his mother's life, when she gave birth to the Alpha King. I turned the page and smiled after reading the many things his mother had written, only suddenly my smile disappeared when I turned to the next page. She had written that as soon as she gave Emmett to his father right after he was born, he began crying. His whole body started burning like someone threw him into a fire but as soon as he was passed back to his mother he calmed down and the feeling went away. I was glued to the diary, quickly turning to the next page. An elderly doctor from the pack who was an expert in magic, told the Luna that the Alpha King was precious and his soul was pious.

The doctor discovered that no one other than his mother would ever be able to touch him without causing him pain except for his mate. Discovering this, his parents were terrified. Only a few people knew about it, the truth was never discussed outside that room. It was kept a secret, but when the Luna Queen wouldn't allow anyone to touch the future Alpha King, rumors began to spread in the palace. People began gossiping and other packs also started to hear the rumors. Watching the deteriorating situation, his mother asked a witch to do something to help her son. The witch said that she could make a pair of gloves that, when worn, he would feel no pain from the touch of others. His mother had to sacrifice a portion of her own skin and it would take the witch three days to make them. The gloves would disappear the moment they were put on and they would only be visible to the wearer. Once donned, the effects would not only shield his hands, but his entire body. After donning them, the Alpha King no longer faced any problems and no one suspected a thing. I read that his mother died of an incurable disease when the Alpha King was only five years old.

Tears ran down my face when I realized that she wrote the last entry a day before her death. His mother had written loving words for her don. She had left this diary for the Alpha King to let him know that his mother loved him dearly. Even though he couldn't bear anyone to touch him, he wasn't alone. She would always be with him in the form of those gloves. The rest of the diary was blank. I regret that I even read it now. I never knew my mother, so I didn't know what a mother's love was like. After reading the diary, I realized that though I had been alone all my life, the Alpha King was equally lonely. The way he kept his mother's diary, I was sure that he must read it every night. Now I understood why he wore those gloves while touching anyone. Only his mother and his mate can touch him. When we first met in the hut, he must have been wearing the gloves but I couldn't see them.

I was about to close the diary when suddenly I saw a page in the middle part of the diary that had been written on. It was strange that, after the death of his mother, someone wrote something in the middle of this diary. It was only one page, so I started reading.

"Today is my 16th birthday…" A smile came to my lips when I realized that it had been written by the Alpha King. He wrote it for his mother. "Today I got my wolf, Emil, at the same time I learned the truth. A truth I need to share with you." I wasn't sure why but I was beginning to feel weirdly nervous. What was this truth that he had to tell his mother? He seemed excited to have gotten his wolf. Why was I scared to read further?

"I'm cursed. I've been cursed to never have a mate. I'm the cursed Alpha," my eyes widened in shock as the diary fell from my hands. He...he was...cur..cursed! I picked up the book and read that line again thinking that I had read it wrong but it was true. He had written that he was cursed. He'd never been bestowed a mate by the Moon Goddess, then how could I be accused of killing his mate? How was that possible? It must mean that somehow he found his mate and then someone killed her. Now I could see why he hated me so much. He had truly been granted a miracle the moment his mate appeared only to have me framed with her murder. I put my hand over my mouth not understanding what had happened. I was doomed. I closed my eyes and leaned my head against the wall. He would never forgive me. He would always hate me. I would never be able to earn his love. I kept sitting there like a lifeless objecting as all the hope I possessed drained out of me. Why did this happen to me?

Suddenly I heard footsteps approaching. It sounded like they were heading toward this room. I quickly got up from the floor and put the dairy back. If the Alpha King knew that I had discovered his secret, I didn't know how he would react. I read it without his permission. I picked up a cloth and started dusting off each book. Half an hour went by, but no one came. Apparently, whoever it was that I had heard was just passing by. I cleaned the entire room and was ready to leave, only to find that I forgot to wipe the big portrait of the Alpha King hanging on the wall. It was too high for me to reach, but I couldn't leave it otherwise I risked being thrown into a cell for a week. Standing on the bed was a good option, but I couldn't climb on it and get it dirty.

He could easily smell my scent on it. Instead I drew a chair over and climbed up onto it, it provided me with enough height to easily reach the picture. While dusting the picture my eyes didn't leave his eyes and lips. My face was so close to his. I felt as if he was really standing right in front of me. My finger traced over his lips. At the party I kissed him, but I didn't remember it. It annoyed me. Why couldn't I remember? I wanted to know what it felt when I kissed him. I let the cloth slip from my hand and leaned in closer to his lips. I wanted to know what he felt like.

As my lips were about to meet with his, I remembered something. *'Yes, it's just a dream. Forget it.'* My eyes shot open when I remembered what he told me between the kisses we had shared. He had kissed me deeply. In my panic, I lost my balance as one of the chair legs broke, I was about to fall. I noticed a large knife that had been left on the table next to me, I could have sworn that it wasn't there before. I knew I was going to fall on it. I was going to stab myself! There wasn't even time for me to yell for help, before I landed a large hand grabbed my waist, directing my body to fall on the bed instead. I found the Alpha King hovering over my body. He hadn't let me fall on the knife, instead he threw me on the bed.

I tightly clutched his coat in fear. My heavy breathing fanned against his face. His eyes that were fixed mine traveled down to my lips. Suddenly he leaned down to my mouth and I closed my eyes. It seemed like he was going to kiss me. I was going crazy just thinking about it, when suddenly his lips brushed my ear and I moaned softly. He gently nipped my ear and I grabbed his arms even more tightly, almost digging my nails into him.

"Stop…" I begged, I was losing my mind. I was close to losing myself to him.

"I want to…but I can't…" He whispered and I opened my eyes. He met my gaze with his own and I saw lust. His eyes roamed over my transparent top. It was like he hated it.

"Never wear these clothes again," he said and I let his coat fall from my grasp which he noticed.

"But you said that I was your whore and a whore wears this type of clothes," I replied with a hurt-filled voice. He didn't say a thing in response, his silence hurt me more than any words could. He was the one who had made me his whore. I tried to push him away, but he put all of his weight on me, completely covering my body with his. I bit my lip at our close proximity. I did my best to not let out a moan.

"You don't need to wear these clothes to let everyone know whether you're a whore or not. The marks on your neck prove to everyone that you're mine. I'll mark every inch of your body with my teeth, if I see you in these clothes again. I'll tear the fabric apart, then your body will be covered with my marks. Trust me, I would love to do that. So don't continue to provoke me by wearing this outfit in front of other males," he whispered.

53. Insecurity and Promise

Natasha

It was one in the afternoon and I had only just woken up. I didn't even go to training today because my neck was still so painfully bruised. Lewis had grabbed my throat so violently that for the first two hours I couldn't so much as make a noise. Drinking lukewarm water helped a great deal, at least father allowed me to take the morning off to rest. When I entered the hall after leaving my room, no one was around. Ever since dad and mom had returned from the palace, the whole pack had been shrouded in a strange silence. I had noticed mom and dad's faces in the palace, they had turned completely white, when they saw Elaine there. I had been just as shocked because I had thought that she had died, but that bitch was roaming around the palace like a queen.

394

I didn't know what the big deal was, but I could tell that my parents were definitely hiding something from us. When I entered the dining room, I found my mom still standing where she had been since Lewis had left last night, at the window that overlooked the parking lot. He still hadn't returned and mom was waiting impatiently for him. It had now been more than twenty-four hours since he had left. Dad didn't seem to care because he was still angry with him, but mom was overreacting. I couldn't help but roll my eyes at her antics.

"How long are you planning to stand there? He's not a child. When he feels like coming back, he will," I said walking to the table as she glanced back at me. I placed a sandwich on my plate as I studied her worried face.

"But it's been over twenty-four hours since he left. He didn't even take his Beta with him. He's already threatened to abandon the pack. I'm worried that he might never come home," she came over to me in a panic.

"He's the only one that you care about! You saw him strangle me! I would've died if dad hadn't walked in and stopped him in time. You only care about your son, not me!" I snapped and got up from the dining table without eating a thing and suddenly mom grabbed my arm.

"I LOVE YOU BOTH EQUALLY!! A MOTHER'S HEAR SIMPLY CAN'T LOVE ONE OF HER CHILDREN MORE THAN ANOTHER, YOU'LL UNDERSTAND THIS WHEN YOU BECOME A MOTHER!!" My mom angrily snapped at me from between gritted teeth.

"If that's the case then I want to be a mother," I countered, she stared at me in stunned silence.

"What?" She asked in disbelief.

"You heard me. Now that Elaine's out of our lives, I'm free to do as I please. That bitch made me hold myself back and she's gone now. She won't be coming back into my life to try to snatch my man from me," I told her and she grabbed my both arms.

"What do you mean by that?" She asked and I smiled.

"I thought that I had made myself very clear, mom. I don't have to wait anymore. I want to marry him as soon as possible," I stated clearly then left the room. The insecurity I had felt while experiencing Lewis' madness last night was terrifying. That bitch had made my evil dominant brother a pussy. It wasn't just him, it seemed that every man went mad over Elaine, this just happened to be the perfect time to get my love back. Soon he would be in my clutches then I would be in his arms. I would have him!

Elaine

"You don't need to wear this type of outfit to let everyone know whether you're a whore or not. The marks on your neck are enough to prove to everyone that you're mine. I'll mark every inch of your body with my teeth, if I see you in these clothes again. I'll tear the fabric apart, then your body will be covered with my marks. Trust me, I would love to do that. So don't continue to provoke me by wearing this outfit in front of other males," he whispered. I was starting to get breathless under his weight. He wouldn't let me get up. At the same time, his proximity was killing me. I wanted him to move away, instead he was leaning closer to my lips.

My heart started beating uncontrollably and I closed my eyes when he was an inch away from my lips. Suddenly a knock interrupted the moment, we both looked at the opened door where Beta Rex stood looking everywhere but at us, I was sure that he had seen everything. Oh shit! I immediately pushed the Alpha King away from me and scrambled off of the bed as he stared at me in disbelief because I had pushed him away.

"I'm sorry," I quickly apologized, picking up the cloth from the floor and continued my work. While cleaning the vase, I glanced at him out of the corner of my eye and saw that he was still watching me. I was trying to act like I was calm, but on the inside I was extremely worried that he would shout at me for pushing him away or punish me. I was already tired and hungry since I hadn't slept well last night, on top of that I hadn't gotten a chance to eat breakfast before I started to work this morning. I couldn't afford to receive another punishment.

"I'm sorry Alpha. It's important, I didn't know..." Rex began to explain but the Alpha King got off of the bed.

"Shut up Rex, just tell me what's wrong!" He cut his Beta off and began to fix his clothes that were wrinkled from jumping on me.

"It's rogues, my King. We caught one who was near the boundary to our territory. It was strange that he was alone. I think he's a spy. Zach is interrogating him now," Rex reported to the Alpha King.

His eyes turned red at the mention of rogues. Both men quickly left the room, I was scared to see the devilishly angry look on the Alpha King's face. I'd only heard about rogues in passing as no rogues had ever attacked the Opal Moon Pack. I wondered who the rogue was that dared to spy on the Royal Pack. He must have had a death wish. I didn't know what the Alpha King would do with him.

54. Rogue

After cleaning the Alpha King's room, I started cleaning the hall. June was able to help me as she had finished with her other chores. Several hours had passed, it was now six in the evening and I hadn't eaten anything since the previous day. Princess Naomi had allowed June to eat but not me. Princess Naomi had assigned me one task after another, so that I just didn't have time to eat, while making me cook lunch for everyone else.

Luna Amanda, Princess Ariel, and Prince Raymond had returned to the palace so I had to make enough food for them as well. In no time, it was a quarter past six. Just as I was about to raise a glass of water to my lips, a woman entered the kitchen. She was very tall, broad shouldered, and looked to be around thirty-five years old. Her long blonde hair was so long that it was brushing her hips.

"You've been ordered to clean the stables," she said.

"Who are you? I've never seen you before," June asked.

"I'm a new member of the pack, I don't work inside the palace so the two of you have probably never seen me. The Alpha King has ordered you to clean the stables as soon as possible, because he's about to go horseback riding," the unknown woman told them, then immediately left the kitchen. I put the glass of water back down on the counter and turned to leave.

"AT LEAST DRINK SOME WATER FIRST!" June yelled after me.

"I'll have a drink once I'm done!" I replied, running out of the kitchen. I couldn't suppress my curiosity. I think Vincent and the Alpha King were both planning to go horseback riding. Vincent had been talking about it this morning. I wanted to see the Alpha King riding a horse, but what did I know about cleaning the stables? Why was I being called to clean the stables when he had servants whose jobs were to clean them and take care of the horses? But I had to follow orders. When I entered the stables a few minutes later, there was no one there except me. It was very strange that the person that was meant to care for the horses was nowhere to be found. I began looking for the man because he needed to tell me what to do, when my eyes fell on a horse.

As soon as I got close enough to him, I let him sniff my hand before my hand slid up to caress his nose. He was a gorgeous white horse. I had never seen a horse before today. While waiting for the stable hand to show themselves, I talked to the horse. That was when I caught the scent of blood. My wolf became alerted by this as I proceeded to walk towards the stench to investigate. It wasn't the smell of old dried blood, but the smell of fresh blood. When I neared the corner of the stables I saw a man, he was lying on the ground. He must've been injured somehow and needed help. Maybe, he was the man I was looking for.

I was running towards him when I heard a growl, a vicious growl. I slowed my steps when I realized that there was another wolf somewhere nearby, but why would a pack member shift inside pack territory? Especially in the stables? Taking two more steps forward, I found the man lying on the staw littered ground in a pool of his own blood. He was dead, but he wasn't alone. There was a huge wolf on top of him, it was the same wolf that had killed the man. I thought about running away, but knew it was too late as the wolf had already spotted me. He lifted gaze to glare at me. I didn't know why, but I felt like he smirked at me. Oh... no! I was dead.

June

Elaine went off to complete yet another task without even being able to take a sip of water first. I felt bad for her because Princess Naomi was constantly giving her an endless number of tasks to do. On top of that, Elaine was being given tasks that wouldn't normally be given to a woman. She made Elaine pick up the heaviest items imaginable and clean spider webs out of a store room that no one used. Elaine had been ordered to clean a room by climbing on top of two tables and a chair that were stacked on top of each other, thus she could have very easily been injured. It was only by the grace of Goddess she was safe. Princess Naomi hadn't even let her have a bite to eat all day under the guise of there being too much work for her to complete. In other words, Naomi was openly exploiting Elaine. I had heard that Naomi was doing this because she was soon going to be our Luna Queen. She was about to become the chosen mate of the Alpha King. What would happen when she becomes our Luna? Oh... shit!

"SHE REALLY IS A BITCH!!" I angrily shrieked. I slammed my hand onto the counter knowing that I was the only one in the kitchen. No one was going to overhear me release my frustration.

"Yeah! She really is a bitch!" Out of the blue, Seth appeared beside me, agreeing with me.

"You're agreeing with me?" I asked him suspiciously, he nodded.

"Of course, I agree with you," he added, sounding sincere.

"Wait! What are you talking about?" I was confused, I hadn't mentioned Princess Naomi's name yet he'd still agreed with me. Why would he do that?

"I'm talking about whatever you're talking about," he replied, his words confusing me further.

"But how did you know I was talking about Princess Naomi?" I asked and he suddenly started laughing very loudly.

"Are you making fun of me?" I questioned, growing angry because nothing I had said was funny.

"Ummm...sorry. I just... remembered something," he said, but I wasn't satisfied with his answer. I knew he was trying to make excuses.

"You always ridicule me then try to cover it up by saying that you just remembered something," I told him sternly.

"Well, forgive me. I'll never laugh in your presence again. I never meant to ridicule you, but your actions are so cute that I have a hard time controlling my laughter," he explained. I immediately stared at him in shock. For the first time in my life someone had called me cute, but I knew that I was stupid. Why did he find me cute? He suddenly stopped smiling when he realized that he had just called me cute. The atmosphere between us changed and I instantly lowered my gaze to the floor.

"Ummm... why are you here?" I asked, trying to change the subject so that the awkwardness would end.

"Oh yes, I remember now! There's a meeting in the Alpha King's office, the Alpha King requests some coffee," he revealed. Well, it was a good thing that I was already making coffee then, so I started pouring some into a cup. It was normally Elaine's job but today I would handle this.

"Why did you come here yourself? I mean you could have sent someone else," I inquired. All my attention was on the coffee I was pouring into the cup until I felt a hot breath against my ear.

"If I didn't come myself, how would I find you? It's not easy to make excuses so that I can come see you," he replied and my eyes widened in surprise. I quickly looked over to where he was standing, but he had already left the kitchen. Damn, that man was fast! What had he meant? Why was he searching for excuses to see me? I knew I was being stupid but I was also struggling with something else. Why did I feel so hot? What was he doing to me?

Emmett

I entered my office with heavy steps. Everyone was already there waiting for my arrival, including Vincent. A rogue incident wasn't a small matter. Seth followed in behind me. Zach, who was already frustrated because of the rogues, stepped in front of me.

"Alpha, I've questioned the rogue intensively, but he's a motherfucker. He's been well trained in anti-interrogation techniques to keep his mouth shut. He's not a typical rogue," Zach reported.

"This means that he doesn't fear death," Rex stated matter of factly, at the same time June entered my office with a tray of coffee. I thought Elaine would bring the coffee, but June came instead. She looked at Seth who stared back at her, but they quickly looked away from each other. Though not before everyone in the room noticed.

"The situation isn't as straightforward as it appears. A rogue appeared near the border and was caught so easily? He didn't take so much as a step towards defending himself and was easily captured by us. It can only mean one thing…" Saying this Vincent looked at me with a frown.

"It means that he was deliberately near our border with only one purpose in mind: to get inside our pack! He's on a mission," I acknowledged, finishing off what Vincent was saying. I understood their plan as my mind burst with anger, simultaneously I felt a strange feeling. Something was wrong.

"So he wanted to enter our pack, but why?" Seth asked. I focused back on the conversation in the room while looking at Rex who was mind-linking with another member of the pack. I don't know why but Emil was getting antsy which was causing me to get distracted. Something was wrong, horribly wrong.

"Alpha, there's an issue," Rex reported in a panic.

"What's going on?" Vincent asked, getting up from his chair.

"The rogue isn't in his cell. He's escaped!" Rex informed me.

"WHAT?!!" Zach yelled in shock, the rogue was his responsibility so the escape was his fault.

"He's still in the pack. According to another pack member, he's near the stables," Rex added, there was a crashing noise that attracted everyone's attention. I looked over and saw June, who had dropped the tray on the floor and appeared absolutely terrified. I walked slowly towards her.

"What's wrong?" I asked gravely, she looked like she was about to cry.

"Elaine…" She said and looked at all of us.

"Elaine, what?" I asked in frustration; Emil was growing even more crazed at the use of her name.

"She went to clean the stables as you ordered. She's at the stables right now," June explained, crying in fear as my eyes widened.

"WHAT?!!" Vincent snapped in shock. I immediately ran out of the office, heading towards the stables as quickly as possible. Everyone else was following close behind me.

"I was with you this whole time, so who lied and told Elaine that you ordered her to clean the stables?" Vincent wondered aloud as he ran beside me. I was downright furious because I knew that she was alone with that rogue. He would kill her.

Arriving at the stables, the first thing I saw was Elaine standing in front of the rogue. The wolf was about to pounce on her! He was about to kill her, so why wasn't she trying to protect herself? I ran towards her at full speed. I quickly pulled her behind me until I stood in front of the rogue as his teeth sank into my arm. I grabbed him by the throat with one hand then with the other hand I grabbed his arm and twisted it painfully behind his back. I heard a snap and he howled in pain.

"EMMETT!!! WAIT!!! DON'T KILL HIM!!!" Vincent yelled, getting closer but Emil had already taken charge. I grabbed his head and quickly gave it a hard twist, breaking his neck.

"Alpha," they all stared at me in fear. Emil was still out of control, but I looked back at her. She was staring up at me, but there wasn't any fear in her eyes. She wasn't afraid of me like the others. She seemed to be in shock, then she closed her eyes and fainted. I managed to grab her just in time so she didn't hit the ground. Her face was buried in my chest as I sucked in deep heaving breaths trying to calm myself. My hand went to her head as I looked down at her innocent face. I couldn't believe I had been about to lose her. Why had I saved her? Why?

55. Someone Wants to Kill Her

Emmett

I slammed my office door behind me as I entered at an animalistic speed. Everyone was already waiting for me. I glared at Zach, who came forward lowering his head.

"HE WAS YOUR RESPONSIBILITY!! HOW COULD YOU BE SO CARELESS?!!! HOW DID THAT ROGUE MANAGE TO ESCAPE WHILE UNDER YOUR WATCH?!!" I bellowed at him and with great difficulty, fought to prevent my hands from snapping his neck.

"I'm sorry Alpha. I openly admit that this was my fault, but I left him chained up in the dungeon. Not only were his hands and feet bound in silver dipped chains, but his neck was also chained to the

406

wall. It was difficult for him to breathe let alone try to escape. When I went to examine his cell I discovered that his chains had been broken as well as the bars of his cell, which would have been absolutely impossible for him to do by himself. The only way that this could have happened is that someone helped him escape. Upon further investigation I found that the lock to the basement was broken as well. All of this happened after I had left the dungeon to come and meet you here. Please forgive me. I know it's my fault. I should've left him guarded," Zach reported all his findings with remorse in his voice. Just as he was lowering himself to his knees to ask for punishment, I demanded that he remain standing.

"What you've just told me makes one thing abundantly clear. Whoever freed the rogue, knows the layout of this palace quite well. They're someone that can easily move around the palace and not look out of place. No one would dare to doubt or question them," Vincent admitted with a shake of his head in disbelief.

"This means that our guess was correct. The rogue was deliberately hovering near our border because he knew that he would be caught. He entered our pack on a mission," Seth grumbled.

"It seems to me as if someone wants Elaine dead. Someone can't bear her presence in the palace," Vincent added. As I listened to him, I remembered what had happened earlier when she had been about to fall off the chair while cleaning my portrait. I had seen from afar that one of the chair legs suddenly broke and she was about to fall on a knife that had been placed on the nearby table. The strange thing was that I never allowed a fruit bowl or a knife to be kept in my room, yet both of those things were on that table and the knife had been poised directly at her chest.

"If he was still alive, we could ask him who put him up to this," Rex pointed out under his breath but everyone still heard him.

"It's a moot point, he's dead now. I tried to stop the Alpha King, but he's the Alpha King. He couldn't control his anger and now the guilty man is dead," Vincent said, heaving a deep sigh. I glanced back at him.

"Why are you here? To bother me? The rogue isn't your concern. You're free to leave," I said coldly.

"Poking my nose in your business is my job. Don't you worry, I'll do my best," Vincent replied with a big smile.

"If you're going to continue to act like this then leave. That's an order!" I replied with my own big smile.

"Okay, if it's an order then I'll go find Peach to accompany me, since my best friend is kicking me out," Vincent teased snidely, getting up from the chair. He was going to find Elaine.

"Wait! Don't go!" I stopped him.

"Why?" He replied, testing my patience.

"JUST FUCKING STAY!!!" I snapped.

"Okay, if you say so," he replied, sitting back down dramatically.

"The question is, who told her that the Alpha King was the one that ordered her to clean the stables?" Rex asked and my eyes went straight to June. She flinched a little when she realized my eyes were on her. She was still a little teary from seeing Elaine in that condition.

"You said that there was a woman that came into the kitchen and told you that I ordered Elaine to clean the stables?" I asked her again and she nodded her head yes, wiping away her tears.

"Yes," she managed to answer.

"Was that woman from our palace?" Seth politely asked as if he was trying to calm her nervousness. His politeness caught my attention.

"Yes... yes, there's no need to panic. Just try to tell us everything you can remember. Seth's here with you," Vincent commented while giving a side smile to Seth.

"I'd never seen this woman before in the palace. She said that she was new and didn't work in the packhouse, so we wouldn't have seen her before. Elaine had to follow the order because she said that it came from the Alpha King. Elaine didn't want to be punished by the Alpha King after being tortured by Princess Naomi all day. So she dropped what she was doing and ran to the stables," June informed them with a bow of her head. She told us everything, but when I heard Naomi's name, my mood soured even further.

"How does Naomi fit into all of this? And what do you mean by torture?" I asked, but I realized that she was incredibly nervous about speaking against Naomi. Seth gestured for her to speak openly without any fear, and we all noticed that this woman was comfortable around Seth.

"Well this morning, Princess Naomi was furious with Elaine so she made Elaine wear that pink transparent dress instead of her normal clothes. She's been giving her impossible tasks to do all day, all the while refusing to let her eat so much as a crumb of food. She wasn't even allowed a moment to drink some water. She kept telling Elaine over and over again that she was your chosen mate, and that she was going to be our Luna Queen soon," June revealed. My brain seemed to short circuit after listening to what June had to say.

"What utter bullshit! After everything that's happened this evening, we have to deal with this on top of it?" Vincent growled, rolling his eyes.

"Looks like I'll have to keep reminding her of Elaine's place here until the day I die," Vincent grumbled, irked beyond belief. After hearing all of this, I was also quite furious. I let June leave as I looked down at my arm, which was healing quickly.

"Emmett," Vincent called from next to me, sounding serious. "Someone wants to kill her. It has to be the same person that locked her in that burning warehouse," he reminded me.

"I know," I casually replied.

"Don't you think it's strange that someone wants to kill an Omega slave?" He asked.

"Yes, it's very strange. Something's definitely weird about this entire situation," I agreed.

56. Possessed by my Possession?

Princess Rose

When I returned to the palace an hour ago, I learned that Elaine had been attacked by a rogue. I wanted to check on her and make sure that she was okay, but I was told that she was still unconscious. Vincent and Emmett told me that I was expected to train every day, today would be the first day but I had to solve the mystery of these rogues.

That's why I had secretly gone down to the prison while in my training clothes. Vincent told me he had hired a skilled trainer to teach me the latest fighting techniques. I was sure that whoever my brother had hired would leave as soon as I didn't appear in a timely fashion on the training field.

The lock to the cell had been broken and there were also broken pieces of thick chains laying on the ground. I touched the chains and I sensed that someone hadn't used a weapon, but a magical power to break them. There was also a familiar scent wafting around the cell that I recognized, but I couldn't place. I closed my eyes to try and remember when I felt someone standing behind me.

I immediately turned around throwing a wild punch to defend myself, but he grabbed both of my arms, yanked me towards him, then jerked both my arms behind me. It all happened in a matter of seconds, I was completely subdued in this person's grasp. All my years of training seemed worthless if I could be disarmed in two seconds, it didn't help that the person was none other than Rex either.

"Might I know what you are doing here, Princess?" Rex asked, the second he called me Princess instead of by name, my blood boiled.

"I'm not obligated to answer your question," I tartly replied, freeing myself from his clutches. As usual he was calm, but he stared at me as if he wasn't able to breathe. His eyes were focused on my hair. My hands subconsciously went up to my hair to try and figure out what was wrong. I could feel that my hair was starting to come undone just when I heard a pin hit the ground as my fingers probed my head. Rex bent down and picked up the pin. I wanted to stop him. I didn't want him to see it, but it was too late. He'd already picked it up and was inspecting it.

"Your hair pin," he offered, extending his hand to return the pin to me. Watching him do this, I felt an unbearable pain. I took my eyes off the pin and looked at him.

"Throw it away. I no longer want it," I ordered him. I thought I glimpsed an agonizing sadness in his eyes after what I said, but ignoring it I made my way out of the cell.

"But once upon a time it was your favorite pin. Do you really want me to throw it away?" He asked, I clenched my fists tightly at my sides. I couldn't believe that I had told him to throw it away. I didn't look back at him, instead I just hollered over my shoulder. "Yes, I'm sure. Throw it away. I used to like it but it means nothing to me now. I've stopped living in the past," I replied without looking at him and left. The decision to get rid of that pin was the right one. With the pin gone then maybe the memories would stop haunting me.

After all, he didn't care about me. Like a bodyguard, he followed along behind me at a distance. When all I wanted was to get as far away from him as possible. The moment that I left the prison, I began lengthening my strides as I headed towards the field, that was when Vincent came into view.

"I've been looking everywhere for you! Where did you disappear to? You should be at training," he chastised me, turning into my possessive brother.

"The trainer wasn't here, so I decided to take a little walk," I came up with a quick excuse, knowing that Rex stood behind me and that he knew I had been in the prison. I had to lie because if Vincent learned that I had been in such a dangerous place, he would've been angry with me.

He glanced at Rex. "The trainer is standing right behind you yet you say that he isn't here?" Vincent asked, raising an eyebrow.

"What?" I asked in surprise. I immediately looked back at Rex. He was looking at me without a single emotion on his face. Now I understood why he had followed me into the cell.

"Apparently Rex didn't tell you. Well, it's his responsibility to train you," Vincent laid it out simply, upon hearing him, the ground seemed to slip out from under my feet.

"Vincent! How can you do this to me?" I asked in disbelief and he just smirked.

"I've thrown you into Rex's arms. I would've thought that you'd be thanking me," he whispered before leaving. No matter how much I tried to run away from him, my bad luck just kept pushing us closer.

Emmett

I entered Naomi's room for the first time without announcement or invitation. She stood in front of the mirror trying on different gowns, her maid stood next to her holding a dozen dresses in her arms handing them over to Naomi one by one. Clothes were scattered around her room as if a tiny cyclone had squeezed itself into her closet, then flung the clothes out and this was the resulting mess. The moment she saw me in the reflection of the mirror she turned around in a panic as her maid immediately bowed her head.

"Oh my Goddess! I never thought that the Alpha King would come to my room. My luck has finally turned," Naomi exclaimed running towards me to hug me, but I threw my hands up to stop her advance. She looked insulted at receiving such treatment in front of her maid, so she signaled for her to leave.

"I'm very happy to see you, but if you'd invited me to your room I would've come," she said seductively.

"I've come to inform you that after today you will not be permitted to enter my room," I said. The smile immediately disappeared from her face and was replaced with an angry frown. Given her expression one would guess that her entire life had been ruined by my proclamation.

"Wh…what? I'm forbidden to enter your room? But why?" Naomi asked as tears welled in her eyes.

"It's what I've ordered. You seem to have forgotten your place and are living under the misconception that you'll be my chosen mate," I told her as she blanched.

"But it's true, isn't it? I will be your chosen mate. I'll be the Luna Queen," she murmured, reaching out to touch me as I jerked away from her touch.

"Maybe you misunderstood me. You're one of hundreds of candidates! That doesn't mean that you'll be my mate. Stop spreading those rumors. If I hear that you're spreading rumors about becoming my chosen mate or Luna Queen again, just remember that the punishment for such slander will be worse than you could ever imagine," I sternly cautioned as she started loudly sobbing.

"Yes, I know that I'm only one in hundreds but I want to be your mate. I love you so much and I know that I'm the right choice for you," she argues through tears.

"I'm the one who'll decide what's the right choice for me and what isn't. Stop fooling yourself with these misconceptions and immerse yourself in reality. Oh, and one more thing! You have no right to order Elaine to do anything. She's my slave and I'll decide what tasks she needs to do and what she doesn't. She'll take a breath whenever I order her to and her heart will beat because I will it to. I don't appreciate a third party interfering with her. If I have even the slightest suspicion that you've violated my orders, you'll be expelled from this palace immediately. You're a guest here, don't forget that! You're to never act as a mistress to anyone that resides in this palace!" I explained to her as calmly as I was capable. So that every word would soak into her mind and she wouldn't be able to misunderstand me. I didn't pay heed to her crying, I just wanted to get out of this perfume-filled room as quickly as possible.

"But you said that within a week you would choose your mate. I'm confident that I'm the only candidate qualified to be your Luna Queen. I won't give up! I will continue to fight to win your heart," she claimed with a sob. I just rolled my eyes and quickly left her room. I'd been hearing this same kind of thing from her since she was fifteen. She swore to never give up on me. I had never given much thought to it and as long as she didn't cross the line I could continue to ignore it.

It was eleven at night when I finally entered my room after finishing wrapping up the rogue matter. I took off my shirt and glanced over at the sleeping woman on the couch. I looked at the food that had been placed on the table for me. My eyes went back to Elaine and I remembered that June had said that she hadn't been given a chance to eat or drink anything all day. It was strange. How could she sleep without eating anything? It was like she was used to going to sleep hungry.

I entered the bathroom and took a cold shower. It felt good after such a hectic day. When I came out, she was still sleeping peacefully on the couch. Picking up the glass of water I started to drink it, but I watched her out of the corner of my eye. Her breathing was weak and shallow. I walked over to her and looked her over carefully.

She was no longer wearing that seductive pink dress. I swore that I was going to tear that off of her, but the truth was that it wasn't the dress' fault. The dress wasn't what was seductive, it was her body, her face, even her eyes that were irresistible. Her innocence alone was enough to seduce me. I sat on my knees beside the sofa and studied her closely. While I was inspecting her features, she slowly opened her eyes and our eyes met.

"You?" She asked in confusion, she must've thought that she was dreaming, but she looked around the room and sat up quickly.

"I'm so sorry. I'll leave immediately," she softly muttered. I was confused for a moment before I remembered that I had kicked her out of my room the previous night. As she got up and passed by me, I grabbed her hand and stood up from the floor.

"I'm hungry," I commented and she glanced at my plate of food on the table that was still untouched.

416

"What would you like to eat?" She asked. I thought she would say that I should eat the plate of food or that she would warm it up for me.

"Anything," I replied and she only nodded her head. Her eyes were on my hand that was still holding onto her. I slowly pulled my hand back. She headed out of the room and I followed after her. When we reached the kitchen, she pulled out eggs and many other things to go along with it. She kept nervously glancing over at me while preparing the food, I kept my eyes on her the whole time.

"Please have a seat in the dining room. I won't put anything bad in the food," she said, cooking quickly. Her words made me approach her, I noticed that she was only making enough for one person. Only enough for me.

"I want some coffee too," I demanded and she looked up at me in surprise.

"But it's so late. Are you sure that you want coffee?" she asked then realized that she had dared to question me. "I… I'm sorry, but I don't think that you should have too much coffee so late at night. The caffeine will surely keep you awake. If you would like, I can make you something else to drink," she offered, but I didn't answer her. She took my silence as a yes and started to make me something else to drink. It was made with milk and she didn't add any sugar. Whatever she was making looked delicious, soon enough the food and drink were both ready.

"Your drink," she said, carefully handing it to me as I continued leaning against the kitchen counter. I took a sip while looking into her eyes, it was very delicious. Coffee couldn't ever compare.

"What's it called?" I asked, there was a small smile on her lips.

"I don't know. I made it once, but everyone said that it was tasteless and awful, like me. So I never made it again, it's nameless," she explained, finally putting the food on a plate.

"Intoxicating," I said, looking at her lips where a small smile still played.

"What?" She asked as she looked up at me and I peered deep into her eyes.

"Intoxicating…it tastes like you," I added as she lowered her eyes without saying a word. I felt her heartbeat again. She was driving me crazy.

"Your food is ready," she remarked, passing me the plate, placing a fork on it.

"I no longer want it," I said, while taking another sip of my drink.

"But…you said…I mean what will happen to this food?" She asked in panic.

"You eat it," I ordered. She looked down at the food and it was clear that she was hungry.

"I can't eat. Princess Naomi said I…" She tried to explain, but I interrupted her.

"I'm the Alpha King, I'll decide what you can and can't do, not her. If I say eat, that means eat," I ordered again and she obediently nodded. I turned to leave the dining room, but when I didn't hear her footsteps, I stopped. Everything was done, so why wasn't she following me? I turned to see what was keeping her, only to find her sitting on the kitchen floor with the plate of food.

"What are you doing?" I asked in confusion.

"You told me to eat," she said in fear. She looked like I was about to beat her because she was eating.

"Yes, but why are you sitting there?" I asked, putting my cup down on the kitchen counter.

418

"Oh... I'm sorry," she replied, quickly getting up from the floor in fear. "I'm really sorry. I forgot that I'm only allowed to stay in the palace as long as I'm working. I'll leave," she murmured, running out of the kitchen with the plate of food. I didn't understand what had just happened and headed back to my room. When I entered my room, I stared out my window and saw that she was eating in the garden. So she went there to eat. Why? After she was done eating, she looked up at the window, but she couldn't tell that I was watching her.

She placed her bag under her head to use as a pillow and closed her eyes. Her face was turned towards my window and the moonlight fell onto her face, making her even more beautiful. I looked up at the moon then back down at her. I just couldn't understand which was more beautiful or was I becoming possessed by my possession?

57. His Strange Behaviour

Emmett

Her innocent face, even more beautiful than the moon, kept me entranced and I refused to move away from the window. I stood there for a long time. I didn't know what time it was when someone knocked on my door.

"Alpha," Rex called as he opened the door. He didn't come in, instead stood just outside. This sudden change in behavior caught my attention. Continuing to stand near the window, I turned to look at where he was standing.

"Why are you standing there? Since when did you start doing this?" I asked, raising my eyebrows, it was only then that he entered my room.

"I decided to keep Alpha Prince Vincent's suggestion in mind after the incident that happened this afternoon. I've decided that from today onwards I won't enter a room without permission, now that you're not alone I don't want to interrupt something," Rex explained. His words and the small smile that was plastered on his face made me narrow my eyes at him. I understood what he was implying. This morning he had walked in on Elaine and I on the bed in a compromising position. When Vincent asked Rex about the spicy news, Rex wouldn't have lied to him. That meant if Vincent and Rex both knew about it, then that meant Zach and Seth were aware of it as well. Those fuckers were playing with me under Vincent's scheming gaze.

"Ohh…" I said, taking a deep breath. "Rex, I need you to find someone for me," I continued as he started to walk towards me.

"Yes, Alpha, who do I need to find?" he eagerly asked.

"Find me a new Beta," I dead-panned as his face turned white. He immediately rushed up to me.

"What? A new Beta? Please don't do this to me Alpha! From today onwards I'll never joke again! I'll never be a part of Alpha Prince Vincent's plan. I promise!" Rex spouted in a panic. "I'm sorry Alpha," he apologized again, but I ignored him.

"Just tell me, why you are here?" I asked and he held out an invitation.

"The Shine Moon Pack is hosting their annual meeting of the Alphas and Lunas of all of the major packs. The Royal Pack is the guest of honor and they won't start the meeting without us, but you haven't gone the past two years. You promised that you'd definitely attend this year. I just came to remind you because you have to leave in the morning if you're going to arrive on time," Rex replied. He left the invitation on the table next to me then promptly turned to leave the room. As I stared at the invitation and the peace I had in my heart suddenly turned into an infinite, unbearable misery.

"Rex!" I barked, not bothering to look up at him. He stopped, waiting to see what I was going to ask.

"Yes, Alpha?" He was nervous.

"I instructed you to investigate the murder of my mate. What did you learn?" My heart was hoping that maybe Elaine wasn't the one that had murdered her. I wanted it to be a misunderstanding, so I had asked him to investigate further into the matter.

"Alpha, this is the fifth time that you asked me to investigate, but the results have remained the same. She really murdered our Luna. I'm sorry if it seemed like I was hiding the facts from you, but I didn't want you to get hurt any further. Please stop seeking any further pain and stop the investigation. I don't want to watch you break down even more," Rex suggested worriedly as he started walking up to me again. I just waved him away, I wanted to be left alone. He followed the order and I let out a long sigh as he left my room, not allowing tears to come to my eyes. She really had killed my mate. Why was that so hard for me to accept? Why had she done it? A deep sorrow slowly filled me. The misery of knowing that no one could possibly understand how I felt, the anguish of knowing that I was truly alone.

This event was held for both Alphas and Lunas, I never wanted to attend because everyone would be there with their mates. I would've attended the event this year if my mate was alive, but she had been murdered! I never even saw her face! I hadn't gotten the chance to tell her that I loved her before she left me forever. Taking my eyes off the invitation, I stared back out the window at the sleeping woman that was responsible for all of my sorrows.

All of my pain and sorrow turned into hatred and anger. I threw my cup onto the floor. No matter how delicious the contents were, it just made me disgusted with myself. That woman disgusted me! Picking up the invitation I tore it into pieces all while my eyes remained fixed on the sleeping figure in the grass.

"She'll pay for what she's done! She'll repay me for all that I've lost! I'll make her life a living hell!" I vowed. I was furious that I believed her fake innocence for a few seconds. I should never have believed her. I refused to fall under her spell. I didn't know why I was having lustful compassionate feelings for her but I'd had enough.

Elaine

It was four in the afternoon and I hadn't seen the Alpha King since that morning. When I was standing at the door to his room with his coffee, he hadn't opened the door for me. I waited for him to come out all day, but he never did. He didn't usually eat breakfast but I thought he would open the door for lunch, but he didn't even open it then. I don't understand what was wrong. Last night he was behaving normally with me, he even praised the drink I made him.

I had smiled all day thinking about last night. He had called me intoxicating. I had nearly gone crazy out of happiness when he said that, even though I tried not to show him. He didn't say anything bad to me and his kindness was so much better than his hateful words and angry eyes. He also told me that I was to obey him, not Princess Naomi. Everything had been normal last night, but now everything seemed to be just as bad as it was before. I noticed that everyone else was permitted to enter his room except for me. He hadn't even opened the door once for my sake. In the afternoon, when Zach went to his room to talk to him about some matter it was June who called to bring in the coffee, not me. For some reason June was called numerous times that day to bring him more coffee.

I felt as if the Alpha King were ignoring me or didn't want to see me, but why? I had witnessed his attitude take a complete 180, hurting my heart profoundly. Now I was in the kitchen, making the same drink for him that he had praised the previous night. I hoped that after drinking this he would go back to normal. I hoped that it would help relieve any tension that remained. As I was thinking about all of this, June entered the kitchen.

"I've entered the Alpha King's room so many times yet I'm still scared!" June said, with a worried look.

"Why are you scared? Did the Alpha King scold you? Is he in a bad mood?" I asked but she gave me an even more frightened look.

"That's the scariest part! You know that there was a meeting going on in his room with Rex and Zach, but only they were speaking. The Alpha King just stood by the window the whole time, looking out. He didn't say a single word, but I could feel a terrifying aura that scared both his Beta and bodyguards just as much as me. His silence in itself is a sign of danger, I don't understand why I'm being called in to serve coffee today instead of you. If I'm called in there one more time I'll go crazy, I might even have a heart attack from the fear! He has had at least fifteen cups of coffee since this morning. Please save me! I don't want to go in there anymore," June pleaded, revealing her pitiable condition. June asked me to take the next coffee service up. She looked like she was on the verge of tears. I had been busy doing other jobs so I had no idea that he had fifteen cups of coffee today! That was too much. He hadn't even eaten anything today.

"Okay, this time I'll take his drink to his room." I told her. Immediately her shoulders sagged in relief. Her wilted face brightened up again as she stood comfortably at the kitchen counter to watch me pour the drink into the cup.

"You have to hurry, I heard that the Alpha King is about to leave for the Shine Moon Pack. There's a meeting of Alphas' and Lunas' and there's also some event that the Royal Pack needs to attend," June explained as I immediately ran out of the kitchen with the cup. I had an idea as to why he would be going to the Shine Moon Pack. They would be having a festival in a few days, but I hadn't realized that it would be so soon. This used to be the one day a year when Marvin and I could talk in peace. No one would disturb us because of their busy schedules, especially Natasha, but I hadn't known that today was that day.

The bodyguards and Beta Rex were making a lot of preparations and there were a lot of vehicles parked outside the palace. I was about to deliver the drink to his room when I noticed Prince Raymond approaching. I gave him a quick once-over, it appeared as if he too was about to go to the Shine Moon Pack. The one positive thing was that he hadn't been spending as much time in the palace so I didn't have to see him as often. I knew he was watching me, but I just kept my head down and continued walking towards the Alpha King's room, ignoring him.

"Ohh... how is it possible that you can look even more beautiful and sexy than the last time I saw you?" Raymond rhetorically inquired as he blocked my path. I ignored him as I tried to walk around him, but he just kept blocking my way.

"Please, let me go," I asked him without meeting his eyes.

"That's not what I want to do, love," he remarked, getting closer to me until I finally looked up at his face. "I want to touch you, hold you, and, in the end, fuck you. Don't you think that's an awesome plan?" He asked, leaning towards my face and once again winking at me. I glared at him in frustration.

"You look even more beautiful when you're angry," he added. Suddenly he bit his lip and came closer.

"Don't come any closer. I'll scream for help," I threatened, but he just smiled at me.

"Really? Then do it, scream. Let's see who'll come to your aid," he countered. Once again I felt absolutely powerless, I knew exactly what he was implying. Who would help a slave like me against a Prince? No one would bother to try and save me, not even the Alpha King. He would believe his step-brother over me.

"Oh...don't start crying. Have you thought about my last warning? You just have to sleep with me. Don't worry, the Alpha King won't know as long as you keep it our little secret. It's just sex, don't build it up to be anything more. After all, that's your job," he said, reaching out to touch my hair. I shoved his hand away. I had decided to slap his face no matter what the consequences were when I sensed Luna Amanda behind me. I turned and saw that she was looking at my hand which was poised to slap Prince Raymond across the face. I wasn't sure whether she'd heard her son or not as she just stared at me blankly.

After bowing my head to her I walked away. Admittedly, I was a little scared of her. She never said a word to me and she never bullied me like Princess Ariel and Princess Naomi. However, I knew she was dangerous, even my wolf was scared of her. Her blank eyed look always frightened me.

I quickly walked away and was nearing the Alpha King's bedroom door which was luckily open. When I finally entered his room he was picking up his shirt. I knocked on the door as I took notice of his eight pack abs. His perfect body took my breath away.

58. My Misunderstanding

Elaine

Oh my Goddess! . I watched him as I entered the room, almost forgetting to ask for permission. He was making me so hot. I'd noticed that the Alpha King was the only one capable of making me feel like this. He tugged his shirt on and raised his head to look at me. His eyes, when he noticed me, cut straight to my heart. I wanted to touch him. I wanted those eyes to never leave me.

"Your... drink," I said, not staring at his body anymore. Due to his overwhelming attractiveness, my legs were shaking at the knees. His gaze flickered to the open door then back to me.

"WHO TOLD YOU TO COME IN?!!!" He yelled, it startled me horribly as I wasn't expecting him to be angry at me.

"I…I…just came…to bring you a drink," I explained, giving him the cup in an attempt to prove to him that I wasn't there to disturb him, but he grabbed the cup from me and threw it on the floor.

"I just want coffee! I hate everything else!" He told me, I just looked down at the pieces of broken glass scattered across the floor. I made that drink for him with so much love, yet he threw it on the floor like it was little more than trash. I glanced back up at him and saw that he wasn't just in a bad mood. He was furious with me, but what had I done?

"But you enjoyed it so much yesterday, so I made it for you again," I explained, leading him to stomp up to me.

"Did I ask you to? Did I say that I wanted anything other than coffee? Why would you do something like that? It appears as if you misunderstood last night's conversation! Just because I drink something that was made by you doesn't mean I like it. It disgusted me like you do, I had to throw it up later. Never forget your place! You're my personal whore. You are only a whore, nothing more," he emphasized as tears rolled down my cheeks. He called me a whore again. I had started to think that after last night things would start to get better but I must've severely misunderstood what had passed between us.

"Oh quit with these fake tears!" He scoffed tightly, grabbing my hair, causing me to yelp in pain.

"What have I done to make you this upset with me?" I asked.

"YOUR VERY EXISTENCE MAKES ME ANGRY!! DO YOU HEAR ME?!! I HATE YOU SO MUCH THAT I CAN'T EVEN BREATH WHEN WE'RE IN THE SAME ROOM!!!" He roared, shoving me away.

"Then why don't you kill me? I don't want to suffocate you. I can't bear your hatred any longer. I'm ready to die," I admitted, but he just laughed.

"Didn't I say that you aren't allowed to die? Don't worry though, I've thought about your punishment. I made you my personal whore, but I won't touch your filthy body knowing that it has been touched by other men. At the end of the week I'll take Naomi as my chosen mate. You'll be thrown out of the palace and placed in a brothel," he warned as my eyes widened. He was going to take Naomi as his mate that soon? That meant I only had three days left in the palace before I was thrown into a brothel and would never see him again.

"But you said that I was yours and no one else could have me," I muttered, peering down at the floor as I slowly all hope seeped out of me.

"Yes, well I changed my mind. I don't want you anymore. The day I mate and mark Naomi, will be the day that you'll go to your proper place. Anyone will be able to purchase your services there. I don't care what you do or who wants to have you, as long as you spend your whole life there and never commit suicide no matter what atrocities occur," he announced as I clutched my skirt in fear. If I was at a brothel Lewis, Raymond, or anyone else could rape me. The Alpha King wouldn't be there to protect me. He was removing me from his life. I didn't bother to look up at him, I just quietly turned to leave the room while trying to control my sobs of despair.

"WHERE ARE YOU GOING?!! I'M NOT DONE YET!!" He snarled so I turned back around. "You're coming to the Shine Moon Pack with me," he announced.

"Why me?" I asked in surprise, he walked up to me.

"Have you forgotten that you killed my mate? Making me mateless? So you'll come with me wherever and whenever I tell you to, seeing as you're still mine to use as I please. You'll be coming with me as my personal whore," he clarified, grabbing his coat before leaving the room. As he left, I let the sobs out that I had been holding in for too long. Why had everything changed so completely overnight?

"Aaahh!" I yelped in shock when someone grabbed me from behind.

"Shhh…" He shushed me.

"My King!" I exclaimed. I thought he had left, so why was he back? Why was he hugging me from behind? Whatever he was doing, it felt wonderful. He had just scolded me, then threatened me to send me to a brothel but as he held me I forgot all of that.

"What are you doing?" I asked, glancing up at him over my shoulder. His eyes were closed and it seemed like he was trying to calm himself. He was taking deep heaving breaths as he held me.

"You're driving me insane," he said, smelling my hair, I could feel his arousal poking me. What was going on? One moment he said that my mere existence made him enraged and was going to get rid of me, then in the next he was holding me and being so tender.

"How?" I managed to ask when his hand went to my waist.

"Everything that I just said to you, I'm the one who's being affected by it," he confessed, but that just made me more confused. Why was he being affected? I should be the one who was affected by it the most.

"Listen to me carefully," he said, only this time I felt his nose rubbing along my neck. Oh my Goddess! He just licked me, my eyes closed as my arousal awakened. "Hate me…" He urged, causing my eyes to snap open.

"What?" I asked, turning around in his arms.

"Yes, hate me like I hate you. Take everything I say as an insult, an offense, a personal affront, or however will work. The next

430

three days should be enough for me to explain myself. Just… leave when I let you. Don't look back and run far away from me," his remarks struck my heart like physical blows. It seemed like he was struggling with something. It hurt me that he thought that I would leave him.

"What if I don't want to go?" I asked. A shocked look crossed his face. I kept my hand on his chest, feeling his heartbeat quicken.

"What? Why?" He casually inquired, but he was still confused.

"I don't want to run away from you, my King. Haven't you given me three days? Then let me stay for those days," I ran my fingers through his hair and buried my face in his chest to inhale his scent. I felt a low growl reverberate through his chest as he began to lose control. He clutched my hair and made me look up into his eyes.

"You're playing with fire, Elaine. Run away before I lose control over my wolf. I won't give you a second chance," his face looked red as he continually argued with his wolf. He didn't have a clue that this was just turning me on even more. I stood up on my tiptoes so that I was closer to his lips.

"Running away from you would be easy, but staying with you is a challenge that I enjoy," I whispered, and his eyes flashed. For a second I saw his wolf's eyes. It was as if he grew excited by what I had said. I felt his hardness against my belly as he leaned towards my face. His lips touched the corner of mine and he growled, holding himself back.

"Little wolf… don't regret your decision," he advised, nipping me once then storming out of the room. It felt so good when he touched me. I bit my lip at the memory of his body against mine. What did that mean? I didn't understand what was happening between us. Why was he so eager to push me away?

When I reached the parking lot I saw that all the cars were already there. Prince Raymond and Princess Ariel had left first with the permission of the Alpha King. Rex and Zach were already standing by the Alpha King's car. Everyone gave me a strange look because no one expected me to be coming with them.

"Elaine, are you going with the Alpha King?" June whispered her question as she followed me out of the palace, but everyone still heard her.

"Yes," I replied with a small, weak smile.

"When will you be back? I'll keep your food in my room even if you don't get back until late tonight. If I don't then Princess Naomi's maid will throw your share away," she whispered back to me.

"I don't know when I'll be back, but it'll probably be late tonight," I answered as it was already evening. She just nodded her head at the same time that Seth appeared.

"Alpha," he called with a bow of his head. "The New Moon Pack's Alpha has requested your help with an investigation," Seth informed. Suddenly I felt June trembling next to me, at the mention of the New Moon Pack, her whole body had become cold.

"What's wrong?" I asked her worriedly because she didn't look good. She seemed terrified, I was worried for her.

"Nothing, I'm good," she answered with a hesitant smile.

"What's going on? What are they investigating?" Vincent seemed to show up out of nowhere, wearing his royal attire. It seemed like he was going to the event at the Shine Moon Pack as well. That made sense because he was also one of the special guests.

"They reported that a slave has run away from the pack and has joined ours. The Alpha of New Moon has requested that the Alpha King find the slave and hand them over. The slave attacked the New Moon Pack Alpha before they ran away. The slave is a criminal," Seth explained, the situation seemed quite serious. The New Moon Pack was one of the top five packs in the Alpha King's realm. The surprising thing was, how had that slave managed to escape the pack in the first place? I could never run away from Opal Moon because every time I tried they would catch me and beat me twice as hard, yet that slave somehow managed the impossible.

"Alright, find the runaway slave and hand them over to the Alpha of the New Moon Pack. This will be your responsibility," the Alpha King told his Gamma.

"Rest assured Alpha that I'll focus all of my attention on this matter until I find the slave," Seth assured, bowing his head. My guess was that he wouldn't be coming with us, only Zach and Rex were. As soon as this conversation ended, Princess Rose appeared. She was wearing a white and pink colored gown which made her look even more beautiful than usual.

"Emmett, Vincent, I don't want to attend this event. What will Ieven do there? It would be better if I just stayed here," Princess Rose argued, looking very annoyed at being forced to go to the Shine Moon Pack.

"You're a Princess, you must attend. There will be no further debate on the matter," the Alpha King sternly stated and Vincent agreed when he suddenly noticed me.

"Peach?" He moved towards me cupping my face in both his palms.

"Why are your eyes and nose red like you've been crying? What happened?" He inquired, seeming to be so worried about me. I just shook my head.

"It's nothing," I answered him with a shy smile, but he turned back to stare at the Alpha King.

"Why are you bringing her with you?" Vincent asked him.

"She's my whore. I could have a need for her at any time. I don't think I need to explain myself further to you," the Alpha King remarked with venom. Everyone looked between the two of us. It seemed like he really wanted to get rid of me. He wanted to kick me out of his life as soon as possible.

"Okay, no problem. You can ride with me," Vincent suggested, leading me towards his car.

"She'll be riding with me," the Alpha King suddenly announced. Vincent stopped and dropped my hand. I lifted my gaze to look at the Alpha King. I didn't want to go with him. I wanted to calm my mind by spending some time alone, but he wanted me to go with him. No, why did you have to make me go with you?

"Rex and Rose will ride together," the Alpha King decided. Princess Rose looked bewildered, immediately looking at Rex as he bowed his head accepting the order graciously. It seemed like she didn't want to go with him.

"Then who should I ride with? Will I be riding alone?" Vincent asked tauntingly.

"Zach will ride in your car," the Alpha King announced, everyone was surprised to hear this. Rex approached him.

"But Alpha, if Zach rides with the Alpha Prince and I ride with Princess Rose, who will accompany you? It's our duty and responsibility to protect you. Please don't send us in separate cars. I want to drive your car," Rex requested, but nothing could change the Alpha King's mind. Vincent and the Alpha King sent him along with Rose. Zach and Vincent left for the Shine Moon Pack next that left only the Alpha King and I. After an important conversation with Seth, he approached the car that I was already waiting near. He opened the door and sat in the driver's seat without paying any attention to me. I sat in the back seat.

"Are you a Queen? Do you consider me your driver?" He asked angrily, raising an eyebrow. I shook my head. " Quickly!Get out and sit in the passenger seat," he furiously ordered, gritting his teeth. Trying not to annoy him further, I immediately got out of the car and sat in the seat next to him. In no time we were on the main road, leaving the Royal Pack. It surprised me that the Alpha King was driving.

He was alone yet has no fear of being attacked. He really was a King that didn't need anyone's protection. There were many rumors in this world, some of which I was slowly coming to realize were the truth. I refrained from looking at him and just kept my eyes facing straight ahead or looking out my window that I had rolled down to let some fresh air in. All of a sudden it became very dark, so dark that the road wasn't even visible.

"Why is it so dark?" I whispered while staring out the window. The car was going full speed down the road as I looked around frantically, trying to catch a glimpse of something. I hadn't even realized that my hand was clutching at his arm, but he noticed it when I grabbed onto him in fear. When I saw him glance down at his arm, I slowly removed my hand hoping that he wouldn't get angry.

"Stay close to me," he whispered and I immediately grabbed a hold of his arm again. I was glad that he was allowing me to hold onto him. I knew that he was able to feel my happiness but I ignored it for now.

"Roll up the window," he ordered. I quickly did as I was asked, sensing the seriousness of the situation. My heart beat rapidly in fear, but I also felt secure in the presence of the Alpha King. Suddenly the moon peeked out from behind the clouds, its light spread across the road to my relief. Now that I could see, I wasn't so scared. I relaxed in my seat, releasing a deep sigh that I hadn't realized that I'd been holding. I was still holding onto his arm as my eyes widened when I saw something appear in front of us.

"WATCH OUT!!!" I yelled as an animal jumped out of the forest onto the road directly in front of the car. The Alpha King tried to swerve away from the animal, but he lost control. I screamed in fear when the car went through the guardrail and off a cliff.

59. Crossroads

Lewis

R olling down the car windows, I let the cold air rush in. I rested my head against the headrest, and closed my eyes as I tried not to think about Opal Moon at all or the fact that I'd have to go back. My Beta had shown up looking for me. I didn't want to go back to my pack, so I decided to stay with my friend. He had just become Alpha a few days ago. When my Beta found me, he told me that mom had created a ruckus in my absence, so dad had sent my Beta to bring me back. Just like in the Shine Moon Pack, Marvin's pack held meetings and special festivals for the Alphas' and Lunas' that were mandatory to attend. My mind wanted to burst with anger over the fact that I didn't want to go back yet I was obliged to obey my Alpha's orders. The word 'Alpha' was slowly killing me.

"Alpha, please calm down. Our Luna is worried about you. I've also noticed that since the Alpha and Luna have returned from the palace, a strange aura has fallen over the pack. None of the members understand what's going on. Everyone is nervous," my Beta told me.

"What do you mean? What kind of change has come over the pack?" Taking interest in this unknown situation, I wanted more information.

"I'm not entirely sure, but the pack members are speculating that there's been a major incident or that something terrible is about to happen," he reported in a confused sense of panic. At that moment the car stopped in front of our packhouse. Everyone was quite surprised to see my face after so many days away. I hadn't shaved since I left so I was starting to grow an impressive beard, nevermind the fact that I hadn't even bothered to put on a shirt. Now that Elaine wasn't part of my life, everything seemed meaningless. My appearance didn't matter to me because she wasn't here to appreciate it.

Passing through the hall, I headed straight up the stairs towards my room. As I walked by Natasha's room I heard her singing loudly. As usual, she hadn't closed her door. She was dancing in front of the mirror like a crazy person wearing just a thong and a low cut transparent bra. I wasn't at all interested in learning the secret behind her happiness. Ignoring the disturbing scene completely, I continued towards my room only to overhear some voices coming from the Alpha's office. When I got closer, I could hear them more clearly. My dad, mom, and Beta Dale were in there and they seemed to be talking about something serious. As I stood near the door, I began to eavesdrop on their conversation. Mom was talking to dad about Natasha's wedding.

She was saying that she wanted to get Natasha married to an Alpha as soon as possible. Dad agreed with her after a few seconds of silence, I was confused. Natasha was 22, like me, she was determined to find her mate. So why were they planning her wedding to another Alpha? Why set up an arranged marriage? I never knew Natasha even liked someone. The biggest question I had was who was this Alpha? I shook my head as I decided to walk away. I didn't fucking care whether she wanted an arranged marriage, to marry for love, or if she didn't want to get married at all. All the girl cared about was getting a big dick up her ass to slake her lust.

I stepped away and began walking towards my room again, only to stop when I heard a name. As soon as I heard this Alpha's name, my eyes widened in shock. Now I knew why Natasha was acting insanely happy. Angrily opening the door to my father's office, I entered without permission. My audacity immediately drew everyone's attention.

"Is that the way you enter my office?" Dad asked angrily, gnashing his teeth.

"Lewis! You've finally come home!" Mom squealed, pulling me into a hug but I pulled away from her quickly.

"Have you all lost your minds? How can you think of having Natasha marry him?" I yelled at all of them. Realizing how irate I was, mom nervously came up to me.

"You don't understand, Lewis. This marriage is happening at Natasha's request. She loves him very much. Plus, it'll strengthen the ties between our packs. We'll become an even more powerful pack, son," Mom explained to me. She started talking about treaties and negotiations, but I took two steps back from her. All of it disgusted me.

"You have no idea what you're doing. What you guys are thinking of doing is a sin! By giving your daughter joy, you're taking away someone else's! He doesn't love her!" I told my parents. Dad slammed his fist down on his desk in frustration then stepped in front of me.

"This matter doesn't concern you as her father, I'll decide who she marries. You just have to prepare to become the next Alpha. I'm going to make you Alpha in a few days, so you should be more concerned about that!" Dad told me then ordered me to leave the office immediately.

I slammed the door shut behind me as I walked out of there. I sucked in long heaving breaths as I tried to calm myself down but it was absolutely impossible. These people didn't even realize what a huge mistake that they were making. After losing Elaine, I was being forced to watch someone else's life get ruined. Standing in front of the mirror in my room I punched it, it quelled my anger a little. As pieces of broken glass scattered onto the floor, I took an oath.

"ALPHA? MAKING ME ALPHA WILL BE THE BIGGEST MISTAKE OF YOUR LIFE!"

Naomi

I dug my sharp nails into my palm when I noticed Elaine sitting in the passenger seat. The Alpha King drove his car out of the pack, slowly vanishing from my sight. I scoffed softly at witnessing all of thay. "He's never let me sleep in his bed. He's never let me in his car. Most surprisingly, he never drives as his Beta always drives him. Yet he's allowing that Omega slave to do everything that I'm not allowed to," I muttered to myself as I tore my gaze away from the window. I focused on Luna Amanda, who was sitting on the sofa in her room.

"So? What happened?" She casually asked me.

"You're asking me what happened?" I questioned as I walked up to her. "I should be the one going with the Alpha King to the Alpha and Luna meeting, not that whore! Why is she taking my place, Luna? Why did he choose her instead of me?" I asked, full of sorrow barely controlling my tears. I was a Princess and I thought that the King would have me accompany him but he took Elaine instead. She hadn't deserved to take my place. I couldn't let her steal my place!

"Because you're not his mate yet and she's his slave, his whore. He's just using her. No man can resist a beautiful woman. It's just a matter of being patient and waiting three days, after that you will be the Alpha King's mate. Then no one will be able to take your place. The position of the Luna Queen will be yours. Of course, you must be patient," Luna Amanda calmly reminded while picking up a glass of wine from the table.

"His mate? Do you know what he said to me last night? He came into my room and threatened me, to know my place and not to push the limits with him. He made sure to remind me that I'm one of hundreds of candidates. He also warned that he would kick me out of the palace if I disobeyed his orders or continued to order Elaine around. Why can't I order a slave around?" As soon as I said this to Luna, I noticed her face change.

"Not only that, Ariel and I were accused of attempting to kill her when she was trapped in that burning building during the market fire. Why would I choose such a difficult way to kill that low life? If I wanted to kill her, I would gladly just strangle her. But I know if I were to do that, then I would be to blame. So I would never do such a stupid thing. The Alpha King would tear me apart if I do much as scratched her. I don't know why Ariel and I were suspected in the first place," I complained.

"So you and Ariel didn't try to kill her? Weren't you the one who set the warehouse on fire?" Placing her glass of wine back down, Luna Amanda asked as she stood in front of me.

"Neither Ariel nor I tried to kill her. I would never do something so stupid because by doing that I would lose my chance at the Alpha King's love," I explained. She remained silent and didn't say a word.

"That's something to think about. Who tried to kill her? And why?" I grumbled, it was a puzzle for me as well. While I was in

440

my room, I discovered that a rogue had escaped from the dungeon and he was about to kill Elaine before the Alpha King saved her again.

Seth

The Alpha's car left the pack but when I turned to look at June, she wasn't there. Where did she go? I had plans to catch her while she was alone today as there was no one in the palace so I could tease her and ...

"Fuck!" I cursed myself. "What the hell am I doing!" I scolded myself but my eyes were searching for that rabbit desperately.

"Umm... Gamma Seth?" The representative from the New Moon Pack attracted my attention but I continued to try and find June but I didn't see her anywhere.

"Yes?" I answered distractedly.

"This has all of the details regarding that fugitive slave. I hope you'll be able to locate and hand them over to us as soon as possible," he said as he handed me a folder. He bowed his head then left after I took the folder from him.

While holding the folder, I went to the kitchen in search of June. There were several maids working there, but not the one I was looking for. Once I reached my room after checking the palace over thoroughly for June, I opened the folder to read over the files. It was very strange that a slave would run away and join our pack. Why would they do that? It would be a huge mistake for a criminal to hide in the palace because Alpha King hated criminals and traitors. If they were caught, then the slave would receive a terrible punishment. Just as I was about to start reading, a maid entered my room with coffee. I expected June to be the one that brought me coffee but some other maid came in her place. I had specifically asked for June. Strange, why was she ignoring me? I wanted to see her and now my heart was beginning to get antsy from not seeing her.

"Where's June?" I sternly asked the woman but tried not to frighten her too much.

"She... she wasn't feeling well... so she's in her room and resting. I... came here because she requested that I help her. I'm really sorry but if you want I'll ask her to come speak to you," the woman said without looking me in the eye, her head was bowed the whole time.

"No need! Let her rest. You may leave," I ordered her then looked at the coffee cup.

"Wait! I no longer want this. Take it back," I ordered her. When she left my room I lay in my bed with the file in my hands and started to read. I had assumed that the fugitive slave was a man but after reading I realized that he was a woman! So a little woman attacked an Alpha and ran away? Unbelievable!

Name: Justina

Age: 17

Height: 5.3

Figure: slim, fair, and beautiful. Big, round, black eyes, small round face, long blonde hair and... a scar on her chest.

As I read each word, the outline of the woman was being formed in my mind and my heart was beating faster. I clutched the paper and got up from my bed in a panic. "No..." My wolf growled in denial.

Vincent

"I'm sorry to disturb you while driving, Alpha Prince, but you're going the wrong way. The Shine Moon Pack isn't this way but in the opposite direction," Zach informed me.

"I know," I answered him tiredly.

"You do? Does that mean you intentionally didn't let me drive because you don't intend to go to Shine Moon but somewhere else?" He asked, predicting my intentions, I just smiled. "Well thanks for that. I didn't want to go either," he admitted, taking a deep breath and looking out the window.

"I know, that's why I chose you," I told him. He turned his attention away from the window and focused on me.

"Is something wrong? You just ordered me to take the passenger seat," he grew serious as he began realizing the seriousness of the situation. After another 2 minutes of driving, I stopped the car and got out. Zach joined me as I stood at a crossroads that was completely deserted.

"Do you know what's special about this place?" I asked him. He was standing next to me, looking in all four directions.

"It's special because one way leads to the Opal Moon Pack and the other to the Shine Moon Pack. The third road where we just came from leads to our Royal Pack, and the fourth road goes to the Alpha King's property which is forbidden for others to thread," Zach explained as I looked back at him.

"Then tell me, if I were to disappear and my last known location was at this crossroads, which path or paths would you search to try and find me?" My question was very simple and clear, he understood it quite well.

"If you were to disappear, I wouldn't find you along the path to the Royal Pack or down the fourth path, which leads to the property of the Alpha King because no one would think to harm you while you're on either of those. I would most likely find you along one of the other two paths, heading toward either Shine Moon or the Opal Moon Pack," Zach rationalized to me. Like a maniac, I whipped my head around quickly and looked down those two paths which were my main focus now.

"So I've found my culprits but only one of them is guilty!" I exclaimed with a laugh.

"Alpha Prince, what is it that you require from me?" Zach asked. He understood that I hadn't brought him here just to ask a random question.

"I need you to find a woman for me. Katrina needs to be found dead or alive, but I have to find her!" I explained, he immediately accepted the task.

"Is she a criminal or something, Alpha?" Zach asked, his words hit me directly in the heart.

"No, she's holding someone's future. She has 15 years of my hard work in her possession. She's holding something precious and irreplaceable..." I replied clenching my fists.

Rex

We were on the way to the Shine Moon Pack. It was a little bit of a drive, more than 25 minutes away but I kept getting distracted by the scent of the beauty beside me. I hadn't known that the Alpha and Alpha Prince would send me with Princess Rose. I wasn't prepared for this and now her sweet scent was driving me crazy. I was trying hard to avoid conversing with her but as the time passed it was getting more awkward.

"Stop the car," she suddenly ordered and I looked at her.

"Here?" I asked and she just looked at me, raising her eyebrow.

"I mean... we're not at the Shine Moon Pack yet. There are mountains everywhere," I explained.

"Stop the car," she coldly commanded again, I had to follow her order. Once the car stopped, she just got out and I began to panic. I quickly followed her.

"Princess, where are you going?" I inquired from close behind her.

"I don't have to tell you a thing. Just go away," she answered. She was holding the long hem of her beautiful gown up with both hands so that she didn't trip over it as she walked towards the mountains.

"What about the Alpha and the Alpha Prince? They'll get angry if they know that you're sneaking away like the little cat that you are," I said, not even noticing that I was being a little too informal. She stopped abruptly and turned back to glare at me. I immediately zipped my mouth shut. Shit! I shouldn't have called her a 'cat'.

"I'm sorry," I hurriedly apologized as she walked up to me. I lowered my gaze.

"A little cat? Are we so familiar that you feel comfortable calling me by such a name?" She asked, which caused me to look her in the eyes.

"No, we're not. I'm sorry, Princess…" I was apologizing when she slapped me across the face. Her eyes were red and there was nothing but contempt for me in them.

"If you're aware then don't cross that line again, Beta Rex!" She said, pushing me away. "Now there's no need to follow me, I'm not a child. I've already mind-linked Vincent and Emmett. Your work here is done. Leave me alone," she ordered before, turning to head down the mountain path. I clenched my fists in frustration. I stole a look at her legs that were long and smooth, definitely not made for walking on that rocky path. She could get hurt. I couldn't help myself, followed her anyway.

Elaine

I screamed in fear though I couldn't manage to close my eyes. I wasn't just watching my own death happen before my eyes but the King's death too. The car was sliding down the slope. I couldn't understand what was going on around me. I felt my seat belt somehow come unlatched, I knew that I was about to die. Then I felt the Alpha King's arm around my waist and the other on my head just before my head was about to hit the ceiling hard. He pulled me towards him, hugging me against his body, and I realized that he had unfastened his seat belt so that he could save me.

"Hold onto me tightly," he advised as he looked for a way to save me. I clung to him as tightly as I could, not letting him leave me behind for even a second. The car kept swaying and I knew that we were going to die. However, even in this horrific situation, where our deaths were only a few seconds away, I felt safe in his arms. What was this feeling? Why did I feel this way only when I was near him? I pulled myself away just enough to glance up at him only to find him looking down at me.

"You said that you've bound the two of us for the next seven lives, didn't you?" I asked him.

"What are you planning?" He questioned as I removed both of his arms from my body. I looked at his lips. I didn't know whether I would survive or not but I wish I could kiss him one last time.

"If that's true, then as long as you're alive I'll be alive too," I told him before shoving him out of the car as he was about to grab ahold of me again. I had noticed earlier that his door was broken. He could've saved himself but because of me he hadn't. I couldn't let him die because of me.

Emmett

She suddenly pushed me out of the car while she stayed behind. As soon as I gathered myself, I saw that the car was still sliding. For almost 2 seconds I just stood in utter confusion. I couldn't understand why that stupid woman pushed me out of the car. I had been about to get us both out. She had done this when we were trapped in the warehouse too. Why did she always do this? She always chose these moments to say something that hits me square in the heart.

I looked at the car again. The car couldn't have landed in something as simple as a ditch. Nope, it was something worse. The car was sliding down a ditch-like slope into a swamp! The car was about to fall into the swamp! I looked up from where I had landed to see where I would be able to safely climb in order to save Elaine. I needed to find a way to get her out, seeing as Elaine and the car were about to fall into the swamp.

"Save her!" Emil screamed like crazy in my head and I couldn't stop myself now. In just 2 seconds, I didn't turn into my wolf, but I used my wolf speed to reach the car quicker. It was dangerous to try and stop the car from the front so I grabbed onto the rear of it and tried to stop the car from falling. I tightened my grip and was able to slow down the car and keep it from falling into the swamp.

My body was covered in a sheen of sweat and the skin on my hands had peeled off. Once the car stopped I quickly opened the car door to grab her. If I didn't pull her out in time, the car could again start sliding towards the swamp. The car door was already broken and she lay unconscious inside.

"Elaine," I called her name but she didn't react. I was holding the car steady with one hand as I bent down and pulled her out with my other hand. When I pulled her from the car, I let go of it and it started to roll down the slope only twice as fast. Then it slowly sank into the swamp until it disappeared completely. If we had still been in the car, it would've been impossible to save ourselves. I looked down at her. She was in my arms and still unconscious as I looked around and saw that we were in a swamp forest.

"Elaine," I called her name again, pulling her close to my chest.

"Elaine, wake up…" I called to her again as I softly tapped her smooth cheeks and she finally opened her eyes. I was glad that she wasn't hurt or seriously injured. I took a deep breath and looked into her eyes which were gazing up into mine. I couldn't help but place a small kiss on her forehead. I hated when her eyes were closed as if they'd never open again. She looked shocked as I kissed her and I realized what I'd done. I tried to look away from her but I couldn't. I wanted to get lost in her big beautiful eyes.

"You..." I started to say before she pulled me into a hug. I stopped talking when I realized how terrified she was. Her heartbeat was so fast that her body was trembling and her tears fell onto my shoulder. She was scared to death.

"Thank Goddess nothing happened to you. What would I do if something happened to you?" She asked, her voice trembling as my heart skipped a beat. Had she been scared for me? She clutched my body even more tightly. My body was starting to react to her touch. I only just managed to keep my hand from touching her trembling one. I couldn't have pushed her away even if I had wanted to. I closed my eyes. Why was this so hard?

60. Dangerous Swamp

Marvin

"Alpha, Alpha Marvin has returned to the pack house," I heard my father's Beta announce the moment I entered the packhouse. As soon as I walked in, the major members, who were already seated in the hall and having refreshments, all turned their eyes to me. Upon seeing me, they all quickly bowed their heads in a panic. I just continued moving forward ignoring every one of them, at the same time I could clearly hear what they were all whispering. My eyes searched for any changes that had been made to the packhouse.

The beautiful decorations adorning the hall were dazzling. It wasn't just the packhouse, as far as I knew every part of our territory had been decorated for this grand event. It took me a few seconds to figure out the reason for the sudden change, then I remembered that today must be the festival celebrating Alphas and Lunas. Thoughts of this festival in particular filled my heart with a fiery rage because in the past this had always been the day I got to spend with Elaine. The festival and every aspect of it from the decorations to the guest list were just rubbing salt into my wounds. I was broken from my reverie when my mom came running out of her room. Perhaps she had heard the Beta's announcement of my arrival as well.

"Marvin," my mom exclaimed, pulling me into a warm hug as tears streamed down her cheeks. I returned her hug as I realized how much sorrow and anxiety I'd caused her. Pulling herself back a little, she gently cupped my face.

"WHERE HAVE YOU BEEN?!! DID YOU EVEN REALIZE I COULDN'T SLEEP WITHOUT KNOWING WHERE YOU WERE?!! WHY DO YOU ALWAYS DO THIS TO ME?!! DO YOU WANT TO KILL ME FROM ALL OF THE STRESS?!!!" My mom angrily lectured me, I could hear the fear that she held in her heart as she hit my chest with her palms two or three times. I gently grabbed both of her hands while I chuckled softly, pulled her into another tight hug so that she would believe that I was really back. She relaxed against me and I knew that she had forgotten her fear, at least for the moment, as she hugged me back.

"It's okay, mom. You're the only reason I came back," I added and she nodded her head.

"WHERE THE HELL HAVE YOU BEEN?!!" My father, Alpha Alfred, angrily yelled as he stomped down the stairs. He was so enraged that his eyes had turned black as if he was about to kill me, but I didn't answer him.

"I asked you a question! Where have you been?" He reiterated the question.

"I just wasn't in the mood to return until now," I replied as no one knew that I was now forbidden to enter the palace or the Royal Pack. The Alpha King's Beta had led me out of the territory that night. I could never go back to see Elaine. Instead of returning home, I went to my mother's old pack as I needed time to come to terms with what Elaine had done to save me. She lied to the Alpha King making it sound like she was a whore, taking all of the consequences for my actions upon herself. She saved me at the expense of her own life. I didn't have any idea what the Alpha King had done with her after that. Having seen the crazed fury in the Alpha King's eyes, I knew that he would never let her go, but I refused to let Elaine continue to live in that hell. I would get her out of there if it was the last thing that I did.

"YOU DISAPPEARED FROM THE PARTY, WE LOOKED FOR YOU EVERYWHERE!! YOU WERE NOWHERE TO BE FOUND!! DID YOU FORGET THAT YOU HAVE PARENTS AND PACK MEMBERS WHO WORRY ABOUT AND WOULD LOOK FOR YOU?? YET YOU STAND THERE TELLING ME THAT YOU ONLY CAME BACK BECAUSE YOU FELT LIKE IT?!!!" Dad barked as he got up in my face while clenching his fists like he was about to punch me. I didn't care anymore whether he was going to kill me or not. I refused to submit to him any longer.

Mom immediately stepped in front of me protecting me like a shield from her mate. "There must've been a reason for him to not return until now. Please give him a chance to explain himself," my mom pleaded, but my dad just shoved her out of the way. A painful scream left her mouth and my eyes widened when I saw blood dripping down her face. My mom's head had hit the wall hard. I immediately went to her to make sure she was okay only to realize that she was in a lot of pain.

"WHAT THE HELL ARE YOU DOING?!!!" I dared to shout at the Alpha as all the pack members that had witnessed the scene trembled in fear. Before dad reacted, mom somehow managed to get between us again.

"It's okay, I'm fine. Nothing happened, just go to your room Marvin, I'll talk to the Alpha," my mom suggested, still valiantly trying to save me. The issue was that this time I wasn't going to back down. I gently pushed my mom to the side and walked up to the disgusting Alpha who always promoted domestic violence and rape within the pack.

"How can you treat your mate like garbage?!" I asked with clenched fists.

"I can because she's my mate! Mine to do with as I please. Mine to abuse!" My father growled in my face. "Plus, now it's time for you to find your own mate. Find your mate and take over the position of Alpha of the Shine Moon Pack!" He continued as if he had already decided my fate.

"That won't be possible. I can't fulfill the fate you just described," I replied and his face darkened.

"What do you mean? Don't tell me that you're thinking of rescinding the Alpha position so that I'll have to randomly choose somefucker to take over my position. I refuse to let that happen. Only my son, someone with my own blood, will take over the position of Alpha in this pack and that's final," he announced and I chuckled.

"I understand quite well, but I don't think that you do. According to the law that you set in place, only a man who has found his mate can become Alpha, correct?" I asked.

"Yes, that's exactly why I'm demanding that you go and find your mate," he repeated and I chuckled again.

"That won't be possible. I don't have a mate," I replied. Once my words registered in correlation with my sadistic smile, it wasn't just my dad's face but everyone's faces turned white.

"You don't have a mate? How is that possible?" My father asked. I could feel the nervous anger behind his comment as he waited to

452

learn what I was going to tell him that would destroy all of his plans.

"The day of the mating ball at the palace, I found my mate and rejected her," I explained, exposing my biggest secret. I had rejected her right there without wasting a second as there was only one woman in my heart, Elaine. Everyone's jaw dropped open at my proclamation.

"HOW DARE YOU?!" My father growled as he slapped me across the face causing my lip to bust open and start bleeding. I didn't react and just wiped it calmly.

"WHY IN THE HELL DID YOU REJECT YOUR MATE?!! THAT'S NOT WHAT I WANTED!! HOW DARE YOU!!!" He screamed at the top of my lungs.

"I don't need anyone's permission to reject my mate. As you've always said, mom is your mate and you can do whatever you want with her. I learned that from you. Now do whatever you want! I don't fucking care," I announced, making him even more angry and stormed towards my room. This was only the start. He expected too many things from me!

Emmett

"Thank Goddess nothing happened to you. What would I do if something happened to you?" She asked, her voice trembling as my heart skipped a beat. Had she been scared for me? She clutched my body even more tightly. My body was starting to react to her touch. I only just managed to keep my hand from touching her trembling one. I couldn't have pushed her away even if I had wanted to. I closed my eyes. Why was this so hard?

"Move!" I coldly ordered. Pulling away slightly, she looked up at my face with her innocent eyes while still hugging me. I gave her a cold glare through narrowed eyes and she seemed to finally realize what she was doing.

"Oh… sorry," she apologized, immediately moving away from me, leading to my wolf, Emil, cursing me as he had been enjoying her proximity.

"How dare you!" I said to Emil while gritting my teeth in anger.

"Don't tell me you weren't enjoying her warmth!" Emil snapped back, with equal amounts of anger.

"I didn't and I don't want to," I replied.

"But I do. You didn't let me finish what I'd started that night we were in the garden. Right now, her touch is making us so horny. Let's fuck her. We're alone and I can feel that her wolf desires us! She'll accept us," he argued.

I immediately blocked him. How dare he think that I was enjoying her warmth. Dusting off my clothes, I got up from the ground. They were nearly ruined due to all the mud that was caked on them. She also got up while nervously glancing at me. When I looked back over at her, she started to look everywhere but at me, purposefully ignoring my gaze. I noticed a torn part of her dress that appeared as if she had mended it previously. The stitching there was ripped open and the cloth was torn even more than before. I couldn't ignore her slim waist that was visible through the tear. She hadn't even realized it. I heard Emil growl again. Did her wolf really want us? Why wasn't she showing me this? She acted cool and calm all of the time. I took my eyes off of her before I did something that I might regret later. It seemed that, after my mate died, my wolf had become a man whore. He was getting turned on at the sight of this murderous she-wolf.

I studied the incline back to the road, it was impossible to climb back up. Then I looked back at the swamp that had already swallowed my car. "Fuck!" I curse under my breath, making her flinch. That had been my favorite car, making matters worse I'd rarely used it. I never imagined that it would be swallowed up by a swamp! I was angry as hell.

"Why don't you…" She suddenly began to speak as she came up to me while looking around us in fear. She was afraid of this place and the creatures that could be hiding nearby. "Why don't you mind-link Beta Rex, Zach, or another one of the pack members? They'll come to rescue us," she suggested.

"Do you think I'm stupid? I already tried to mind-link the members of the pack, but we're too far away. Mind-link doesn't work with this much distance between us," I told her while studying our surroundings. We were trapped here, I couldn't find a way out of the swamp. I started to look more thoroughly around for a path so that I could get us out of this hell as soon as possible.

"I think there is a forest path over there where there seems to be land rather than swamp," she informed me. Hearing her, I went over and inspected the area. It was clear that the forest started here, but as far as the swamp was concerned, it still seeped into at least forty-five percent of the forest, which looked like normal land. Similarly to my precious car, our bodies might soon be swallowed up by the swamp. I began walking in that direction and she followed me.

Elaine

After entering this forest, I realized that the swamp extended into here too. I felt stupid for telling him that there was no swamp here. The good thing was that the Alpha King was walking ahead of me, letting me know where I should place my feet. The forest was becoming more and more terrifying as we ventured further inside. My heart beat faster with anxiety. Back in the Opal Moon, I had spent almost every moment inside. I had only been allowed to go to the market, otherwise I would face unbearable beatings if I even thought about going anywhere else. I had always been terrified of the forest because I had been told that if I tried to escape the pack, I would be killed or enslaved by the rogues that lived there.

My biggest fear in this forest came in the form of those rogues. What if they attacked us? I was relieved that the Alpha King was with me. His presence gave me the strength to not give into my mounting fears. I was forced to walk with a few feet between us so that he wouldn't get upset with me. Fifteen minutes passed and we were silent as I followed him. He never bothered to look back to make sure that I was still there or say a word to me. He was treating me like I was invisible. Until I suddenly stepped on a sharp rock. Pain shot up my foot all the way to the top of my head, making me scream out in pain. I immediately covered my mouth with my hand because I was worried about my scream attracting the rogues.

I didn't want to cause the Alpha King any more problems. Placing a hand on a nearby tree for balance, I lifted my foot and pulled out the rock. At least I knew that it would heal quickly, now that I was getting proper food and water. I wasn't as weak as I used to be in the Opal Moon Pack. Lowering my foot back down, I lifted my head to follow the Alpha King again, only to quickly realize that he was no longer there. I panicked as I frantically looked around. He was nowhere to be found. I was alone in the forest. He had continued walking and left me alone. He must not have heard my muffled cry. Had he thought that I was still following him? Everything seemed scarier than before, in his absence.

Lifting the hem of my dress up slightly, I started to run in the direction I had last seen him walking. I had to also be aware of the swamp so that I didn't accidentally fall in to never be seen again. I followed his scent, but after a little while it completely disappeared. I stopped, finding myself surrounded by trees and a terrifying darkness. I knew that I was lost. I could hear animals scurrying around, I quickly found a large stick to use to protect myself. I wasn't going to shift unnecessarily because I didn't know how to fight. Holding the stick, I followed the unknown path feeling completely abandoned. It was the scariest feeling that I've ever known. Why had he left me? I stopped walking and let the stick drop to the ground.

The Alpha King had already planned to abandon me in three days anyway when he took Princess Naomi as his chosen mate. If I couldn't bear being separated from him now, then how would I be able to spend the rest of my life without him? Tears gathered in my eyes before they trailed down my cheeks. I looked up to the sky, searching for the moon, but it seemed to have abandoned me as well. Suddenly I heard footsteps that were approaching me from behind. Was it a rogue? Would they attack me? Would they murder me? My wolf immediately went on high alert as I tightened my grip on the stick to attack the approaching rogue. I didn't look back in the hopes that they would leave me alone. The footsteps didn't stop, they only continued to get closer. I waited until it sounded like they were right behind me, then I turned around and swung the stick with all the strength that I could muster. My eyes widened when I saw that I had not hit a rogue but the Alpha King. The only positive thing about the situation was that he had caught the stick with his hand so that it didn't end up hurting him.

"I'm... I'm so sorry," I immediately let go of the stick while I apologized. I thought he had left me behind but he had come back for me. He came closer to me, tossing the stick onto the ground. I took a few steps back in fear, I knew that he was going to beat me because I had dared to attack him. I closed my eyes in terror, only to immediately open them again when I realized he hadn't hit me but gently touched my cheek instead.

"Why are you crying?" He asked, running his thumb through my tears as he made me look deep into his eyes. Did he care about me? Or was I just misunderstanding the situation again? His touch was causing my heart to beat out of control. I didn't want it to stop. I wanted him.

"I...I thought...you were... a rogue," I answered while his thumb continued stroking my cheek and his fathomless eyes devoured me. I lowered my gaze and eventually he also let go of my face. I quickly wiped away my tears.

"Don't disappear again, follow me closely," he ordered, quickly walking away. This time Imade sure that I was only four steps behind him. I didn't want to get lost again. After walking for a few minutes, he stopped and seemed as if he were looking at something. His large body kept from seeing whatever it was, so I decided to look over his shoulders only to quickly realize that it was no use seeing he was so tall! Then I figured that it would make more sense to peek around him. He noticed me doing this and I saw that he had a surprised expression on his face. Ignoring him, I saw that there was a house in the middle of the woods.

Emmett

I stared at the only house that we'd come across in this forest. Yes, of course I would like to request assistance from them, but I found its location quite suspicious. Why would someone live in this forest that's surrounded by swamp? Then, I noticed that the little woman behind me was peeking around me. She was incredibly curious to find out what I was looking at. Ignoring me, she started to look around me at the house. I turned my attention back to the suspicious house and decided that we wouldn't approach it, when the over-excited woman next me got a big smile on her face.

"We can ask them for help!" She happily told me. I was about to refute that statement, but before I could she grabbed my hand and began to run towards the house. What the hell? Her excitement must have been contagious because somehow I was running alone with her. I was about to yell at her for such childish behavior, but with my hand clasped in hers I forgot everything else. So I just decided to quietly follow her. She was small, but running fast towards the house in the hopes that they could help us get out of this forest. Her hand was warm and the smile that graced her face was incredibly intoxicating. I couldn't keep my eyes off of her. Before I knew it, we were in the garden of the house.

"No, this house is suspicious. On top of that, we don't need anyone's help to get out of here," I told her.

"But why? If someone lives here, then they know the best way of getting out of this forest. There's nothing wrong in asking for help," she argued, making me chuckle irritably.

"I don't trust anyone blindly. I've learned that they're equally as likely to eat you as they're to help you," I warned as she came up to me.

"Not everyone has evil intentions. Try to have a little bit of trust. The whole world is based on trust even if it's just a little," she said. I moved back in alarm, she smelled so good! I could fuck her right now. Why didn't she understand the danger I posed to her?! I need to keep my distance.

"I refuse to trust anyone or anything blindly in this world. I'm leaving this place and don't you dare follow me. If you dared to argue with me, you'll be getting back to the palace on your own," I cautioned. I sensed her panic at my statement, but Ileft with a parting glare to ensure that she didn't try to follow me. I vanished into the shadows, but my heart pounded with anxiety in my chest at leaving her in these woods alone. I stopped and stood in the shadows of a tree to watch what she would do next.

For a few moments she just stood there, staring in the direction that I had gone. Was she hoping that I would come back for her? Then she approached the door, taking baby steps, scared of her surroundings. The door opened shortly after she knocked. A tall man in his thirties appeared in the doorway but didn't fully exit. He was a lone wolf.

"Ummm…" She began to say. "I'm sorry to bother you so late at night but I'm lost and trying to find my way out of this forest. Could you please…" She stopped abruptly because she was distracted by the enormous smile that had spread across his face. Why was he smiling?

"A beautiful woman lost and alone in these dangerous woods?" He smirked, trying to pretend that he was worried for her, but he was too excited. His excitement bothered me so much that Emil growled in my mind. It wasn't until then that the man had exited his house completely, seeming very interested once he learned that she was alone. She gave him a nervous smile at seeing his strange behavior.

"Could you please tell me the way out?" She completed her earlier request.

"Yes, of course! First you'll have to tell me where you came from so that I'll be able to point you in the right direction," he playfully inquired, his eyes slowly raking over her body. I noticed that his eyes stopped on the torn part of her dress. She also noticed this and immediately tried to cover the exposed part of her waist. Her small fist was unable to do it.

Elaine

The man who opened the door was acting strange. He was handsome, but acted like a creep. While he was talking to me I noticed that he stared at my waist. That was when I realized that a part of my dress was torn. I was beginning to feel uncomfortable while speaking with him, but it was the only house in this awful forest and he was the only one who could help me to get out of here. I regretted arguing with the Alpha King. He had left me due to my own stupidity.

The man's eyes were still focused on my waist, making me very uncomfortable. The Alpha King was right, I shouldn't trust anyone. I just kept my hand on my waist trying to cover as much of my skin as I could. While I explained my situation to the man, I tried to see if I could sense the Alpha King's presence around me, but found nothing. He wasn't here. He really had left me. This realization increased my anxiety.

Where had he gone? What if he went back and I was stuck in these woods for the rest of my life? I knew that he hadn't wanted me to come back. If I didn't return, then it would be easier for Princess Naomi to have the Alpha King all to herself. Of course, that meant I lost those last 3 precious days with him. I wanted to go back to him. I kept talking while all of this was racing through my head, when that man suddenly got even closer to me.

"I get what you're saying," he interrupted my thoughts.

"Thank you, can you please tell me the way back?" I asked again.

"I wish I could," he said sadly.

"What do you mean?" I asked in confusion.

"My eyesight is bad at night so I can't travel or tell you the way," he replied and I was quite shocked to hear this. He seemed to be in good physical condition, plus he was a werewolf. It didn't seem like his eyesight was bad, but it would be rude for me to question him. Of course, he could've told me this before, so why had he asked for all of the details about my journey?

"No problem, sir. Thank you so much for your time. I'm sorry that I bothered you. I'm sure that I'll be able to find my way," I replied, deciding to take my leave, when he grabbed my arm.

"Why don't you stay here for the night? I can lead you the way out in the morning when I can see better," he proposed, which was quite a scary proposition.

"Thank you so much, but I would rather not," I politely declined with a small smile.

"What? Why? I can't let a beautiful woman walk alone in the woods. Maybe you don't know this, but there are rogues in these woods," he whispered conspiratorially, totally shaking me to my core. My suspicions were correct. There were rogues in these woods. I looked behind me again. The Alpha King was nowhere to be found.

"Come inside. I'll take good care of you," he urged, but I pulled my arm out from his grasp, my instincts were screaming at me to get away from him.

"No thank you. I'll manage, I'm not alone," I lied.

"Oh? Who's with you?" He asked with a raised eyebrow.

"I'm with my husband," I quickly lied. I knew that the Alpha King wasn't here so he would never discover that I had referred to him as my husband.

"You don't need to lie. I know you're alone. Trust me and come inside," he coaxed as he grabbed my arm again and opened the door of the house. I couldn't believe what I saw inside. There was a woman sleeping naked on the bed with another man who was also naked. Who were they?

"NO!" I screamed, pulling my arm back and losing my balance in the process. He tried to catch me so that I wouldn't fall, but before he could I felt a strong arm wrap around my waist and pull me against a firm chest that was very familiar. It was the Alpha King!

"Don't you dare touch my wife again," the Alpha King growled, making me look up at him in shock. What was he doing here? I thought that he had left. The man took a few steps back in fear when he saw the Alpha King's elongated claws. I swallowed in fear. What was he planning to do? What was going to happen? And why was my wolf jumping with joy at the realization that he had come back for us?

61. Lost

Rose

Fifteen minutes passed by as I sat here on this hill. Coming here after two years was like a dream. This was why I had left the palace today, not to visit the Shine Moon Pack so that I would be stuck with arrogant people overly inflated with their own self worth. All of that was just a pain in the ass. Attending the festival had been an excuse, so that I could leave the palace without a bodyguard, but I had no idea that Emmett would send Rex with me.

I had a great view of the natural splendor all around me. I was surrounded by hills, a waterfall, and dense forest. It was my good fortune that I had been able to visit this location after two years. I had both good and bad memories attached to this place that were flowing through my mind, it wasn't helping that I could feel Rex standing a distance behind me.

Despite the fact that I had dismissed him, he kept shamelessly trailing behind me. I thought he would stop following me after I slapped him, but that wasn't the case. For the last fifteen minutes he'd been standing like a sentinel by the same tree a few paces behind me. I could feel his gaze on me. He hadn't let his eyes drift to the beautiful nature that surrounded us that was bathed in moonlight.

After two years, the two of us were here again, but the situation had completely changed causing me unfathomable pain and sorrow. My wolf was both annoyed and happy at his presence, but I was just angry. Sitting in the same place, I turned my head to the side and looked at him. He was leaning against the tree with both arms crossed over his chest, and he looked unbelievably handsome. As expected his eyes were fixed on me, but my heart went crazy when I realized that he was checking me out! My face flushed and my wolf was jumping with joy in my mind. I felt as if he were fucking me with his eyes. My face turned red and I got up from the ground before my panties started to get wet.

"I TOLD YOU TO LEAVE! I DON'T NEED YOU! I JUST WANT TO BE ALONE SO YOU CAN GO!" I yelled at him not just because I was upset, but I was also trying to control my hormones that were going crazy because of the pheromones he was releasing. Why was he acting like that! He never looked at me with lust before.

"I'm sorry but I can't. I can't leave you alone in the forest, no matter how many times you order me to leave," he replied, pulling away from the tree while dusting off his shirt. I gritted my teeth in frustration at his response.

"So, you're daring to disobey a direct order?" I asked, raising a single brow. He began to make his way over to me and I didn't know why but I found it playful! What was wrong with me? Was I imagining that he was walking towards me like he was going to devour me or something? He stopped when there was only a step between us.

"Yes, I'm disobeying you Princess... Rose..." He replied, towering over me. He was so tall that I had to tilt my head back to meet his eyes. I knew that I should be nervous when he said that he wouldn't obey my orders, especially here in the woods when I was alone with him, but I didn't know why my fucking heart found him so hot and sexy. The gap he had placed between 'Princess' and 'Rose' just poured more fuel onto my hormones. I only wanted to hear him say my name a few more thousand times, he could forget about my title. I was turned on even though I didn't want to be.

"You... you'll be punished..." I coldly stuttered, trying to cover the nervousness that he had created. It was going to be embarrassing if he sensed my arousal. His lips turned into a sly smile as he leaned down towards my face, he stopped only a few inches away from my lips.

"Maybe I want to be punished," he whispered against my lips, turning me on even more. I was two seconds away from jumping on him for a kiss or more than that. Fighting against these feelings, I pushed him back and ran away. I was running back to the car. Shit! I hadn't known that the situation would turn out like that. That shouldn't have happened! I got aroused by a few scant words. It was embarrassingly unexpected. I didn't want to see his face until I had both my wolf and body under control otherwise, I would become a laughing stock. So using my speed, I reached the car as quickly as possible, luckily in that time I was able to control myself by shifting my attention.

The one positive thing was that he hadn't followed me like he had the last time, but about ten or fifteen minutes later he showed up to find me sitting in the car. I completely ignored him as I stared out the window while the car started moving towards the Shine Moon Pack. I had never been consumed by so much shame before in my life. His silence was enough to convince me that he had intentionally not followed me because he knew how I felt about him. He knew that I was aroused. I wanted to die. Please Moon

Goddess, strike me dead! I pleaded in my mind, regretting the whole thing.

I didn't know how many minutes or hours passed when I finally saw the Shine Moon territory appear in the headlights, it caused relief to shoot through me. Every second spent in this car felt like years, it hadn't helped that my face had been red the entire time either! As soon as the car stopped in the Shine Moon Pack, I jumped out of the opened car door. I didn't even give him a chance to open the door for me as I got out and started walking towards the crowd, but I was unlucky in that everyone was bowing their heads and giving me space to go where I pleased. I hurriedly made my way in the other direction when Vincent arrived with Zach. I was quite surprised to see him get out of the car as I expected him to be here already. I wonder what had caused him to be delayed? He looked annoyed.

"I received your mind-link about not attending, I also noticed that you immediately blocked me after that," Vincent sternly lectured because he was very angry with me. I just smiled at him.

"Don't worry I was just joking with you. As you can see, I'm here. I didn't run away. How could I possibly ignore a direct order from my brother?" I smartly countered saving myself from his scolding. Of course, Rex was standing behind me listening to every word and he obviously knew that I was lying. Well, I was well aware of the fact that he would never tell the truth before I did.

"Hmmm..." Vincent replied, narrowing his eyes at me. He knew that I was messing with him. He looked at Rex in the hopes of getting some information, but he didn't tell my brother anything.

"Where's the Alpha King?" I asked while looking around. I wanted to see Elaine. Even though our car had left for Shine Moon before his car, he should have arrived by now seeing we had taken a little detour. With that question, Rex and Zach went on high alert and started searching for the Alpha King all over the place.

"That's weird that the Alpha King hasn't arrived yet," Zach said, looking around in confusion.

"There must be something wrong! I'm going to go find out where the Alpha King is!" Rex stated while Zach went with him, but Vincent stopped them.

"There's no need to go anywhere," he ordered the two of them with a playful chuckle.

"Do you know where the Alpha King is then?" Rex asked, confused.

"I don't know," Vincent replied.

"If that's the case then we should start searching for him immediately! I knew I shouldn't have left the Alpha King alone," Rex muttered worriedly.

Vincent rolled his eyes, "Don't be thick! Why would you go looking for him? Especially when he's not alone. Remember that he has a beautiful woman, Elaine, with him. I don't think he needs anyone to come to his rescue. The Alpha King is with a nymph from heaven, I don't think you should disturb him," Vincent explained and all the men had smirks on their faces. I just rolled my eyes at these idiotic men. Their minds were filled with dirty erotic thoughts. Imagining the inevitable truth, they all started laughing and I knew that when Emmett returned, they were going to give him a hard time. Ignoring all of them, I entered the packhouse and saw that Alpha Alfred was waiting there to welcome me.

"Welcome Princess," he said bowing his head, I looked at his handsome son who was nearby.

"Marvin, show the Princess around our pack. This is the first time that she's visited our home," Alpha Alfred suggested. I noticed that something unusual was going on between the two of them. I started to walk with Marvin, but I glanced back to where Vincent, Rex, and Zach were standing. Alpha Alfred was welcoming them, but Rex wasn't paying attention to him, his eyes were focused on me and Marvin.

"Princess," Marvin called, attracting my attention as he offered me a drink. I took it with a small smile.

"You really are beautiful, Princess," he suddenly said and I laughed.

"Are you sure?" I asked, playfully raising my eyebrows.

"Do you think I'm lying?" He countered with a small laugh.

"I thought Elaine was the most beautiful woman to you," I argued, my words making his smile completely disappear when he heard her name. "I saw what happened on Luna Amanda's birthday," I added. He just smiled sadly, proving me correct.

"What about you?" He suddenly asked.

"What about me?" I was confused.

"Beta Rex can't seem to keep his eyes off of you. Are you two…?"

"No… we're not…" I immediately cut him off, not letting him finish.

"You're a Princess. You're…" He muttered as I clutched my glass tightly. I could feel Rex getting closer to us. I was panicking. This wasn't good. Marvin had shaken my heart and mind with his comment. I couldn't face Rex right now.

"Me too…" saying that, I quickly hugged Marvin and he was shocked by my sudden actions. I felt Rex stop in his tracks.

"Please… just go with it…" I whispered into Marvin's ear.

"Sure," he whispered back conspiratorially, while returning the hug as if he were in love with me. I felt Rex's anger rising in his blood as I hugged Marvin more.

"Let's have coffee tomorrow, Princess," Marvin suggested and I pulled myself away a little. "In my room," he added and I smiled.

"Sure… I'll be there," I answered, giving him another hug. Turning around, I looked Rex in the eyes and they were filled with anger as I passed by him. He had no right to be upset, he lost his chance two years ago.

62. Best Day And Kiss

Elaine

My heart was beating wildly, I was sure that it was so loud that the two men could hear it. My wolf, on the other hand, jumped with joy when the Alpha King called me his wife. Even though he had only said that to get the man to back off, I had never been so happy. Wait! Did that mean he'd heard me when I referred to him as my husband? Watching his claws extend, I grew worried that he was going to kill the man. The stranger immediately got down on his knees when he felt the terrifying aura of the Alpha King.

"I should be given the death penalty for thinking poorly of the Alpha King's wife," the man said. He sought the death penalty because it was common knowledge that if someone begged for

470

forgiveness from the Alpha King after committing a crime, then they would be buried alive. He was so terrified that he trembled with fear and was sweating so much that his shirt was saturated with it. He didn't dare look at me anymore as he wept in fear. Upon hearing him speak, both the man and woman got out of bed with only a blanket or towel wrapped around their bodies. Seeing the angry face of the Alpha King, they were both shocked then in the next second both got down on their knees as well.

"What's going on?" An old lady's voice drew our attention in the other direction. An old woman with a bowed back and shaking hands showed up along with an old man. I was surprised to learn that neither of them were werewolves, they were humans. Knowing that they had weak eyesight, the Alpha King ordered the two men and the woman to stay still, signaling them to keep their mouths shut.

"Ummm… we were just passing by. We got lost in the forest, when we saw the hut we came to ask for help getting out of here," I said, trying to handle the situation as quickly as possible. Luckily, the Alpha King wasn't going to punish these people in front of humans.

"So you two have lost your way?" The woman walked up to me holding onto the old man's arm, I guessed that he was her husband.

"Yes," I answered her with a sad smile.

"These poor people have lost their way as well and we allowed them to stay here for the evening seeing as it was already dark," the old man explained. This meant that all three of those wolves were trying to take advantage of other lost people, on top of taking advantage of the generosity of these two elderly people. I couldn't even imagine the Alpha King's fury over the situation he'd walked into, he absolutely loathed treachery and deceit, I hated to admit that those three were guilty of both.

"Could you please tell us how to get out of the forest?" I asked the woman and she nodded.

"You'll need to go straight due east then after traveling a long way, you will see a small mountain. Once you've crossed that you'll be able to find the way out of the forest," the lady disclosed to us, with delight, I looked back at the Alpha King. I knew that he wasn't going to thank them seeing as they were human and he disliked humans.

"Thank you so much. You've helped us a great deal," I said.

"I would like to advise you not to go into the forest at night. This forest is full of treacherous swamps. It's impossible to distinguish between the land and swamp when it's so dark," the woman sincerely advised.

"No, we won't be staying here. I just want to get out of this place as soon as possible," the Alpha King announced then started to walk away. I knew why he had said this. Human eyes couldn't differentiate between swamp from the land, but wolf eyes certainly could. Of course, there was still a great deal of danger. The Alpha King was being rude to these kind people, he hadn't even thanked them for their generous offer.

"Please don't mind him. He's just stressed because we've been lost and wandering for a while now," I explained to them and the man suddenly smiled at me.

"Young man..." The old man suddenly called to the Alpha King, making him stop and look back.

"Didn't you just stand up to those people over your wife's safety? If you love her and care about her well-being then stay here for tonight. We have extra huts," the old man suggested. I was quite shocked that the elderly couple seemed to know about what had happened. Maybe they'd overheard the conversation then acted unaware, but he said that the Alpha King loved me. I wish that were true. The Alpha King glanced at me after the old man's comment. We just looked at each other.

"I think you misunderstood. I don't care about her. She's not my wife," the Alpha King callously replied. Each of his words stabbed my heart like a dagger, slicing it to pieces.

Emmett

I cleared everything up with this elderly couple, afterward I noticed there were tears in Elaine's eyes. Why? Didn't she know that?

"Oh...I'm sorry, I thought you were husband and wife," the woman apologized to us.

"No apology needed. I lied to protect myself from that man when I said that he was my husband, but he's not. He's not someone that anyone can easily claim," Elaine acknowledged, looking into my eyes. I wasn't expecting her to say something so complimentary after what I had just said about her. "He's not mine. The truth is that I'm his slave that he's planning to get rid of in three days," she continued explaining to them while maintaining eye contact with me. I didn't know why, but her words hurt me. My hand went to my chest. I felt the pain that she was experiencing right now. Three days? Why did she need to tell these strangers that? It was as if she was challenging me or something.

"Young man," the old man called to me.

"We have another hut. You should stay there for the night, there are rogues in the forest. Your confidence tells me that you're not too worried or afraid of them, but think about this woman. It's just one night," the old man suggested. Of course at the same time the old woman was telling Elaine about the other hut that was only a few steps away. The two of them went in that direction leaving us behind. I quickly looked around so that I could finish dealing with those lowlifes that had already been here, but it seemed that they had run off while we were talking to the elderly couple. It had been a smart choice on their part.

Elaine looked back at me, "I know you don't want to stay here, but I request that we don't continue on tonight. You don't need to worry about me. I won't enter the hut. I'll stay away from you. I'll sleep outside," she explained before walking towards the hut. A few seconds later, I decided that I would stay here for the night even though I was very hungry. I hadn't eaten anything all day, I'd only consumed an over abundance of coffee while in the palace. When I reached the hut, it was small but beautiful. I sat on a big wooden log as I watched her. She pulled her long hair up into a messy bun then unexpectedly ventured into the forest. I didn't understand, what was she doing? I stared in the direction where she vanished into the forest.

Ten minutes passed, but she hadn't come back. The forest was full of wolves, rogues, and swamps. I quickly got up wanting to bring her back. Of course, the moment that I took my first step towards the forest, she came out carrying vegetables in her hands. I was quite shocked. She went into the forest to get vegetables? After washing the vegetables and slicing them, she built then lit a fire. There were utensils in the hut that she had brought out as well.

I sat back down on the same piece of wood and watched her diligently work. I was drooling from the smell of the food and eagerly waited for it to finish cooking. From time to time, she would glance up at me. She was roasting sweet potatoes over the fire. I'd seen her cook in the kitchen but now she was cooking under the light of the moon. My eyes kept getting drawn to her hair, a few pieces had fallen loose from her bun. The hairs kept falling in her face and she kept swiping aside again and again.

"The food's ready," she announced as she handed me a big leaf that acted as a plate. It was a mix of the vegetables that she had gathered, all roasted to perfection. I had never eaten such unceremonious food before, but my mouth watered at the sight of it. I could tell just from its scent that it was going to be wonderful. As soon as she handed me the food she turned to leave, and my eyes went towards the abandoned utensils. I could see that there wasn't any more food near the fire.

"Where's your food?" I asked, grabbing her hand to stop her. When she looked back at me, there was weariness in her eyes, and I could tell that she was very tired.

"I didn't go very far to gather vegetables so I couldn't collect much. I'm not hungry, so I don't want to eat," she offered before trying to leave again, but I didn't let go of her hand.

"Then why did you cook?" I inquired because I hadn't ordered her to cook for me.

"I knew that you must've been starving since you'd only had coffee all day. Plus, we still have to get out of the forest, so you'll need your strength tomorrow. Please eat, I'll go arrange the rest," saying that she tried to leave again. This was the first time someone had genuinely taken care of me since my mother died. I felt warm as I immediately pulled her towards me. She fell down at my feet in the exact same position as when I met her for the first time. She knelt between my legs as I sat above her. The panic and fear clearly visible in her innocent eyes, as if she were also recalling the events of that day.

"If I need strength, then you do too. The both of us are getting out of this forest, but if you faint on the way I won't be carrying you out over my shoulder. So, start eating and don't argue," I urged, putting a sweet potato in her small mouth before I started eating. I couldn't believe that I was sharing something with someone else. I'd never done that before, be it food, toys, or what have you. Only I had the right over all things. The cool breeze and the moonlight were lovely, this was my first experience eating like this. She slowly began eating, only hesitating slightly.

I saw her face up close in the light of the moon for the first time, and my hunger and thirst disappeared on seeing her. How could anyone maintain such innocence? As soon as she glanced up at me with those big eyes, my hand instinctively moved towards her face. She held her breath in surprise when I touched the corner of her lips. Her pink lips were so soft and seductive. I tasted them for the first time when I bound her to me forever under the moon. Now she wasn't wearing a single bit of make-up and yet she put any other Princess or Queen to shame with her beauty.

"What are you doing?" She quietly asked me; it was only then that I realized what I was doing. I immediately pull my hand back. My stomach felt full from having watched her eat.

I didn't reply so she continued eating. I was solely focused on her lips and they were torturing me. I grabbed her hand, pulling her closer to me. She was startled and looked confused, thinking that she had done something wrong. I drew nearer to her lips until I was only a few inches away from having them. I felt joy running across my skin and throughout my veins. My eyes snapped open, I locked my gaze with hers. What was I doing? Why did I crave her so badly?

"What's wrong?" Her voice was so soft when she inquired, not knowing what my intention was. I leaned down and licked the corner of her lips. She closed her eyes and moaned in pleasure.

"There was some food," I whispered, pulling her against me. She nodded slowly without looking at me and I continued. There wasn't any food. I lied to calm myself and in the depths of my heart I thought that she was aware of that as well. I pecked at the corners of her lips to try and satisfy my lust before I left her there.

Sometime later, I went to check the perimeter so that I could get an idea of the security, but as I walked, I saw that the door of the hut was open. When I entered, I found that she had made a mattress for me to sleep on using dried grass.

"I've made all the arrangements, now you can sleep comfortably. I'll be near that big tree outside the hut. Give me a call if you need anything," she told me. After studying me carefully one last time she bowed her head and left, closing the door behind her. Why did she look at me as if it would be the last time? Why was she doing all of this? Was she showing off? Was it to prove herself useful or was it something else? I stared at her through the window. She lay down on the damp soil under the big tree that she had mentioned.

It was midnight and the sound of the wild animals doubled. I could see that her entire body was trembling with fear, but she didn't come to the hut. She just tried to cradle herself the best she could in her own arms. What was she doing?

Elaine

Horrible sounds echoed in my ears. I was sleeping out in the open in the forest where any wild animal could jump out and attack me. At least the Alpha King was only a short distance away in the hut. I always slept facing the window of his room, but now I slept with my back to his hut so that he wouldn't think that I was watching him. It was the early hours of the morning; the temperature had dropped so much that my body was trembling with the cold as much as the fear. I wish I knew whether he was asleep or not. Was he cold too? Suddenly I felt some movement behind me, I clung tightly to my clothes while holding my breath.

It was as if someone was doing something behind me, but I didn't have the courage to look back. Then, all of a sudden, I felt an arm wrap around my waist. I cried out in fear, but the arm belonged to none other than the Alpha King. I tried to look back, but he wouldn't let me. In a matter of seconds, I found myself on the same dried grass bed that I had prepared for him inside the hut, but why had he brought it outhere? My head and back were glued to his chest. His warm arms were clasped around my waist.

"What are you doing out here?" I asked, silently wishing that I could see his face.

"I'll be unaware of any danger if I'm inside the hut, so I've decided to come and sleep out here," he explained and I just nodded. So he came out here for security reasons? I wish he would have come for me.

"But…" I was about to ask him why he was holding me like this before he interrupted me.

"Your scent alone is enough to invite danger, so you'll stay with me like this all night. That way your scent mixes with mine," he told me. I just nodded again, but I had a smile plastered across my face. The thought of our scents mixing was kind of erotic and more than a little seductive. I wish it could always be that way. It wasn't just the scent but the heat that I was getting off of his body that was intoxicating. I never thought that I would be able to sleep in his arms. I didn't think it actually happened, but for a moment I swore that he smelled my hair. I thought I was just imagining things, but then I felt his lips against my neck.

"Aaahhh…" I moaned softly under my breath, but he heard me clearly. His proximity was driving me crazy.

"My King… please... don't touch... me…" I helplessly begged him. I tried to move away from him, but he clutched me even more tightly.

"Don't move. I'm cold," he whispered into my ear. I closed my eyes enjoying the warmth of his body. It was hard to get control over myself but I tried, eventually drifting off to sleep.

In the middle of the night, I turned onto my other side and realized that his handsome sleeping face was only a few inches away from me. If he were to wake up and immediately see my face it would only make him angry so I decided to move away. I tried to move his hand, but he just pulled me closer to him in his sleep. I found myself even closer to his lips. I didn't know when I would ever be able to see him this close again so I decided to not move away from him again. I stupidly moved closer to his lips instead. I only had three days left so I deserved at least one kiss, right? He was sleeping so he wouldn't know if I kissed him, right? No, he would wake up if I did this. I smiled sadly to myself and gave up on my idiotic idea.

"I don't deserve it," I mumbled to myself, moving away from him. Suddenly he opened his eyes and the next thing I knew his lips were crushed against mine. I stopped breathing. He was kissing me.

My eyes were wide open in shock as they peered into his eyes. He pulled me closer as he deepened the kiss. I just closed my eyes as I began to kiss him back. I didn't know what he was thinking or why he had kissed me, but this had to be the best moment of my life. I wished that this night would never end...

63. Left

Elaine

With some fruit and vegetables in my hands, I reached the hut of the elderly couple and thanked them for letting us stay the night. I felt awful that I could do nothing to repay their kindness, so I gave them the vegetables and fruit that I had gathered. Both of them were very satisfied with this and hugged me lovingly. I had never met humans before, but this first experience was very good. It seemed that not all humans were bad. I turned back and looked at the Alpha King who was standing a short distance away.

"I think you should go. He's waiting for you," the elderly woman told me.

"Yes, he also wanted to thank you, but he's in a bit of a hurry so he doesn't want to waste any more time. I'll thank you on his behalf," I said and bowed my head to both of them, but the woman laughed.

"Maybe you didn't know, but he already thanked us and gave us an animal that he had hunted as a gift," the woman unexpectedly revealed. This shocking news made me look back at the Alpha King again as he continued to monitor the surroundings. Now I knew where he had disappeared to that morning. When I woke up, he hadn't been next to me. He must have gotten up early to go hunt. I smiled thinking about it. I knew quite well that he wasn't a bad person, and that he had a big heart. He just didn't necessarily know how to show his true feelings to anyone.

After saying goodbye, I joined the Alpha King and we both started to walk in the direction that would lead us out of this forest. Like before, he walked ahead of me and I followed him. Like the old lady had said, the ground was littered with swamps. Luckily, there was also a river where we could take baths and drink from. It was refreshing. At the same time, I kept thinking about last night. I was scared of how I would face him in the morning as I had kissed him back. I was embarrassed, but when I saw him after he came back after bathing he acted normal. It was like I was the only one that remembered what happened last night. Looking at his face, I could tell that he either didn't remember or didn't care about the kiss we shared last night.

It was kind of sad, thinking that I was the only one who valued that kiss. For him, it was just a quick and sudden physical reaction that made him kiss me due to our close proximity. He had kissed me out of the blue then quickly forgot about it. It was quite painful but I was trying to act normal. I decided not to forget about it as it was the best memory of my life. After two hours of walking, I realized that the forest was thinning out. Finally, we had made it back to the main road and I walked beside him.

First, he narrowed his eyes at me and I thought that he would tell me to get back behind him, but he didn't. Walking beside him gave me a good feeling. I knew I was being crazy, but every moment that I spent with him was precious. A few minutes later, I looked up at the Alpha King and saw that he was mind-linking someone. He must have been speaking with a pack member to let them know we were on the way to the Shine Moon Pack.

Rex

"It's morning and the Alpha King still hasn't returned. I'm really worried about him," Zach admitted to me. We were seated at the giant dining table at the Shine Moon Pack with the other guests. We were all waiting for the Alpha King to arrive seeing as without him the meeting couldn't start. Arrangements had been made for everyone to stay here overnight, but Alpha Prince Vincent had mysteriously disappeared last night. In the absence of the Alpha King and the Alpha Prince matters couldn't even be discussed. I was worried about the Alpha King too, but at the same time I'd kept a close eye on the packhouse. Finishing the drink in front of me in one gulp, I slammed the glass down on the table. My blood was boiling and Zach was surprised by my change in behavior when Alpha Prince Vincent entered the dining room. Seeing him, everyone's face brightened as they bowed their heads and began welcoming him.

"What's the matter? Why are you so angry?" He asked me while picking up a glass of water. He could read the emotions on my face from across the room.

"Nothing, I just couldn't sleep so I have a slight headache and my mood seems to be a bit tumultuous," I explained, glancing towards the packhouse where I could clearly see the window of Alpha Marvin's room which was still closed! Why has he kept his window closed!!!

"By the way…" Alpha Vincent began to say as he watched me closely, so I removed my gaze from the window. "I was told by Rose that she was having breakfast with Marvin. Is she with him now?" He inquired; I replied before Zach who I noticed had opened his mouth to answer.

"Yes, both of them have been alone in Alpha Marvin's room for the past hour," I answered, letting him know that his precious sister was alone with another male.

"Okay, it seems that Rose and Marvin have become friends. It's good that she's making friends," Alpha Prince Vincent said. I was surprised by this.

"No, the Princess shouldn't be friends with Marvin. He's dangerous and I don't trust him," I tried to get him to see my side of things.

"Dangerous? I don't think he's dangerous. By the way they were hugging each other last night, I think…" Zach trailed off, falling silent at a look from the Alpha Prince. Their silence just made my heartbeat faster.

"They're mates," the Alpha Prince hazarded to guess, completing Zach's unfinished sentence and my eyes wide in surprise.

"NO! THAT CAN'T BE TRUE!! IT'S IMPOSSIBLE!!!" I yelled, losing my temper in blind fury, as I slammed my fist down on the table. All the Alphas sitting around us could hear my outburst. Zach advised them all to ignore us with a glare.

"Why not? Why can't they be mates?" The Alpha Prince inquired, raising an eyebrow and I immediately fell silent. He was asking me even though he knew everything. At that moment, Princess Rose and Alpha Marvin exited the packhouse. I didn't know what they were talking about, but they both looked very happy. For the first time in two years, I saw the Princess laughing. Her laughter lit up her face, making her look even more beautiful. I immediately looked away because my wolf was growing sad as well as angry. The Princess sat down next to the Alpha Prince to speak with her brother when I suddenly received a mind-link from the Alpha King.

"What's wrong?" Alpha Prince Vincent asked, he knew that I had to be speaking with the Alpha King.

"I just received a mind-link from the Alpha King. He told me that he was heading to the Shine Moon Pack, only on foot. His car crashed, falling into the swampy forest and he was stuck there all night. I'm going to go pick him up," I explained to everyone making sure that the Alpha's could hear me so that they knew that the Alpha King was going to be arriving shortly. All the members of Shine Moon Pack started to prepare for the upcoming meeting, but when I reached the car, I noticed that the Alpha Prince had followed me.

"You can take my car. If he was stuck in the swamp, his clothes must be a horrible mess. I have some fresh new clothes that he can change into, but a change of clothes for Elaine will have to be arranged," the Alpha Prince remarked. Just as he finished saying this, the Princess walked up to us and placed one of her beautiful dresses in my hands.

"Take my clothes. I refuse to let her enter this place as a slave or whore," she told me then immediately looked away.

"That's my baby sister," the Alpha Prince proudly said, hugging her. Watching their interaction, I smiled as well.

"Now I understand why Alpha Marvin is showing so much interest in you. Who wouldn't want to have such a beautiful and intelligent Princess on their arm," Alpha Prince said and hearing his words made my mind crack. I remembered everything all over again.

Marvin

There was a stir in the pack as soon as it was known that the Alpha King was about to arrive. Everyone has been anticipating his arrival since last night. Alpha Fabian and Luna Wilma went to help my parents welcome the Alpha King. The two sinisterly hypocritical Alpha brothers had been talking to each other for a long time, about what I had no interest in discovering. I didn't know why Natasha was behaving strangely either.

I knew it was a big festival, but she had dressed as if the Alpha King was coming to marry her. She was wearing excessive make-up, which she didn't need, and she kept smiling while stealing looks at me. For a moment it seemed as if she was waiting for me, but why? I glared at her like always. I hated that sadistic bitch. Being around her made me feel even more uncomfortable and suffocated than before. So I left and went back to my room because Princess Rose didn't need me anymore. She was busy with her brother now. I was watching everyone from the window of my room. As usual, everything was beautiful and everyone was happy, but the most important person in my life wasn't here to enjoy this with me.

"Elaine…" I murmured her name. I wished I could see her. I wished she was here too. The sound of the door to my room opening caught my attention. When I glanced back, I saw that my dad had closed and locked the door behind him. He never entered my room, he would rather have me come to his office. This change was quite surprising but I knew why he had come here.

"If you've come to tell me to try and not fuck up when the Alpha King arrives, I already know. Please leave me alone," I calmly stated, but I knew that it wouldn't be so easy, so I decided to leave but he was standing in front of the door blocking my exit.

"I've come to speak with you about something else," he said, looking very serious.

"You're to take over my position in a few days. The time has come for you to take your place as Alpha," he announced and I was quite surprised to hear this.

"But I've rejected my mate so I can't be Alpha. That's your law," I reminded him of his own stupid law that had ruined so many lives throughout his reign as Alpha.

"I KNOW QUITE WELL WHAT LAWS I HAVE MADE AND WHAT LAWS YOU HAVE DARED TO BREAK!!!" He angrily barked at me which relieved me. I couldn't hold back my smirk. "That's why you'll get married," he added. My mind was blown away at what I was hearing. Since I had rejected my mate, he decided that he would choose another woman for me.

"I NEVER THOUGHT THAT YOU WOULD STOOP SO LOW TO SATISFY YOUR EGO AND STUBBORNNESS!!!" I snapped at him.

"YOU HAVE NO IDEA HOW FAR I'M WILLING TO GO!!" He yelled back at me.

"Whatever happens, I refuse to marry another woman. I'll live the rest of my life alone and under my own will!" I stood by my decision.

"You will marry the woman that I have chosen and that's final. I've already made all of the arrangements with her parents and the date has been set. I didn't come to ask for your approval, but to tell you what has been decided on your behalf. Prepare yourself for the wedding. She loves you more than her own life," he said. Just from the way he was talking about the woman he had arranged for me to marry, I realized I was in a huge mess.

"Which woman have you arranged all of this with?" I asked, looking into his eyes with fury.

"Alpha Fabian's daughter, Natasha," he replied, hearing the name of my bride, I broke out in goosebumps. Now I could see all the links connecting. The answer behind what the two Alpha brothers had been talking about earlier, why their Lunas were behaving like sisters, and above all why Natasha was casting those glances my way.

"NO!!!" I shouted, refusing this match at the top of my lungs. I glared at him with disbelief. "HAVE YOU GONE INSANE?!! NATASHA IS YOUR NIECE!! SHE'S MY COUSIN!! I'VE NEVER LOOKED AT THAT WHORISH BITCH WITH ANYTHING BUT DISGUST!!! I WILL NOT MARRY THAT WHORE!!" I roared everything out in a burst of anger in the hopes that my words would make it through his thick skull.

"But she's never seen you as a brother. She loves you. It doesn't matter if you two are cousins anyway," he said simply, which caused me to become even more furious.

"You might not mind, but I do! I refuse to marry Natasha. That bitch must have gone mad if she wants to marry her own relative. I might as well be Lewis to her! Her brother! I can hardly bear to look at her! She's the greatest source of grief in my life. I loathe her as much as I hate you. I'll never let her dream come true and neither will yours. If you want to kill me or kick me out of the pack, you can. You can't force me to marry her," I threatened. Suddenly a smile appeared on his face.

"If that's the case then be prepared to watch your mother suffer," he warned, only his threat wasn't aimed at me but at my mom.

"What do you mean?" I asked.

"If you don't agree to this marriage, then I will reject your mother. She'll no longer be my Luna and I'll declare her a rogue," he explained, turning my whole body cold.

"You can't do that," I muttered in disbelief.

"I can and I will. I've already warned your mother of this possibility so she's well aware of it. If you don't want your mother's life to be ruined, then prepare to marry Natasha and become the next Alpha," he said. After delivering his ultimatum, he finally departed and I was left feeling completely helpless.

I could hear the delighted voices of Natasha and Luna Wilma from afar. They were saying that the idea of threatening to reject my mother had been Natasha's because she knew that I loved my mother a great deal. That by doing so I wouldn't have any other choice but to marry her. Hearing this, my anger overtook me and I completely destroyed my room. Just then my Beta, Eric, entered my room and saw that my hand was covered in blood.

"Alpha…please control your temper. The sounds of you growling in anger are radiating from your room and every guest can hear it. People are asking Alpha Alfred about it," he pointed out, which didn't help me reign in my emotions at all as I continued to destroy my room until I heard a sob. I looked up to find my mom standing near the door, she was watching me as she held back tears looking broken.

Elaine

Beta Rex stopped the car in the Shine Moon Pack. Returning back to this place after so long made me very nervous, I could clearly see that many people had gathered to welcome the Alpha King. Even the Prince and Princess were there. Rex immediately opened the door for the Alpha King, but I was hesitant to step out in these clothes. I didn't know that Princess Rose would send me one of her own dresses to change into. I had only ever worn old, torn clothes, but I was wearing this soft and comfortable princess gown, which felt very strange. People were going to make fun of the Omega slave dressed in the clothes of a Princess. As soon as Rex opened the door for the Alpha King, I saw that someone had come around to open the door for me, it was none other than Alpha Prince Vincent.

"Welcome Elaine," Vincent said, welcoming me as he extended his hand towards me. I exited the car while placing my hand in his. He was treating me carefully as if I were a Princess. I felt pampered. Once out of the car, Vincent brought me over to the Alpha King and stood beside me. Everyone was surprised to see the Alpha King and I, but the Alpha King and I looked at each other. Standing with him like this in front of everyone, made me feel as if I were his mate, as if we were a couple. Everyone was surprised to see me in these clothes and with the Alpha King. I looked at Natasha, who was glaring at me as if she was just about to snatch the clothes off my back or burn them. Her eyes were red with anger, probably because she had no idea that I was going to be here. Despite all of that, no one was laughing at me. They didn't dare make fun of me, probably because I was standing between the two most powerful males in the realm.

"Alpha, everyone's waiting for you," Zach urged as he came over. The Alpha King was ready to walk in, when all of a sudden I saw Princess Naomi. I had absolutely no idea that she would be here, but how could I forget that she was a Princess so she would be expected to attend. Looking at me from head to toe with both surprise and hatred, she came running up to the Alpha King and stood by his side, placing her hands in his.

"I've been waiting for you since last night. I was really worried about you. Let's go inside, my King," Princess Naomi suggested, discreetly pushing me away as she stepped on my feet with her sandals. My feet were in pain from her stepping on them, but the jealousy in my heart was greater than any other pain I had ever experienced. She quickly led the Alpha King away from me while I was left standing there until Princess Rose came up to happily hug me .

"I knew it. You look gorgeous in this dress," Princess Rose exclaimed and my cheeks turned red from her praises. Like every other year, the Shine Moon Pack had organized the meeting to take place in the garden; the only difference was that today the Alpha King was in attendance. Everyone had a smile on their face, but on the inside everyone was scared. The meeting started and many things began being discussed.

I did my best to completely ignore Prince Raymond who arrived with Princess Ariel, but I could feel his eyes lingering on me. Lewis was sitting with Alpha Fabian and I heard that he was going to be Alpha in a few days. I was anxious about seeing him again. The whole time he had been looking at me while I did my best to ignore him. Luna Wilma was very angry to see me there.

This wasn't like a normal conversation because in most meetings the different parties speak about their issues then they try to agree on a solution together, but here only the Alpha King and the Alpha Prince spoke. They seemed to be the ones who were making all of the decisions while the other Alphas were just receiving orders from them. No one dared to disobey their orders or to question them. My feet hurt from standing for so long and I had nothing to do with any of the issues being discussed. So I passed the time by quietly talking to Princess Rose. We were talking about nothing and everything, we were both just enjoying each other's company.

"I don't want to be here any longer. Let's go somewhere else," Princess Rose suggested. I agreed because I didn't want to be here either, until I suddenly saw Marvin. The smile on my face disappeared the moment I saw him, he seemed to be in pretty bad spirits. His eyes were red and he had completely let his appearance go. Something awful must have happened to him. I realized that he was approaching me, as soon as I took note of that I became very nervous because the Alpha King was nearby. If he saw Marvin and me together, then there would be bloodshed in the Shine Moon Pack.

"I'll meet up with you in a little while," I told the Princess then immediately began walking in the other direction, but Marvin was following me.

Emmett

The meeting went on for a long time, but my entire focus was on Elaine. When she stood in front of me after changing her clothes, I couldn't believe what I was seeing. She looked exactly like a nymph. The beauty of any woman attending the meeting didn't hold a candle to her. She was laughing with Rose as they stood a short distance away. I had never seen her laugh before. Seeing the joy on her face made a completely different feeling arise in my heart. Even though I was sitting alone in the meeting of all the Alphas and Lunas while the chair next to me remained empty, I didn't feel incomplete, like I usually did.

For the first time. I wasn't angry seeing the mate marks on the neck of many of the wolves in attendance because my eyes were fixed on the most beautiful woman here. From time to time she glanced at me and it was clearly visible that she was shy about wearing the fancy dress, but at the same time I noticed that she was drawing the eyes of the unmated males. Especially Lewis, the son of Alpha Fabian. Seeing the men's eyes on her, the jealousy in my heart was beginning to increase and my wolf wanted to rip their heads off for looking at what was ours. Then I noticed that she suddenly stopped laughing and smiling and was looking in another direction. Following her gaze, I saw that she was looking at Alpha Marvin. He was totally disheveled, but what made me livid were his eyes! They were filled with love! His eyes were full of love and it was all for her. She quickly started to walk in the opposite direction.

I clenched my fists when I saw that he followed her. So, she only came here so that she could meet her lover. They were meeting behind my back. My mind went blank as anger flooded my heart. Vincent noticed the change in my behavior and thought that I would leave the meeting or stop it, but I didn't as I had other plans.

Many hours passed and it was almost evening now. The festival was going to be long-lasting, but I had decided to leave. Vincent didn't want to stay any longer either. After having a final conversation with Alpha Fabian and Alpha Alfred, I left for the parking lot. I sent Rex and Rose together like before. Vincent had gone with Zach in his car, and I was seated in the driver's seat and she was sitting next to me. I wasn't able to control my wolf when I smelled Marvin on her. He touched her. That was the only thought running through my mind, it drove me crazy.

Elaine

The car finally exited the Shine Moon Pack as I watched the sun setting. Today had been a very peaceful day as Natasha and Lewis couldn't bother me with so many other people around. I had also been able to see Marvin, but I was worried about him. He was very worried about something, but he wouldn't tell me what. I knew he was hiding something big from me, but I couldn't get him to tell me. I had to end the conversation with him quickly, but before leaving I told him to forget about me and to move on with his life, not that he wanted to hear that. He just kept saying that he would only love me and that he would find a way to get me out of the palace. Seeing his condition, the burden on my heart increased. I knew that I was responsible for his condition.

As I thought through all of this, my eyes began to grow heavy and I didn't realize that I began to doze off. Fifteen minutes later, the Alpha King stopped the car with a jerk, which caused me to open my eyes in a panic. I looked around frantically, thinking that we had gotten into another accident, but I found the car parked on the road in the dark forest.

"Get out!" He ordered. I looked at the Alpha King realizing that he was very angry.

"What? Here?" I asked nervously. He was asking me to get out in the middle of this dangerous forest?

"I SAID GET THE FUCK OUT OF MY CAR!!" He barked and I almost screamed when I saw his wolf's eyes. I had to obey him, but when I was getting out my long dress got stuck on something and I fell to the ground. He immediately closed the door as I stood up. I was terrified when he drove away, leaving me alone.

"My King, please don't leave me here alone," I begged him while banging my hand on the window.

"You'll get back using the power of your own two feet! Don't worry, I'm sure that you'll encounter plenty of rogues who will be more than willing to flirt with you. They'll keep you entertained like Marvin did today," he sneered before speeding away. I panicked when I heard him and started to run after the car, but he just drove away faster. I looked around, finding myself in the middle of an unknown forest. I didn't know the way back to the palace. I never thought that he would leave me alone in a place like this.

64. Yes Mate...

Rex

Our car had finally returned to the Royal Pack territory and the Alpha Prince's car was in front of me. I loved the feeling of being alone with Rose for hours like this, even though she didn't seem too thrilled about the situation and wasn't talking to me. I could hear her heartbeat quicken as it always did in my presence. She was hiding her face from me using her hair as a sort of veil, she wasn't wearing the hairpin that she always wore. Her lovely fragrance filled the car, but as soon as we arrived at the palace I knew that she would leave taking that beautiful fragrance with her. I wish this journey would never end, but at the same time my blood was boiling over that precious diamond hair pin in her hands.

I overheard the conversation between Princess Rose and Elaine in which she had explained that the hairpin had been given to her by Alpha Marvin as a gift. A gift to celebrate their new relationship! Fuck their new relationship! The two of them hadn't even known each other for more than twenty-four hours and he had already started giving her gifts. She was smiling as she looked at that hair pin, I felt like breaking it into pieces and eating it. My emotions were on edge already when I noticed her wearing that hair pin. I immediately applied the brakes even though we hadn't arrived at the palace yet. Due to the sudden jolt, she was startled and the hair pin had fallen from her hand.

"Why did you stop so suddenly?" She asked in surprise, frantically looking around. It was obvious that we hadn't made it to our destination yet.

"I thought there was a cat in the road. Sorry about that" I simply replied.

"Oh no! The pin fell from my hands," she said and hearing the sadness in her voice over the loss of her gift made me even more upset.

"If it's lost, then let it go," I flippantly remarked, then began driving the car again as the main gate of the palace opened as we approached.

"No, I couldn't have lost that hair pin so easily. Marvin said that it's invaluable and was made just for me. I'll look beautiful wearing it. I can't lose it before I even have the chance to wear it," she grumbled, still looking for the pin at her feet and my own, without looking at me. She was upset at having lost the precious pin because Marvin had given it to her! Enough was enough. I couldn't bear it any longer. I stopped the car in front of the palace, unbuckled both of our seatbelts, and pulled her close to me. She peered up at me with her big beautiful eyes in shock.

"What are you doing?" She asked bewildered.

"Don't move," I whispered, leaning down towards her small face. I grabbed the tendril of hair that had fallen into her face, preventing me from admiring her beauty. I pulled it back as she always did and secured it with the hair pin that she had asked me to throw away the other day. Her hand reached up and touched the hairpin. She had recognized it just by touch as she looked up at me again.

"This…" She started to say as my hand traveled down to her cheek.

"The hairpin isn't what makes you beautiful. Your presence alone makes things desirable. You're beautiful…" I whispered near her lips. My greedy eyes were fixed on her soft red lips. I wanted to kiss her, but suddenly she closed her eyes. I closed mine as well and was only an inch away from kissing her when a car entered the palace driveway at full speed. Rose and I both opened our eyes as she pulled herself away from me, I knew that the moment was ruined. She got out of the car immediately. I shook my head in irritation. Why had I done that? Why couldn't I just keep myself under control? I exited the car and walked over to the Alpha King's car.

"Alpha…" I greeted as I opened the door for him, noticing that Rose was looking for Elaine. Alpha Prince Vincent came over and everyone was waiting for Elaine to exit the vehicle, but she didn't.

"Where's Peach, Emmett?" The Alpha Prince asked, searching the back seat for her.

"I don't know. She's probably still in the woods," the Alpha King replied nonchalantly and everyone was shocked that he had left her in a dangerous forest in the dark. But I hadn't missed the fact that he kept looking down the driveway as if he was worried for her too. He was definitely worried for her but didn't want to show how much she made him worry. His wolf was desperate for Elaine but for whatever reason he continued to hold himself back.

"Did you two have another fight?? I'll go and get her," the Alpha Prince suggested, only to receive a deadly glare from the Alpha King in return.

"Of course, you can go and bring her back. Once you have finished with that, there's no need for you to return to my palace. Rose is welcome to continue to stay here while you return to your own palace," the Alpha King coldly replied. This made Vincent stop in his tracks.

"WHY?!!" He yelled at the Alpha King as they just stared at each other.

"BECAUSE I SAID SO!!!" The Alpha King yelled back like a small child. "She has legs that she can use to walk back. Anyone who leaves the palace to go get that woman doesn't need to return. That individual will be kicked out of my pack!" the Alpha King announced. It thoroughly pissed off the Alpha Prince Vincent, but he couldn't say anything. He knew that he couldn't leave to bring Elaine back now without risking his relationship with Emmett. The Alpha King started to enter the palace even though he continued to steal glances down the driveway out of the corner of his eye. We were all following him inside when the Alpha of the New Moon Pack suddenly arrived.

"My King," he said with a bow of his head, at the same time Seth and Zach appeared. It was like Alpha Kevin had been waiting for the Alpha King to return.

Seth

The Alpha of the New Moon Pack had entered the palace. I was very surprised to see him because he should be at the Shine Moon Pack, not here. Taking in his appearance, he seemed quite disheveled and rather panicked.

"Have you found my runaway slave?" He asked, I was rather surprised by his question. The Alpha himself had come to retrieve a runaway slave. That was very odd.

"I only received the information regarding the runaway slave twenty-four hours ago. The search continues," I told him which made him very angry.

"YOU'VE HAD TWENTY-FOUR HOURS AND YOU STILL HAVEN'T FOUND A SLAVE THAT'S ONLY A SEVENTEEN-YEAR-OLD WOMAN?!!!" He barked at me, I was about to answer him when Zach forward to help me with the situation.

"You need to speak politely and I wouldn't risk raising your voice either. Remember that you're speaking to the Alpha King's Gamma. If the Alpha King were to find out that you dared to disrespect Gamma Seth in the manner you just did, then rest assured your tongue would be cut out," Zach informed him which just made him more furious. He seemed to be one of those males with a trigger temper. I put my hand on his shoulder and advised him to remain calm.

"The number of servants in the palace and Royal Pack far exceeds the total number of members in your pack. If you want your slave back, you're going to have to be patient," I calmly explained to him, at that very moment the Alpha King entered the palace.

"Alpha Kevin, why are you here?" The Alpha King asked. He appeared to already be in a fowl mood, which wasn't helped by the presence of the Alpha of the New Moon Pack.

"Have you come here looking for that runaway slave?" The Alpha Prince asked Alpha Kevin.

"Yes, but I was just told that she hasn't been located yet," he replied, but it seemed as if he was asking the both of them for help in finding the slave as soon as possible.

"Seth, haven't you found the culprit yet?" The Alpha King inquired.

"I haven't found her yet but the matter has my full attention. I just need some more time," I explained to the Alpha, but Alpha Kevin was in a hurry which frustrated me. I hated to be rushed.

"Zach, help Seth find the fugitive. I want the criminal brought in front of me as soon as possible," the Alpha King ordered before going inside the palace. Alpha Kevin exited the palace shortly after.

Zach had been groomed since childhood to be the Alpha King's bodyguard and had a knack for tracking down criminals. Now that the Alpha King had assigned him to this case along with me, I knew that he was going to be relentless in dragging the criminal to justice.

"All female servants, gardeners, and cooks working in the palace, no matter the age, even if they're sick, must be brought to me immediately," Zach commanded the guards. Slowly every female was brought to, they were understandably terrified of the situation as Zach and I questioned each of them.

In the absence of the Alpha King there had been a lot of responsibilities on my shoulders, so I hadn't been able to focus all of my efforts on finding the criminal right away. The Alpha knew that, so he sent Zach to help me.

Keeping in mind the physical appearance of the woman mentioned in the letter, we looked over all of them. Half an hour had passed but we hadn't found the culprit.

"The woman we're looking for isn't here. All these women are between twenty-five and thirty years old, only a few are twenty-two or twenty-three years old. The information we have says that the fugitive is seventeen. Do you think the Alpha of the New Moon Pack was mistaken?" Zach asked as I studied all the women there. If we didn't find the criminal soon, the Alpha King would be very angry. That was when I noticed that with all of the women there, I had missed the absence of one particular woman.

"Where's June?" I asked, clutching the file that held the information related to the criminal. Everyone looked at each other then one of the women spoke up.

"She was with us when the guards brought us here, but I don't know why she isn't with us now," the woman said in horror as Zach looked down at the paper in his hand again. He was re-reading the criminal's description.

"If I'm not mistaken, that's the same suspicious woman who was snooping around the palace on the day of Luna Amanda's birthday. I also believe that she's seventeen years old. All the information written on this paper could be applied to her. I think we've found our culprit," Zach announced after reading the paper then folding it up, putting it in his pocket and looking at me.

"You knew, didn't you? You must've had your suspicions," Zach asked me as all the women were sent back to their jobs.

"It could be a lie, Zach," I argued and he turned towards me.

"Why do you feel that way? You haven't known her for that long and yet you'd blindly believe her?" He pointed out.

"My heart says that it can't be true and my wolf agrees," I told him.

He got all up in my face then said while looking into my eyes, "If she was innocent, she would've shown up with the others instead of running away. Do you really think that she's innocent?" He questioned as anger flowed through my blood. Each accusation that came out of his mouth was correct. When I had first read the information regarding the criminal, I had already suspected that it referred to June but my heart wasn't willing to accept it. She had run away, I felt as if I had been deceived. My wolf and I were drowning in misery.

"Gamma, we've received information that a woman is trying to escape the pack," a guard said as he came up to the two of us.

"In which direction is she running?" I roughly asked the guard, Zach was surprised to hear the anger in my voice.

"East," the guard answered. I immediately ran out of the palace and proceeded eastward through the gardens. I could tell that Zach wasn't coming with me. That's when I got his mind-link.

"You don't need me to help catch your woman," Zach said. Increasing my speed I reached the area where the guard had told us

June had last been seen. I could smell her scent and followed it as it got stronger, knowing I was getting closer to her. After another ten seconds, I saw her running ahead of me. She must have realized that I was following her because she started running even faster. Seeing her run away from me only caused my anger to increase even more. In the blink of an eye I was only five steps away from her. Using my long arms, I wrapped them around her and she cried out in fear.

"LET ME GO!! LET ME GO!!!" She shrieked while banging her small fists against my chest as she tried her best to remove herself from my grasp.

"YOU'LL NEVER BE ABLE TO RUN AWAY FROM HERE!! AS SOON AS YOU STEP FOOT OVER THE BORDER YOU'LL BE BRUTALLY KILLED!!!" I screamed at her, while pushing her up against a big tree, we were only one hundred meters away from the border. As soon as she had crossed the border, the guards patrolling there would have sliced through her body with arrows.

"THEN LET ME DIE!!" She yelled back at me. "I know you'll just drag me back there and turn me over to Alpha Kevin, but it would be better if you just killed me. If I can't escape, I'll accept that death is my fate!" She told me as I pressed closer to her.

"You should have considered the consequences before you tried to kill Alpha Kevin," I told her.

"No, that's a lie! Alpha Kevin's lying to you and everyone else. I didn't attack him. I just ran away to save my own life. I picked up that dagger to try and protect myself, I just cut him on the arms. As soon as I got the chance, I ran away from him," she explained, but I was getting even more angry listening to her because she had no proof to back up her claim.

"BUT WHAT COULD HAVE POSSIBLY HAPPENED TO MAKE YOU ATTACK YOUR OWN ALPHA?!!!" I yelled at her in frustration.

500

"He's not my Alpha! He's a monster. I was the daughter of the Beta in my pack. My pack was very small, one day Alpha Kevin attacked my pack. The Alpha and Luna, my parents, and everyone else were all killed. Only a few Omegas and I were taken captive. I didn't even know that when I was forced to become a slave, that I wasn't to be a common slave but a sex slave for Alpha Kevin. He would exploit me wherever and whenever he saw fit. He not only raped me but physically abused me. He's a sadistic bastard. He scratched up my whole body not with his claws, but with his favorite dagger. Harming me gives him pleasure. He loved seeing me in pain. After raping me that day, he sliced my chest with a dagger. I was in so much pain that I screamed and looked to his Luna for help,she as usual walked away completely ignoring me. In the end, I wished he would've just killed me, but I knew he wouldn't. So I decided that I would run away. With my feeble strength I picked up the dagger and managed to escape by attacking his arms. After wandering in the forest for about four days, I decided that I would hide in the palace as that was the safest place for me. I thought that he wouldn't look for me here, but he showed up anyway. What I did, I did in an effort to protect myself, I don't think that I've done anything wrong. I think any other woman would have done the same thing in my place. I don't want to go back to his pack where I'll slowly wither and die under that sadistic monster's control. That's the whole story. Please believe me," June revealed. She was holding onto the end of my shirt in fear as she looked up into my eyes.

Her innocent eyes were full of tears and my heart said that she was telling the truth, but all the evidence was against her. The fact that she had tried to run away today was also not helping her case. She had decided to run away instead of coming to me and telling me the truth. Removing her hands from my shirt, I took a few steps away from her.

"I can't believe you," I told her, even though it just about killed me. She looked devastated. Tears rolled down to her cheeks as she nodded her head.

"I know…" She admitted and I saw her hand traveling over her blouse. Slowly she lifted her top completely removing it, letting it fall to the ground. Until she stood in front of me in only a long skirt and bra. My eyes widened as I broke out in goosebumps when I saw her body. There were so many scars from what was probably a dagger beside bite marks all over her body. Her body had been badly bruised and the entire area from her waist to chest had been disfigured.

My eyes traveled over each mark in horror. Every single mark on her body was proof of the cruelty that had been committed by Alpha Kevin. She was ashamed to show her body to me, but her desire to prove herself innocent outweighed her shame. I walked up to her and hugged her tightly. She sobbed loudly when she realized that I now believed her. She returned my hug with trembling arms. She then noticed Zach and Rex standing behind me who had overheard and saw everything. She clutched my shirt tightly in fear as she was half naked in front of them.

"Don't send me…back to him. Please…let me go…now," she begged, burying her face into my chest. She was afraid of them, especially Zach who's face looked as cold as ice.

"No," I replied and she looked up at my face.

"Why?" She asked, suddenly the moon shone over our heads. It was past midnight and a new day had come. Suddenly I felt my wolf acting strange as my eyes met June's.

"MATE!" My wolf exclaimed in my mind. Her teary eyes widened along with mine. I guess that today was her eighteenth birthday. She was my mate! She looked horrified. I was about to tell her to calm down or she was going to have a heart attack. My wolf was screaming in my mind that this beautiful woman was my mate. I was over the moon. Now I understood why my wolf was so attached to her and why I had been falling for her. She blinked and the next second she pushed me away.

"What's wrong?" Rex asked as he watched her run away.

"ZACH!! CATCH MY MATE!!" I yelled at him. Rex and Zach were both shocked, but Zach immediately grabbed her around the waist. She couldn't never dream of beating Zach's speed. She was crying and struggling in his arms. I walked over to her while pulling my shirt off.

"Please let me go...I don't want to go back...Don't send me back to him," she loudly whimpered as she was surrounded by all three of us. I pulled her out of Zach's arms and pulled my shirt over her head.

"No one is going to send you anywhere," I replied, peering deep into her eyes. I wanted to make sure that she believed me. She looked up at me in disbelief trying her best not to cry.

"Really?" She asked as I tenderly kissed her cheek.

"Yes... Mate..." I replied.

65. I Hate You

Lewis

The Alpha King left two hours ago and everyone was happy and enjoying the party since no one had gotten on his bad side during the meeting. My pack was also partaking in the festivities while I continued to sit in my chair all alone staring at the spot where Elaine had been standing. I had absolutely no idea that she would be attending the festival. What had seemed even more amazing was that she'd arrived wearing a gown fit for a princess. I always knew that if she had been allowed to wear fine clothes, that she would be more beautiful than any queen. I had planned to dress her like a queen when I made her my Luna, but that was never going to happen now and she was no longer here for me to admire. She had arrived with the Alpha King and departed with him.

In spite of the noise of the crowd, I was able to clearly make out everything that my insidious family was saying. Marvin was being forced to marry Natasha. I could see Natasha's feet moving quickly around as she danced like crazy and drank an absorbent amount of alcohol with her friends. Marvin was nowhere to be found, but he didn't seem to be in the mood to attend the festival.

All of these things were proof that my father and his had laid a trap to ruin yet another innocent life. Listening to Natasha and my mom laughing, my mind began bursting with even more anger. I was suffocating in this place, but I had to stay because of my dad's order. That was when a sweet and lovely fragrance entered my nostrils. My wolf was overjoyed. I lifted my gaze and found that the woman standing in front of me was my mate. A chuckle escaped my lips when I realized who my mate was. The daughter of Alpha Eric, Danica, whose father had been murdered by my own many years ago. How ironic that the daughter of my father's enemy was my mate. She sat in the empty chair next to me and looked towards her brother, who had taken over the position of Alpha after his father's death.

"I don't want you as my mate. I hate you," she spat out, still looking at her brother not even bothering to spare me a glance.

"I couldn't agree more," I replied as she finally looked at me.

"Then let's reject each other otherwise I'll end up killing your whole pack," she casually threatened, proving that she was the strongest female Alpha that I've ever met.

"Then do it," I egged her on, making her raise her eyebrows. "You want revenge, right?" I asked, getting up in her face. She didn't move away, instead she kept studying and listening to me calmly.

"Don't try to fuck with me using sly words," she replied with a sterned look.

"I hope that you haven't forgotten that my father killed yours, making you an orphan when you were only seven years old. How he left you crying beside your parents' corpses after making their faces hard to recognize, so disfigured…" I goaded, but she didn't let me continue as she immediately grabbed my coat. There was no anger in her eyes, but there was a volcano that had been waiting several years to erupt.

"I'll torture your father, I won't kill him swiftly! Just as I was forced to witness the murder of my parents, I'll slice open every vein of your father while you watch," she told me as she tightened her grip on my coat. Every word she said was like music to my ears. Grabbing her murderous hands that were soon going to wrap around my neck and snap it to satisfy her blood lust, I gave her a sly smile.

"What if I said that I could help you achieve your greatest desire?" I asked and there was a change in her eyes, which was a mix of suspicious surprise.

"What do you mean?" She inquired and I immediately got up from my chair while holding her hand in mine.

"Everyone! May I please have your attention?" I asked while Danica stood beside me confused because she had no idea what I was planning. My parents, Marvin's parents, Natasha, Danica's brother, and everyone else in the room looked at the both of us and frowned.

"WHAT IS GOING ON?!!!" My father angrily barked when he saw our hands clasped together. Her brother, Alpha Rick, was also boiling in rage, but he was intently focused on his sister. Maybe they were mind-linking with each other.

"I would like to introduce my mate, Danica," I announced as my parents' jaws dropped. After having the mind-linked with his sister, Alpha Rick was calm.

"You must be joking!" Father exclaimed, taking long strides towards me. I knew quite well what his next words would be, that I would have to reject Danica. I smiled at my father and he stopped as if he knew exactly what I was about to do. Pulling Danica closer to me I stared at my parents while leaning down towards her neck, I watched their horrified reactions as I sunk my canines deep into her neck, completely marking her as mine in front of everyone. I pulled away a little so that she could mark me as well. I licked my lips, which were covered in her blood. My family, Marvin's family, and the members of the other large and small packs had witnessed it. Both of the evil brothers were angry, but I noticed Marvin had carefully watched everything.

Vincent

It was two in the morning and there had been a stir throughout the whole palace caused by that fugitive criminal. It was difficult to sleep with such a ruckus, so I went to the kitchen. I was craving some coffee made by my Peach's own hands, but she wasn't available. So I decided to make my own coffee for the first time. It couldn't be that hard, I thought. I had just pulled the coffee grounds from the shelf when June suddenly entered the kitchen with Rex, Zach, and Seth. Three men with one woman? What was going on?

"I'm making my own coffee. Would anyone like to have some? It's a once in a lifetime opportunity," I asked all of them. With the criminal still around, they had been up late and looked exhausted.

"Please let me make that for you," June suggested as she immediately ran towards me. I hadn't even said yes before she had the pot out and was already making the coffee. That made me realize how lazy I was. It was such an easy thing to do. I stood there by the kitchen counter studying all of their faces.

"What happened? Did the criminal get away?" I mockingly inquired of the three of them. All three of their appearances told me that something had happened or that the criminal had escaped.

That was when Rex and Zach pointed to June, who was still making coffee, only her hands were trembling.

"So she's the culprit?" I asked the three men, only two of them nodded because the eyes of the third were fixed solely on June. It was then that I noticed that June was wearing Seth's shirt.

"It seems like your mate's in trouble, Seth," I quipped as June looked up at me in surprise that I had come to the conclusion that they were mates so quickly on my own. Her nervousness had proven me right.

"Yes, she is. I was actually hoping that you could help us, Alpha Prince," Seth said, sounding slightly desperate.

"What kind of help are you hoping for? I'm powerless here as this isn't my Kingdom. I'm basically useless," I replied, already knowing exactly what he wanted from me but I needed to know how far he was willing to go for his criminal mate. All three of them narrowed their eyes when I referred to myself as powerless and useless. I only chuckled.

"June is innocent. Alpha Kevin lied when he claimed that she tried to murder him. The truth is that the man is insane, sadistic. He dared to lie, not only to you, but to the Alpha King as well," I frowned at this information.

"Explain everything to me. Don't leave out a single detail," I ordered as they sensed the enraged aura growing around me. Who would dare lie to Emmett? Seth told me how Alpha Kevin attacked June's pack, made her his sex slave, and committed countless atrocities against her. Now I understood why Alpha Kevin had been so desperate to capture the fugitive slave. He feared that if June told someone what had been done to her that Emmett would find out about it. He wanted to continue on with his depravities in private. Of course, he had no idea that when she ran away from him, June would choose to hide in the palace, which was the most dangerous place for Alpha Kevin. Seth also explained that he had seen the marks from the dagger and his cruelty all over her body which was quite horrifying. Rex and Zach also confirmed that they too had seen the scars and bruises with their own eyes just as Seth had.

"Hmmm…" I replied, taking the offered coffee cup from her hand. She hadn't dared to look at me, most likely thinking that I would force her to undress so that I could confirm the men's story. I was sure that she would start sobbing if I demanded that of her.

"So what is it that you want from me?" I asked while taking a small sip.

"The Alpha wants to have the culprit apprehended and brought in front of him as soon as possible. The moment he knows that the culprit has been caught, he'll deliver the sentence immediately, and none of us will dare to speak before him. You're the only one that can explain the situation to him in advance," he said. I narrowed my eyes at the three of them. They were all giving me puppy dog eyes, hoping for my help.

"Why are you scared of him? You're his Beta. Surely he'd listen to you?" I asked Rex.

"Being his Beta causes me to be even more scared," he replied. I was quite surprised that Zach was giving me puppy dog eyes,that was unacceptable.

"Zach, don't give me that look. It doesn't suit you. Just be cold and rude as you always are, that suits you a lot better," I remarked off handedly and he smiled.

"Okay," I finally relented, Seth's eyes shone. He immediately grabbed a scared June and tried to calm her. She was barely holding back tears, thinking that she would be thrown back into the hands of Alpha Kevin. Everyone released a long sigh of relief as they picked up a coffee mug.

"But not now, I'll wait until later in the morning," I added when they had taken a few sips of coffee. They all panicked again because they wanted me to talk to Emmett right now.

"But why Alpha Prince?" Seth asked the question they were all dying to know.

"Wait a minute! I think I know why," Rex said and I smirked. After all, he was Emmett's Beta. How had they not noticed?

"What do you mean?" Zach inquired.

"The Alpha King isn't in the palace," Rex pointed out then everyone looked to me to see if I knew the reason behind his absence.

"Where's the Alpha King?" Everyone asked me together, but I just smiled and enjoyed the coffee in response.

Emmett

When I entered my bedroom after finishing the work that had been left due to my absence for twenty four hours, it was midnight and my body ached from sleeping on the hard ground last night. As soon as I thought of the ground, I walked over to my window and gazed out at the garden where she slept every night. For the last few days, she'd been sleeping out there after eating dinner but not tonight. Only her belongings could be seen, but she wasn't there. Stepping away from the window, I took off my clothes and went to take a shower. When I closed my eyes under the stream of water, I remembered the river where I bathed with her in the forest. I had no idea that she would ask me to accompany her for a bath because she was too afraid to go alone. When we arrived I realized that she had wanted me to guard her and kept repeatedly warning me not to look back at her!

She had ordered the Alpha King not to look at her when she wasn't wearing anything, but how could she have forgotten that she was my property? Despite her order, I took a peek at her out of the corner of my eye, she looked like a beautiful mermaid. I immediately took my eyes off her before I became so aroused at the sight of her naked body that it became impossible to control my wolf. Under the shower spray, I was still able to remember her fair chest and round breasts. My breathing became labored when I thought about her pink nipples which turned me on. I growled in frustration when I realized that I was as hard as a rock just from thinking about her.

I was as bad as a teenager who couldn't control their hormones! I blamed my wolf, he was acting like a pervert! Now I needed to take care of this! While jerking off, I thought about her and her sexy curves. When I finally exited the bathroom, I went back over to the window and peeked out. She still wasn't there. I glanced at the clock. She should have been here by now. I smirked as I thought about how she must be walking slowly because she must be exhausted. She deserved it! How dare she set up a secret meeting with her lover behind my back! Now she would never dare to act so innocent in front of me. After throwing the wet towel on the sofa, I picked up the plate of food and began to eat while stalking back over to the window. When I put a bite of food in my mouth, I found it tasteless.

This food wasn't comparable to the food that she made for me in the forest. That salad and roasted vegetables, just thinking about that meal made my mouth water. It was so simple, yet delicious. I again looked down at the food, finding it tasteless, colorless, and completely unappetizing. Putting it back on the table, I laid down on the bed and stared at the clock. It was half past one in the morning now. She should have come back by now, no matter how slow she was walking. Crossing one ankle on top of the other, I kept watching the clock. I couldn't keep my legs still or distract my mind enough as I watched the hands of the clock tick by. As soon as it was quarter to two in the morning I sat up in bed.

Had she run away? There was no one to watch over her and I wasn't with her. This was a great opportunity for her to run away from me, I thought. As I was thinking this, Emil grew very angry with me for what I'd done.

"NO! SHE WOULDN'T DARE RUN AWAY!!!" I yelled out loud before looking at the clock yet again. There were only five minutes before it would be two in the morning. I may have told her that there were rogues out there, but that was a blatant lie. That area was quite safe and the time to travel from there to the palace was only three hours if you walked, but it had now been six hours since he left Elaine. There could only be two possible answers for why she hasn't come back yet. Either she didn't know the way back or something must have happened to her. My eyes went to the clock for the hundredth time as the clock read two in the morning. I immediately picked up my car keys, headed to my car, and exited the pack.

As soon as I drove out of the pack, I hit a wall of rain. Strangely it seemed that it was raining in some areas, but it hadn't been raining in other areas for the last several hours. That was why I hadn't realized it earlier. It was an oncoming storm. I noticed that trees had been uprooted as I was speeding the car towards the forest where I had left her several hours ago. My eyes were scanning everywhere for her as she had been heading back in the direction of the palace, so she could be anywhere along the road. Half an hour passed while I drove around but I couldn't find her anywhere. The road was completely deserted, there weren't even animals visible. Where had she gone? As every minute passed, my anger only increased.

"When I find her, I'm going to teach her a lesson about wasting my time!" I snapped, punching the steering wheel. A few minutes later I had to stop my car because a huge tree had fallen across the road, blocking my path. I grew even more frustrated and decided to take another way, but I noticed something that made me get out of the car. In a few seconds I was soaked from the heavy rain. Pushing the tree a little I found a small piece of fabric. It was a piece of the gown that she had been wearing. I clutched it tightly when I saw that it had blood on it. I sniffed it and knew that it was hers. I quickly looked around because I knew that she had to be nearby. I closed my eyes and tried to feel her because there was no way to catch her scent around me. It was raining heavily which was causing her scent to be washed away and hidden. I concentrated for a few seconds before Emil felt her. I looked straight ahead and knew that she was in that direction.

Right now, I didn't want to contemplate the reason behind why I was feeling her, but I was able to feel her through my soul. I began running at full speed, still holding onto the piece of her bloody dress. I knew that I was getting closer to her as the feeling in my soul got stronger. I was desperate to see her. The smell of her blood increased with each step that I took. I could see that there was a lot of blood on the road. It was as if someone had attacked her. Had... had rogues attacked her? Just the thought of this had both Emil and I losing our control. I was furious.

I stopped when I finally laid my eyes on her. She was sitting under a tree moaning in pain. Her clothes were completely soaked through and incredibly dirty, but as soon as I saw her left leg I knew that she was injured. A leg-hold trap was near her feet, probably left by hunters to catch their prey, and it was stained with her blood. Due to the darkness and the storm, she must have inadvertently stepped into the dangerous trap. She was biting her lip so as not to cry out in pain, but tears were pouring down from her eyes.

"Elaine..." I gently called to her as I moved towards her, she stared at me in disbelief for at least two seconds before she began loudly sobbing. Seeing her crying like this, I could no longer control myself, I ran towards her. When I reached her, I immediately hugged her soft fragile body. I closed my eyes in relief. I had found her. She was safe.

"Don't cry... I'm here. I came back for you," I said, her whole body was trembling from the cold, pain, and fear. She shook her head.

"I...hate you...I hate...you..." She stuttered between sobs while pushing me away. She was expressing her displeasure, but I just kept holding on to her even more tightly as she tried to push me away.

"Don't...touch me...I hate you..." She kept telling me over and over again.

"Okay… okay… I understand," I cooed, kissing her forehead and wiping her face. The rainfall had increased even more and both of us were completely drenched. I gently cupped her face, still wiping her tears away.

"Why...did you...leave me? Why?" She asked between sobs. Her question made me stop for a moment. I wasn't sure why but I suddenly found myself thinking about when I was fifteen years old and there was a little girl who had also been sitting under a tree getting wet and was afraid. Her eyes had been as innocent as Elaine's. Right now looking into Elaine's eyes I thought that she was the same girl from my past. I couldn't remember her face, but as I watched Elaine sob I was remembering her. She was...my first love…

"Why?" She asked again and I ran my thumb through the tracks of her new tears.

"I'm sorry…" I replied, looking deeply into her eyes and she stopped. I felt like time itself had stopped. I had never apologized to anyone. So why right now at this moment? Why her? Why did I always do things with her that I never did with anyone else? Why? The weather grew worse as it started thundering and lightening with more frequency. When she flinched from the thunder, I came back to my senses and looked at her injured foot.

"AAAAAA…NO…" She shouted in pain, not allowing me to touch her injury. She had been in the rain for too long and her wound could get infected if it was not taken care of soon. I studied her face and it was clear that she wouldn't be able to stand, let alone walk.

"Come here," I said, scooting closer to her and pulling her body against mine. I slipped one arm under her legs and the other behind her back then stood up while holding her tightly against my chest. I began heading back towards my car that was parked a good distance away. I listened to her painful moans as my steps jostled her foot. I looked down at her and saw that she was staring back at me with teary eyes. We seemed to be glued to each other as I kept walking.

"I…was scared," she softly admitted, clutching my shirt tightly.

"Me too…" I confessed while I kept her cradled in my arms and she rested her head against my chest.

To Be Continued

ABOUT THE AUTHOR

Pooja Rao is an Indian author, born in 1997. She loves to travel, try different types of food, and spend time alone reading. She became addicted to reading when she was ten. It all started with short stories from newspapers and comics. She wrote her first book that was inspired by events in her own life then mixed with her imagination. Writing is her happy place, it helps her breathe. She strongly believes in love and by writing her stories, if she can make even one person feel that warmth, excitement, and joy of that feeling, she has achieved her goal.

Facebook: Author POOJA Stories

Instagram: pooj_a6710

ABOUT DREAME

Established in 2018 and headquartered in Singapore, Dreame is a global hub for creativity and fascinating stories of all kinds in many different genres and themes.

Our goal is to unite an open, vibrant, and diverse ecosystem for storytellers and readers around the world.

Available in over 20 languages and 100 countries, we are dedicated to bring quality and rich content for tens of millions of readers to enjoy.

We are committed to discover the endless possibilities behind every story and provide an ultimate platform for readers to connect with the authors, inspire each other, and share their thoughts anytime, anywhere.

Join the journey with Dreame, and let creativity enrich our lives!

ATTRIBUTION

Image By Freepik

Made in United States
North Haven, CT
07 July 2024